Praise for Elizabeth Chadwick

'Picking up an Elizabeth Chadwick novel you know you are in for a sumptuous ride. Beautifully strong characters and a real feel for time and place'
Daily Telegraph

'Blen authentic period details with modern convention for emotional drama'
Mail on Sunday

'Enjoyable and sensuous'
Daily Mail

iculous research and strong storytelling'
Woman & Home

writer of medieval fiction currently around'
Historical Novels Review

THE AUTUMN THRONE

ELIZABETH
CHADWICK

sphere

SPHERE

First published in Great Britain in 2016 by Sphere
This paperback edition published in 2017 by Sphere

1 3 5 7 9 10 8 6 4 2

A CIP catalogue record for this book
is available from the British Library.

ISBN 978-0-7515-4820-4

Typeset in Baskerville MT by Palimpsest Book Production Limited,
Falkirk, Stirlingshire
Printed and bound in Great Britain by Clays Ltd, St Ives plc

Papers used by Sphere are from well-managed forests
and other responsible sources.

MIX
Paper from
responsible sources
FSC® C104740

Sphere
An imprint of
Little, Brown Book Group
Carmelite House
50 Victoria Embankment
London EC4Y 0DZ

An Hachette UK Company
www.hachette.co.uk

www.littlebrown.co.uk

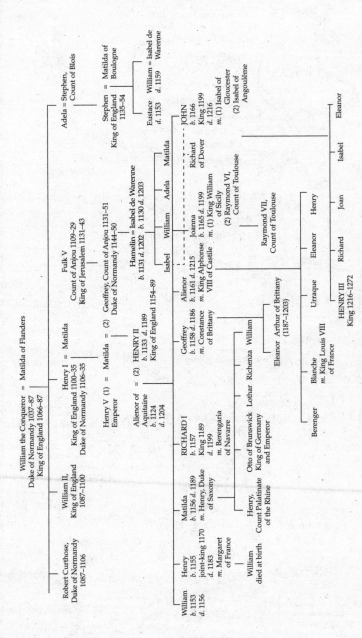

The Norman and Angevin kings of England

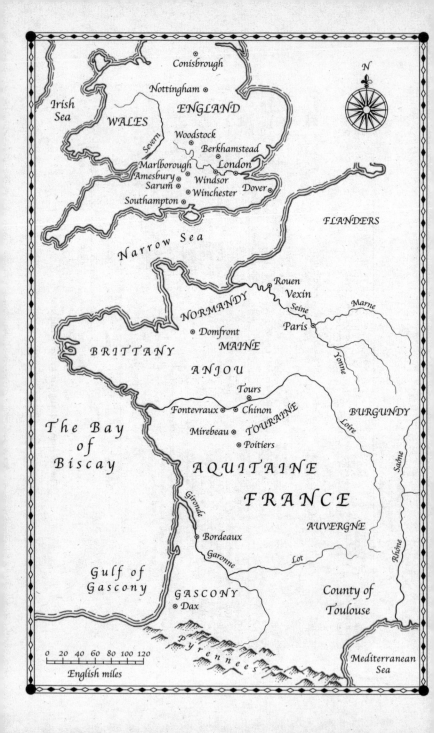

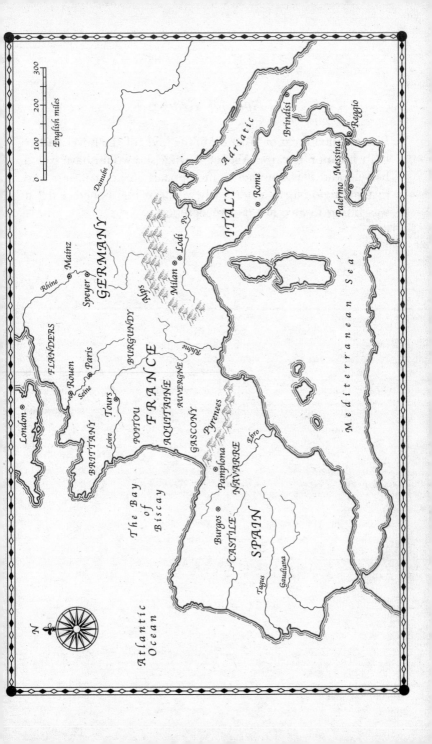

Note for Readers

I have called Eleanor 'Alienor' in the body of the novel, rather than Eleanor, because Alienor is what she would have called herself and it is how her name appears in her charters and in the Anglo-Norman texts where she is mentioned. I felt it was fitting to give her that recognition.

1

Palace of Sarum, Wiltshire, April 1176

Alienor, Duchess of Aquitaine and Normandy, Countess of Anjou, Queen to King Henry the second of England, gazed around the bare, cold chamber that had been her prison for almost two years. Pale spring sunlight splashed through the window arches, and pooled in tepid gold on the floor boards. The hearth had been swept clean of ashes, and her few portable furnishings were loaded on the baggage cart waiting in the courtyard.

A chill breeze brushed her face. All winter the wind had swept across the Downs, howling around the white-washed palace buildings like a hungry wolf. Her joints had grown stiff, and her thoughts had become as turbid as the mud at the bottom of a frozen pond. It was difficult to stir, to awaken and face the world. A cramped limb returning to life always caused an agonising tingle. Holding out her hands she noticed the soft fawn age-mottles, but they bothered her less than the way they shook.

Her wedding ring glinted. Despite all she had suffered at Henry's behest she still wore it, for while it adorned her finger, she was his queen and duchess. Even incarcerated on this wind-scoured hill top, her titles retained their potency. Henry in his usual ruthless way had isolated her here. The world moved and she had been banished from moving with it, her sin that of defying his will in rebellion and interfering with his policies. He accused her of betraying him, but the greatest betrayals had always been his.

What news she received was filtered through her gaolers, who were disposed to tell her little, and then only details that brought her low while exalting her husband. Now, however, he had summoned her to attend his Easter court at Winchester, and she was suspicious of the reason. Forgiveness in the season of Christ's rising? She doubted it. Further punishment? He must want something from her, even if only to parade her before his nobles and prove he had not had her murdered. He could ill afford to have another such accusation on his hands – not after his Archbishop of Canterbury had been hacked to death before the altar of his own cathedral by four knights of the royal household.

Hearing footsteps in the chamber beyond, she faced the door, concealing her anxiety behind regal hauteur. Much as she desired to leave this place, the notion of stepping into the world made her anxious because she did not know what she would find, or how long this reprieve from isolation would last.

She was expecting her gaoler Robert Maudit, and was astonished when the door opened and her eldest son stood on the threshold, dazzled in spring sunlight from the squint window on the stairs. His fair-brown hair was wind-tousled, and a magnificent white gyrfalcon rode on his gloved right wrist.

'Look Mama,' he greeted her with a broad smile. 'Is she not a beauty?'

Alienor's heart clenched and she felt as if all the breath had been snatched from her body. 'Harry,' she gasped as her knees started to buckle.

Immediately he was at her side, his grip firm beneath her arm as he escorted her to the window seat. 'I thought they would have told you.' His gaze was full of tender concern. 'Shall I summon your women?'

'No . . .' She shook her head and retrieved her stolen breath. 'They tell me nothing.' Her voice fractured. 'I am blind and this is too much.' She covered her eyes with a trembling hand.

He set his arm around her shoulders and she pressed into him, inhaling the scent of his healthy male body; feeling his

2

strength and vitality – qualities sapped from her own store by years of strife and then imprisonment.

The gyrfalcon bated her wings, jingling the silver bells on her jesses and uttering a series of harsh, piercing cries. 'Gently.' Her son's soft tone might have been either for her or the bird. 'Go gently.'

By the time Alienor had recovered sufficiently to look up, the falcon had settled down too and was diligently preening her flight feathers.

'My father sent me to bring you to Winchester.'

She gazed at the gyrfalcon, trapped on his glove. She could not fly until he released her, no matter the power in her wings. 'What does he want of me – other than to prove to the court that I am not dead?'

Harry's smile diminished. 'He says he wishes to speak with you – and make peace.'

'Is that so?' Bleak laughter lodged in Alienor's throat. 'And what will that entail?'

He avoided her gaze. 'He did not tell me.'

She looked round the empty room. What would she give to be free? More importantly, what would she not give? 'No, I do not suppose he would.' She struggled to contain her emotion as she thought of what might have been had Harry succeeded in overthrowing his father three years ago. 'I have so many regrets, none of them about reconciliation. Most of all I am sorry about being caught. I should have made better plans.'

'Mama . . .'

'I have had little to do here but think on what happened and my cup is full of remorse that I hesitated for too long and therefore lost the impetus.' She surged to her feet causing the gyrfalcon to dance on Harry's wrist. 'If your father has sent you to bring me to Winchester, it is because you are reconciled and we must go on from this. Truly, I am overjoyed to see you.' A grown man in his twenty-first year, the age at which his father had become England's king. 'Who else is at Winchester?'

3

'Everyone.' Harry stroked the bird until she resettled. 'Richard, Geoffrey, John, Joanna.' His smile was flippant and did not reach his eyes. 'Wives, bastards, kith and kin, all living cheek by jowl; you know how it is. No fights as yet, but plenty of opportunity.'

It would be like going from starvation to glut in a single step without time for adjustment. Her body was strung with tension as she faced leaving this chamber that was both her cage and her sanctuary. 'Well then' – her light tone was a shield – 'let us go and make the most of opportunity.'

Life's luxuries at Sarum were few and it required but a single cart to bear her belongings the twenty miles to Winchester. Harry had arrived to fetch her with a full complement of knights – mostly of his father's household, but with a few of his own retinue among them including his tutor in arms William Marshal, who awaited her at the bridle of a docile dappled-grey palfrey.

'My liege lady.' The instant he saw her, he knelt and bowed his head.

The sight of him, steadfast and strong, and his gesture of homage made Alienor tearful. 'William!' She touched his shoulder, signalling him to rise, and as he did so his dark eyes met hers in acknowledgement. Eight years ago as a young hearth knight he had saved her from ambush but had been captured himself while fighting off her attackers. She had purchased his liberty and entrusted him with protecting her eldest son while training him to knighthood. They were allies through thick and thin.

'You look well, madam.'

She gave him a reproving look. 'I find you guilty of flattery, messire. I know what I must look like after two years walled up in this place.'

'Never less than a queen,' he replied with gallantry, and she had to blink hard to clear her vision as he assisted her to mount the grey. The saddle faced sideways, with a padded

4

back support and footrest, a genteel style she had always eschewed in favour of riding astride. Chair seats slowed the pace and made her feel vulnerable and less in control. Typical of Henry that he would send one of these, thus putting her in her place before all.

'Madam, at court they say you are in fragile health and have been resting at Sarum,' William said with tactful neutrality.

She gathered the reins, her mouth twisting with contempt. 'I suppose such an excuse serves as a bandage of concealment.'

He said nothing, but his look was expressive before he turned to his horse.

Harry joined her, his chestnut palfrey dancing and arching its neck. 'Papa thought it best that you travelled like this because it is a long time since you have ridden.'

'And because it suits his purpose, Harry. I have not lost my wits or my ability to ride, only my freedom.'

Harry had the grace to look chagrined but swiftly brightened and fixed her with his disarming smile. 'Even so the sun is shining, and it is a fine day for riding – whether aside or astride.'

Alienor bit back the retort that it would be finer still to have a choice. Harry had the ability to live on the surface which she did not – to be a butterfly and enjoy a fine moment for as long as it lasted.

With a few adroit movements he transferred his hawking gauntlet and the white gyrfalcon to her wrist. 'Take her, Mama.'

She felt the balanced weight of the bird, the grip of the sword-grey talons on the padded glove, and gazed into its fierce ink-drop eyes.

He gave an approving nod. 'Now you are a great queen and duchess going about her business.'

Tears pricked her eyes once more. Until her incarceration at Sarum she had always kept a white gyrfalcon in her chamber and had taken fierce joy in flying her to hunt. The females were larger and stronger than the males. She had given Henry one at their marriage and every day she wished that gift undone.

'What is her name?' she asked.

5

'Alienor,' Harry said.

She bit her lip and strove not to weep. 'I will think of her soaring high and free,' she said when eventually she could speak.

As the cavalcade rode out from Sarum, the wind herded fresh white clouds across a sky of pale April-blue. Skylarks sang high above the Downs, the wind hissed through the new grass, and the pain in Alienor's heart was exquisite.

By the time they reached Winchester, at nightfall, Alienor was reeling with exhaustion and pain. Henry's doubts concerning her riding abilities had been borne out with a vengeance. Confined at Sarum for two years, deprived of exercise and company, she was both physically and mentally overwhelmed.

The gyrfalcon had been returned to her carrying cage several miles back and the symbolism of being shut away had not escaped Alienor. More worrisome to her was the fact that she almost envied the bird's enclosed security.

Summoning her last reserves, she projected a façade of regal detachment as they rode under archways and through sentried gateways, eventually drawing rein in a dark courtyard. Servants hastened out with lanterns that swayed in the gloom creating dances of ragged gold light. William Marshal was swiftly at her side, helping her to dismount and steadying her while she found her feet. Briefly she clung to his solid strength before pushing herself upright. To onlookers it must appear that she was indeed in fragile health and her arrival at night would only serve to compound that impression. No fanfares, no colourful parade through the street to celebrate the entry of a great and vibrant queen, but instead something subdued and nocturnal to greet a weary shadow-woman.

She turned to Harry who had been dismissing his entourage with good-humoured jests and shoulder slaps. 'It is late.' Her voice wobbled. 'I . . . I would retire immediately.'

'Of course, Mama, I should have realised.' Immediately he was attentive, issuing swift commands, and very soon a lantern bearer was escorting her to the apartments she had always kept as Queen when staying at Winchester.

She swallowed tears as she was greeted by the soft light from hanging lamps of thick green glass, walls clad in colourful hangings and a bed made up with a coverlet of silk and fur. Two books bound in leather and panelled in ivory lay on a bench with a hinged seat, and a chess set stood on a table beside a rock crystal flagon and cups. A delicate smell of incense threaded the air and braziers filled with hot coals gave off welcome heat. All the luxuries she had taken for granted before her imprisonment. After two years of privation, this unsubtle statement by Henry about what he could give and what he could take away juxtaposed feelings within her of rage and antipathy that were almost paralysing.

As she eased down on the bed, servants arrived with bread, cheese and wine. Others brought her baggage into the room, supervised by her chamber lady, Amiria. She was the widowed sister of a Shropshire baron. In her mid-thirties, she was efficient and quick about her duties, but quiet and religious, preferring to avoid the stratagems and politics of the world – precisely the kind of attendant Henry deemed suitable. No servant of Alienor's was to have the remotest capacity for subterfuge unless they were reporting to him.

Amiria knelt at Alienor's feet to remove the cowhide ankle boots her mistress had worn for riding and replace them with a pair of soft sheepskin slippers.

Harry sauntered into the room on the heels of the baggage and glanced round with a proprietorial air. 'Does this suit you, Mama? Is there anything more you need tonight?'

She shook her head wearily. 'Only that which I cannot have.'

'I would give it if I could, you know I would.'

She drew in her feet as Amiria completed her task. 'Yes, we are each constrained in our different ways.'

He poured wine into one of the cups and brought it to her. 'It's all right,' he said when she hesitated. 'It's from my household, not Papa's.'

7

Alienor took a cautious sip. The usual state of the wine at court was halfway to vinegar. However, this was smooth and rich, tasting of her Poitevan homeland and bittersweet because of it.

'Shall I summon the others?'

'Not tonight,' she said with a jolt of trepidation. 'Let me sleep first.' She was desperate to embrace her other offspring, but they could not see her like this, tired, tearful and over-whelmed – especially Richard. Henry she could not bring herself to think about because her hatred for him curdled her stomach. 'You should go too.'

His look of relief worried her, for it was one she had seen children bestow on ageing relatives to whom they owed a duty. 'I will make sure you are not disturbed, Mama.'

'I am sure the guards outside my door will do the same.'

When he had gone she lay down and bade Amiria draw the bed curtains. Curling in upon herself, she sought the oblivion of sleep, too exhausted to bother disrobing.

2

Winchester Castle, April 1176

The morning brought an initial moment of disorientation as Alienor woke and strove to remember where she was. She was stiff and sore, and the inside of her mouth tasted parched and stale. She gazed at the canopy above her head, painted with silver stars, while she drew herself together and sought the wherewithal to rise and face the world. Outside the curtains she could hear Amiria whispering to another maid and suspected that the hour was late. But why bother to rise at all? Why not just lie here and let time slide away?

Another woman addressed the maids, the voice gently enquiring, but firm with authority. An instant later the bed curtains rattled aside and Alienor's sister by marriage, Isabel de Warenne, stood in the rectangle of light, a goblet in her hand.

'I've sent away last night's wine and brought you fresh spring water,' Isabel announced. 'There is new bread and honey and I have taken the liberty of sending for a bath.'

Bemused, Alienor took the goblet and drank. The water was clear, cold and refreshing and the sight of Isabel comforted her sore heart because here was a true and stalwart friend.

'Harry told me last night you had arrived but insisted you were not to be disturbed, otherwise I would have come to you straight away.'

Alienor set her drink aside and opened her arms. Isabel fell into them and then burst into tears, which made Alienor cry too.

'You foolish woman,' she sniffed, wiping her eyes as she pulled away, 'look what you have made me do.'

'I cannot help it.' Isabel dabbed her face daintily on her sleeve lining.

'Your heart is too tender,' Alienor scolded. 'That is why I could not have borne to see you last night. I am not sure I can bear it even now.' She picked up the goblet again. 'Ah Isabel, it is so hard, to leave the grey and return to colour. You cannot begin to know what he has done to me.'

Several maids arrived bearing a tub and pails of steamy water.

'Perhaps not, but I want to help you.'

Alienor concealed a grimace. Isabel had a penchant for doing good deeds to better the lives of the afflicted. She suspected she was one of them in her eyes. 'Do not dare pity me,' she warned.

Isabel's hazel-brown eyes widened with hurt. 'I would never do that! You malign me.' She produced a vial of rose attar and, going to the tub, tipped some precious drops into the steaming water, causing a wonderful fragrance to billow into the room.

'You cannot help yourself.' Alienor softened the comment with a smile, although Isabel continued to look reproachful.

Once disrobed by Amiria, Alienor stepped into the tub and sank down into the blood-hot rose-scented water, uttering a soft gasp halfway between pain and pleasure.

Isabel refreshed Alienor's cup. 'John and Joanna were so excited to know you were coming,' she said.

Alienor's throat tightened. When Henry had shut her away from the world for rebelling against him, he had shut her away from her children too. Isabel, who was wed to Henry's half-brother Hamelin, had temporarily taken them into her household to raise with her own children, which had been one small grace amid the devastation. 'How are they faring?'

'Well indeed – as you will see,' Isabel said fondly. 'Joanna is a fine young lady and John and my William have become close friends as well as cousins.'

'It has been a great comfort to me knowing they are safe in your hands.'

Isabel waved away the acknowledgement but looked pleased. 'It has been my privilege. They are both so clever. I have never seen anyone so adept at working an exchequer board as John, and Joanna reads aloud with never a stumble.'

Alienor glowed with pride at Isabel's acclaim, but felt a guilty frisson of resentment. She should be the one praising such intelligence instead of hearing about it from the lips of another woman, even if Isabel was her sister by marriage and a good friend. Nevertheless, a new mood was clearing her path, like sun burning through fog. She had been shaken back to life and there was no turning back.

'Do you know why Henry has brought me to Winchester?' she asked as Amiria helped her to don a clean chemise, and a gown of scarlet wool. 'Harry says he wants to make peace, but I fear his motives will not be to my advantage.'

Isabel shook her head. 'Hamelin has said nothing.'

Alienor sent her a sharp look. 'He does not know, or he will not tell you?'

Isabel dropped her gaze. 'I do not know that either.'

And she would not venture to ask: Alienor knew Isabel's propensity for refusing to see life's harsher realities in their true light.

'I hope you can make peace,' Isabel said anxiously. 'It is no life for you at Sarum.'

Alienor curled her lip. 'I expect Henry will use life at Sarum as one of his levers. He imprisons me there for nigh on two years, denies me all contact with the world and my children and takes from me all things of grace and luxury. Now he brings me to Winchester and showers me with everything that I lack. But I tell you this: I will never yield him Aquitaine, if that is his price. I would rather return to Sarum. Indeed I would rather be dead.'

'Alienor . . .' Isabel extended an imploring hand.

'Do not look at me like that!' Alienor snapped, and then drew a long breath up through her body, filling herself with life and banking down her irritation. 'I bless you for waking me up,' she said in a gentler voice, and kissed Isabel's cheek. 'I may not be ready to speak to Henry, but I am desperate to see my children.'

Alienor had just finished breaking her fast on bread and honey when John and Joanna arrived with their nurses and Isabel's four offspring, their cousins. Alienor's heart turned over, for she barely recognised the son and daughter whom she had bidden farewell at Sarum's gates two years ago. Aged nine and ten they were still children, but standing on the final stepping stone before the perilous leap into adulthood.

John was first to come forward, smoothly bending one knee. 'My lady mother,' he said. Joanna curtseyed and murmured the same. Her hair was plaited in a gleaming braid, the light brown shot with distinct glints of her father's auburn.

11

The constraints binding the situation were like taut ropes at full strain. In a sudden flurry, Alienor slashed through the formality and gathered her youngest children to her heart. 'How you have grown!' She fought tears. 'Ah it has been too long but I have thought about you every day and prayed to see you again!'

'We prayed too, Mama,' John said, his expression innocent and open.

'Yes, they did,' Isabel confirmed. 'I never had to remind them.'

Wiping her eyes on her cuff, Alienor took John and Joanna to sit in the embrasure with her, while she recovered. Eventually she was able to greet Isabel's son and three daughters with composure and was astonished at how they too were no longer tender little infants but thriving youngsters on the swift path to maturity. Isabel's son William was the same age as John and the pair had formed the sort of young male bond that involved continually testing the boundaries and each other in cub-play while being united against the world. Isabel's eldest daughter, Belle, was a similar age to Joanna and possessed the alabaster skin and striking green-blue eyes of her grandsire Geoffrey, Count of Anjou, who had been famed for his beauty. 'I can tell this one is going to strew the road with broken hearts.' Alienor smiled. 'Have you betrothed her yet?'

Belle preened at the compliment, but kept her lids modestly lowered.

'No, we want her to be older, and to have a say in her choice.'

Alienor raised her brows. 'What if she sets her heart on a kitchen boy or a minstrel with pretty words in his mouth and nothing in his purse?'

Isabel waved her hand. 'Obviously there are limits, but within them she shall have a choice – as shall all my girls.'

'What does Hamelin say?'

'He agrees with me. There is plenty of time, and no one has yet made an offer we are unable to refuse.'

Alienor said nothing. For a conventional woman, Isabel could be stubborn and wayward in matters of the heart and home. Some might call her brave and truthful, others indulgent and foolish. She could see why Hamelin would agree with her. Henry's half-brother ruled his domestic household with benign but absolute authority and would be reluctant to change that state of affairs by giving his daughters in marriage at a young age and exposing them to the influences of other men. Alienor's own daughters had made matches before puberty in order to secure binding political alliances, but there were fewer onuses on Isabel and Hamelin.

She heard the sound of approaching male voices raised in jovial banter and an instant later her older sons surged into the chamber with their father, bringing with them the fresh scent of outdoors and stirring the atmosphere with vibrant energy. All four were laughing uproariously because Henry's favourite terrier had absconded with the Bishop of Ely's jewelled fur hat and had proceeded to murder it round the back of the stables.

Alienor's gaze went straight to Richard, the heir to her duchy. Her heart was open for all of her sons but Richard was its light. Count of Poitou, future Duke of Aquitaine. His red-gold hair gleamed with vitality, his eyes were the rich summer blue of cornflowers, and he was the tallest among them.

Abandoning the joke, he came to kneel at her feet in formal greeting and receive the kiss of peace. Alienor used the ritual to maintain her dignity, although her emotions were spiralling like a whirlwind. Their eyes met, filled with a multitude of things they dared not say in front of Henry and the others.

Richard rose and yielded his place to his brother Geoffrey, a year younger, brown-haired and slighter of build. He was being groomed to rule Brittany and was betrothed to Constance, its heiress duchess. Still waters in Geoffrey ran deep and the open expression on his face was not necessarily indicative of the complex thoughts flowing beneath. 'My lady mother.'

Taking her hand, he pressed it to his brow. His manner was pleasant but his eyes were guarded and inscrutable.

Harry kissed her warmly and squeezed her hand in reassurance. 'Are you feeling better now, Mama?'

'I have donned my armour,' she answered with bleak humour. Was she feeling better? Different perhaps; ready to do battle.

'These are for you.' He poured half a dozen gaudy jewels into her palm, including a large amethyst drilled with two holes, from one of which dangled a thread with scraps of squirrel fur attached. 'Spoils from the kill; don't tell the Bishop of Ely.' His eyes gleamed with laughter.

Alienor clasped the stones in her fist for a moment, knowing their value and how they might be put to good use. Henry would not confiscate them when there were so many witnesses and it was all part of the jest. Having locked the gems in her jewel casket, she turned, her body taut with resistance, to face her husband who had deliberately let his sons go first so that he could observe her interaction with them. She did not curtsey and he did not bow.

'Madam, I trust your sojourn in peace and solitude has been of benefit?' His eyes were as hard as chips of flint.

'Indeed, sire. I have had time to think on many matters and to see them more clearly than I did before.'

'I am pleased to hear it. As you see I have come to an understanding with our sons and there is no reason why we cannot all dwell in peace together.'

There were many reasons for the opposite but Alienor bit her tongue.

He held out his arm. 'The court awaits us in the hall, if it please you.'

'Would it matter if it did not?'

'I think we both know the answer to that,' he said pleasantly, although his gaze remained cold.

She did not want to touch him, but she made herself place her hand on his sleeve and walk with him, knowing he had

14

no desire for this contact either, except as a means of exerting his power. She had perforce to play this game until she found out what he was up to, and then they would see.

3

Winchester Castle, Easter Court, April 1176

Alienor sat in a window embrasure with Isabel, embroidering the sleeve on Joanna's new gown. It was intricate work but her stitches were swift because her reprieve might end at any moment. At Sarum her sewing consisted of plain linen shirts and chemises for the poor and the sick – deemed part of her penance for encouraging her sons to rebel against their father – and it was a joy to work with silk and beauty again.

Yesterday had been one of family gathering and reunion, as bright on the surface as sunlit water concealing turbid undercurrents. Everyone had smiled, and at times the laughter had been genuine, but darker emotions lurked beneath the surface and no one had spoken of the matters that had caused the rifts. Instead there had been jesting and tales of the hunt. The demise of the Bishop of Ely's fur hat had been reprised several times, and the Bishop himself had taken the incident in good part, graciously conceding the gems to Alienor's custody. No mention was made of the strife that had turned son against father and resulted in Alienor's imprisoned isolation at Sarum, yet it was an episode of such enormity that there was no room in the chamber for anything else, and every breath and word was tainted with its presence.

This morning Henry had gone hunting with their sons, at pains to show her the hearty masculine rapport that existed between them. *See, they are mine. You tried to take them from me and you did not succeed.* That was the version he was vigorously

15

promoting, but while it hurt like a ripped fingernail, she did not believe him.

Joanna and her de Warenne cousins were occupied with small embroidery projects of their own, as were Harry's young wife Marguerite and her mousy-haired sister Alais who was betrothed to Richard. Constance of Brittany, Geoffrey's future wife, was reading to the women from a bestiary, and had just informed them, grimacing, that camels would rather drink dirty water than clean, stirring it up with their feet to create slime.

'Did you see camels when you went to the Holy Land, Mama?' Joanna asked. 'Did they do that?'

'Not that I noticed,' Alienor replied. 'You must remember that not everything learned men write is the truth. I rode a camel once in Jerusalem. Louis was horrified at the impropriety, but that did not stop me.'

Joanna's eyes widened. 'What was it like?'

'Sore.' Alienor made a face. 'And I felt sea-sick. They are taller than horses so you can see further, but they are not as sure-footed, nor do they respond as swiftly to commands. A fast Arabian courser though – ah, now that is different.' Her eyes lit up at the memory. 'Louis disapproved of that too. He hated to see his wife racing about the desert on a horse as fast as the wind. I suspect he thought I might run away from him – hah, and he was probably right! I wish I had an Arabian horse now, or even a camel; but then if wishes were horses, I would have been in Poitiers, in my own hall, long ago.'

Isabel gently touched Alienor's hand and gave her a sympathetic look that nevertheless held a warning.

'Concerning the eagle,' Constance's light voice continued, 'it is known that when the eagle is old, it becomes young again in a strange manner. When its eyes are darkened and its wings are heavy with age, it seeks out a fountain, crystal and pure, where the water bubbles up and shines in the clear sunlight. Above this fountain it rises high up into the air, and fixes its eyes upon the light of the sun and gazes upon it until the heat thereof sets on fire its eyes and wings. Then it descends into the fountain where the water is clearest and brightest, and plunges and bathes three times, until it is fresh and renewed and healed of its old age.'

Alienor's eyes stung with tears. If only it were as simple as that.

The reading was rudely interrupted by Henry who swept into the chamber from his morning hunt, all fiery with the energy of the chase. Mud stained his boots; there was a tear in his cloak and twigs in his hat. Alienor could smell his sweat. There was no sign of their sons, and Henry was minus attendants. Her heart started to pound. So now they came to it, the moment of barter.

He tossed his hat and cloak to a duty squire, dismissing the youth at the same time, and approached the embrasure. 'Leave, all of you,' he commanded with a brusque wave of his hand. 'I wish to speak with the Queen in private.'

'I want to stay.' Pouting, Joanna leaned against Alienor.

'Want all you wish, but do as I say,' Henry said shortly. 'This conversation is not for you.'

'Come, Joanna,' Isabel cajoled, 'I need to sort through my jewel casket and you and Belle can help me.'

Joanna gave her father a swift look that was almost a glare but, unable to resist the lure of her aunt's jewels, flounced him a curtsey and departed with Isabel.

Henry hissed through his teeth. 'Daughters,' he muttered as he sat in the place Isabel had vacated.

Alienor picked up her sewing. 'It is to be expected. She is reaching an age when she understands a great deal.'

'She is also reaching an age when she needs to behave with dignity and decorum,' he said irritably, 'and to obey her father.' He pinched a strand of gold embroidery thread between forefinger and thumb and examined it in the light from the window. 'Envoys are on their way from Sicily to finalise a marriage proposal on behalf of King William, and I am of a mind to accept if the terms are advantageous.'

Alienor made a couple of intricate stitches. An alliance with

Sicily had been mooted several years ago, and put to one side, but not as a rejection. Another daughter given to far-flung lands, probably never to be seen again. And yet in its climate and culture, Sicily was not unlike Aquitaine, and might suit Joanna well. William of Sicily was perhaps ten years older than their daughter – an age gap that could be either a short step or a gulf. 'Does Joanna know?'

'No, but I will tell her soon. If the negotiations are straight-forward, she will leave before autumn.'

Alienor looked down at her work. Hating to ask, but swallowing her pride, she said, 'Will you let me stay and spend some time with her?'

'I might see my way to it.' He heaved an exaggerated sigh. 'I have always done what is necessary for the unity of our realms. My sons understand that now, and I hope your time to reflect has brought you to a better sense of reason. How are we meant to inspire kingship and loyalty if people do not see us as united?'

My sons, she noted, not *our sons*. 'I have had little else to do but ponder the matter,' she said, and turned the fabric to look at the back of her stitches. 'Since you have slackened my chain and brought me to Winchester, you clearly have something in mind. Harry said you wanted to make peace?'

He wound the glittering filament of thread round his fore-finger. 'Do you remember when we visited Fontevraud together?'

An interesting gambit. 'That was a long time ago.'

He gave a twisted smile. 'Yes, in the good years.'

Her mind filled with an image of strolling with Henry through dew-damp grass, hand in hand, the abbey's walls pearled in early morning mist, a nurse following with their firstborn carried high in her arms. A future of endless oppor-tunity stretched before them and her heart had brimmed with certainty and exultation. But Will had been tomb-dust for more than twenty years, and the memory was but a swift sun-flash on perilous water. She had visited Fontevraud many times since, but never with Henry. 'What of it?'

'You have always found balm for your soul there. I do not believe you have the same connection with Sarum?'

Alienor stopped sewing and gave him a narrow look. 'Your point being?'

He rose and went to the window. The movement released the acrid smell of the hunt from his body and garments. 'The abbey at Amesbury is to come under the rule of Fontevraud and will require an abbess. It would be a worthy project for you without stigma. You would be honoured.'

Abbess! So that was his plan. Pack her off to a nunnery and expect her to spend her time in prayer and charitable works and perhaps a little socialising sufficient unto the dignity and standing of a noble lady of the Church. A small and pretty death – and presumably a hard and cold one at Sarum if she resisted.

'I would not put pressure on you once you were there,' he said smoothly. 'You could do as you pleased – go out riding, entertain visitors of rank and be an asset to our dynasty, not a liability.'

Alienor eyed the back of his head. His hair was thinning and the once ruddy gold was the hue of dusty sand. 'I think I would prefer to spend time in Poitiers,' she said in a conversational tone. 'In another two months the cherries will be ripening and early summer is always beautiful there. That would truly be balm to my soul.'

He turned round. 'That would not be appropriate. After what has happened, you can never return there.' His stare was as hard as the stone against which he had been leaning. 'I have been talking to various Churchmen and they tell me it can be arranged that we are no longer married.'

Alienor was neither shocked nor surprised, for she had been down this dusty path before. 'You are speaking of an annulment?'

He shrugged. 'Of that kind, yes.'

'Let us be clear and not mince words. You do mean an annulment. What else of "that kind" is there?'

He looked down at the twist of gold thread between his fingers. 'Yes, if you will have it baldly stated. An annulment.'

'You wish to make me nothing.' Her voice was low-pitched with angry contempt. 'You wish for me to just disappear, to not exist.' A sensation filled her stomach like heavy stones dropping, one on top of the other. She would not let him do this to her. 'I ask myself what benefit there is to you from such an offer?'

He shrugged. 'I do not see why you should object. It means we can go our own ways and cease this acrimony.'

If there was acrimony it was because he had belittled her at every turn and was still doing so. Hiving her off to a convent and denying her the right to visit her own duchy. Perhaps he was looking to take another wife – a threat she could not ignore because if a new queen bore him children, her own offspring might be endangered. She would stand in front of a sword to protect them.

Alienor set her sewing to one side and rose to face him. 'I have no intention of seeing our marriage annulled, not for what you offer in exchange. The prospect of a fairer prison will not sway my intent.'

'You will find you have little choice, madam. I can obtain documentation to prove our marriage was consanguineous and unlawful from the start.'

She gave a contemptuous laugh. 'I am sure there are many reasons for us not to be married, Henry, but they were all overcome and dealt with when we were first wed. Whatever evidence you provide, I can show equal that will give yours the lie. I may not have armies at my disposal, but that matters not in this arena. After what happened to Thomas Becket, there are many in Rome who will be delighted to uphold my case. Moreover, you have to keep me alive, because after Becket, it would be too easy for men to believe you capable of murdering your queen as well as your archbishop.'

Henry flushed scarlet, the broken veins a purple script across his cheeks. He raised his fist. 'By God, madam, you go too far!'

'Then strike me,' she challenged with a proud toss of her head. 'Send me back to Sarum and then explain why to "your" sons and see just how they answer you.'

They stood within the embrasure, heaving for breath, glaring hatred at each other.

'By God, you shall give me what I want,' he snarled.

'I care not what you do,' Alienor retorted with bravado. 'You have already brought me low; whatever you do, makes no difference.'

'Oh, but it does. Think on it well, madam. I will ask you again before this Easter gathering is over, and by then I expect you to have come to your senses. You know the outcome if you do not.' He shouldered her out of the way, making her stagger, and stormed from the room.

Alienor's knees gave way. She fumbled behind her until she felt the cushion on the window seat, and sank down, trembling. Dear Christ; he wanted an annulment so he could shove her into a convent and forget her. She had very few weapons to hand, but refusal was one of them and she would fight him all the way.

Isabel tip-toed into the chamber and approached Alienor where she sat in numb silence. On seeing her condition, she waved the other women away and brought her a cup of wine herself.

'He wants an annulment,' Alienor said stiffly. 'He wants me to go to Amesbury and take the veil.'

Isabel gasped. 'Oh my dear!'

'He wants to make a nun of me and take away Aquitaine.' She trembled with her hatred and revulsion of him. 'He says it will be honourable; he says I will have peace and freedom from strife, but people say that about death, do they not?' She looked at the wine, its surface shimmering in her unsteady hand. 'One day I may embrace the cloister, but not yet. My child-bearing years are behind me, but I shall not be treated like a used-up old nag put out to grass for her last days.' She shot Isabel a fierce look. 'I will never consent, never!'

Isabel sat down beside her, and after a moment said hesitantly, 'I know it must be difficult to consider, but is it not better than returning to Sarum or being kept under lock and key at Winchester?'

Alienor tightened her lips and looked away towards the light from the window. The strand of gold thread Henry had been winding around his finger sparkled on the floor. 'No,' she said, 'it is not.'

'But you will have the company of other gentlewomen, and books to read and all manner of matters to keep you occupied.' Isabel touched Alienor's knee, her tone coaxing and sympathetic. 'You will have fresh air and daily comforts, and you will be honoured. When you think about it, is it really so bad what he is asking?'

Isabel's determination to see the good in every situation even if it meant taking the path of least resistance had always exasperated Alienor and now, because of what had just happened, it spilled over into fury. 'You do not understand, you never do!' she lashed out. 'I am a queen and this thing he asks of me is not my role. It sweeps me out of his way like dust.'

Isabel made a gesture of appeasement. 'I did not mean to offend you; I mean it for the best.'

'The best? Hah! He would make me nothing and you condone it because you refuse to see the world as it is.'

'Alienor—'

'Oh go away,' she spat. 'I do not need your kind of advice.'

Isabel bit her lip. 'I want to help you, that is all.'

'You cannot help me,' Alienor snapped with miserable anger. 'I mean it, leave me; I do not want you here.'

Isabel rose to her feet, her chin dimpling. 'As you wish, madam.' She formally curtsied and fled the room.

Alienor closed her eyes and covered her face with her hands. She almost called Isabel back, but pride and anger fettered her to her seat.

No one approached her, for who would risk the lioness's den? She was alone. After a while she lowered her hands to her lap and raised her chin, her expression taut and regal. In a strange way she felt expanded and filled with purpose. She would deal with whatever came her way on her own. She was a queen, and by the very nature of the role she was set apart from other women, even those she thought to call friend. This incident with Isabel had proved to her yet again that the only person she could rely on was herself.

4

Winchester Castle, Easter Court, April 1176

Hamelin de Warenne, Earl of Surrey, was relaxing before the fire enjoying the ministrations of his three daughters. They fussed around him, voices bright as songbirds as they combed his hair and bathed his sore feet. He had been on them all day, attending to the demands of his energetic royal half-brother, and this respite was a blessed relief.

He thought with complacence how fortunate he was in his family. His son was a clever lad with a quick mind and robust strength that boded well for the future of the earldom, while his daughters enriched his life with a warm glow of family and fulfilment. One day they would marry, and their husbands would be fortune-favoured to receive such wonderful wives – and would know it from him constantly. But not yet; he and Isabel could take pleasure in the girls for a little longer. Belle, although beginning the journey into womanhood, was not yet twelve, Adela was seven and Matilda five. Unlike Henry's daughters, there was no rush to tie them into grand dynastic unions.

He glanced at his wife who was busy sorting through a clothing chest, her back turned and her movements erratic as she tugged and pulled, but he thought little of it, other than to note she was engaged as usual in some mysterious female domestic business.

'Belle, play for me,' he said.

His eldest daughter fetched her harp and perched on a footstool at his feet. Her plait of rich brown hair swung forward and she flicked it back with a graceful movement of her wrist and a smile for her father. She was an accomplished musician, her fingers pliant as ribbons, weaving the tune through the strings. Matilda clambered into his lap for a cuddle and he curved his arm around her lithe, small body in tender protection. Having been closeted with Henry for most of the day he was in desperate need of this family moment to cleanse himself of the murk of the court. He constantly praised God that he had such joy at the heart of his family when others lacked all sustenance.

Later, after the girls had kissed him and retired to bed, overseen by their nurses, and his son had similarly departed, he turned to Isabel and patted the bench.

'Come, you have been very quiet tonight. Bring me a cup of wine and sit a while.'

She did as he asked, but he marked her preoccupation. Something was gnawing on her bones, but she would tell him in her own time and he was not the kind to seek trouble unnecessarily. He took the wine and stretched out his legs towards the fire. 'I suppose you have heard about Henry's plan to annul his marriage to Alienor?' he asked.

When she did not answer he looked up and was in time to see her face crumple as she burst into tears. Astonished and dismayed, Hamelin took her hand. 'What is it?' he asked. 'What's wrong?'

'Nothing,' she choked. 'I will be all right by and by.'

'Come now, is it what I have just said?' He wondered if she believed her own position was threatened by the news. 'It is not as though I am going to ask for annulment from you. Why are you so upset?'

'I . . . I'm not upset,' Isabel sobbed, mortified that she could not hold herself together in her own household which was supposed to be Hamelin's haven of peace and tranquillity.

24

'To the contrary I can see that you are. Tell me.'

'It's Alienor,' she wept. 'She . . . she turned on me when I suggested that an annulment was for the best. Told me to go away and that I did not understand. It was as if I was her enemy, and all I have ever done for her is as nothing!'

Hamelin grimaced. Much as he loved his wife, her sensitivity sometimes made matters awkward, and he had no intention of becoming embroiled in a woman's spat. Whatever Henry's foibles, schemes and rages, they were far more easily dealt with than issues involving women. 'Calm yourself, my love,' he soothed. 'I have lost count of the occasions Henry has ordered me from his presence because he has disagreed with something I have said, or just because he is angry with everyone. He needs me when it comes to the crux – as Alienor needs you, whatever she says to the contrary.' He made a wry face. 'We are their props even when they spurn us. Have some wine and dry your eyes. It will pass.'

'So,' he said when eventually her tears had turned to occasional snuffles and he had refreshed her cup. 'Alienor is not disposed towards an annulment then?'

Isabel gave a small shake of her head. 'No. She was like a lioness when I said it might be for the best.' She twisted the damp square of linen she had used to mop her eyes. 'Even if Henry sends her back to Sarum or puts her in a dungeon, she will still refuse him.'

A pained expression crossed Hamelin's face. Henry and Alienor's marital difficulties were a cause of friction far beyond their personal arena. He wasn't at all surprised at Alienor's contrary response to Henry's suggestion.

'Has Henry told you why he wants an annulment?' she asked.

'He says he desires a clean cut to sever himself from Alienor. She will be honourably occupied with duties at Amesbury and he will be free to continue with his own life.'

'Alienor thinks Henry is belittling her.' Isabel gave him a searching look. 'The rumours have not gone away that he is planning a marriage to Alais of France or to Rosamund de Clifford.'

Hamelin shrugged. 'The gossips will always create fire from sparks. Knowing my brother he will do neither because of the upheaval it would cause. One is betrothed to his son and the other is a mere baron's daughter. He is not that foolish.' He pulled her to him and gave her a kiss. 'You must distance yourself. That is the only way to stay safe and survive.'

'Yes, you are right.' Isabel leaned into him, seeking comfort.

'I have some other news that might be more to your taste,' he announced after a moment. 'Henry tells me Sicilian envoys will be arriving with a marriage offer from their king to our niece Joanna. If their terms are acceptable, Henry is going to agree.'

'I knew it had been mooted, but I had not realised . . . it is far away for the child.'

'It is Joanna's destiny to make a great marriage and foster good relations between the countries. She knows that, and you have prepared her well. By all accounts the bridegroom is handsome and well disposed, and the Sicilian court is one of the most prestigious in Christendom.'

'It is a good match and I am pleased for the great future she will have, but I shall miss her. So will Belle.'

'It is her duty,' Hamelin said firmly. 'It is what she was born to.'

'I was born to it too. I might have been England's queen.' Isabel thought of her first husband who had been heir to the throne and had stepped aside for Henry. If fate had been different, Alienor's crown would have been hers. 'I am glad I am not; it would have broken my heart to let our daughters go at so young an age. How soon must Joanna leave if it is agreed?'

'By the autumn.'

Hamelin's white gazehound leaped up on the other side of the bench, circled several times and then settled, resting her muzzle on Hamelin's thigh.

'Henry wants me to escort her there and see her safely bestowed.' A smile lit in his eyes. 'You are to come too, so the time for parting is not quite at hand. What do you say to that?'

Isabel pulled back from him and then she laughed in surprised pleasure. 'I do not know what to say! It is a prestigious undertaking, and there will be much to do.' She thought of all the items for a bride's wedding chest, and the new garments and trousseau that would have to be assembled, not to mention the organising of a new household for Joanna. Henry would not allow Alienor to do it, that was for certain. She hastily stopped thinking about Alienor before she began crying again.

'Indeed there will, but say nothing for now,' he warned. 'Do not go making a great display of packing the baggage.'

'Of course not!' She gave him an indignant look. 'I can keep secrets!'

'I know you can,' he mollified her, and then grinned. 'It will be a fine opportunity to bring home silks from the Sicilian workshops for gowns, and wall hangings, hmm?'

Isabel gave a mock flounce. 'I might just suspect you of offering sweetmeats to comfort me.'

'What is wrong with that? What pleases you pleases me because it brings harmony to my household – and I value that above all things.'

'I value it too.' She bit her lip in contrition. 'I am sorry.'

'For what? Having a gentle heart?' Tilting her face to his, he kissed her. 'I treasure that in you too.'

Isabel responded warmly before drawing back again. 'You say it will pass, but words are easier than deeds. What should I do about Alienor?'

He gave a pragmatic shrug. 'Do nothing. Let the dust settle. Alienor has few enough allies that she can afford to spurn your friendship and counsel. Let her come to you, but do not expect an apology. Neither she nor Henry has it in them.'

Isabel shooed the dog away, and perching in Hamelin's lap,

curled her arms around his neck. 'I never want that to happen between us,' she said with vehemence, 'that we should come to a divide in the path and go our separate ways in anger.'

Hamelin wrapped his arm around her waist. 'We must all sleep alone in the tomb, my love, but in life we are joined as one flesh – as our children attest. I am not Henry, you are not Alienor – God forbid.'

They went to bed and made love thoroughly and tenderly, something they had not done in a while, because the routines of life and the court had left no time or energy for such expression. When they fell asleep, they were spooned against each other like a complete chirograph, two halves of one whole.

5

Winchester Castle, Easter Court, April 1176

Alienor sat across a chess board from Richard. A damp spring dusk was darkening into nightfall; the shutters had been closed and lamps and candles cast the chamber in grainy amber light, deep with shadows. Henry was absent, as was the Archbishop of Canterbury and the Bishop of London, which was ominous, but not in a way that gave Alienor cause for fear. Rather she was sourly amused, for she knew perfectly well what was taking place.

Between moves on the board, she pressed on with her sewing despite the poor light, determined to finish the embroidered piece before she and Joanna parted company – which might be imminent if Henry sent her back to Sarum in punishment for her obstinacy.

Richard rubbed his chin, considering his next move. His red-gold hair tumbled over his brow and she suppressed a maternal urge to push it away from his eyes. He was very much the man now and any soft gesture from her would be interpreted as fussing.

He had more pieces than her, but although she seemed to be at a disadvantage in terms of what she had left, she continued to hold him off. She was making him work hard, and a deep frown made two vertical lines between his eyebrows as he moved his knight.

Alienor deliberately responded with a ploy that loosened the situation and allowed him through. In part it was a sacrifice, but it was also a trap, because depending on his judgement he could either win or be destroyed. He reached out strong, slender fingers, but then hesitated. A slow smile curved his lips as he changed his mind, and made a different move that avoided her trap. He looked at her, acknowledging her ruse, and exulting that he had seen through it.

'I am proud of you,' Alienor praised. 'In the old days you would have moved first and cursed yourself afterwards.'

He gave a narrow smile. 'I would be a fool not to have learned from past mistakes.' His frown returned with increased intensity. 'Mama, I wish there was something I could do about . . . about your situation.'

She reached across the board and took his hand. Although smooth across the back with youth, it belonged to an active man, and his palms were callused. 'As do I, but we must be practical. For the moment your father controls the board and you must decide how best to serve your future. If it means cooperating with him do so, but never lose sight of your own goals.'

His mouth twisted to the right, a mannerism from young boyhood when confronted with something distasteful. 'He has set me the task of keeping order in Poitou, and I need more resources to quell the unrest. Aimery de Thouars is up in arms because Papa has denied him his wife's inheritance rights and has used them instead to enrich my little brother.'

Alienor grimaced too. 'The only matter in which your father

29

can be trusted is to make life difficult. He will employ you in Poitou but he will still control the finances and keep you beholden to him. Be on your guard.'

'That goes without saying, Mama.'

They finished their game, Richard winning because she had deliberately given him the chance in order to see how he would react. As he leaned back from the game and took a drink from his goblet, she said, 'Your father has asked for an annulment to our marriage, and I have refused. I have told him that hell will freeze over first, and that is why he is currently shut away with his bishops. He desires to send me into retirement as the new abbess at Amesbury.'

Richard almost choked on his wine and anger flashed in his eyes. 'Dear God, Mama, is this what he calls making peace?'

'I do not think the religious life would suit me, it is true.'

A red flush crawled up his face. 'He cannot do this. I shall—'

'You shall do nothing,' she interrupted firmly. 'Let me deal with it.'

Richard's flush darkened. Even if he had managed to control his impetuousness, the lesson was not yet ingrained. 'But he disparages you, and he sets us all at naught. I will not let him do this!'

'What did I say about learning to look before you leap? It behoves you not to become involved because you need his resources to manage Poitou. While you have that military control, you have power of a kind, even if you still owe it to him. Do not worry; he shall not have his annulment.'

Richard breathed out hard. 'Have you told my brothers?'

'Not yet; I have not had an opportunity to speak with them. But I want all of you to behave with restraint.'

Still fulminating, Richard flicked at one of the chess pieces, revulsion plain on his face. 'You must have heard the rumours about him plotting to marry Alais. Everyone treats it as an outrageous jest but I am not so sure.'

'Who knows what your father would and would not do,' Alienor said with contempt, 'although taking Alais to wife would not seem like wisdom.'

Richard's expression was edged with defiance. 'I certainly have no intention of wedding her. There are heiresses who would better suit my needs. Rather a wife from lands bordering Aquitaine than a French mouse.'

'I agree. It was never my desire to see any of my sons betrothed or wedded to France,' Alienor said with distaste. 'For Harry it is too late, and Marguerite may suit his needs if we are being practical, but I vowed when your father forced you to make your pledge to Alais, you would never be bound by that oath if I could help it.'

'It will not happen.' Richard's jaw was set with determination. 'For now my father will procrastinate because it keeps the power in his own hands.' He sent her a look from under his brows in which she read anxiety, even though he was trying to be hard-headed. 'There is the de Clifford girl too. You do not think he would take her to wife?'

Her smile was caustic. 'It is a moot point since he is bound to me until one of us dies, but again, I doubt such a thing of him. Taking a girl of the lower nobility for a mistress is one thing, but making her his wife quite another. No, he wants this annulment in order to cut off the roots of my power, and remove me from all areas of influence. Retiring me to Amesbury is more convenient for him than keeping me locked up at Sarum – more civilised he would say. What use am I when he has loyal sons to do his bidding?'

Richard scowled. 'He should not treat you like this.'

'That has never stopped him. It is the way things are – for now.' She tapped the chess board with her forefinger. 'Strategy.' She made sure he took her point. 'Do not waste your time, but bide it.'

Clad in a simple shift of filmy Cambray linen, Rosamund de Clifford sat in Henry's bed, plaiting her silky hair into a single long braid. A ring of pearl and gold that had once belonged to Henry's mother gleamed on her heart finger and she was humming softly to herself as she worked.

The braid ended in a thick tassel at her waistline and she placed her hand just below it and smiled, thinking of the new life growing inside her. Henry's child, a prince of royal blood, conceived at the Christmas gathering, on the very anniversary of Jesus's birth. She had been Henry's mistress for almost ten years, but this was only the second time she had conceived. The first had ended in a miscarriage before she had quickened, but this time she had reached her fourth month and her belly was showing the first gentle swell of fruitfulness. Come the autumn, she would present Henry with his new heir and by then, hopefully, she would be his queen.

He said she was his wife in all but name, and had given her his mother's ring in token of that bond. When she was younger she had been satisfied, but now she wanted more. It was not enough to be at Henry's side at court and in his chamber at night because without the sanction of the Church she was just another concubine; it wasn't the same as being a wife. His queen had that title and privilege, although she did not deserve it for what she had done to him, urging his sons to rebel and dishonouring his name. Alienor was barren now too, dried up with years and redundant, whereas she was ripe with child and could give Henry everything he needed. It would be best for everyone if Alienor agreed to an annulment and ended her days as a nun.

She heard voices outside – Henry bidding his squires goodnight – and she quickly tidied away her toilet items and straightened the covers. Henry entered the room and immediately her heart sank, for his lips were set in a tight line, and he was limping, favouring the foot with the sore toenail.

She hurried to take his cloak and bring him a drink. 'You look troubled, sire,' she said softly. 'Come, let me rub your feet.'

Henry grunted and sat down heavily before the fire while

she pulled off his boots and socks. His right big toe was puffy red around the nail bed.

'You should summon the physician, sire.'

'Tomorrow will suffice.' He took a single swallow of wine before setting it aside. 'Tonight I do not care to be examined and prodded and made sorer than I am already.'

Rosamund took his good foot in her hand and began to gently massage it. 'Have you spoken to the Queen?'

'For what good it did,' he growled. 'She refuses to consider an annulment. I knew she would.'

Rosamund swallowed disappointment. She had thought so too because refusal was all Alienor had left, but she had hoped. 'I am sorry, sire.'

Henry rubbed his brow. 'I did not expect her to consent on the first asking, but a few more months at Sarum might make her see matters more clearly.'

Glancing up, Rosamund saw the flinty look in his eyes, the one he always got when Alienor was the subject of their conversations. She wanted to ask him how long it would be before the annulment was achieved, but knew better than to press him while he was impatient and in pain. However, she did not have 'a few more months' if this child was to be born legitimate.

'As you say, sire,' she said softly. 'I will pray for a successful outcome.' She looked at him with loving anxiety. 'I want to give you what she cannot and openly in the sight of God. I want to help you and have the lawful right to be at your side. I hate to see you tired and sore like this.'

He slanted her an enigmatic look that she could not read, even though she studied hard to know his soul. 'You are queen of my heart.' He pulled her into his lap. 'No one cares for me as you do. Do not fret, all will be well.'

He did not say he would marry her; he did not say she would wear a crown.

He loosened the ties round the neck of her chemise and pulled it down so that he could bury his face in her warm, white cleavage. Rosamund put her arms around him, pressed her cheek against his thinning hair, and sent up a fervent plea for God to answer her prayers.

6

Winchester Castle, Easter Court, April 1176

Alienor watched Joanna at play with Marguerite's fluffy dog, her gown swirling about her legs and her face alight with laughter as she threw a leather ball for him to chase. She was tall and well grown but not yet showing the physical changes of womanhood; however she possessed the self-assurance of a young lady who knew her worth.

Isabel entered the chamber and after a hesitation crossed to Alienor's side and curtseyed. 'You asked for me, madam?' she said stiffly.

'Indeed I did.' Alienor gestured Isabel to sit beside her on the cushioned bench.

It was three days since the women had parted company in strained circumstances. Alienor was not sorry for what she had said, but in hindsight, she had let her irritation overrule her diplomacy. She had so few people she could turn to, and Isabel was a true friend, even if she was infuriating. Isabel wanted everything to be perfect. If there was a crack in the table, she would cover it with a decorative napkin or candlestick and pretend it wasn't there; but it was her nature, as was her kindness and staunch devotion.

'We misunderstood each other a few days ago,' Alienor said. 'I want to tell you that I do sincerely value your friendship, and your counsel.'

Isabel smoothed her gown over her knees and did not reply, although her chin trembled.

Alienor handed her a knotted skein of embroidery wools. 'See if you can unpick this for me. You have a delicate touch and my patience is exhausted – as you well know.'

Isabel took the wool and began to pluck at it with delicate movements. Alienor hoped she had snarled up the thread sufficiently to keep Isabel occupied while the atmosphere settled.

'Has Hamelin told you about the envoys from Sicily arriving to discuss Joanna's marriage?'

'Yes, he has.' Isabel's careful teasing found an end on the thread.

'You are to accompany her there if the negotiations go well, I hear.'

Isabel gave her a wary glance.

'I am glad about it . . . truly. Joanna loves and trusts you, and I know you will ease her journey into a new life.'

Isabel's taut expression softened and ready tears glinted in her eyes. 'I promise to hoard every memory like a jewel and tell you everything when I return. I will bring you silks from the workshops in Palermo. Henry will not dare confiscate a gift from me and Hamelin.'

Alienor gave a rueful smile, recognising that Isabel too was mending broken bridges, and probably feeling guilty that she was adventuring to Sicily whereas Alienor's horizons were little more than prison walls. Even had Alienor been free, she would still have had to wave farewell to Joanna from a quay- side. A queen bore daughters and lost them before they were properly women. 'I would like that.'

Isabel picked carefully at the tangle in the middle of the skein. 'Does Joanna know yet?'

Alienor shook her head. 'Only what is in the air. Henry is going to speak to her today.' And then her life would change. She gazed at her daughter in the last hours of her childhood.

'She is a lovely young lady,' Isabel murmured. 'She laughs and is giddy like all girls at times, but she has a noble heart and the will to do the right thing.'

Alienor forbore to comment. Isabel was talking in platitudes again. All that she said was true, but Joanna would need steel to survive, although not so much that it broke her will.

Isabel returned the knotted threads to her. 'I have done what I can, but that section in the middle will never come free unless you cut it out.'

'Like a heart,' Alienor said, and looked round as Henry arrived on his way to the hunt, his tread swift and business-like. Ignoring Alienor, save for a single hard glance, he sat down before the fire and commanded Joanna to come before him.

She did so with lowered eyes, her earlier high spirits subdued into wariness because her father was the King and unpredictable.

'Sire.' She spread her skirts in a curtsey.

Hamelin, who had come to stand at Henry's right-hand side, gave her a reassuring smile and the twitch of an eyelid that might just have been a wink. Noting the gesture, Alienor felt grateful to Hamelin for that support.

'Daughter,' Henry said after a heavy silence and rubbed his fingertips back and forth across his whiskers. 'I want to talk to you about a matter of alliance.'

Joanna eyed him warily. 'Yes, Papa.'

He beckoned her closer and took her hand, clasping it between his hard weathered ones. 'You are to wed William, King of Sicily, should negotiations with his envoys prove satisfactory. He is my ally and good friend, and you will be well settled with him.'

Joanna visibly swallowed. 'Thank you, sire,' she whispered. Alienor could see the wide, almost fearful look in her eyes, and was utterly proud of her daughter when she pulled the right answer from somewhere deep within. 'I am honoured.'

'Good.' Henry squeezed her hand, released it, and stood up. 'Your mother and the Countess de Warenne will tell you what you need to know.' Satisfied that he had fulfilled his part of the business as far as informing her went, he left the chamber, already talking to his attendants about which spears they should bring with them on the hunt. Hamelin followed him with a brief glance over his shoulder for the women.

Joanna looked at Alienor and Isabel, still clearly stunned by the speed and enormity of what had just happened.

'Sicily is beautiful,' Alienor said. 'A little like Aquitaine. I shall be sorry to part from you, but your father is right, it is a good match.'

'You will have fine gowns and clothes,' Isabel said in a kindly voice, 'and a court and ladies all of your own. It will seem strange at first, but we will help you prepare, and I shall be accompanying you – that is already decided.'

Joanna nodded, and some of the light returned to her eyes.

Alienor sent Isabel a grateful look that helped to further mend the bond between them. In this at least they were united. 'You have a while yet. You will not go to Sicily before the summer's end. As your aunt Isabel says, there is much to do. Come.' Alienor drew her daughter to the window seat and sat her down. 'I will tell you what I know of Sicily and what I remember, and you can ask me anything you want. I do not know your husband-to-be, but his father welcomed me when I was on my way home from Jerusalem, and I believe you will settle there well.'

Joanna nodded and straightened her spine, sitting erect as if testing the weight of a crown and new responsibilities. 'Yes, Mama,' she said dutifully.

'Even if distance parts us there will still be letters and messengers; and you shall have your own household and people you know.' She squeezed Joanna's hand more gently than Henry had done. 'You are bound on this course and you must do your duty to the best of your ability. That is part of being a queen. I know you understand this in your heart.'

'Yes, Mama,' Joanna said again, biting her lip.

Alienor kissed her with compassion but did not draw out the moment because maintaining regal dignity in difficult circumstances was another part of being a queen and something Joanna had to learn.

* * *

37

Alienor walked in Winchester Castle's garden, enjoying the fresh spring morning. Bees trundled industriously from flower to flower on trees laden with apple blossom thick as snow and the air was scented with delicate perfume. At least Henry had not denied her the pleasure of this place even if he was watching her closely and giving her no opportunity to speak to anyone of influence. He continued to press home the detail that he controlled the chess board and her only way out was to agree to the annulment. Yesterday at dinner he had disparaged her by seating her down the table away from him while he conducted a conversation with a Winchester gold merchant. The times she was not invisible, he was marking her as of no consequence, and it would only worsen.

'Mama . . .'

Turning, she saw Harry walking down the path towards her. He was wearing his travelling cloak and a feathered cap. Here, in part, was the reason matters would deteriorate. Her sons were leaving for their duties one by one and there would soon be no support from that quarter. Richard had already departed for Poitou armed with fresh funds for his war against his rebellious vassals. Now Harry was going to join him via a visit to his father-in-law in France. Only Geoffrey remained, but he would soon go to Brittany.

'Are you ready?' Her smile was strained. She had been hiding in the garden, trying to gain the serenity to bid him farewell. He wore a guilty expression because he was leaving her, but she could also see the gleam of anticipation. He was impatient to be gone. Henry had given him funds too and the money would run through his fingers like water because he had no responsibilities to anchor him to reality. The coin would be squandered on clothes, on parades, on fine horses and days spent hunting and tourneying.

'Yes, will you come and bid me farewell?'

You are a queen, she reminded herself. *That is what keeps you strong. That is what you tell your daughter.* 'Of course. I wish you were not leaving, but I know you must.'

She set her arm on Harry's sleeve and walked with him from the garden to the stable yard where everyone was gathered, either to ride out or bid Godspeed to those on their way. Some farewells would be longer than others. Her glance flicked to Joanna who had just embraced Harry's wife Marguerite and was crouching to bid farewell to Marguerite's fluffy little dog. Alienor suspected the latter was the greater sorrow of the parting, although when her youngest daughter became Queen of Sicily she could have as many lap dogs as she desired.

Harry gave Joanna a pretty intaglio ring with a carving of a small lion. 'I will escort you part of your way to Sicily after you have crossed the Narrow Sea and I promise to visit you when you are queen,' he said, hugged her again, and then turned to Alienor.

'Travel safely, my son,' she said. 'I may not hear word of you because of my circumstances, but know you are always in my heart.'

He bestowed his brightest smile on her, the one he could turn on anyone and make them believe they were the most important person in the world. And then he grew serious. 'I will not forget, Mama, on my soul, I won't.' He squeezed her hands. 'He is my father, but I am also my mother's son.'

'And that is why you are taller than he is.'

He laughed aloud, kissed her cheek, and turned to mount his horse.

'Look after him,' she said fiercely to William Marshal who was making final checks on the harness and equipment and giving orders to the squires. 'I trust you.'

'Madam, that is my life's task and my honour,' William responded with a bow. 'I shall do everything I can to keep him safe.'

They exchanged a meaningful look. To protect him from himself as much as from others was the awareness that went unspoken. William tugged a small jewelled cross from inside his shirt and kissed it; a cross she had given him in the days when she had such largesse to bestow on those whose service she valued. Tucking it away again, he turned to his horse.

Henry arrived at the last moment to bid his son farewell and gestured Harry to remain mounted. 'Godspeed you,' he said gruffly. 'And try to keep your purse strings closed for once.'

Harry gave his father an ironic salute, and turned his rein.

Alienor watched them ride out, a handsome cavalcade with hawks and hounds, their harnesses jingling with silver bells. Silk banners fluttered in their midst and her throat swelled with emotion at the sight of such pride and beauty, and at the knowledge that she could not ride with them.

'Well.' Henry turned to her as the guards closed the gate. 'You have had your time to think about Amesbury. Do you have an answer for me?'

Alienor faced him. 'Indeed I do, and it has not changed. Amesbury is out of the question. You may have your annulment if you set me free to go to Aquitaine.'

His face contorted with a mingling of anger and exasperation. 'Then you condemn yourself to a life of confinement. You leave for Sarum today – immediately.'

'So you punish Joanna too?'

'You think she cares about a mother such as you?' he scoffed. 'All the value you are to her is as an example of how not to be a queen.'

Alienor set her jaw. 'Do as you will, but you will not break me.'

'You think not? Watch me.' He walked away, flexing his shoulders like a fighter.

An instant later, Alienor was surrounded by guards who gripped her arms and escorted her from the courtyard in front of everyone who had gathered to bid farewell to Harry, including John and Joanna.

She held her head high because contrary to what Henry said, she would show her daughter how to be a queen, especially under duress.

Without ceremony, Alienor was bundled into a travelling cart with a plain canvas cover. No horse for her this time, no bright escort, just grim-faced soldiers intent on obeying their lord's bidding. She had been permitted three weeks in a gilded cage among all the finches and eagles of the court. Now it was back to the windswept coop and solitary confinement. Gazing across the wain to the grimy linen canvas on the other side, she made her mind blank in order to endure. Either she would die or Henry would, and then it would be over.

7

Palace of Sarum, August 1176

Once again Alienor settled into the stultifying routine of life at Sarum. The endless sewing of plain seams, the days confined to her chamber save for rare moments when she was permitted to walk the castle's precincts or attend services in the cathedral, under strict supervision. Once more news of the outside world was cut off. She made a pet of a white dove and fed it crumbs on her sill, taking pleasure in watching it pirouette and coo, until the day one of the knights hunted it down with a peregrine from the mews. She ceased feeding the doves after that.

Occasionally she would pick up pieces of information but they were like the discarded ends of linen thread on the seat where she sat to sew the interminable pile of shirts and chemises. Henry had gone to his hunting lodge at Clarendon and Richard had won a victory against the Poitevan rebels at Butteville, but the details were scant and passed down through so many hands that they had little value when they came to her ear. Once or twice her days were enlivened by visiting clergy, but always they came on Henry's behalf, saying if she would only consider becoming the Abbess of Amesbury all this would end and be beneficial for everyone. In a perverse way Alienor looked forward to such approaches because they gave her an opportunity to exercise her wiles on the men, leaving them discomfited and aware in no uncertain terms that her stance on the matter remained firm.

One parched afternoon in mid-August, Alienor emerged from prayer in the cathedral. The sun struck the stonework like a hammer on a white anvil and the still air was as hot as a forge. Raising her hand to shade her eyes, she started to walk towards the castle, Amiria at her side, guards following at a discreet distance. And then she stopped because Isabel was standing in the courtyard shaking out her skirts, and with her were John and Joanna, and their cousins Belle and William.

Alienor thought for an instant that the blazing heat had created a mirage, but the scarlet-faced soldiers tending to the horses were far too solid to be ephemera. And Isabel, although neatly dressed as always, had the look of a butterfly newly emerged from the chrysalis wings all crumpled.

It took all Alienor's will not to run to her visitors and to approach them at a measured walk. 'What a surprise, but it gladdens my heart to see you!' she said in a voice that was close to cracking. What was Henry up to now?

'We're visiting before we leave for Sicily,' Isabel replied as they embraced. 'I have permission.' She showed Alienor a folded piece of parchment in her hand with a seal attached. 'I have Henry's safe conduct. Hamelin persuaded him. I know you think I bow to my husband's every whim, but I asked him at the right time and in the right way and he agreed to intercede. Sometimes it pays to conciliate.'

Alienor was amused and a little irritated. Clearly their earlier disagreement remained a tender subject with Isabel. 'It depends what you have to lose by doing so, but I am grateful. I had resigned myself to never seeing any of you again.' She hugged John and Joanna, and wondered at Henry's motives for allowing the visit. Perhaps he was hoping that several more months spent in isolation at Sarum had pressed home his point and would make her more willing to reconsider. If so he was sadly mistaken; the experience had just made her more determined to defy him.

She brought her guests to her chamber in the north tower of the complex. Isabel made no comment as she gazed at the spartan surroundings, but Alienor saw shock in her eyes. And pity. 'My penitent's cell,' she said. 'At least it is cool in this heat.'

Joanna sat down in the window seat, her expression and posture making it plain that she had not expected to find her mother dwelling in such reduced circumstances.

Isabel's maid was hefting a large willow basket and Isabel removed the folded tablecloth covering the contents and bade Amiria spread it upon the room's bare trestle table. 'I have good wine,' she declared with determined gaiety as she produced a stone costrel from the depths of the basket. 'And roast fowl and white bread. The guards dared not refuse the King's own sister by marriage arriving under safe conduct.'

Alienor raised her brows. 'Does that not constitute an act of defiance?'

'Not at all.' Isabel tossed her head. 'I am merely exerting my rightful authority.' She presented Alienor with a cone of parchment filled with sticky brown squares. 'Hamelin knows how much you like gingerbread and wanted me to give you this.'

The warm scent of exotic spices blended with honey filled Alienor's nose as she took her next breath. She and Hamelin did not always see eye to eye. As Henry's brother he always supported him; at times he could be a self-righteous pedant; but he had a thoughtful side and he was not vindictive.

'You must thank him and tell him I appreciate his gift,' she said, feeling almost tearful. 'It is kind of him and I am not accustomed to kindness these days.'

Isabel turned pink at the praise. 'Indeed I shall. And this is from me.'

She gave Alienor a small rock crystal bottle wrapped in a square of purple silk. The bottle was carved with a swirling labyrinth pattern and when Alienor removed the stopper, a wonderful perfume of roses, nutmeg and woody balsams from the oil within transported her to the gardens in Poitiers with the summer roses and honeysuckle trellising the wall.

'I will treasure this,' she said when she was able to speak. 'You have brought comfort to my day; indeed to all my days here.' She hugged Isabel and wiped away a few treacherous tears on the back of her hand.

Once the table was ready, they sat down to eat.

'I am to be betrothed,' John announced as he broke a piece off the loaf.

Alienor turned to her youngest son in surprise, although not shock. He had once been betrothed to little Adelaide of Maurienne but the child had died soon after Alienor's imprisonment. It stood to reason that Henry would find someone else for him – and that he would not see fit to tell her.

'Indeed? To whom?'

'Hawise of Gloucester.' He curled his lip. 'She's my second cousin but Papa says he can arrange a dispensation.'

Alienor frowned. 'Hawise of Gloucester?'

'She was born not long before you first came to Sarum,' Isabel said.

'Ah, yes.' Not that she had known about the child, but she had seen her father around the court at Winchester.

'She's only three.' John sprinkled his bread with salt. 'Of course she might die before I marry her like the last one, but if that happens Papa says he'll give me Isabelle de Clare. That means Chepstow and Pembroke and Ireland. She's older; she's four.' He bit into the bread. 'And Normandy too,' he added indistinctly.

'And when is this betrothal to take place?'

'In a few weeks in London.' He chewed and swallowed. 'It's the land that matters. The Gloucester ones are better than the Chepstow ones though.'

He spoke in a knowing way that suggested he had checked for himself rather than repeating what someone had told him. His eyes were a quenched green-grey and it was difficult to tell the expression in them, or to see past the half-mocking smile to what lay beyond. Even as an infant he had always seemed more like an adult – a scheming, manipulating one at times. If he was angry, the recipient of that anger would only find out when they discovered one of their possessions damaged or else sat on the nail that had mysteriously appeared on their chair. Yet he could also be devastatingly sweet and amusing.

'You seem to have considered it thoroughly,' Alienor said.

'I wanted to know.' He laid down his knife. 'I also know why Papa wants an annulment.'

Alienor lifted her cup. 'Is that so?'

'Rosamund de Clifford is with child.' His eyes glinted. 'The baby's due in the autumn and he wants to marry her and make her queen.'

Alienor sipped her wine while she assimilated the news and composed her expression. 'And that is worth sending envoys all the way to Rome? I somehow doubt that is your father's intention.'

'She is with him all the time,' John said, with narrow eyes and a fixed look. 'She is always in his chamber touching him and petting him.'

'That does not mean he will marry her even if she is with child. You need not worry on that score.'

'I'm not worried.' He shrugged but she could see he was unsettled – or perhaps jealous. 'She's nothing,' he said with a curled lip. 'My father's stupid whore.'

Isabel made a small sound of protest because it was inappropriate talk at the table, and the way he spoke possessed an undercurrent of violence.

'Yes she is,' Alienor replied, 'and therefore beneath your notice. It only matters if you let it matter because then you make it more than it is.'

John continued to scowl but finished his meal in silence and then went with his cousin William to poke about the palace.

Alienor changed the subject and asked Isabel how the preparations for Sicily were progressing.

'Well indeed.' Isabel was as eager as Alienor to sail the conversation into less fraught waters. 'Joanna has four new gowns, haven't you, my love?'

Joanna joined the conversation, her expression alight with pleasure. 'King William sent merchants with bolts of silk damask cloth,' she enthused, and went on to tell Alienor of the painted chests that had been constructed to hold her trousseau – sheets and coverlets, bed hangings, candle holders, napery and silver dishes. Her excitement at going as a bride to the King of Sicily far outweighed her fear of her new situation now she had had time to grow accustomed.

Alienor was pleased for her, but sad too because beyond the clothes and jewels, beyond all the appurtenances of royalty, she knew what it meant to be the wife of a king. 'You must write to me often. I shall help you if I can, and I will always be your mother. I want you to remember that.' Her heart filled with pain because locked up here what influence did she have and what kind of an example could she set?

She gave Joanna two jewelled combs she had managed to secrete in her baggage from Winchester, carved with acanthus scrolls pin-pointed with tiny sapphires and rubies. 'Remember me whenever you use these, and pray for me as I shall pray for you,' she said, and embraced Joanna who reciprocated, but with an air of reserve as if shielding herself from the difficulty of imminent parting.

'Belle is not coming with us,' Isabel said with a gesture to her own daughter. 'As our eldest, she must look after the others and wisdom says we keep her at home.'

Belle said nothing, her eyes downcast.

'She is disappointed of course,' Isabel said. 'She will miss Joanna's company and friendship, as I know Joanna will miss hers, but it is part of becoming a woman learning responsibility. She shall have an important role at home as chatelaine of the household.' She sent her daughter a proud look and Belle responded with a modest half smile.

After the children had retired, Alienor and Isabel talked long into the night over more wine.

'Did you know about Rosamund?' Alienor asked.

Isabel turned one of her rings. 'Yes, but not until recently. I swear to you I did not know at Easter and neither did Hamelin.'

'Henry did not tell him?'

Isabel rubbed her finger over the gem in the ring. 'Hamelin keeps out of Henry's amours. He focuses on his brother, not the girl in the bed behind him.'

Alienor almost laughed for Isabel's comment conjured up a vivid image of Hamelin attempting to have a conversation with Henry while trying to ignore the mistress in her chemise. 'Even if Rosamund desperately wants to be queen it will not happen,' she said with weary contempt. 'Knowing Henry, even if he does care for her, his eye is already on pastures new and untrodden. He would see marriage to her as just another trap. Ah, enough of this talk. What of other news?'

Isabel began telling her about the castle Hamelin was building on their land at Conisbrough in Yorkshire. 'It is his retreat from the court and a secure fortress facing north to pass on to Will.' She cast a glance heavenwards. 'In truth, he has discovered such a delight in the building that at times I think I might as well have married a mason. You should hear him enthuse over the fireplaces.'

Alienor laughed. 'I do believe that listening to Hamelin wax lyrical upon stone and mortar is a pleasure I can forgo, even if I do love him dearly for sending me gingerbread.'

In the morning they attended mass in the cathedral, and then with the clouds rolling in over the Downs, the visitors mounted their horses and prepared to return to Winchester.

Alienor kissed Joanna a final time. 'I am proud of you,' she said. 'Be proud of yourself.'

'Yes, Mama.' Joanna's response was dutiful, her gaze already on the path beyond the gate.

Alienor kissed John too. 'Be honourable in all that you do, and whatever the circumstances of your match with Hawise of Gloucester, remember kindness.'

'Yes, Mama.' John gave her a warm, guileless smile that somehow managed to be as distant in its quality as Joanna's stare.

When they had gone, Alienor walked around the perimeter of the walls encircling the hill like the bounds of a coronet. Queen of all she surveyed – for what little it was worth.

8

Winchester Castle, September 1176

Henry pressed a kiss on Rosamund's soft pink lips and held her as close as he could, given that the curve of her belly was as round as a full moon. Rosamund stroked his beard and smiled even though she was unsettled and a little sad. He continued to call her his queen but nothing she said or did would spur him into making it fact. Instead he gave her jewellery or cloth for a new gown and cajoled her with empty words. Her only hope was that he would change when she gave birth to the perfect male child to eclipse his other sons and begin a new dynasty. She often shared that vision with the baby in her womb when it kicked and turned. She never, ever thought the word 'bastard' about their child because she wore Henry's ring and was his wife in all but the vows made before a priest.

'I will send word to you as soon as the baby is born,' she said. 'If you have a moment, think of us.'

'Indeed I shall do, often, and pray for your safe delivery.' He placed his palm on her belly in a salute that was also a preliminary to farewell.

Sensing his anxiety to be away, she turned his face to hers, making him meet her gaze because it was important to have that acknowledgement. 'You promise?'

He grasped her hand in his. 'I promise.' An expression of regret briefly replaced his impatience. 'If I could stay, I would, but matters of state will not wait.'

And I will, Rosamund thought. *I will always be waiting.* 'I understand.' She was glad she had made him look at her and take notice. 'Go with God.'

'And may he keep you.' He drew her hand to his lips, kissed her fingers, and was gone. She stood at the window and watched him ride away. The King of England, her lover, the father of her child and keeper of everything that mattered to her in this life.

An hour later a servant arrived bearing a gift from Henry of a circlet of woven wheat stems, jewelled with the blood-red seeds of the wild dog roses that had bloomed in the hedgerows all summer long. Rosamund placed the crown on her brow, imagining Henry's hands setting it there in regnal gold, and smiled wistfully.

A few days later at dawn Rosamund's labour began, but as the contractions intensified, she started to bleed. The midwives attending her exchanged glances as they worked and reassured Rosamund, who could not see the red trickle that emerged on each contraction, that all was well.

'Soon, my lady, it will be soon,' Dame Alicia said, her voice comforting and calm. 'Just you drink this tisane and rest yourself.' Turning away, she murmured instructions to one of the other ladies in attendance to fetch the priest and have him on hand.

The sun rose to its autumn zenith and began its journey westwards, filtering through the trees. On the bed Rosamund thrashed in agony and screamed for Henry as the blood pooled between her thighs.

The baby was born easily enough – a little boy, but he was pale and lifeless, and a red gush followed him that the midwives could not staunch even though they massaged Rosamund's belly in a desperate effort to make her womb clench upon itself.

The priest arrived, his expression taut with distaste at the stench of blood and the sight of the red carnage on the bed, but he made haste to administer the last rites and placed a cross in Rosamund's hands.

'God have mercy on your soul, my lady,' Dame Alicia whispered with compassion, her eyes wet as she knelt at Rosamund's side, clasping her prayer beads.

Rosamund's face was grey and her skin clammy as she fought for breath. 'Tell Henry I am sorry,' she gasped. 'Tell him I died thinking of him . . . tell him I died as a wife doing her duty. I am so sorry I failed him.'

Rosamund was deeply loved by the community at Godstow. Beyond her youth, beauty and sweet nature, she had always remembered the nuns in her prayers and sent them gifts on feast days. She had brought the King's patronage to the convent and made it a place of wealth and influence amid the local community.

Sorrowfully, the nuns accepted her body and buried her with her stillborn red-haired son wrapped in her arms. After much debate they left her wedding ring on her finger, and interred her in a place of honour before the choir in the fading gold of a late September day.

Belle tilted her nose in the air and tried to ignore the sniggers and low-voiced exchanges coming from her brother and their cousin John. The boys were supposedly playing chess but they kept looking across at her and making remarks, their expressions sharp with mischief bordering on malice.

They had been lounging around the court, getting in everyone's way and playing pranks all week. John was usually the leader and William followed, although sometimes an idea would spark, such as his notion to 'accidentally' leave a gate open so that somehow the pigs got into the vegetable garden and trampled a recently planted bed of cabbages. Innocence was always sworn and never believed. Only yesterday John had tied together a cat, a dog and a rooster for the fun of watching the ensuing, bloody mayhem. Her uncle Henry seemed to think their japes amusing and dismissed their antics as the common nature of boys; he had better things to do with his time than listen to petty complaints about their behaviour.

Had her papa been here, Belle knew John and Will would never have got away with such mischief, but her parents were not due home from Sicily until Christmas. She sometimes thought she would have liked to accompany them, but then again, she would only have been a handmaid and Joanna would have stolen all the attention. At least when her mother and father returned, Belle would not have to compete with her pretty royal cousin and there would be gifts too – ivory combs, jewels and rich silks – from the famed Sicilian work-shops. She was eagerly awaiting those.

John whispered something, and as Will turned to look at her and grin she saw John sneak one of Will's pieces from the board and secrete it in his palm. Realising she had observed his trickery, John shot her a warning look, which she returned with superior contempt. There had always been friction between her and John. He would pull her hair, spit in her cup, break her possessions, and she would tell tales on him to her father, pinch him, and until recently push him around, although he was growing too strong for that and she was more wary these days, especially while she did not have the cushion of her father's protection.

His recent betrothal to Hawise of Gloucester and his father's plans to make him King of Ireland had made John far too full of himself. He had developed a swagger which she hated.

She picked up her sewing basket which contained a tunic band she was embroidering for her father's return, but on removing the woven lid she recoiled from the vile stench of decay and then shrieked to see a decomposing rat on top of the fabric, its corpse leaking stains onto her painstaking toil. She hurled the basket across the room and the rat flew out, striking John across the arm and chest, leaving a vile smear on his cloak. He flung himself backwards with a shout, but swiftly recovered, seized the rodent's scaly tail and slung it back at Belle, while Will doubled over, helpless with laughter.

A stocky young man with wavy auburn hair walked into the midst of the furore. 'What is this unseemliness?' he shouted, hands on hips. 'Are you brawling, peasant brats?'

'I thought that was your inheritance,' John drawled insolently. 'Wasn't your mother a common whore?'

Belle's eyes widened in horror at John's insult, but with an underlying secret glee because of the challenge to authority – it was exciting and something she would never dare. Jeoffrey FitzRoy was the King's oldest son, but bastard-born. He was the royal chancellor, designate Bishop of Lincoln and John's half-brother.

Jeoffrey strode over to John, grabbed him by the shoulders and shook him. 'I have no time for your foolish insolence,' he snapped, grey eyes bright with anger. 'Yes, foolish, not clever, however you may smirk.'

John writhed and tried to push him off without success. 'Don't touch me; I'll tell Papa.'

'Oh yes, carry the tale and see how far you get,' Jeoffrey scoffed.

John's expression grew narrow and mean but he pressed his lips together. Jeoffrey released him with a final shake and John shrugged away and straightened his clothes, defiant but wary. The obnoxious reek of dead rodent filled the air.

'He put the rat in my sewing box and spoiled all my work!' Belle was determined that John was going to pay the price. 'I'll have to throw it away now and it was going to be a band for my papa's tunic.' She did not have to feign the quiver in her voice. It had been a lot of hard work. She sent Jeoffrey a look intimating that he was her champion and would see justice done.

Jeoffrey eyed the ruined basket and a look of revulsion

crossed his face. 'You will be compensated; I will personally make sure it happens.'

Belle said nothing. How could there be compensation for all her time and effort?

John shrugged sulkily. 'It's a fuss over nothing, a silly piece of embroidery.'

Jeoffrey stared at him with contempt. 'It would not be a fuss over nothing if the item belonged to you; indeed you would be the first to complain. Why do something like this? It benefits no one, it's not funny. You should have grown out of such pranks by now.'

John shrugged again. 'Very well, I am sorry,' he said in a way that suggested he was anything but. 'I didn't mean to cause harm. It was in jest.'

'You did mean it.' Belle continued to be aggrieved. 'I'll never forgive you.'

John curled his lip. 'You think I care?'

'Peace!' Jeoffrey bellowed. 'You should care, because one day you will need friends and allies. What will you do when all turn against you because of what you have done to them in the past?'

John set his lips and Jeoffrey dug one hand through his hair in exasperation. 'I'm warning all of you to stay out of the King's way and mend your behaviour. He's just received bad news and his mood is vile.'

John immediately pricked up his ears. 'What sort of bad news?'

Jeoffrey lowered his hand. 'Rosamund de Clifford has died in childbirth and the baby with her.'

'Good.' John's smile was sharp. 'She got what she deserved. She was a whore like all the others. He will soon forget her, he always does. There will be another one in his bed before Christmas.'

'Do not let our father hear you say that or you will not sit down for a week.' Jeoffrey shook his head in baffled disgust. 'Why are you so full of poison?'

John lowered his eyes, disengaging from the contact, and fell silent.

'Just watch your step,' Jeoffrey warned. 'And stay out of trouble if it's within you to do that.'

Belle knew it wasn't within John at all. She hated him, but at the same time, that look in his eyes, a dagger gleam between narrowed lids, gave her a frisson of horrified attraction. She found it very exciting, the way he walked so close to the edge.

Henry sat before the hearth in his chamber, his head bowed and his body racked with painful spasms. He could not believe that Rosamund had left him; that their last farewell had been final. It was a wound so deep he could not deal with it. Indeed, he could not face it at all, because he was a king, and if he broke under the weight of his grief, then so did the Crown.

He had been alone for several hours. The one person he might have allowed access to this room was Hamelin and he was in Sicily seeing Joanna safely married. He had gone out riding earlier to try and outrun his grief but had only succeeded in half killing his horse. Why had God not taken Alienor instead? That would have been justice.

A string of women had frequented his bed, some for longer than others, but he had only ever had two proper mistresses and both were in the grave. It felt like betrayal. He would never give of himself to anyone again. As powerful as he was, he could not control death, and when people died they took pieces of him with them into the grave, leaving him with raw wounds that would never heal.

The door creaked open and he turned ready to do battle, but was surprised by the sight of his youngest son tip-toeing into the room. 'What do you want?' he demanded.

John hesitated. 'Nothing, Papa. I left my knife on the stool.' He pointed to a leather sheath gleaming in the edge of the firelight.

Henry pinched the bridge of his nose. 'You disturb me for this, boy?'

'I wanted to see how you were,' John added disarmingly.

'You can see how I am.' He looked at his son in the dim light of candles that were burning down to their stubs because no one had come to replenish them. John was like a wary, half-feral cat, padding softly in the shadows, ears pricked. If John was asking how he was, it was for his own purpose, but Henry could not be bothered to know what it might be. 'Let me give you some advice,' he said. 'Harden yourself. The world is a harsh place. Trust no one, especially those who smile on you because one day they will steal everything from you, and when that happens, the betrayal will be so bitter it will choke you.'

John picked up the sheath from the stool and drew the knife to examine the blade and make sure the rat blood hadn't rusted it. He had reached that conclusion himself. And that the world was a place where those who had power could do what they wanted and those without it were the victims. The world would try to make him its victim, so it was always best to strike first. 'You can trust me, Papa,' he said. 'I won't betray you.'

Henry watched him sheathe the knife and sighed. 'You're a good boy. Come here.'

John joined his father at the fire and Henry ruffled his hair. 'You are my youngest, but that does not mean I value you less – indeed perhaps the opposite. I see myself in you and what you could become; I do not see your mother.'

John didn't see that either and his father's words were like being given a glowing jewel worth braving his chamber for. One day he would be a king and of more than just Ireland. And he would be better than his father.

At Sarum, Alienor listened to the wind whistle around the keep as dusk fell. Summer's heat was over and this chilly autumn bluster had snatched the first of the leaves from the trees. She had been sewing until it grew too dark to see the thread against the cloth. Amiria had gone to fetch food and

55

candles, but Alienor had grown accustomed to sitting in darkness and to eking out the light. No more profligate use of wax and lamps, burning into the night, sometimes until matins. The thought of spending another winter at Sarum did not bear contemplating.

Breathless from her climb up the tower, Amiria returned bearing a tray of food and the requisite candles. As she set the bread and wine on the trestle she said, 'I heard some news in the courtyard just now.'

Alienor eyed her maid with cautious interest. Not all news was equal, but if it was sufficient to animate Amiria, it must be important. 'Indeed?'

'They are saying that Rosamund de Clifford has died in childbed and the baby too – a boy stillborn.'

Alienor experienced no flood of triumph at the information, rather a weary trickle. What did it matter? It was just more detritus. 'God rest her soul,' she said. *And damn Henry's.*

Amiria set about lighting the few candles she had brought. 'Forgive me, madam, I thought it would please you to hear it.'

'I am more saddened than anything.'

Amiria chewed her lip, clearly agitated about something, and eventually she could not contain herself. 'She is to be buried at Godstow and the King says he will pay for a shrine before the choir for her and daily prayers. It is not fitting!'

'No, it is not, but much good it will do her now.' Alienor imagined Rosamund lying in state at the nunnery like a queen. How often would Henry visit? As often as he went to see Thomas Becket? More often than he visited Reading and the tomb of their firstborn son? 'I pity her, and that is the truth.'

She attended to her simple meal of bread and cheese and thought with longing of beef stew simmered with cumin and ginger, of spiced wine and her favourite sugared pears. She was not starved here, but the food had no savour. She had long ago finished the gingerbread from Isabel and Hamelin even though she had eked it out.

Her meal over, she retired to pray at her small portable altar. It was one of the few items of high wealth in her chamber, studded with sapphires and rock crystal, and under the marble top was a fragment of the finger bone of St Martial. She prayed for Rosamund because it was her Christian duty. She felt angry contempt for Henry for the way he had paraded the girl at court, but Rosamund had only possessed the fleeting power of the bedchamber and Alienor had never seen her as a serious threat to her queenship. Poor, silly girl.

Amiria came back from returning the used food bowls to the scullions and announced that she had more news.

Alienor raised her brows. 'This is indeed a feast day in the midst of famine,' she said tartly. 'What have you heard now?'

Amiria flushed at her tone. 'A wine merchant was telling one of the guards that your son the Young King and his queen expect a child next summer.'

Alienor was assailed by two emotions at once: pleasure at the thought of a grandchild from her eldest son, and upset that she had had to find out like this – as overheard gossip from her maid rather than a salutation from an official messenger. How much else of the warp and weft of family life and politics was passing her by? The child would be born to parents who had no lands to call their own, only allowances doled out by Henry, spent almost before they touched the sides of Harry's coffers.

'It is indeed good news,' she responded to Amiria, because she had to say something. It was too much to hope that Henry would now give Harry the dignity of lands to govern. It would be utterly wrong should Marguerite bear a son for him to have a father who still had not so much as a yard of earth to his name. Henry was only forty-three, and his grandfather, the first King Henry, had been almost seventy when he died.

Still, new life was new hope. 'A toast.' Alienor directed Amiria to fill her cup. 'To my son, his wife and their unborn child, may they prosper and flourish.'

9

Palace of Sarum, July 1177

Beyond the palace walls a burning summer sun had stolen the blue from the sky. The Downland grass was parched and sere and the cathedral gleamed like a white lantern in the bleaching heat. It was early in the year for thunderstorms but that kind of oppression crackled in the air. Sick of being cooped in her chamber even though the walls kept the room cooler than outside, Alienor bade Amiria leave her sewing and come for a walk.

Beyond the shelter of the tower, the sun's heat struck like a fist. Two guards crouched in the shade, their weapons propped against the wall. They were playing a desultory game, throwing small round stones to try and strike a larger one, and after a glance at the women and a swift obeisance, they paid little heed to what was a daily routine. What attention they could dredge from their heat-induced lethargy was focused on some women collecting buckets of water at the well. Gowns tucked through their belts, exposing bare legs, they were splashing each other and laughing. A small boy dashed through the sparkling rainbows of water, wearing nothing but his shirt. The sight reminded Alienor of her own sons doing the same when they were that age, and she smiled with nostalgia.

For the last fortnight, masons had been busy constructing a new gatehouse and a wall around the inner compound. Their presence was a welcome distraction to the mundane daily routine and helped Alienor believe that Sarum was not a forsaken place at the back of beyond, but somewhere worthy of attention. Why Henry was bothering with these renovations was a puzzle. Surely she was not so much of a threat that he needed to add new walls and defences to keep her enclosed? Perhaps it was a warning to others that there was no chance of springing her free.

The women at the well stopped their sport to curtsey. The little boy with no understanding of etiquette continued to caper and splash. When his mother moved to grab him, Alienor shook her head. 'Let him play,' she said. 'I would join him if I could.'

She moved on, aware of the women's constraint. The masons toiled on the scaffolding of the new gatehouse. A labourer had stripped to his braies and Alienor appreciated his wiry musculature. The linen clung to his buttocks and thighs, leaving little to the imagination, and her eyes glinted with appreciation. Amiria averted her gaze.

The guard on watch suddenly reached round to the horn slung on his baldric and, placing it to his lips, blew a long, loud blast. 'The King!' went up the cry. 'The King is here! Bow to your sovereign lord!'

The labourer in the revealing braies dropped to his knees and his companions downed tools and followed suit. Soldiers hastened to open the gate and the guards who had been lounging outside the royal apartments came at the run, cramming helmets on their heads.

Despite the heat of the sun, Alienor felt as if she had swallowed a bucket of ice. What was Henry doing here?

Two by two the knights of the royal escort entered the yard, Henry riding in their midst. It was not the full court, but a conroi of about twenty men including Henry's half-brother Hamelin. Watching Henry dismount she noticed the way he tensed as he landed. His face was fiery red with sunburn despite the shade of a straw hat and he sported the belly girth of a middle-aged man. As usual his impatience was palpable, but he seemed bogged down, as though his energy was a ball of iron with a solid core.

As grooms and servants took the horses, he started towards the palace, limping heavily on his right leg, but he checked as he saw her. Alienor positioned herself to stand like a host receiving a guest. Sarum might be Henry's castle but it was her residence and the only way to deal with this was to be the Queen, not a prisoner. She observed etiquette by curtseying to him, but did not wait for him to bid her to rise. Henry's expression tightened with annoyance.

'This is a surprise, sire,' she said. 'I bid you welcome.' Her tone was pleasant, but corrosive with sarcasm. 'Will you come within and refresh yourself?'

Henry gave her a hard look. 'Enough of that, madam, I am not here to play games.'

Her lips straightened. 'Neither am I – and I know very well why I am here.' She gestured round. 'All this new building is impressive I admit, but surely you do not fear me so much that you need to build these extra defences?'

They began to walk towards the keep. The glare of the sun on the lime-washed walls dazzled their eyes. The women had vacated the well, dragging the child with them, and all that remained of their presence were damp patches on the housing flags, swiftly drying out.

'I do not fear you as well you know,' he retorted, his voice harsh and dusty. 'It is part of a general refurbishment; the same as at Clarendon so that the place is ready for any purpose.' He spoke in a preoccupied manner, his mind clearly elsewhere.

They entered the great hall but Henry continued on through to the chamber beyond, bereft of furnishings save for a trestle and a couple of chests. He unfastened his belt and tossed it across one of them, followed by his hat. 'Ah God, it's too hot.' He rubbed his leg and winced. His old injury, she thought, as well as his toenail. His horses often kicked him, but one such blow had caused permanent damage to his thigh and intermittently broke out, causing inflammation and fever.

Servants arrived with watered wine and Alienor sat down at the trestle bench. The floor was dusty and a puddle of wax had congealed near her feet. She still did not know why he was here and a glance at Hamelin left her no wiser for his expression was like a firmly locked door under tension. The other knights had remained behind in the hall.

'To what purpose do I owe the honour of this visit?' she enquired. 'I cannot think you are here to socialise?'

Henry drained his cup and poured a fresh measure into it. 'That would be the last thing on my mind. Were it not for an understanding you claim I do not possess and a desire to see how the work is progressing, I would have ridden straight to Clarendon.'

'Understanding?' She arched her brows. 'What "understanding" would that be, sire?'

He swept a callused palm over his face, leaving sweaty streaks. 'We had news from France the day before we left Woodstock – from Paris.'

'Marguerite? She has had the baby?'

A look of sour amusement crossed his face. 'I am surprised you have not already heard. I am sure despite all my measures aimed at allowing you to lead a life of retirement, you have ways of finding things out. Yes, the child is born – on the first day of July. A boy, christened William. Our heir now officially has an heir.'

Alienor would rather not have heard the news from Henry but at least he had not withheld it from her and it came to her fresh. A baby boy, a grandson. She had other grandchildren from her eldest daughter Matilda, but they were not destined for an English crown – unlike this newborn. 'I am delighted, especially for Harry and Marguerite.' It was an achievement for her son, something his father could not take from him, something over which Henry had no power. 'Surely you will give him some of his inheritance now he has an heir to raise?'

Henry sat back on the bench and his expression closed. 'I will think about it.'

And do nothing.

'I will write to him.'

'And I will be glad to send your message by my swiftest courier.'

Having first vetted the content.

'That is generous of you,' she said neutrally.

He continued to rub his chin. 'Louis presses me to marry Richard to Alais, but I am not inclined to do so.'

Alienor stifled a grimace. She had promised Richard he would never have to marry the girl, but there was little she could do from Sarum. 'There are rumours you are having an affair with her and that it's one of the reasons you were seeking an annulment from me – so you could make her your queen.'

'There are always rumours, some more preposterous than others.'

'I have even heard it said she is your consolation for Rosamund.'

His sunburn reddened and his grey eyes were very bright. 'There will never be any consolation for Rosamund.' The look he gave her was hard, almost hostile, but she saw the grief there too despite his effort to conceal it. 'Louis' milksop daughter could not begin to fill her place, but if it allays your concern I will tell you that Rosamund's second cousin Ida is of great solace to me.'

Alienor eyed him with contempt. She did not know her, but expected she was another vulnerable, impressionable girl over whom he could exert his power and will. They always were.

'Alais is part of the business of government. I will not be dictated to by Louis, or by my son. I will decide when the wedding takes place, not Louis or the Pope, and not Richard.'

Alienor said nothing, for his attitude accorded with her own desires. However, she did not trust him. He would change his mind on a whim if it suited his purpose.

While servants set up tables to provide a meal for the guests, Henry took the opportunity to go and have his leg tended to by his physician. Alienor surmised that the old injury was troubling him more than he would admit.

'It will never heal if he does not rest it,' she said to Hamelin. The latter handed his empty cup to a servant to refill. His own face was burned brown by the sun, but being less auburn than Henry, he had not suffered as much. 'I try to make him sit still, but he will not.'

They looked at each other. Conversation was awkward because of her situation and Hamelin's fierce loyalty to Henry, yet his wife was Alienor's sister by marriage and one of her dearest friends.

'Isabel is well?'

'Indeed,' he said. 'She is at Conisbrough for the moment. There is still much work to do – as here, the masons are busy this summer – but the hall is habitable. She has some silk cloth for you and some gifts from Sicily when next you meet.' He made a rueful face. 'Doubtless she will give you all the details about our mission that a man would think of no importance yet by which women set great store.'

Alienor smiled. 'I am sure despite your shortcomings you are able to tell me if Joanna was well settled.'

Hamelin looked taken aback, but then gave a reluctant smile at her riposte. 'Joanna took immediately to her new surroundings as if she was born to it. Everyone was welcoming; the King is a fine man and most gracious, and he was kind to her. The palace was a sight to behold – I have never seen such wall paintings and columns, or such magnificent gardens.'

Trying to get Hamelin to describe something beyond the mundane detail had always been like pulling teeth. He was not insensitive, just lacked the poet's eye and vocabulary. 'Yes, I saw it all myself long ago in another lifetime. Perhaps in hindsight I should have stayed there. I am glad my daughter received kindness from her husband. I wished it for her.'

'She will flourish,' Hamelin replied. 'She showed sense and fortitude on the journey and she knew her role when we arrived.' He cleared his throat, slightly embarrassed. 'She took my hand as we were leaving and asked to be reminded to all in England, especially her lady mother.'

Alienor bit her lip. A lady mother she barely knew given the many times they had been apart.

Henry returned, limping worse than before after having the wound probed and dressed. Alienor suspected that the scarlet hue of his face she had first put down to sunburn might be caused by fever. Unable to prevent a wince, he sat down and directed a squire to pour him a fresh cup of watered wine. The glare he sent round the room challenged anyone to comment.

A squire approached, leading a messenger, whom Alienor recognised as Wigain, one of Harry's clerks who often rode as a messenger when personal business was involved. The man's garments were sweat-soaked and his satchel was powdered with chalky dust kicked up by the speed of his horse.

'Sire.' He knelt and, with head bowed, handed Henry a letter.

Henry broke the seal and opened the parchment to read it. The impassive expression on his face did not change, except to set like stone.

'Sire, I am sorry. I tried to catch the first messenger, but he had too great a start on me.'

'Get out,' Henry snapped.

Wigain was swift to obey, like a rabbit down a hole with the hound on its tail.

Henry palmed his hand over his face and then looked at Alienor. 'The child is dead. Found unbreathing in his cradle.'

She clapped her hand to her mouth. 'No!'

'He lived for just three days.' He swallowed.

'God rest his poor little soul.' At least he had drawn breath in the world and thus had been baptised and would go to heaven, but it was little consolation. 'Harry and Marguerite – dear sweet Jesu, they must be distraught.'

Henry said harshly, 'You see now why I cannot put any trust in him? You lean on him and despite the promise when it comes to holding fast there is nothing there. First a child and then no child.'

'You do not mean that.' She was appalled. 'It is your grief

and disappointment speaking. Our firstborn only lived for three years. Would you say the same of yourself?'

He clenched his fists. 'I was not there when he died,' he said. 'Do not blame me for your lack.'

Alienor recoiled as if he had hit her, and could not speak, all words stolen by his cruelty.

Henry pushed himself upright and turned to Hamelin. 'We are not staying. Tell the grooms to saddle the horses; we'll push on to Winchester.'

'I am sorry,' Hamelin said. He looked at Alienor to include her in his words. 'Such news always tears the heart.'

Henry made an impatient sound. 'There is nothing to be done. If you fall off a horse, you get straight back in the saddle. The child is born, the child is dead. Grieving will not bring him back. They must try again when Marguerite has been churched.'

Hamelin did not reply but a muscle flickered in his cheek. 'I will give the order to the grooms,' he said, and left the room.

'Have you no compassion?' Alienor demanded in a broken voice, and then shook her head. 'No, I am foolish even to ask.'

'Of course I am sorry the child is dead,' Henry snapped, a feverish glitter in his eyes. 'He would have been my grandson and added lustre to my line. But it is pointless to weep over something ended before it is begun. Say your prayers, madam, and have done. They are young; there will be others.'

'So you say, but you take God for granted at your peril.'

'God!' Henry spat the word as if it were a molten ingot and he the accused being made to carry it over the distance of trial by hot iron. Clamping his jaw, he limped from the chamber.

He was running away but Alienor knew it was futile, because what he was running from would always dog his heels, and one day it would catch him.

10

Palace of Sarum, Winter 1178

December was an iron month; the ground had been hard with frost since the first week and although the shortest day was over, the daylight barely seemed increased and Alienor felt as if she was spending all her time in darkness. She had received few visitors over the past eighteen months and news of the outside world was hard to come by. Sometimes the Bishop of Salisbury brought her crumbs of information, but mostly she was kept in ignorance. She heard in passing that Henry had been threatened with interdict over his refusal to set a marriage day for Richard and Alais, but that, like the marriage, it had not come to pass.

The building work had been completed and now a full wall curtained off the palace making her surroundings more oppressive than ever. Henry had gone to Normandy, returning in late summer and had spent Christmas at Winchester. She had half expected to join him, but no summons had arrived.

On the feast of the Nativity she had attended mass in the cathedral, the interior lit up like the heart of a frozen dark jewel. Her breath had clouded the midnight air and the cold had so utterly enmeshed her that by the end of the ceremony she could barely move and her very sinews seemed to be made of ice.

There had been no company, no merriment, music or feasting. A freezing fog had descended that night and Sarum had become a pale crown of bones caught fast in clinging droplets of cloud. Alienor felt as though she was disappearing, becoming a wraith. This place would vanish with her walled up inside it and only other damned souls would know she was here. The Christ child was born, but where was the light?

In the gathering dusk of the third day after the Nativity Alienor wrapped herself in her cloak and went for a walk in order to stretch her legs and relieve the monotony by gazing at a different set of walls. The cathedral bell tolled the hour of vespers and the sound hung on the air as she walked past the solitary guard, clapping his mittened hands together in a fruitless effort to keep warm.

She made her way across the compound towards the boundary of the main gate now enclosed in its high curtain wall and discovered that the gates themselves were open and riders were milling in the courtyard and dismounting in clouds of vapour. A baggage cart rumbled into view drawn by two sturdy bay cobs. The contents of the cart were concealed under a tied-down canvas, and two lads who had been riding on the end hopped off to see to the horses.

Amid the masculine voices of the visitors, she recognised a boy's lighter tone, and her heart gave a tender lurch. She saw a handsome young man wearing a crimson cloak, his arm thrown across the shoulder of a boy in blue. Geoffrey and John. On seeing her, they quickened their pace and then together knelt in greeting.

'My lady mother,' Geoffrey said. At twenty years old, his voice had the full ring of manhood. John murmured the same and gave her an inscrutable glance.

Alienor bade them rise and embraced them joyfully. 'What a welcome surprise!' She bit her tongue before she said she had almost given up hope of seeing anyone this season. 'I am ill prepared for visitors, but you shall have the best of what I can provide.'

'We have brought you gifts.' Geoffrey indicated the laden baggage cart. 'There are fur covers, and wine, and pheasants and venison.'

'Papa allowed us to,' John qualified. 'He said if it would

make Geoffrey hold his peace for a minute he would let us ride over to Sarum.'

Geoffrey reddened. 'All I said was that it was not far to Sarum and I should visit Mama since I had not long returned from across the Narrow Sea.'

John cast a malicious look at his older brother. 'You also said it would be a charitable thing to do.'

Geoffrey cuffed John across the top of the head. 'What else would I have said to our father? You know how he is. You chose to come too – to make trouble I am beginning to think, or perhaps as Papa's spy.'

John looked wounded and straightened his hair. 'I can't help it if he likes me better than he does you.'

'I hope you are not going to spend your time with me in argument and sniping at each other,' Alienor reprimanded with dismay.

'No, Mama, I apologise.' John gave her a look from his repertoire, wide-eyed and angelic.

Despite herself, Alienor was amused at his incorrigibility. 'However you managed to visit, I am touched. Come within, warm yourselves, and tell me your news.'

The food Geoffrey had brought from Winchester included such delicacies as spiced wine, smoked eel, pheasant, and her favourite chestnuts which they roasted on a pan over the hearth fire.

For entertainment Geoffrey had brought his own small troupe of minstrels, a jester with a monkey, and two acrobats he had picked up in Southampton. At first Alienor found it difficult to laugh. As before, it was like returning to life from a living tomb, but gradually the colours seeped back into her awareness and words started to have meaning.

John had just celebrated his twelfth year day and she had nothing to mark the occasion for him beyond prayers. Henry had given him a fine hunting knife in a decorated sheath, which John had been showing off and waving around throughout the meal. Henry had also presented him with a black palfrey with red leather harness and a gilt-edged saddle cloth. She learned that John was to enter the household of Master Ranulf de Glanville the justiciar to further his education and was being groomed for Irish kingship. Much of his conversation was punctuated by 'my father says' and Alienor could clearly see Henry's influence at work. He was a miniature version of her husband. His attitude towards her had changed; more wary now, more judgemental. Still, the fact that he had chosen to visit told her that there was still a bond there of sorts.

Her relationship with Geoffrey was less complicated. His mind was deep and he only let her see the surface, but what he did show her was pleasant and sincere. He was genuinely regretful at the estrangement between his parents, and shocked at how she was living.

'You should have better than this, I told my father as much.'

'And his reply?'

'He said he would talk to you at Winchester at Easter and in the meantime he agreed to send you furs and bolts of cloth for robes and more lamp oil.'

All concessions that did not cost him the earth but were sops to keep Geoffrey from complaining too much. So she would be summoned to Winchester for Easter. She did not want her heart to leap but it did.

'Harry will be here at Easter too,' Geoffrey said. 'He has promised to come – before the jousting season starts in earnest.'

Alienor bit her lip. Harry was squandering his life by sporting at tourneys but she did not blame him. What else was he to do when his father refused to give him land and responsibility? Richard and Geoffrey both had more than he did although they were younger – and John would too if he became King of Ireland.

'I tourneyed with Harry for a while last summer and found it instructive,' Geoffrey said with a glow in his eyes. 'You have to have your wits about you; it's a brutal sport, but I know why men are drawn to it. There's glory in the surge through your body as you level your lance, spur your horse and feel the power.'

Alienor's stomach lurched. 'It is dangerous too.'

Geoffrey rubbed his soft new beard. 'Yes,' he conceded, 'and that is part of the attraction. But it is not as dangerous as war and there is a structure to it that fills the days with routine as well as excitement.'

A fairground of fighting then, she thought with a shiver of dislike for her son's enthusiasm. Young men parading from place to place in a dazzling summer cavalcade of bell-sewn harness, banners and armour. Jongleurs, troubadours, dancers, swordsmiths, thieves. Bright triumphs like flocks of small finches, sometimes overshadowed by the crow wings of death.

'William Marshal is truly a master of the art.' Geoffrey was warming to his theme. 'I have never seen anyone wield a lance or control a horse as he does. If my brother wins all the prizes this year, it will be because of the work the Marshal has put in with his knights in the fallow season. Some say the Marshal is too eager for his own advantage, but they are envious, because of the way he sweeps all before him.'

Geoffrey's words were certainly instructive, but did nothing for Alienor's peace of mind. 'As long as he remembers his duty to protect your brother,' she said tautly.

Geoffrey looked thoughtful. 'He does it better than some of them in Harry's entourage, but there is no mistaking that the Marshal is the real champion and Harry his pupil – I am not sure Harry appreciates that.'

'Didn't your father say anything about you going off to join Harry at the tourneys?'

Geoffrey looked amused as he replenished his cup. 'It was Papa's suggestion after I was knighted at Woodstock. He told me to go and enjoy the sport for a while. Of course he wanted me to report on what Harry was doing – I am not a fool, I knew what he was up to.'

'He did not think you would turn and conspire against him between you?'

Geoffrey gave a short laugh. 'With what, Mama? He knows that for now he has us leashed. Besides, it is no bad thing to let other princes see what handsome, accomplished sons the King of England has bred. King Louis' heir is afraid of horses. He's a weakling when it comes to sword play and his faults are very obvious when measured against our brood. Papa likes to rub it in.'

Alienor experienced a glow of pride tempered by trepidation. 'He should be careful; Louis is not to be trifled with. You may think you can run rings around him, but he knows how to bide his time and he will raise his son the same.'

Geoffrey eyed her curiously. 'I always thought your opinion of Louis was that of a milksop monk.'

She shook her head. 'He was never a milksop. And I have known several monks who are less than saintly.' She reached to her wine and, keeping her voice casually neutral, asked, 'What of Richard? Is he to join us at Easter too?'

'I suppose it depends on whether he can spare the time from his campaigns in Poitou,' Geoffrey answered, shrugging. 'There is still widespread rebellion and I doubt he thinks spending Easter in the bosom of his family is the best use of his time. But he will need to make a report to Papa and ask him for more funds.'

And then Henry would parade her as a hostage and a warning to his sons to be obedient to his will.

She touched Geoffrey's wrist. 'And what of you, my son?'

He gave her a twisted smile. 'I am the quiet one, Geoffrey the thinker. I don't have Harry's charm or claims to inheritance, and I am not a fire-eater and heir to Aquitaine like Richard, but fortunately I have an inheritance, courtesy of my future wife.' He reached to his cup and contemplated his wine. 'For now let us say I am content to bide my time.'

John remained silent and toyed with his new dagger.

71

11

Winchester Castle, April 1179

Walking in the garden at Winchester, Alienor was enjoying the green flourishes of spring. Violets and celandine carpeted the beds and daisies spotted the lush turf. The sky was a clear pale blue decorated with rabbit-scut fluffs of cloud. Harry walked at her side, hands clasped behind his back and his head inclined towards hers. As always he wore a smile, but beneath that polished surface Alienor could sense his grief and turbulence.

'I understand your pain.' She touched his arm. 'I wrote to you, but I do not know if you received my letter.'

He drew a deep breath. 'I do not know either, Mama. In truth I remember little about that time. He was in the world barely a moment. I saw him, my own flesh and blood, lying in the cradle, and then he was gone – his life snuffed out as easily as extinguishing a candle.'

Alienor tightened her grip in compassion.

'Perhaps God has decreed I should have everything and nothing,' he said bitterly.

'That is not true, never think that! There will be other children.'

'So everyone tells me,' he said. The dazzling smile was back on his face – the glittering façade. 'Have you heard how well I am doing in the tourneys? Geoffrey must have told you.'

'Yes, he did, but sons risking themselves in tourneys is not something a mother desires to hear about, even while she is proud of their skill.'

'They are good for making alliances and friendships, and for recruiting likely men. They are fine places to display prowess and generosity.'

'So I hear.' She gave him a censorious look. 'I understand from others that no sooner does your father fill your purse than it is empty again – almost as if you are challenging him to an eating contest except with money.'

His expression grew petulant. 'Richard practises war in Poitou and you do not complain. He is always running out of money too and coming to Papa with his hand out. Do you approve of that? I am making my way by politics and diplomacy in a different way, that is all.'

'I have a mother's natural fear for her offspring,' she soothed him. 'I worry for both of you. I wish it was different.'

'What else am I supposed to do when I have nothing to govern?' he demanded. 'My father uses me as a diplomat at the tourneys and at the French court. I am his representative in areas where he cannot make that kind of show – the sort he used to depend on Thomas Becket to provide until Becket abandoned him for God and then chose martyrdom. If I go to aid Richard, then it is Richard who commands the troops, not me. When I am at my father-in-law's court I hear their whispers – that I have neither power nor influence beyond the smile on my face and my father's money in my purse. They bow to me and then they smirk behind their hands. Nothing has changed, Mama, nothing, except for the worse.' Tears filled his eyes. 'Now they say I cannot even beget a living son.'

Alienor winced, feeling sympathy for his pain, but she was also exasperated. 'You should not listen to the back biting and gossip of courtiers. I can do nothing about your situation. Once I tried and I paid with my liberty. If you have smiles and money to your account, then I have nothing. Like me you must bide your time, but mind how you spend it.'

His expression soured. 'I have been hearing that ever since my coronation and that was nine years ago.'

A headache began to throb at Alienor's temples. 'I have no remedy, Harry,' she said wearily. 'I wish I did.'

Rounding a corner they came to an arbour. In the summer roses and honeysuckle would trellis around the seat but at the moment the lats were bare. Two young women decorated it now, surrounded by a gathering of eager young courtiers. There was a lot of giggling and laughter but it ceased abruptly as Harry and Alienor arrived, and everyone hurried to bow and curtsey.

Alienor flicked her gaze over the group. Alais was there, Richard's betrothed. The continued delay of the marriage was a source of deep friction between England and France. The girl was sixteen, slim and fair like her father with grey eyes and thin, fine features. She reminded Alienor of a mouse. The other young woman was petite and vibrant, with a cherub mouth, dimpled cheeks, and large brown eyes. After a single startled glance at Alienor, she dropped her gaze and stared at the ground. Standing beside her was Roger Bigod, heir to the earldom of Norfolk, but currently denied that position because his father had sided with Harry's thwarted rebellion six years ago. He too looked discomfited, as if caught with his hand in the honey jar.

A fluffy terrier not much bigger than a rat began a high-pitched yapping at Alienor and Alais swiftly picked him up and held him to her breast. 'We were taking Trynket for a walk,' she said.

Alienor felt like an intruder even though hers was the greater right to be here. What else did she expect of the young? It was natural to find places like this to huddle and socialise. She made an impatient gesture. 'You have my leave to go.'

They made their respects and departed in a haste of colour. The pretty dark girl still had her head down. Roger Bigod murmured something to her and she shook her head and quickened her pace. Harry looked after them, eyes narrow.

'Do you want to join them?'

'No, Mama.' He gave her his glittering smile. 'I would rather spend time with you.'

'I am not so certain about that,' she said, wryly. 'Who was the young lady with Alais? I have not seen her before.'

Harry's mouth twisted. 'Ida de Tosney, Papa's latest concubine. She's Rosamund de Clifford's second cousin.'

'Yes, he told me.' Another girl of tender years; an heiress in Henry's care. She could read the pattern so well in him. 'Does he think to replace Rosamund with this one?'

'She is a sweet girl. I receive the impression that far from scheming herself into Papa's bed, she would rather it had not happened.'

'Roger Bigod was paying her close attention.' Alienor sat on the seat and surveyed the garden.

'I expect when Papa tires of her, he will sell her marriage to an interested party,' Harry said. 'Bigod is making that interest known. Still, he should be careful. Treading the young hen while she's still the rooster's favourite is dangerous.'

Alienor looked at him. He had shown no inclination to take a mistress himself even though his wife was still in Paris and their relationship was one that functioned on duty not passion. If he had other women, at least, unlike his father, he was discreet about it.

'They make him forget his age,' Harry said. 'That's why he always has the fastest horses to stay ahead of everyone else.'

'And they always kick him. He cannot bear to relinquish control to anyone. That is why he likes such women too. They do as he says – they are in his power and they do not struggle to escape.' Unlike his ageing wife, who he had to keep under lock and key, build walls around and set spies upon. She gave an embittered smile. What it was to make a king afraid.

Later, during an informal gathering in the hall, Alienor took a moment to draw William Marshal aside and speak to him. 'I am reminding you to take care of Harry,' she said. 'He is a grown man and would not thank me if he heard me speak thus to you, but tourneys are dangerous places, and I fear that living life dangerously has too much glamour for him just now.'

William's easy smile gave way to a more serious expression. 'Madam, I have sworn to guard my lord with my life.'

'Then do not lose your focus, William. I hear many tales of your prowess and I see how men look at you in this room – and women too. It would be easy to become carried away by adulation and by the abilities in arms you possess. I do not want you or my son to endanger your lives. You must be aware for both of you. Do not reply that it goes without saying, because it does not. It has to be said before it can be put to rest.'

William dipped his head. 'I understand, madam, and I take it to heart. In serving my young lord, I serve you also, and I swear I will not let you down.'

Alienor gave a firm nod and was satisfied, knowing that William's reply, while courtly, was sincerely meant. Many young men would have taken umbrage at her warning, but he had accepted it in the spirit with which it was meant, and was sufficiently secure in his own manhood not to feel challenged.

Alienor returned to Sarum after the Easter gathering and prepared to spend another summer on the wind-burned hill top. Harry escorted her there and stayed for three days. He took her hawking on the Downs, which was a rare and wonderful treat, before he rode away to rejoin the tourney life and left her to the confines of the palace.

The masons continued with their building: plans were afoot to construct another secure tower at the postern end of the complex. Alienor eyed the foundations of the embryo building and wondered at Henry's desire to strengthen the security at Sarum, since she doubted he was ever going to stay here himself.

In August, Richard surprised her with a swift visit, arriving in a flurry of coloured silk banners that declared here was a presence to be reckoned with. Neglecting a formal greeting, she flew into his arms and embraced him with a cry that was half joy and half pain.

His arms were hard and strong as they enfolded her and she clung to him in the utter pleasure of reunion before pushing him away, greedy to take in the whole. 'Let me look at you!' She had not seen him for three years and the youth had been completely banished by a tall, beautiful man, his features strong yet refined, his body lithe, with supple power in every movement. He had Henry's thrust and energy, but tempered with grace because of his height and coordination.

He smiled at her. 'Do I meet with your approval, Mama?'

'How could you not?' Laughing, crying, she hugged him again and then took his arm to lead him towards the keep. 'But even putting aside my bias as your mother, I would challenge anyone to find fault.'

'Even my father?' he asked, lifting his brows.

'Why, what has he done now?'

He shook his head. 'I was jesting.' His gaze followed the line of the new curtain wall with thoughtful interest.

'He says it is to bring the defences up to a better standard than they were in the time of his grandsire, but it is oppressive. I know I am prisoner, but this serves to emphasise the detail. He is also building a secure tower apparently, but whether to house me or part of his treasure I know not.'

They entered the cool interior of the great hall and servants brought refreshment and attended to Richard's entourage. Someone had already run to the top of the tower to fly his banner from the battlements. Richard removed his light travelling cloak and handed it to a squire.

'So,' Alienor said, as a servant set down a platter of honey cakes, 'do you have news for me? I am starved for information here except for what I manage to pick up like a bird pecking crumbs from under the table. Your father isolates me as much as he can. How is Poitou?'

Richard bit into a honey cake, chewed and swallowed. 'Still in rebellion, but learning that the harder they press, the more determined I am, and that my resources and tactics are better than theirs. For now there is calm. I do not suppose it will last, but many of the perpetrators have sworn to take up arms in Jerusalem instead.'

Alienor noted the gleam in his eyes with misgiving. Richard had been a warrior almost from the day he was born, from preference rather than necessity. For him the gauds of the tourney were so much frippery when the true kernel of prowess was on the battlefield.

'They said Taillebourg was impregnable, but it fell,' he said. 'I took it and I razed it, and Geoffrey de Rancon knelt to me in surrender.'

Alienor gave a pragmatic nod. Her bond with the de Rancon family had been close in the past; indeed her tie to Geoffrey's father was part of the past she would never reveal to anyone. But time and a changing political landscape had frayed the cords and they were not as securely attached to a younger generation. There had always been unrest in Aquitaine, each lord striving to hold as much power as he could.

That Richard had taken and razed Taillebourg surprised her because it was reputedly impregnable. She had consummated her first marriage there when she was barely more than a child, her young husband fumbling in the dark and both of them frightened and excited. Perhaps it was a good thing that the place with all its whispers and memories had been torn down.

'You have done well.' It was indeed a great achievement for someone not yet twenty-two.

He shrugged but looked pleased. Finishing the honey cake, he took another. 'I do not trust any of them even if they are out of my sight on the road to Jerusalem, but it will give me an opportunity to establish my government.'

'If your father will let you.'

'He said he would. Not that I trust him either, but he seemed pleased with my progress. He said he would leave matters in my hands and that he thought me capable.'

'Did he?' Alienor was not impressed. Richard was her heir specifically and when she died, Aquitaine would be his by right, independent of any paternal heritage. It did not surprise her that Henry was doing his utmost to keep Richard in his camp and out of hers. 'I know you are more than capable, but be aware you are still on his leash, even if he has slackened it for the time being.'

78

'Yes, Mama, I have it in hand.' He made a face. 'Indeed, we did argue, but it was not about my rule in Aquitaine.'

'Then about what?'

'You.' His complexion darkened. 'I told him it was shameful that he still kept you locked up like this; I asked him to set you free if it really was his intention to have peace and co-operation in all of his lands.'

Alienor was darkly amused. 'And what did he say to that?'

'What he usually says when pushed into a corner where he does not have a good answer. That he would consider it well and let me know at a later time. That it was not as easy as forgiveness and clemency, and he had to think about the wider implications – which means he will do nothing.'

'It is simple. While I am locked up here I cannot cause trouble for him. I doubt he will ever apply forgiveness and clemency to me.'

'I told him I intended visiting you, and he did not object, but we both knew it was a sop because he had refused my other request. I will set you free, Mama, I promise you that.'

She did not answer. While not doubting his determination and sincerity, she knew what was and was not possible. He might have the military skill to reduce the fortress of Taillebourg to rubble, but it was not within his power to spring the locks at Sarum.

'So, will you return to Poitou now you have made your report and been granted permission to return and rule as you will?'

He nodded. 'I am on my way there now. My baggage wains have gone to Southampton.' He hesitated as if deciding whether to say more.

'Tell me,' she said. 'What else?'

Richard swept his hand through his hair leaving deep finger marks in the coppery waves. 'While I was with Papa he received messengers from France. Louis is coming to England to pray at the tomb of St Thomas. That sickly son of his has a fever and he desires to pray for his safe recovery. It is best for me

79

to be absent because Louis will want to see his daughter, and if we are together, he might just moot a wedding.'

'And that would be disastrous.' Alienor was unsettled at the thought of having her former husband on English soil with her present one. 'I am surprised your father granted Louis' request.'

'He says it is an opportunity for them to talk diplomacy on his territory and as compassion from one father to another.' Richard rolled his eyes to show what he thought of that particular gambit. 'They have to meet anyway, so best to take advantage and make it now. Doubtless Louis will be praying to St Thomas for more than just his son's life; he'll be asking for French victories over us, and Papa will be reciprocating with entreaties the other way.'

'Undoubtedly, but Louis never could resist a shrine and the chance to amplify his pleas to the Almighty by invoking the saints. When we journeyed to Outremer, he sought out every one he could find in order to worship and collect a handful of dust or a relic to put in his coffer. He was obsessed. His army went home and he stayed because he hadn't finished shrine-visiting.' Alienor shook her head in remembered exasperation. 'Abbé Suger kept writing to him begging him to return because France was threatened with rebellion. He listened eventually but he was reluctant. He'll be desperate to worship at Thomas Becket's tomb – it was Thomas that gave him a son in the first place by blessing his marriage bed.'

Richard gazed at her, his mouth slightly open.

'Louis always needed the sanction of the Church to help him beget his children.' She waved her hand. 'Unfortunately with me and his second wife the clergy's blessing only brought him girls even when the Pope got involved, but Philippe was born nine months after Louis granted Becket succour in France during the quarrel with your father.'

Richard grinned. 'So in a way Thomas Becket is Philippe's surrogate sire? How wonderfully ironic!'

Alienor laughed. 'Oh, your visit has lightened my mood. It is so good to talk to you.'

'I would bring you back to Aquitaine if I could, Mama. Stow you away in my baggage and set you free the moment we crossed the Narrow Sea.'

Her laughter faded. 'I long for freedom with all my heart, but how long would it last?'

Richard placed his hand over hers. 'I mean it about setting you free, Mama. It is a promise I intend to keep.'

When she did not answer, he squeezed her hand. She looked at his fingers, young and smooth, but hard too with a warrior's strength and adorned with the sapphire ring of St Valerie that was part of the regalia of the Counts of Poitou.

Intent was one thing and accomplishing it another, but if she believed in him, then at least it was another spar to cling to when despair threatened to drown her.

12

Palace of Sarum, November 1179

Alienor knelt at prayer in the private royal chapel dedicated to St Nicholas. Outside a chill rain-laden wind was blowing across the Downs, buffeting the palace walls, and the lowering clouds sent little daylight through the window above the altar. However, the candles provided illumination within and the chapel was painted with scenes from the life of St Nicholas in vibrant colours that brightened her surroundings.

The prospect of winter daunted Alienor, with the dark days contracting her world and the news from outside so meagre. Gazing at the depiction of the saint pushing a bag of gold coins through the window of a house that belonged to a poor man with three daughters who had no money for their dowries and faced prostitution, she wished that someone would push hope through hers.

The stormy weather eventually blew out to sea, leaving a stripe of golden sunset edged with charcoal cloud. Alienor returned to her chamber and played a desultory game of merels with Amiria, her emotion one of grey boredom – until Robert Maudit came to tell her that the Countess de Warenne had arrived.

'Bring her to me!' Alienor seized on the moment like a drowning swimmer to a rope. 'And see that suitable accommodation is prepared. This is my bag of gold through the window!' She laughed as Amiria and Maudit gave her baffled looks, clearly thinking she was losing her mind, and she sent a prayer of gratitude to St Nicholas.

Isabel was on her way to her Norfolk estate at Acre to join Hamelin before travelling on to Nottingham for the Christmas court, but had detoured with her daughters to visit Alienor. Her son William was keeping John company as they studied in the household of royal justiciar Ranulf de Glanville.

'It is so good to see you again!' Alienor cried as they embraced. 'And my nieces, all so grown up!' Belle at fifteen was a beauty. Her silky brown hair was plaited round her head and revealed the delicate sweep of her neck. The style emphasised the blue-green sea colours of her eyes and her skin was clear and luminous. Adela and Matilda at eleven and nine were pretty and vivacious but still children, lacking their big sister's allure.

Isabel returned the smile, but with a slight strain at the edges. 'Yes, indeed,' she murmured.

'Hamelin is well?'

'Yes, and sends you his good wishes – and more gingerbread.'

'He let Belle paint his beard blue,' Adela announced with a giggle. 'And then Mama was cross with him because he was going to meet the King of France.'

Alienor looked between mother and daughters and for the first time in an age was moved to genuine laughter. 'Truly? A blue beard?'

'It was folly,' Isabel said primly. 'He should have known better and so should Belle. What must people have thought?'

'It was nothing,' Belle retorted. 'You are always so serious, Mama!' She turned to Alienor. 'We were watching some cloth being dyed and Papa was telling me he had read that the people of long ago used to dye their skin with woad. So I said his beard was going grey, and he let me paint the end of it, that is all.' She shot her mother a defiant look.

'It was irresponsible,' Isabel said. 'Everyone was laughing. And your father had to go clean-shaven to court. You should have taken more thought for the consequences.'

Belle compressed her soft pink lips and looked down in apparent submission, but Alienor could see the rebellion in her and even understand it a little. 'Henry would do things like that,' she told her niece. 'I remember once he rode into Thomas Becket's hall all spattered from the hunt and slung a fresh dead hare across the dinner table – and that was in the days when they were friends.'

Isabel shook her head and tutted; Belle gave a half-hidden smile and darted Alienor an almost conspiratorial glance.

'I am sure no one paid much notice to Hamelin's shaven chin,' Alienor soothed, and changed the subject. 'Were you at Canterbury? Did you see Louis?'

Isabel nodded. 'I have never met him before, so I cannot judge him on past appearance, but I must say he seemed rather frail.'

Alienor frowned. 'In what way?'

'He was tall, but stooped over, and thin I thought, perhaps from fasting. He was unsteady on his feet and his attendants had to stand close all the time ready to catch him if he stumbled. He was an old man, Alienor.'

Alienor had often hated Louis with all the venom in her heart for what he had done to her, and for the failure in him that had ended what might once have been a workable marriage. Yet there were moments of softer emotion when she remembered the early years – a boy and a girl thrown together by the machinations of others, bewildered, but taking shelter and comfort in each other. 'I am sorry to hear that.'

'He was deeply moved by the tomb of the Archbishop,' Isabel continued. 'He openly wept. I think Henry was taken aback.'

'Louis was always one to weep and prostrate himself at the tombs of martyrs,' Alienor replied. 'I expect he felt duty bound to do so at Becket's even if his tears were genuine. Did he meet his daughter?'

'Yes. He praised her manners and demeanour – it was all of duty and piety – but he has not seen her since she was a babe in arms.'

'And she is female which he has always found a difficult proposition,' Alienor said with asperity. 'Did he speak of marriage between Alais and Richard?'

'Hamelin said he did in counsel with Henry. Apparently Louis told him the matter had dragged on for too long and that the marriage should be solemnised.'

'And what did Henry say?'

'He agreed with him.'

Alienor sat up straight. 'He promised he would not! He told me he had no intention of doing so!'

'No, no.' Isabel waved a denial. 'He agreed in order to put him off. He said that indeed it was past time but Richard had been busy in Poitou. He agreed that Louis was bound to have concerns as a father, and he promised he would look to finalise a date for the wedding. Louis was either too tired or too much the diplomat to push matters through there and then. They agreed on some time next year, but Henry told Hamelin later that it would be as he chose and no one would dictate to him.'

Alienor knew that she and Richard were part of the 'no one' in that remark, but at least for now the danger had passed.

Isabel hesitated. 'You should also know that Ida de Tosney has retired to Woodstock. She is to bear Henry's child some time between Christmas and Candlemas.'

The news was little more than a muted blow on old scars and Alienor's only emotion was dull sadness. Indeed, she was sorry for the girl – yet another of Henry's victims. 'I do not suppose Henry will keep her in attendance once she has been churched. He changes his women almost as often as the laundress changes his sheets. He will find a marriage for her among the men at court and in the meantime, someone else will catch his eye.' She turned to address her nieces, who were agog. 'You may think it exciting to be the mistress of a great man,' she cautioned, 'to be the centre of attention and have silks and jewels and the best morsels set before you at table, but it is a dangerous thing, because you are dependent on his whim and he can discard you with a snap of his fingers.'

'Is that not like being a queen too?' Belle asked.

Alienor looked sharply at her niece. The sea-coloured gaze was perceptive – almost knowing. She had used the word 'dangerous' and it came to her that this girl with her nurtured, cosseted life and protective parents was in search of excitement to whet her existence, even if it meant breaking something. 'You might see it like that, but my husband took those things from me. He did not give them because they were mine in the first place. It is the way of the world, so be on your guard.'

Belle's cheeks turned pink. 'My uncle has made an endowment to Godstow nunnery in memory of Rosamund de Clifford. She has a magnificent tomb and he has turned it into a shrine.'

'Belle, enough!' Isabel hissed.

Alienor waved away Isabel's chagrin. 'No, it is better to speak of these things than to hide them in dark corners.' She faced Belle. 'Rosamund was your uncle's mistress for many years. He was never going to marry her, but he has honoured her in death more than he has ever honoured me in life. Yet what good does it benefit her to have the tomb of a queen? She is still a rotting corpse under the slab.' She exhaled scornfully. 'The King is good at shrines for the dead. One for Thomas, one for his mistress – and one for me, a living one here at Sarum . . . But not all of us are prepared to lie as quiet as the grave.'

*   *   *

85

When the girls had gone to bed, Isabel and Alienor sat before the dying embers in the brazier, drinking wine and playing merels as they had often done in the old days at court.

'I hope Belle did not upset you,' Isabel apologised. 'She is at an age when she is no longer a girl, but not yet a woman. One moment she plays like a child and the next she demands all the privileges of an adult. It is not easy.'

Alienor shook her head. 'I have gone beyond those sort of hurts, and I can remember what it was to be that age and constrained by the company of older women – although by that time I was already wed to Louis.'

'We have started to look for a husband for her,' Isabel said, 'but it is a slow process and we want her to be well settled.'

'If I was free, she could serve as one of my ladies and have opportunities, but as it is she would be unlikely to meet any personable young men at Sarum, and would probably wither away from the boredom.' Alienor leaned forward to make her point. 'But you must give her things to do beyond sewing and looking after her sisters. Let her be the chatelaine – give her one of your households to manage so that she will be occupied and well prepared.'

Isabel pursed her lips. 'Perhaps you are right; I shall think on it.'

The women resumed their game but were interrupted when Robert Maudit arrived, his expression sombre and his manner subdued. 'Madam, there are grave tidings from France. I am sorry to tell you we have received news that King Louis has suffered a debilitating seizure.'

Alienor stared at him and Isabel uttered a soft gasp.

'It is uncertain whether he will live,' Maudit continued. 'He has recovered consciousness and is being tended by his physicians, but he cannot speak – that is all we know for now.'

Alienor heard his words but found them difficult to absorb. An image came to her of Louis at seventeen, tall, narrow-hipped and graceful, silver-blond hair waving to his shoulders and a coronet of sapphires on his brow that matched the deep blue of his eyes. He had been a beautiful youth and she had loved him in that long, hot summer, whatever had changed in the years since.

'God have mercy on his soul,' she said. 'And thank you for telling me.' She spoke the words by rote. 'I will pray for his recovery.'

Maudit hesitated, bowed and left the room.

'Oh my dear, is there anything I can do?' Isabel extended a compassionate hand.

'I am sad, not distraught,' Alienor said. 'Tomorrow I will pray for him and have masses said for his soul.' Rising to her feet, she held out her hands to the last warmth from the brazier. She felt cold, as if the news of Louis' illness had sucked some of the life from her, but it was a temporary thing and her political brain was stirring and asserting itself. 'Louis' heir is only fifteen years old and malleable. Who knows what will happen now? Those in power surrounding him will now have opportunity to make their play.'

'Harry and Marguerite will be at his court,' Isabel said, 'and he has known them for several years.'

'Indeed, and Harry can charm the birds out of the trees if he sets his mind to it, but he will have to contend with others too.' She frowned thoughtfully. 'Henry may find Philippe a difficult proposition because he is closer in age to our sons. He will not be able to control him as he does them and there are no ties of old acquaintance. Louis was thirteen years older than Henry, and now Philippe is more than thirty years younger than Henry. The balance of time is no longer in his favour and this alters the landscape entirely.'

'Are you worried?'

'There is nothing I can do, so there is no point.' She looked across the brazier at Isabel. 'But Henry should be.'

Belle shivered with delicious fear as she followed John into the dark passageway, heavy with the scent of moist stone. They had left the royal chamber where the adults were socialising and gone for a walk around Nottingham Castle's grounds in the overcast December afternoon. It had begun raining and John had dared her to come with him and investigate one of the many caves tunnelled into the soft sandstone rock on which the castle was built. Nottingham itself was honeycombed with underground dwellings and cellars of which the castle had its share. The lantern in his hand cast sufficient light to illuminate the way but heightened the blackness behind and beyond.

'Careful,' John whispered. 'You might tread on a rat.'

Belle shuddered, imagining a yielding furry body under the thin sole of her shoe. He had said it to scare her and she was determined not to let him know he had succeeded. 'So might you,' she retorted with bravado. She touched the wall and felt the gritty stone under her fingers, scored by the chisel marks of the men who had cut these caves in the soft stone.

'There are worse things than rats,' he whispered. 'They used to chain prisoners down here on the night before they were executed.'

'I don't believe you. It's just a place for storage.' Belle looked surreptitiously over her shoulder.

'Yes, storage of bodies. You can hear the fetter chains of the condemned rattling sometimes if you listen.' He had just turned thirteen and his voice had developed the grate of young manhood.

'You don't scare me,' she said scornfully, but strained her ears nevertheless. All she could hear was their breathing, the scrape of their soft soles on the tunnel floor and a distant plink-plink of dripping water.

He turned a corner, ducking under a thick archway, and then another, bringing them into a chamber hollowed out of the rock. 'In the town people make their homes underground,' he said. 'There are cockfighting pits and ale houses.'

The smell of stone was powerful and musty. Belle was intensely aware of his presence and the lantern light making a disturbing mask of his features, half golden, half dark.

'They say the tunnels go for miles and you can walk all the way out of the city if you know the way – and under everyone's feet without them ever knowing.' For an instant his air of world-weary cynicism was replaced by one of fascinated speculation. 'Truly there could be enemies under your bed . . . or even in it.' He turned towards her.

A frisson of fear and something less easily defined shivered down Belle's spine. It was indeed unsettling to imagine a dark, subterranean world underfoot. She gazed round the irregular circle of the cavern. A stone plinth ran round the edge almost like a bench. 'It's boring.' She affected disdain. 'There weren't any prisoners chained down here; it's just an old storage room.'

She made to push past him and return the way they had come, but he blocked her path, holding out his arms. The lantern swung and the shadows climbed the walls.

'Even so, people have come down here, unsuspecting, and never been seen again.'

'Let me past.' She pushed at him, beginning to feel afraid. 'I have had enough of your folly.'

He gave a soft laugh. 'Is that what you think? But surely you were the foolish one to come here in the first place.'

'John, I mean it; let me go.' Panic started to rise within her.

'Or what? You'll tell your papa? What will you tell him?' He watched her, eyes avid like a cat playing with a mouse.

Belle felt queasy with fear but there was a strange, sweet heaviness in her loins.

'He will not let you out of his sight ever again if you cannot even be trusted to go walking with your cousin without causing trouble.'

She gasped at the unfairness. 'How dare you!'

'Because I am a prince, the son of the King!' He lifted the lantern. 'When the prisoners were kept down here, they had no light; they were kept in pitch blackness. Did you know that, cousin?'

'There weren't any prisoners, you're lying!'

He pointed to a chain secured high up on the wall and,

attached to it, a fetter cuff. 'No? If you were taller, your wrist would fit in it. Do you wonder what it would be like? You do, don't you?'

Belle glared at him, trying not to show her fright. 'Don't be stupid.' She shouldered past him into the corridor.

In a sharp puff of breath he blew out the lantern and plunged them both into blackness. The scream left Belle's throat before she could prevent it. The darkness was absolutely black, like thick smothering cloth.

'Now who is stupid?' John purred.

'I want to go back.' Her fear was becoming terror. John, with his aptitude for trickery, might go on ahead and hide somewhere further up the tunnel in order to leap out on her, or he might just abandon her here.

'Do you think this is what it is like to be eyeless?' he mused. There was a clink as he set the lantern down.

'I mean it,' she quavered. 'I want to go back.'

His voice came to her, soft and husky. 'When you have no eyes, you have to rely on your other senses.' She felt his fingertips lightly brush her cheek, and then trail down her throat. 'It is my thirteenth year day today, will you not give me one kiss and see how it feels?'

Belle trembled, balanced between terror and a surge through her body of different physical sensations. Outside in the daylight she would have had control and perspective, but here in the pitch dark, he was in command.

'Just one,' he coaxed, and his hand whispered over her breast and came to rest at her waist. 'And then we'll go. No one has to know; this is a place for secrets, and this one will be ours.'

She stood very still. Should she run and hope to find her way out on her own, or should she yield? Her mother would be horrified, but then her mother was horrified at everything, and what did she know? At home she was the good girl, the darling, but her compliance masked a simmering discontent. That was what attracted her to John: the danger on the edge.

Someone who would dare her and say, 'Do it, there is no harm.' Someone who would leave her in darkness and threaten her with 'just one kiss'. If she yielded then everything would change, and at the same time, because it was a secret, all would remain the same – on the surface. One life in the light, and another underground.

Belle groped in the dark until she found his face, and then she curled her hand round the nape of his neck, pulled him in close to her and pressed her mouth to his. His lips were soft, tender almost, and the feel against hers was not unpleasant. It was like kissing a warm, slightly moist cushion. His hand tightened at her waist and he held her, but by mutual consent not constraint, and the kiss lengthened.

Eventually Belle drew away and gasped for breath. 'There is your kiss and more. Now take me out of this place.'

She felt the rapid rise and fall of his chest, heard his ragged breathing, and was empowered and emboldened.

'And if I don't?'

'Then I will find my own way, and I will tell my father, and who do you think he will believe?'

'Hah, you would do it too, wouldn't you? Papa's perfect daughter. Come then.'

He took her hand in his and together they felt their way back along the passageways towards the light, bumping against each other, half playful, half challenging. Each time his body touched hers, she felt the contact like a lightning jolt, and she thought it must be the same for him. He was the one who had asked her for a kiss after all. He took her hand and squeezed it hard enough to make her gasp, but then she pinched him, using her fingernails, and he writhed away with an involuntary yelp before rounding on her and pushing her up against the cave wall and snatching another kiss. This time she bit him, but not too hard.

'You like games, don't you?' he said.

'It's not a game.'

Belle could see the entrance, smell the rainy air. Nearby a

dog was barking. She shoved him away and walked briskly now towards the normality of the mundane. And then from a walk to a run. She expected him to chase after her, but he didn't, and she emerged into the cold late December afternoon alone. She raised the back of her hand to her lips, fancying she could still taste him, and looked over her shoulder, but still he did not come.

She had no intention of waiting until he did, and returned to the domestic chamber, slipping quietly into the room, removing her cloak, going to kiss her father on the cheek. He was playing a game of chess with Henry, and patted her hand with dismissive affection. She joined her mother and the other women who were sewing and gossiping and became that perfect demure daughter with downcast eyes and a modest expression, enhanced by the slightest curve of her lips. Glancing at the other women she thought that they didn't know a thing about desire and all the delicious, disturbing feelings that such darkness aroused. She pitied them and was scornful too, and perhaps a little afraid because her world had changed irrevocably. This year at least, the Christmas feast was not going to be boring.

13

Palace of Sarum, June 1180

The door opened and Alienor looked up in surprise as her gaoler Robert Maudit entered the room followed by several servants bearing sacks and chests. Accompanying him was a robust young woman with an olive complexion, red lips and lustrous dark eyes. She dropped a deep curtsey and bowed her head.

'What is this, messire?' Alienor rose to her feet.

'Gifts from the King, madam,' Maudit said neutrally.

Trying not to look astonished, Alienor left the window and

came to appraise the goods. One chest held panels of furs including sable and squirrel from the lands of the Rus. Another was piled with bolts of fabric for winter robes. There were scarlet bed hangings and candlesticks of enamelled silver. A large brass bowl. Chess sets, dishes, and even a chest of books.

Alienor studied the largesse with suspicion. Why would Henry relax his austerity? She did not believe he had suddenly forgiven her and mellowed. Until recently he had still been trying to make her agree to take vows and become Abbess of Amesbury.

'Who are you?' She gestured the young woman to her feet. 'Speak, mistress.'

'Madam, may it please you my name is Belbel de Rouen,' she answered in a musical voice, deep for a woman. 'I am a seamstress and lady of the chamber sent by the King to attend on you and fashion new garments for your wardrobe.'

Two perspiring servants hauled another chest into the room, followed by a man bearing a saddle of red leather and a matching bridle gilded with silver.

'The King of his clemency says you have leave to ride out suitably escorted, madam,' Maudit said, 'and provides you with the necessary harness.'

Alienor noticed the flicker in his cheek and almost felt sorry for him. She was mystified as to why Henry was doing all this, but whatever the reason, she was delighted.

Once Maudit had departed about his business, Alienor turned to the matter of her new maid. 'Well,' she said, 'it pleases me to have another attendant to grace my chamber, especially one with the capability to improve my wardrobe.' She regarded her narrowly. 'But why are you really here?'

The woman curtseyed again. Her gown of deep red wool was plain but exquisite and enhanced her figure without being tasteless or lewd. 'Truly, madam, I am to serve you in any way you wish, but my particular skill is with the needle and that was the King's intention in appointing me.'

'He chose you personally for this task?' Alienor raised a

cynical eyebrow. She would not put it past Henry to have engaged this woman as a spy, and wondered what his relationship with her was, although she seemed a tad too old and voluptuous for Henry's usual tastes.

'Yes, madam.' The woman was unfazed by Alienor's stare. 'I was employed to make a tunic for the King and he was greatly pleased with my work. He said he was of a mind to have new gowns made for you and that he would provide the cloth and the seamstress.'

'That is interesting, since my husband has a singular disregard for his appearance. I have known him go to church still bloody and mired from the hunt.'

'I understand he was pleased because the tunic flattered his girth,' Belbel said steadily.

Alienor was amused. Last time she had seen Henry, his barrel chest had been spreading south to include his gut, and that might be a point of concern to a man eager to keep up with younger men. 'Well then, let us hope you can perform similar miracles for me and restore my figure to what it was thirty years ago.'

A spark kindled in Belbel's eyes, composed of humour and acceptance of a challenge. 'Madam, it will not take much work, but it will be a pleasure.'

'Then I am immediately wary of a flatterer!' Alienor retorted, but smiled. 'Amiria will find you sleeping space and show you where to put your belongings.'

In the weeks that followed Alienor decided that Belbel was a godsend. She was vivacious, intelligent and perceptive. Alienor played chess and backgammon with her and enjoyed an astute opponent who gave of herself honestly and without deference. Belbel had a forthright personality, yet knew when to be silent and was tactful when the occasion demanded. She was as content to sit and quietly sew a seam with Amiria, or pray in church, as she was to accompany a heavily escorted Alienor for rides on the Downs.

Belbel's supreme skill lay in her ability to assess fabric and turn it into beautiful garments. With clever cutting and stitching, she created gowns that delighted Alienor with their stylish elegance. The drape and the arrangements of the laces did indeed restore Alienor's waistline and lift her breasts, giving her a defined figure without making her look like an older woman desperately chasing her youth. The clothes made Alienor feel powerful and attractive, reminding her of what had once been hers to command. She was still baffled, however.

'I do not understand why the King has sent me all this largesse,' she said to Belbel, who was kneeling at her feet to adjust the hem on the latest gown of green silk, patterned with gold. 'He must have an underlying motive.'

'Perhaps he thinks it is time to mend the breach between you, madam.'

Alienor tried to gauge the nuance beneath the words. Belbel had rarely spoken about how she came to work upon a tunic for Henry, other than having been recommended to him by other clients. 'Did you ever hear him say as much?'

Belbel set a silver pin into the gown and sat back. 'No, madam, but I think he was lonely.'

'Indeed?' Alienor raised her brows.

'He has his courtiers and companions, but it is not the same as having a queen. At times I thought him a little lost.'

Alienor moved away from Belbel and walked to the window to look out on the cloudy September daylight.

'Forgive me, madam, if I have spoken out of turn.'

'No,' Alienor shook her head. 'Rather you have given me food for thought.'

Henry as a lost soul. She had often thought that, and damned him to perdition. But somewhere deep within her that hard knot of resistance had become less tight of late. If he was thinking of conciliation, then perhaps she might consider being more amenable herself – something she would not have contemplated even a few months ago, but things had changed. Louis had been consigned to a living death by the seizure he had suffered, Belbel had arrived with these chests and trinkets, and their son Geoffrey had married his bride Constance of Brittany, who perhaps even now was with child. The passage of time was like a brush, sweeping and blurring what had once been clearly defined.

'You are a clever young woman,' Alienor said with a hint of challenge. 'Did it not occur to you to take that seat at his side? To become a mistress?'

Belbel screwed up her face. 'Yes, madam, but for as long as it takes to drink a cup of wine. I would not have succeeded because I am not what he seeks. I am too old, too knowing, too worldly for his taste. I may be a fine seamstress but that does not mean I would make a good concubine.'

Clever indeed to walk away from what might seem like a great position, but in the end would lead nowhere. It had occurred to Alienor that Henry had sent Belbel to spy on her, but even if that was so, Alienor could cope because it was a usual state of affairs. Belbel had indeed given her food for thought.

As dusk fell, Alienor went to pray in the chapel adjoining the hall but had barely knelt at her devotions when Joscelin, Bishop of Salisbury, arrived to see her. He had grown old in Henry's service and the years had not been kind. He had to struggle to kneel before the altar, and the hand he raised in genuflection was swollen and twisted out of shape. The amethyst cabochon ring of his office bit into the middle finger of his right hand, where the skin was slick and mottled like an old leaf. He bowed his head in prayer and then waited in silence until she had finished hers. And then he told her that a messenger had brought the news that Louis, King of France, was dead.

'We are praying for his soul that it may find a place in heaven, but we do not doubt it is so.'

Alienor had been expecting the news for several months, but still it jolted her to hear the words, and to know that her first husband no longer breathed in this world. There was a sinking feeling inside her like water running through dry sand.

'God rest his soul,' she said, and her voice wobbled with sudden, unexpected tears.

'Daughter?' The Bishop's rheumy eyes held concern and compassion.

'I did not think I would still care,' she said. 'But a part of my life has gone with him into the grave, the memories we shared.' She swallowed. 'They were not all good memories, but they belonged to both of us and now there is only me to keep them.'

'Daughter, when you reach my age, you understand that well.' The Bishop covered her hand with his gnarled one. 'Let us pray for his soul, and for succour in grief.'

Alienor bowed her head, and behind her eyes the memories ran like a stream with her prayers, both the good and the bad. The shining young prince with the sweetest smile. The lover in her bed, damp with the sweat of lust. The father looking at her and their newborn daughter, the disappointment in his eyes verging on disgust. The tonsured penitent returning from burning the people of Vitry inside their own church. The pilgrim – Louis the pious as he had come to be known – prostrating himself at every shrine along the way. The embittered spouse whom she had escaped, only to bind herself to the young Henry FitzEmpress with new and stronger fetters.

'God save you, Louis,' she said. 'And God help me.'

14

Lewes Castle, Sussex, July 1181

Belle rose from her seat in the window embrasure and watched John and her brother Will ride into the courtyard amid a small group of companions. She was suddenly alive with excitement as what had been another boring day of routine became rife with possibility. Abandoning her sewing, bidding the women stay where they were, she ran down to greet them, although as soon as she reached the doorway she smoothed her gown, composed herself, and walked out as regally as her aunt Alienor confronting the King.

'Welcome.' She gave John a cool, gracious curtsey as befitted the lady of the house to a guest. 'My father is absent about his business, but he will be happy to see you when he returns. For now, may I offer you hospitality?'

John inclined his head and his lips curled in a mocking smile. 'Thank you; we would be glad of refreshment – and a bed for the night.' The words were spoken with the utmost civility into which nothing could be construed, unless one was especially looking for a nuance. 'We are on our way to meet my father on his return from Normandy.' He looked round. 'Your lady mother is not here?'

'She is at Conisbrough with my sisters.'

Belle's face was hot under his scrutiny. She turned to Will, who had been speaking to a groom, and embraced him with a sisterly hug, but her awareness was all of John. His very presence made her skin prickle with expectation.

'I knew you would come,' she murmured to him as she walked beside him to the keep. He had grown again and a fledgling beard edged his jaw. She had not seen him for several months. He had been busy at his studies with Ranulf de Glanville and she had been occupied in her role of chatelaine here at Lewes while her father was about his business in the locality. She had enjoyed the duty at first, but had soon grown bored. There were times when it was almost like being buried. She understood now how her aunt Alienor must feel.

Last time she and John had met, in the early spring, he had taken her into a dark corner, reminding her of the caves at Nottingham, and pressed himself against her in a way that could not be mistaken. She had evaded him but then proceeded to tease him mercilessly, enjoying her power. However, it was a double-edged sword, and her own feelings of attraction had become a gnawing hunger. Now he was here, and she was intoxicated by all the dangerous possibilities of the underground game.

She saw to the comfort of all, providing refreshments and water for washing hot hands and faces. Although she had initially led them to the keep, by mutual assent everyone soon repaired to the gardens to take their ease with wine and sweetmeats. Chess boards and dice games came out. Belle played her harp and sang, eventually passing the instrument to a knight who wanted to sing to his own accompaniment. Her brother sat down to dice with a couple of companions, and was soon engrossed in his game.

'Papa's chestnut mare had a new foal yesterday,' Belle murmured to John who was watching the dice play with folded arms but not taking part. 'Do you want to come and see him? Papa says he will make a fine destrier when he's grown.'

John's glance flicked to Will. 'Of course,' he said.

Walking side by side, they left the garden and headed towards the stables.

'So you are chatelaine here on your own?' he asked.

'Yes,' she said, 'on my own.' Saying the words gave her a frisson of fear and anticipation. 'But my father will be here soon.'

'But not yet.'

'No.'

The mare was in a clean stall piled with straw, and a spindle-legged colt foal tottered at her side. He was black with a round white star between his eyes. His mother swung her body side-on to protect him from John and Belle.

'Indeed, a fine little beast,' John said. 'She must have had a good stallion to service her.'

Belle's stomach leapt at the innuendo. 'From the Bigod stables at Framlingham.'

'But we didn't really come here to talk about horses, did we?' He tugged her into the adjoining empty stall.

'Didn't we?'

99

He put his hands to her waist and drew her against him. 'Not unless you are going to speak in terms of mounting and riding.'

'Someone will come, someone will see.' She pushed at him in half-hearted protest.

'That was already in your mind before you brought me here.' He was breathing hard. 'You enjoy taking risks, otherwise we'd still be with the others. If your father is going to be home soon, we have no time to waste.'

He lowered his mouth to hers and ran his hands down her spine. Belle wrapped her arm around his neck and stroked his hair where it curled at his nape. The daring, the danger, the arousal were heady. When she felt his hand beneath her gown on her naked thigh, she started, but she did not draw away, and when he laid her down in the hay and lifted her skirts, she did nothing to protest until he was on top of her.

'We shouldn't . . .' She gripped his shoulders to hold him off.

'Then why did you invite me?' he said hoarsely. 'You knew this would happen.' He kissed her lips and throat and moved his lower body against hers in slow, tantalising circles. 'It will feel good, I promise.' He nuzzled and gently butted his hips.

Belle swallowed. She wanted to do it, but it was the biggest dare of her life and making that leap was frightening. Too fast, too far, and yet she had committed herself. 'I—'

He shut off her words with another kiss and thrust inside her. She clutched his shoulders and stifled a scream by biting into the cloth of his tunic. It hurt, dear God it hurt, but it was good too, and while he arched over her, pushing and pushing, exerting his dominance and his will, she felt powerful because with this act she was binding him to her irrevocably.

Three months later at Conisbrough, Isabel de Warenne straightened up and, rubbing the small of her back, eyed with relief the row of packed baggage chests, assembled ready for attending the winter gathering at Winchester. All was finished, save for small items and last-minute additions.

She turned to ask Belle if she had packed the ivory coffer

for her ribbons and pins, but her eldest daughter was not to be seen.

Belle had returned home, having travelled north with her father and the court during Henry's progress throughout the late summer, but her presence was proving to be a mixed blessing. Her stint as chatelaine at Lewes did not seem to have settled her down; if anything the opposite, although several weeks of travelling with the court might well be to blame. Her moodiness since she had returned home made Isabel want to tear her hair with exasperation.

'Where's Belle?' she demanded of her younger daughters.

'She's sick again,' said Matilda.

'What do you mean "again"?' Isabel frowned. She had not noticed Belle being unwell, but she had been preoccupied with other matters, and Belle had been avoiding her company.

'Every morning she is vomiting either out of the window or in the garderobe. She said we weren't to say anything to you and that it was nothing.' She bit her lip and flicked a glance at Adela. 'She might be very ill, I had to tell.'

A cold fist squeezing her heart, Isabel went from the chamber to the latrine recess and found Belle hanging over the hole, clutching her stomach and trying to retch silently. Shocked, Isabel put her arm round her daughter's quivering shoulders. 'What is this? Why didn't you tell me you were sick?'

'It is nothing, Mama.' Swallowing convulsively, Belle pushed her away and stood up.

Isabel took in her pallid face and dark-circled eyes and then dropped her gaze to her belly. There was little to see, perhaps a slight thickening of the area, but her bosom looked fuller.

'Dear God,' Isabel whispered, 'do not tell me you are with child?'

Belle set her jaw and raised her chin.

Isabel became aware of Adela and Matilda standing behind her, craning their necks, saucer-eyed, and she rounded on them. 'Go and take the dogs for a walk round the bailey with Sarah. I need to talk with your sister.'

'Mama, what's wrong with Belle, is she—'

'Go!' Isabel shouted, waving her hands, and thought she might be sick herself.

As the girls left with anxious glances over their shoulders, Isabel drew Belle back into the chamber and sat her down on her bed. She could not believe it yet the evidence was staring her in the face. Her daughter, her beautiful, perfect daughter, her father's princess. 'How did this happen to you?' she demanded. 'Who has done this to you? Why didn't you tell me sooner?' It had to have been rape. The poor child, keeping it all to herself. Small wonder her moods had been difficult. Tears scalded Isabel's eyes and she pulled Belle into her arms. 'Tell me who did this to you, and he shall be dealt with.'

Belle had not spoken to answer her mother's first demand, but now she drew away. 'It was my cousin John,' she said flatly.

Isabel stared at her in disbelief. 'How can that be, he is barely more than a boy!'

Belle shook her head. 'No, Mama, he is most certainly not a boy.'

It was as if a knife had cut a cord and stopped everything. 'Did he force himself on you?'

Belle did not answer but her look was enough: the defiance and fear, but also the slight curve of her lips holding bitter and destructive triumph.

Isabel's world came crashing down in pieces. This must have been going on under her nose and she had not seen it, and that meant she was to blame for leaving the door wide open to opportunity. 'I trusted you, and you deceived me,' she said in a shaken voice. 'You bring shame on our house and you have given me this grief to bear. You repay all the love and care you have had by bringing disgrace on us, and on John too, for all I know that he must have led you on in some way. This is a dishonourable act – so dishonourable.'

Still Belle did not answer but there was no remorse in her expression.

'You have had every privilege in life and have destroyed it for what? For lust? For some misguided notion of love? Why?' Isabel's heart cracked with grief. 'Had you no thought of what it would do not just to your own reputation but that of your sisters?'

Belle looked down and tightened her lips.

Isabel felt as though her life had been a beautiful reflection in a mirror, and now the glass was crazed and shattered and she was looking instead into a terrible place all fractured and distorted. 'This cannot be hidden; your father will have to be told and we will all have to face the consequences.'

Belle did look up then, and Isabel saw the jolt of alarm cross her face.

'Yes,' she said grimly. 'You have destroyed more than your own life and honour. You have broken everything.'

Isabel buried herself in the final arrangements for court, although she knew that Hamelin might be the only one going now. Still, the bundles, chests and coffers were all neatly arranged near the door ready to go onto the packhorses, because such activity could be controlled and she would have done violence if she had not had an occupation for her hands. When Hamelin returned an hour later, she sent out the servants, Adela and Matilda, leaving only herself and Belle.

She poured him wine and knelt to remove his boots and replace them with another pair of soft kidskin. He sighed with pleasure, lifted his cup and then stopped as he saw her face.

Isabel said stiffly, 'Your daughter has something to tell you that is best not heard by others, although I fear already the gossip must be rife.'

Hamelin put down his cup and turned to Belle. She had been sitting silently on the bed, but now she rose and stood with her hands clasped in front of her. She drew a deep breath and jutted her chin.

'I am with child, Papa.'

Isabel watched the shock slam through her husband; saw

103

the arrested breath before he forced air into his lungs and turned to her, seeking explanation and reassurances that she could not give.

'I am sorry,' Isabel said, tears spilling down her face, 'but it is true: Belle is with child. I did not want to believe her, but I am afraid I must. All she tells me is that it was her cousin John who did this work and that it was with her consent.'

Hamelin looked at his daughter, standing before him, trembling but defiant. 'You whore!' His voice was thick with fury as he stood up and struck her across the face.

The crack of the blow made Isabel cry out in distress. Belle uttered no sound but dropped onto the bed and put her hand to her cheek.

'How dare you put this family's reputation in the gutter!' Hamelin roared. 'What cause have we ever given you to do such a deed? All you have ever wanted you have had and more, and yet you set it at naught and repay us in this whorish coin! I account you good for nothing but the Church. You must go and beg forgiveness of God, for you will not have it from me. You must shrive for your soul, my girl. Go and make your confession to God. And I will have satisfaction from John in this too and see what his cause is and why he should do such a thing to betray our trust and the honour we placed in him within our own household.'

'Papa . . .' Belle whispered as her father's tirade pierced the shield she had raised to protect herself. She reached out to him but Hamelin turned his back on her.

'Take her to the church, madam, and let her confess on her knees,' he snarled at Isabel. 'I do not want to see her; I do not want to talk about this.' Pivoting on his heel, he stormed from the room.

'Come,' said Isabel tersely, 'you must do as he says.'

'John loves me.' Belle's voice, although it quivered, still held defiance. 'And I love him.'

Isabel was appalled and very tempted to slap her daughter too. 'Neither you nor John know the first thing about love, or about respect and duty, because if you did you would not have committed such dishonour for a moment of lust. You have ruined us all. You will come now, and you will seek forgiveness and think upon what you have done, and then we will decide what we are going to do with you.'

Henry looked up from the letters he had been studying as Hamelin was announced into his presence. His ushers had told him that his half-brother had arrived in Winchester earlier that afternoon, but he had not necessarily expected to see him today. Hamelin had clearly availed himself of a flagon since that information because his cheeks were flushed and he was swaying on his feet. The sight of him the worse for drink was enough to make Henry put down his work and stare.

A bitter early November wind blew rain against the shutters, and the youth who tended the hearth took the bellows to the fire to work up the flames.

'What is it, brother?' Henry asked with jovial curiosity. 'Have you come to keep me company tonight?'

Hamelin approached the trestle where Henry was working and rested his knuckles on the wood. 'No,' he said. 'I have come to seek justice from you on a matter that concerns your son John.'

Henry raised his brows, wondering what his scoundrel youngest son had done now. Since he was close friends with Hamelin's boy, Henry suspected that the youths had had some kind of quarrel that had gone badly for Hamelin's heir. 'Indeed?' He gestured Hamelin to sit.

Hamelin hesitated, but then slumped onto the bench opposite Henry and palmed his face. 'John came to Lewes in the summer,' he said. 'He and my daughter . . . they . . .' He swallowed hard. 'Belle is with child.'

Henry had to bite his cheek to stop an inappropriate guffaw. Somehow he succeeded in keeping a straight face and gazed at his brother with concerned sympathy. 'You are sure of this?'

'As sure as my daughter's belly is swelling, and I have no

105

reason to doubt what she tells me. The child is John's.' Hamelin grimaced. 'I took him into my household and treated him more like a son than a nephew, and now he betrays the sacred bond of family . . .'

Hamelin's throat worked and Henry pushed his own cup of watered wine towards him.

'Indeed, I agree, it is a shocking thing, but young men . . .' Henry opened his hands. 'We have to be realistic; these things happen.'

'Not to me, not to mine.' Hamelin's eyes flashed. 'This is a disgrace, one I will never live down.'

Henry studied his half-brother. Bastard-born of a court whore, Hamelin was overly sensitive on the matter of family honour, occasionally to the point where a perverse facet of Henry wanted to see him fall flat on his face – and now it had happened, spectacularly. He suppressed the quip that they would now be joint grandparents. 'It is unfortunate, I grant you, but you must put it in perspective. It happens to many. It is raw at the moment, but it will fade in time.' He gestured airily. 'Belle's reputation won't be too damaged by this. It will be over and done with in a year or two and no one will know the difference. Besides, it may even have benefits. A prospective husband will know that your girl is capable of bearing children, and the link with me as the child's grandsire will be an asset not a liability.'

Hamelin's gaze was dark with anger and misery. 'But I will know the difference, and whatever you say it still does not prevent it from being a dishonour.'

Henry shrugged. 'You should not work yourself into such a fury.' He leaned back in his seat. 'I will see matters put to right. The child will be well provided for if you do not wish to take it in.'

'And John?' Hamelin demanded belligerently. 'What of John in all this?'

Henry rubbed his chin. 'I will see that John is punished and that he does penance. I am as much a father in this as

106

you are. It is not a situation I condone. All I say is that we should deal with it practically.'

Hamelin's cheek muscles clenched. 'See that you do.' Shoving himself to his feet, he staggered from the room, flinging the door wide open and leaving it ajar.

'Oh God.' Henry rubbed his chin but there was a glimmer of sardonic amusement in his eyes. He could understand why Hamelin was so chagrined, but still . . . He had had his first woman when he was fourteen – although she had not been his cousin – so he understood the drive and the temptation. He would have words with the lad, but he could not help feel a secret touch of pride.

Striding through the palace, Hamelin felt bitter rage that it should have come to this. He had had to live with the burden of being illegitimate all of his life, even if he was the son of a count and the brother of a king. He had not wanted that for his children. He had wanted something pristine and beautiful, and to have this visited upon him was the worst irony God could concoct. The wound went deep and he had seen from Henry's manner he would do little to staunch it. The conciliatory words, the promises, meant nothing; they never did.

Arriving in the stable yard, calling for his horse, he stumbled to a halt because John was there, talking to several cronies. The young men had recently returned from a ride and were gathered together laughing in their fine array. All Hamelin saw was a snide youth who had everything and who was intolerable because of the way he chose to behave.

John looked up, saw Hamelin advancing on him and stiffened.

Fit to burst, his heart hammering in his chest, Hamelin seized John by the throat of his tunic and butted him up against the wall. 'What do you mean by entering my household like a wolf in sheep's clothing?' He brought his knee up into John's groin, doubling him over. Wrenching him to the ground he kicked him, and felt satisfaction as his boot connected with John's ribs. He kicked him in the groin again, and John choked.

The gathered youths watched in shock, but an older man who had been talking to a groom stepped forward – John FitzJohn, Henry's Marshal. 'Sire, you should not,' he said.

'Stay out of this,' Hamelin snarled. 'I ought to kill him for what he has done.' He launched his foot into John's ribs again. 'He should have had respect and decency thrashed into him long ago.'

FitzJohn hesitated a moment longer, but when Hamelin put in another kick he intervened and seized Hamelin's arm. 'Sire, you will indeed kill him; stop, I beg you. He is your nephew, your kin.'

The words sickened Hamelin but had the effect of checking his madness. He shook the Marshal off and stood back, panting. John was doubled over, holding his stomach, and wheezing.

'You know what this is about,' Hamelin said harshly. 'Do not pretend you do not, and do not think to hide behind your father. You shall make reparation for this, I swear.'

Turning away, Hamelin shouldered through the men and made for the stables. His dun palfrey greeted him with pricked ears and a questing whiskery muzzle, but Hamelin had no treat for the horse. Taking a fistful of dark mane, he pressed his face against the warm golden neck fighting tears, wondering how it had come to this.

Henry found his youngest son playing chess in a window embrasure with one of the youths from his entourage. John FitzJohn had visited Henry a short while ago and told him about the altercation at the stables. Henry had not been surprised, and had even thought that in some ways it was a good thing because it would drain some of the rage from Hamelin while sending John a warning about the consequences of rash behaviour.

As Henry crossed the room towards the embrasure, John looked up, his gaze filled with wariness and a tinge of alarm. He was hunched over the chess board but plainly trying his best to behave as if nothing was wrong.

Henry waved a dismissal to John's opponent and waited

until the youth had scuttled away. Then he punched John playfully on the arm, knowing how much it was going to hurt. 'I hear you have been up to no good, my lad, and I want to know from your own lips what has been happening.'

He watched John struggle to hide his pain at the blow before fixing him with an innocent stare. 'Sire, if it is about the chess set, I can explain.'

Henry raised his brows. 'I am sure you can.'

'I know it belongs to Jeoffrey, but I promise to put it back in his chamber when I have finished playing.'

Henry flicked a glance at the board and pieces. It was indeed the property of his oldest bastard son Jeoffrey and had once belonged to Henry's mother. As such it was a treasured possession and John was treading dangerous ground here also. 'See that you do, but this is not about these gaming pieces as well you know.'

John lowered his gaze and said nothing. Shy as a maiden some might think, but Henry knew better.

'Come, my boy. Your cousin is a pretty girl; just what have you been doing?'

John slowly raised his head. 'I did not mean to,' he said, wide-eyed, 'but she led me on. She wanted me to.'

Henry sat down opposite John and regarded him over his folded arms. He was indeed swiftly maturing into manhood, something which he had not really noticed until now. His bones were lengthening and new adult angles had started to develop, as well as fledgling fuzz across his upper lip and upon his chin. And obviously his organs of procreation were sufficiently advanced to sire a child.

'Indeed, it may have happened like that; I have always thought your cousin less innocent than her parents would have her. But you are no lamb led astray.' Henry unfolded his arms and leaned forward to move a piece on the chess board. 'Do not let it happen again. Hamelin is my brother and your uncle. He is staunch in his support and the last thing you should do is defecate on his doorstep. I say this crudely to make it plain.

By all means have your sport, but not at home, and not where others end up having to clean up your mess. Do I make myself plain?'

'Yes, Papa.'

Henry eyed him narrowly. He did not for one minute believe John's look of sincere and injured innocence, but the lad was intelligent enough to understand what was at stake. 'I hope I do. For now you must make reparations. Go and confess your sin to your chaplain who will advise you on your penance – and I must counsel him not to be easy on you because the court will be watching.'

John nodded and refrained from commenting that his father had done no such thing when he got Ida de Tosney pregnant and she had only been Belle's age. His youngest half-brother William FitzRoy was toddling around the nursery at the moment and Ida had been married off to Roger Bigod.

Henry stroked his beard. 'Since your uncle and aunt are often at court, and you share your lessons with their son, you must treat with them too. I cannot speak for how you deal with Will, but for your uncle and aunt you must have the right attitude. Keep your distance for now, but when you are in their company, be serious and know your place. That doesn't mean you have to grovel. The girl has to take her share of the blame. You are very young to have fathered a child but now you must learn the responsibilities of a father. It is your child and you have a duty to raise it. Do you understand me? Be a man.'

'Yes, sire,' John said, and looked as if he had been given real food for thought rather than something to be lightly dismissed or mocked. There was also triumph in the set of his lips. He had been expecting far worse than he had received. Reaching across the board he kissed the sapphire ring on his father's right hand.

Henry's lips twitched, but his gaze was hard. 'I mean it.'

'So do I, sire,' John replied. 'I promise to take my responsibilities seriously.'

'I will make sure you do. Indeed, everyone will be watching.'

John's eyes flickered at that and Henry clapped his hand to his shoulder in father-to-son rapport, but also by way of warning.

15

Winchester Castle, November 1181

Alienor arrived in Winchester on a murky afternoon in late November with dusk already falling over the city. Her chamber had been prepared and she was glad to go straight there and warm herself at the fire while her servants brought in her baggage which was more plentiful than of yore. Under Belbel's skilled direction, several new gowns had been cut and sewn, some with luxurious fur linings for the winter season, and she had ridden to Winchester proudly and in full view this time. The crushing sense of impotence was still there but at least now she had leave to ride out; she had more servants and books to read, and did not have to resort to biting her nails and pacing her chamber end to end in a restless rhythm for hours on end.

She was informed that the King was busy with other matters but would visit on the morrow, to which she raised a knowing eyebrow. 'Other matters' were usually either of state or women, and always excluded her. However, Ingelram her chamberlain announced that the Countess of Salisbury was already here and requesting an audience. Alienor's spirits immediately lightened. 'Bring her at once,' she commanded, 'and bid her not stand on ceremony.'

As Isabel entered the room, Alienor hastened to embrace her and was immediately shocked at how thin she had become. Isabel had shed weight like a tree shedding its leaves in autumn to leave only stark branches. Her cheeks were gaunt and dark shadows haunted her eyes.

'It is good to see you.' Alienor drew Isabel to the fire, 'but you look tired. What has Hamelin been doing to you?' She spoke with a smile so that Isabel could treat the words as a jest if she wished, and was appalled when her friend's eyes filled with tears.

'Nothing,' Isabel said. 'But it is so difficult between us just now. I . . .' She put her face in her hand and struggled for composure.

Alienor curved a comforting arm around Isabel's shoulders. 'Come, come, what is wrong?'

'I am overburdened and do not want to add to your woes,' Isabel sniffed, 'but I have no choice because it concerns you and you will hear soon enough. The gossip is already rife.'

Alienor was suddenly wary. 'What do you mean it concerns me?'

'It's Belle.' Isabel's voice cracked. 'She's with child.'

'Belle?' Alienor was taken aback. Isabel was a protective mother and she could not imagine her letting a fox into her coop, although she had sometimes wondered about the girl. 'Do you know the father?'

Isabel swallowed. 'Yes,' she said. 'It's John.'

'John who?'

Isabel bit her lip. 'Your son John. He visited Lewes in the summer on his way to Canterbury and she . . . they . . .' She waved her hand to serve for the rest. 'And numerous times after that while they were travelling with the court.'

Alienor stared at Isabel in open-mouthed shock. 'Dear God. He is not yet fifteen. Did he . . .' She could not finish.

'It was not rape. They both colluded in the deed – it was lust. I had no notion, no idea. I trusted her, and I trusted too much.'

'I am so sorry.' Alienor clenched her fists, feeling powerless. This was what happened when a ship only had one oar. What sort of example had John learned from his father who consorted with the young women he was supposed to be protecting? She sat down beside Isabel on the hearth bench, feeling wretched. 'When you look at them as babies in the cradle, you never know what they are going to become, but you always hope for the best.'

'What could you have done from Sarum? Do not take it upon yourself.'

Alienor gave a bitter laugh. 'No more than you take the blame upon your own shoulders.'

Isabel shrugged forlornly.

'I suppose Hamelin has taken it hard.'

'It has broken his heart,' Isabel said, wiping her eyes. 'He does not want to see Belle. He has sent her to the convent at Shaftesbury – his sister is abbess – and I shall join her there after Christmas to await her confinement. The baby is due in the spring.' She hesitated and then told Alienor what Hamelin had done to John. 'If he had to be in the same room just now, he would kill him, but they will have to come to terms.'

'Indeed yes.' Alienor thought how awkward it would be. Only time would heal the rift, and a long time at that. 'If anything positive is to come from this mess, let it be that we are sisters by marriage and we shall share the gift of a grand-child.' She embraced Isabel again and the women clung together for a moment before each withdrew to sit in silence with her thoughts.

'Isabel told me about John and her daughter,' Alienor told Henry. He had been hunting, but had spared time to change his tunic and boots, although a beaded scratch on his cheek gave evidence of his impetuosity in the chase, and she could still smell his sweat. His limp was barely noticeable today and the vigorous way he was pacing the room reminded her of the early days of their marriage.

'Young fool,' Henry growled, pausing by the brazier. 'All youths sow their wild oats, but not on their own doorsteps. I have ordered him to do penance and warned him to be more careful. It's distasteful and an embarrassment.'

'It is a pity no one noticed until it was too late. Surely there were indications?'

'I am his father, not his keeper,' Henry snapped. He sat down by the fire and used a poker to dig out new red flames from the half-burned logs. 'Her parents should have been watching her too if they didn't want her belly to swell. Where were they? John says she led him on, and I can believe it. It's in the blood. Hamelin's mother was a whore after all.'

'I hope you did not say that to Hamelin.'

'Credit me with a little sense. He is my brother and I need his support. As it is, he is bruised and barely speaking to me. He thinks I should have clapped John in irons and had him flogged. He will get over it.' Henry gave a dismissive wave and rested the poker at the side of the fire. 'Worse things happen. Someone will be glad to take the girl in marriage. She's well connected and proven to be fertile. The child, if it lives, will prove useful either for the Church or administration. There are always places for well-born bastards.'

'As you have often proved yourself. I hear you have Ida de Tosney's little boy in the nursery at Woodstock? Do you try out all your wards before you marry them off?'

Even in the dull firelight she could tell that Henry's face had darkened. 'Your tongue, madam, could slice stones.'

'What should I say? What kind of example does it set to your son when he sees how you behave at court? He will either follow you down, or hate you. Before the de Tosney girl there was Rosamund, and she died in childbirth did she not?'

Henry seized the poker again and rammed it into the heart of the fire. Alienor watched him, and although her stomach lurched, her expression remained impassive. There was bitter entertainment in goading him, but it was desolate too.

'You are one to talk of examples to set to children.' He watched the end of the poker glow red. 'What have they learned from you save perfidy and rebellion?'

'I did not teach them that. They had far more instructive examples to follow.'

He threw the poker down and rose to pace the room once more. 'Ah, I am sick of this.'

'So am I.' Her voice was flat with pain. 'But that makes no difference. We can go neither forward nor back. We are in limbo. I did not set out to defy you. I married you in good faith, and see what it has brought us.'

She stared into the flames rising out of the log where he had stabbed the poker into its heart. 'You sent me chests of cloth and fur in the summer,' she continued. 'You sent me a maid to fashion fine garments and keep me company. You gave me a palfrey and a red leather saddle to set upon her back. Why did you do that? I hardly think it is because you have a troubled conscience, or that you are guilty of compassion. What is your own lack, sire, that you should be generous to me after all you claim I have done? What do you want from me?'

For an instant she thought he was going to leave, crash from the room as he usually did and give instructions that she was to be taken straight back to Sarum. However, he paused at the embrasure, hands gripping his belt. 'I want a truce,' he said. 'Even the bitterest enemies withdraw from their battles in the winter season.'

'A truce?'

'We are never going to resolve our differences, but if we agree on that, then perhaps we can be civil when we do meet. But I am beginning to think it is not possible.'

'And if not, you will strip me of your goodwill and send me back to Sarum?'

'You will cut off your nose to spite your own face?' he retorted. 'The decision is yours.'

Alienor had heard those words before, but a truce was easier to swallow than the notion of a convent. In the past she had indeed cut off her nose to spite her face. Were golden fetters better than ones of rusting iron? Perhaps it was time to find out, and a truce might lead further down a road to freedom. Heaving a sigh, she lifted her hand in weary acquiescence. 'Very well. Sit for a moment if that is possible, and send for some fresh wine that isn't vinegar, and we shall see about the matter of a truce.'

Henry hesitated and then went to the door. She heard him issue gruff orders to his squire and her mouth curved with a humourless smile. Knowing the state of Henry's cellar, obtaining decent wine was perhaps even more problematical than a cessation of hostilities.

Returning, Henry complimented her on her gown and she thanked him for sending her Belbel.

'I thought you would enjoy her company.'

'I did wonder if you had set her upon me as a spy, but I am sure you would be more subtle than that in your choice. Is that the tunic she made for you? She is good at hiding a multitude of sins.' When he looked at her sharply, she smiled and gestured to her dress. 'I have a figure again, something I thought never to possess after bearing so many children.'

One of Henry's squires arrived with wine and a platter of small fried pastries drizzled with honey and sprinkled with chopped almonds.

'Now you are indeed making your point,' Alienor said with a wry laugh. 'If this is a truce, I will adhere to it.'

She took a pastry and bit into the hot, crisp shell with greedy delight. Yet with guilt too because sweetmeats and fine clothes were no substitute for her liberty, and once again he was showing her what he could give and what he could take away.

'So,' she said when she had swallowed. 'Speaking of children, I hear that Geoffrey's marriage to Constance has been satisfactorily concluded.'

Henry nodded. 'At Rennes. That is the matter of Brittany settled and I expect him to govern well.'

Alienor heard the reservation in his tone. 'But?' She wondered if it was because he found it difficult to hand control to his son.

Henry shrugged. 'I can never tell what Geoffrey is thinking. He smiles and agrees with me, but I receive the impression he is paying lip service while playing his own game . . . and just what that game is, only he knows. I know where I stand

116

with Harry, with Richard, and even John despite his escapades. I know I can grab them by the scruff and haul them back, but with Geoffrey there is nothing to get hold of.'

Again it boiled down to trust, and trust was something Henry did not have, and which he never received either. 'But he has proved himself competent and steady.'

'Thus far,' he acknowledged grudgingly. 'But I need him to answer to me even when he rules in his own right. I am still his overlord.'

'You have to let him make his own path.'

Two deep furrows appeared between Henry's brows. 'He is like Harry – he has too many romantic notions of what being a ruler means, but he does not wear such notions openly for the world to see, and he is always ready to add subtle seasoning to any brew of trouble his brothers concoct.' He took one of the pastries and ate it with vigorous rotations of his jaw.

And Henry's refusal to allow his sons control was the reason there was a brew in the first place. 'Shall I see any of our sons at the Christmas feast, or do they all have business elsewhere?' she asked.

Henry swallowed. 'They are busy helping Philippe of France deal with his rebellious Blois vassals. The less influence that faction has over the boy the better. After that they will keep the Christmas feast in their own domains, except for John.'

Alienor almost grimaced. A Christmas spent with Henry and John seemed like more of an endurance test than a joyful occasion.

'I wish I could see all of our sons.'

'Indeed that can be arranged in the future,' Henry agreed blandly. 'Write to them for now, send them gifts, and they will do the same for you.'

And Henry would vet all of her letters.

'This truce of yours, does it mean I may remain here when you leave?'

Henry reached for another pastry. 'If you choose to,' he said impassively.

He invited her to play chess as they had done in the days before he had shut her away to rot at Sarum. Watching him set up the board reminded Alienor to ask after his bastard son Jeoffrey with whom she had often played, and who owned a precious set of pieces given to him by his grandmother the Empress.

'He has renounced the bishopric of Lincoln,' Henry said. 'He may yet take holy orders, but for now I have employed him as my chancellor and he performs the task very well.'

Alienor narrowed her gaze. She had an uneasy truce with Jeoffrey. He was Henry's firstborn son begotten on a favourite mistress now deceased. She suspected him of ambitions above his station and those fears were resurrected now, especially as he had forsaken holy orders. 'Indeed? Then I hope to see him over the coming season.'

Henry allowed her to make the first move. 'Do not worry. I love him, but we both know his place.'

The statement was ambiguous, deliberately so she could tell.

As the game progressed, she took pleasure in pitting her wits against his. Their verbal sparring was satisfying, the rough edges smoothed out by the boundaries of their truce. Henry seemed to be enjoying it too, and she realised that despite being surrounded by courtiers and men with whom he had long-standing social relationships, he was still alone. The King on his pedestal. He had removed his consort, his queen, from hers and there was no one to hold that place in her stead. Substitutes such as Harry's wife Marguerite did not fulfil that role with the same gravitas. Perhaps he was trying to set her back in her place, only he dared not let her stand in too much light. She must be under control and subordinate.

She played her game with skill and determination and eventually they arrived at a stalemate. Henry gave her a sardonic smile as he pushed to his feet. 'Enough for tonight,' he said. 'Tomorrow I will win.'

Alienor arched her brows. 'Are you so certain of that?'

He gave a soft laugh. 'Oh yes, I only deal in certainties.'

When he had gone, Alienor sat before the dying fire, wrapped in her fur-lined cloak, and finished her cup of wine. She had learned long ago that nothing was certain.

16

Winchester Castle, September 1182

Alienor approached the cradle and looked at her baby grandson gurgling on the soft lambskins. He had recently been fed by his wet nurse and was content with the world. Fine golden-brown hair glinted on his skull and feathered his brows. His eyes were the mutable blue of all small infants, and his face soft-featured without definition. He was long-limbed and sturdy though, and the sight of him made her smile.

She had several grandchildren born to her daughters but only knew of them through letters and messengers, although that state of affairs might soon change. Her daughter Matilda, Duchess of Saxony, had been sent into exile with her husband and three of their children over a dispute with their overlord, Emperor Heinrich. They had sought refuge at Henry's court in Normandy. Henry had welcomed them and was trying to negotiate a reconciliation that would allow them to return home, but it might take a long time even with intensive diplomacy.

It was a sweet pain to Alienor knowing they were so close to her, yet inaccessible. The truce between herself and Henry did not extend as far as permitting her to cross the Narrow Sea to see them.

'He is beautiful,' she said to Isabel as the baby gave her a gummy smile. She could not resist picking him up and holding his delicious weight in her arms. It was a long time since she had cuddled an infant and he was a bundle of innocence, even if he had been born of circumstances that no one discussed.

'I have never known one with so sweet a nature.' Isabel was smiling too, but her expression was careworn and apprehensive. 'I do not understand why John insisted he be called Richard though, and Henry has endorsed it.'

Alienor carried the baby to the window. 'Who knows why John does anything? Were I to hazard a guess I would say it is because Richard is a proven commander performing a man's work as Count of Poitou, and if he grows up to be like his uncle Richard then he will be exalted.' She stroked the infant's cheek and thought too that here was something Richard did not have, and she would not put it past John to give his son the name in order to goad his older brother. 'How is his mother?'

Isabel bit her lip. 'It was difficult for her. It was not an easy birth – he was a big, strong baby. He went straight to the wet nurse and she has had little to do with him – better that way. Hamelin has had a good offer of marriage for her from Robert de Lacy. He is an older man, steady and decent.'

'And Belle?' She stroked her grandson's cheek. Rewarded with another beaming smile, she experienced a small flood of painful joy.

'She shall do what is expected of her,' Isabel said flatly. 'She knows her choices are limited and that if she is ever to win herself back into Hamelin's good graces she must behave in an exemplary manner. It is not enough to be good; she has to be better than good, for her own sake and that of her sisters. For now she bides her time at Shaftesbury with her aunt.'

Alienor's stomach tightened. She knew what it was to be a prisoner; yet the girl had made her own fetters by choosing to do as she had done. She felt guilty that John had been involved and had made his own dishonourable choices, but there was nothing she could do.

'I am glad you brought him for me to see. Has it been decided what will become of him?'

'He is to be raised at Woodstock with Ida de Tosney's child,' Isabel said. 'I am taking him there myself.'

'You are not keeping him?'

Isabel shook her head. 'It would be unwise, and anyway, Hamelin would not allow it. He . . .' Tears sparkled in her eyes. 'Ah, let it be. Time will heal the wounds; that is the only remedy.'

But it would leave scars, not least on her friendship with Isabel for all that their blood was mingled in the veins of this child.

The next morning Isabel set out for Woodstock with the wet nurse and the baby. Alienor waved them farewell with a forced smile and a heavy heart. Worse things happened as she had cause to know, but it would take a long time for the ripples from this to smooth out and settle.

Returning to her chamber she began composing a letter to the Bishop of Worcester but was interrupted when a messenger arrived from her daughter Matilda. When the man was admitted to her presence she was surprised to see Robert of London, one of William Marshal's tourney companions. He was a young hearth knight of proven ability on the battlefield and she would not have expected him to be bearing messages, unless there was a problem.

His complexion was flushed and his eyes glittered with fever. Kneeling to her, he almost toppled over. Alienor was immediately concerned, thinking that something dreadful had happened to Harry or Matilda, but the letters he presented from her daughter were routine matters. He could have been coming to England anyway and been chosen as an opportune messenger, but he appeared to have travelled in urgency, and he was clearly suffering.

'Messire, you are not well.'

'It is nothing, madam, a chill picked up along my journey.' His voice was rusty with congestion. 'I should have stayed in the deck shelter when I was on board ship.'

She noted the covert sign he made with a forefinger to tell

her there was more to his message than met the eye. Her curiosity intensified, as did her concern.

'Madam, I—' He started to speak but hunched over, coughing so hard that he could barely breathe.

'See that this man is found a wholesome chamber and fetch a physician,' Alienor commanded the servants who came at her signal to half carry him away. Gazing after him, she wondered what was afoot.

Later she visited him on the pretext of concern for his well-being and found him lying on a rope-framed bed in a well-lit chamber often used by the scribes. A physician had bled him to relieve his raging fever and he had been wrapped in a scarlet blanket to further assist recovery.

'How are you feeling, messire?' She gestured him to stay where he was when he struggled to rise.

He screwed up his face. 'As though a thousand demons are playing drums in my head, madam,' he said hoarsely, 'but I hope to recover soon thanks to God's mercy and the care I am receiving.'

'You should drink your tisane.' She took the cup standing at the bedside and helped him sip from it.

He drank a small amount to soothe his throat and then said, 'Madam, I have to tell you' – his gaze went beyond her to the servants going about their business but easily within earshot – 'that I am very grateful for your care.'

Alienor picked up the bowl and cloth standing on a stool at the bedside and sent the nearest attendant to refresh it and instructed another to bring some nourishing broth. 'Now,' she said, the moment they were alone. 'What do you have to tell me that is so important and secret I have to dismiss my servants?'

He swallowed painfully. 'William the Marshal has sent me to tell you that he has been accused by men of his lord's household of engaging in a secret affair with the Young Queen. They say that the Marshal is a usurper in my lord's bedchamber as well as on the tourney field.'

Alienor was horrified. 'Oh, that is preposterous!'

The knight coughed. 'I assure you on my life, madam, that it is not true. The Marshal is an honourable man who would rather die than do such a thing; he is very wronged and has asked me to make it apparent to you so that no distrust may come between you and no dishonour touch you as it has touched his reputation.' Febrile tears glittered in his eyes. 'I would not have borne you this message save that it was necessary for you to know, and that the Young King is being badly advised.'

'I do not believe a word of it,' Alienor repeated. 'William would never do this.'

'He is under threat of banishment at court. My young lord no longer invites him to share his trencher or dine with him at table. He has forbidden men to speak with him and his position has become untenable.'

Alienor knew well how dangerous the court could be, with factions vying for influence and seeking to destroy their rivals by whatever means they could. William, with his prowess, his charm, his closeness to her son, had long been a target for jealous men. He had a great deal of influence with Harry, and if he was ousted from that position, others would rush to fill the gap – others, who unlike William, had no allegiance to her.

'I fear the Young King is being fed bad advice from all quarters,' Robert said throatily. 'William says he will appeal to the King for justice in this matter when the court comes to Caen at Christmas, but if it goes ill for him, what is to be done?'

Alienor clucked her tongue in annoyance. Appealing to Henry would do no good because he was ambivalent towards William and as likely to make him a scapegoat as exonerate him, depending on his political requirements. To deprive Harry of his very competent marshal might just be something Henry wanted to do.

'When you are well,' she said, 'return to William and re-assure him that I know better than to give credence to gossip from such sources. He has my goodwill always, and I will do what I can for him.'

A look of deep relief crossed the knight's flushed features. 'Thank you, madam, thank you.'

'I will write to the King and to my son.' For what good it would do, but her role as Queen allowed her to intercede. William had saved her life once, and she would do her best for him. 'How is my son?' When Harry took to listening to flatterers and deceivers, it always meant he was unsettled and seeking comfort in their assurances. Men who would furnish him with a tapestry of lies instead of the truth so that all he could see was the tale they wove and not the truth behind it. He needed William Marshal to hold him to reality.

Robert of London dropped his gaze. 'He is well, madam, but a trifle restless, as to be expected.'

The servants returned from their errands and Alienor and the knight ceased their conversation. She had much to think about. There was danger here. Her life had fallen back into a daily routine that was comfortable enough to breed a kind of stultifying complacency. She had her ladies, she had jewels and clothes. She was permitted to go riding, to write letters and receive them, although she knew they were opened and vetted. It was like wading in a sea that looked calm and smooth but in fact was seething with undercurrents so dangerous that a single shove would be enough to push her under and drown her. Harry was bound to be unsettled when he saw his younger brothers governing their own territories and being given responsibilities that never came his way. She felt for him and feared for him too. He needed William at his side to protect him from himself and everyone else.

While Robert of London recovered from his malady, Alienor wrote to Harry, entreating him to be careful and think well on the political ramifications of what he was doing. She wrote to Henry too, in an understated way that he would not take as a challenge, saying she had heard disturbing rumours, and that he should not trust those who spread them. She did not write to William. Robert of London could convey verbally what she had to say when he was well enough to leave, and she would send William a gold ring in token of her support. He would know what it meant.

17

Winchester Castle, April 1183

Alienor laughed as she watched a litter of four kittens tussling in a garden flower bed. The boldest was a golden tabby with a snowy chest and paws. He wriggled his little rump, hunched his shoulders and then pounced on two of his plain tabby siblings. The fourth kitten, mostly black with a white blaze on its forehead, crouched, waiting its moment. Their mother, a green-eyed beauty with a mottled coat of blended agate, washed herself in the warm spring sunshine.

'There you have my four sons,' Alienor said over her shoulder to Belbel who was making fond sounds in their direction. 'Richard, Harry, Geoffrey and John. I don't need to tell you which is which.'

'Indeed not, madam,' she said. 'And I will not make a comment about their lady mother.'

Alienor chuckled. 'Indeed, for then you would be guilty of impertinence. Perhaps it would be good to change places with her just for a moment – although I doubt she would consider the exchange a fair bargain.' The cat looked up and fixed the women with her exotic eyes. 'See, she understands what I say to her.'

'You should bring her into the bower,' Belbel suggested.

Alienor shook her head regretfully. 'The dogs would chase her and she would scratch the bedding and sharpen her claws on the chairs. Let her have her freedom.'

'So you would not want a kitten when it was weaned?'

Belbel looked longingly at the tussling bundles of fur. 'Not even Richard?'

Alienor laughed again. 'Having either cat or man confined to my bower would create far too much trouble.' Her expression sobered. Her sons created far too much trouble as it was. She had written to Harry about the situation with William Marshal and received no reply beyond a fond but formal message that told her nothing of the state of his mind. Such news as she had received was either vetted by Henry, or gleaned from scraps obtained by her women or by discreet bribery of servants and merchants. She had learned from her alternative sources that William Marshal's appeal for justice had been ignored. He had been banished from court, whereupon he had gone on pilgrimage to pray at the shrine of the Three Kings in Cologne and seek divine intervention. Other high-ranking barons and princes had been vying for his services ever since, although he had not accepted any of the offers, saying that his loyalty to his lord remained staunch. Alienor suspected that the loyalty was to her as much as to Harry. That Henry and her son could think for one moment that William was having an affair with Marguerite was preposterous. William did not have a dishonourable bone in his body, and Marguerite was hardly the kind of young woman to drive an experienced courtier like William so wild with lust that he lost his reason.

She had heard that at Christmas in Caen, Henry had tried to make Richard and Geoffrey swear allegiance to Harry to try and assuage the latter's growing disaffection, but it had only worsened the situation. Geoffrey had agreed to swear, but Richard had refused, declaring that his allegiance for Aquitaine was to the King of France, not his brother. Harry had accused Richard of fortifying the castle of Clairvaux which lay in his territory and outside Aquitaine. The quarrel had escalated, although as far as she knew a reconciliation had finally been patched together. Richard had yielded Clairvaux to his father and sworn loyalty to him, but the foundations were built on sand. Her sons fought like those kittens, but with deadlier intent. She had no doubt that young Philippe of France was egging them on too because the more they quarrelled the stronger his own position became.

Belbel was still eyeing the kittens with longing.

'A cat will scratch the fine cloth you are sewing and tangle your embroidery silks,' Alienor warned.

'You are right, madam, but they are so pretty and a delight to watch.'

'That does not mean you should turn your enjoyment into a rod for your own back. I—' She looked up as she heard male voices at the garden gate, the tones brusque and filled with business. The mother cat ceased washing and slunk away into the cover of a myrtle bush, and the kittens, already alert to danger, tumbled after her.

Robert Maudit advanced down the path, walking briskly and accompanied by three guards. Seeing the hard set of his mouth, Alienor clasped her cloak together at the throat.

'Madam, you must prepare to leave,' he said. 'The King requires you to return to Sarum immediately.'

Alienor gazed at him in shock. There had been no sign of this on the horizon. She was comfortable at Winchester and the thought of returning to that windy hill-top palace filled her with dread. 'Why?' she asked. 'Why does the King require this?'

'I cannot say, madam, but I must see his command fulfilled.'

'He must have a reason.'

Maudit said nothing, his lips compressed.

'I am not prepared. I have all my baggage to pack.'

'That will be sent on. Horses are being made ready for you and your ladies. Madam, if you please.' He gestured to the path.

'And if I do not please?' She looked at the knights beyond him.

'Madam, I pray you, come with us,' Maudit reiterated. 'It is necessary.'

She composed her expression to one of regal hauteur. She had fought such orders on occasion, but always to a futile and painful outcome. In Antioch when she had refused to go with

127

Louis and told him she intended divorcing him, he had sent his henchmen to abduct her by force in the middle of the night. And Henry was no better. She knew what men were capable of doing. Head high, she swept past Maudit to the garden entrance. She had done nothing save counsel her sons to have a care in all they did, listen to good advice, and be cordial to each other. Her conscience was clear. Obviously something bad had happened, something she was not allowed to know, but she would find out one way or another.

Belbel entered Alienor's chamber, the basket over her arm domed with pink-gilled field mushrooms. 'Look what I found in the market,' she boasted with the fierce delight of a hunter returning from a successful foray. 'Aren't they fine? Freshly picked this morning and still with the dew on them.'

Alienor admired the produce. Being a prisoner taught one the art of appreciating small pleasures. Taking an interest was a part of avoiding the black cavern of despair. 'I thought you went to buy needles.'

'I did.' Belbel patted the pouch at her belt. 'But I saw these and they were too fine to ignore.' She handed the basket to a servant with instructions to take the mushrooms to the kitchen and, having firmly closed the door, returned to her mistress.

'And did you also find any fish worth frying?' Alienor enquired.

'Madam, I did, but I am not sure you are going to find them to your taste.' Belbel drew a deep breath. 'The King has arrested and imprisoned the Earls of Leicester and Gloucester and is putting a close watch on anyone in England he considers may strike against him.'

'Why should he do that?' Alienor's heart quickened. Henry had gradually been relaxing his grip, but this spoke of a fresh crisis.

'Madam, the Young King and the Count of Brittany have turned upon their father and the Count of Poitou. The King's men have been attacked and an attempt has been made on the King's life. An arrow was shot at him while he was under a flag of truce and it pierced his cloak.'

Alienor shook her head. Harry's disaffection had been bound to spill over again and there was nothing she could do incarcerated here. 'Go on, I take it there is more.'

'It is said that the King intends having the rebels excommunicated, even to the point of bringing down the wrath of the Church on his own sons.'

Alienor gazed at Belbel in dismay verging on despair. She understood Harry's frustration and anger, but to drag Geoffrey into the fray and to attack Richard was petulance. 'Truly,' she said, 'how can grown men brawl like children?'

'I am sorry, madam, I wish I had gleaned better news for you.'

Alienor made a weary gesture of negation. 'Better to know.'

'I heard also that the Young King has sent his wife to France. Supposedly it is to keep her safe, but there are rumours about her and the Young King's Marshal.'

'That is no more than wicked gossip,' Alienor snapped. 'If William Marshal was with my son he might have prevented this from happening, or at least have dissuaded him from the worst of his follies.' She was so frustrated at being shut up in Sarum without influence. All she could do was write letters of exhortation and pray for a truce, but she suspected from past experience that neither would be effective.

Two weeks later on another foray into the market place, Belbel encountered a royal pack train collecting treasure from the recently built stronghold tower and learned from a serjeant that Harry had pardoned William Marshal and recalled him from exile. The situation had not improved. Harry remained focused on rebellion and was now raiding and burning in the Limousin. Alienor wondered if half a prayer answered was better than none. Perhaps William would be able to draw the rein on the runaway horse, but she suspected Harry had recalled him for his military prowess rather than to receive wider advice.

Alienor dined that day on fish stew, a favourite of hers, enhanced with the subtle flavour and rich golden hue of saffron, the juices mopped up with plentiful fresh white bread. And then hippocras and sugared fruit. At least Henry was not keeping her in penury, and to assuage the hollow feeling inside she ate until she was bloated – and then immediately felt regretful.

Her discomfort lingered and eventually she went for a walk around the castle grounds to aid her digestion. The summer heat had bruised the sky to a pink and purple dusk. Swifts swooped and dived through the breathless air, hunting on the wing, their cries as keen as silver needles. Alienor's stomach churned, refusing to settle, and she wondered if the fish had been bad. She asked Belbel to return to the chamber and prepare a tisane of mint leaves, and, accompanied by Amiria, went to say her evening prayers.

The chapel of St Nicholas was quiet and dark except for a lamp over the altar and a few candles burning in niches. It was blessedly cooler than outside for which she was grateful as she crossed herself and bent her head to pray. Her stomach was churning and her mind empty of thought, as if there was a gap between her and God. She prayed for guidance and asked the Almighty to keep her sons safe whatever their folly, but her entreaties stayed solidly within her. She felt too listless and weighed down to reach out.

Beside her, Amiria whispered her own prayers, hands clasped, head raised to the vaulted ceiling with its ribs arching like the spine of an animal. Alienor looked up too, and then back down, feeling nauseous. She closed her eyes to see if it would help and her vision immediately filled with an image of Harry, but as if painted in an illuminated manuscript. Gold leaf gleamed and the colours bore the richness and depth of the most expensive pigments. He sat enthroned with gilded leopards either side, an orb in his cupped right hand and a sceptre gripped in his left. He wore a crown, set with gemstones and pearls, the gold glinting with light. Above his head blazed a second coronet, so bright that it dazzled her, and that brightness expanded across her vision in a flash of white brilliance that made her cry out and open her eyes. For a moment she was blind, and she reached out in panic.

'Madam!' Amiria took her arm, her voice filled with alarm.

Alienor's eyesight returned, but it was murky and zig-zagged by flashing, lurid colours. Her stomach heaved and she clapped her hand to her mouth. Making a tremendous effort not to defile the chapel, she staggered to the door and hunched over, vomiting. A vile headache was tightening around her skull like a crown of molten iron. Amiria cried for help and a servant came running.

As the worst of Alienor's spasms subsided, they helped her to her chamber and laid her down on her bed. Belbel brought a cool cloth to press over her brow. Alienor still felt nauseous, but purged and light-headed. 'When I was in the chapel, I saw Harry,' she told Belbel as she slowly sipped the mint tisane to cleanse her mouth. 'On a throne with an orb and sceptre in his hands.'

'That is surely a good thing, madam,' Belbel said. 'And he is in your thoughts and prayers, so he must be on your mind.'

'Perhaps.' The impression left by her vision was of something portentous and exalted, but disturbing too. Did it mean Harry was going to succeed in his endeavours this time, and if he did, what did that mean for Richard? Why had she seen Harry and not Richard?

She lay down and the maids closed the curtains. The headache continued to pound at her temples and random flashes of light darted before her eyes so that it was almost like suffering a thunderstorm inside her skull. Eventually she slept, and she had neither dreams nor visions. When she woke several hours later the headache had retreated to a dull pain, but her thoughts were made of fleece and she had to perform every action with sluggish deliberation.

Alienor recovered slowly from her bout of illness. The very notion of fish stew made her feel sick and for several days the only nourishment she took was light broth, but gradually she started to feel cleansed and normal. The vision of Harry she had experienced continued to worry her and she wrote to him, telling him what she had seen and exhorting him to consider his actions carefully.

A little over a week later, she was sewing in her chamber when the Bishop of Salisbury asked to see her. She had been expecting a request for he was a stalwart supporter of Henry's and although elderly and growing frail he still exuded authority and power when he chose to exert his will.

Leaving her needlework, and accompanied by Amiria, Alienor followed the escorting knights of the Bishop's household from the palace to his lodging in the cathedral enclave. The clouds were high in the sky with wide expanses of glorious blue between them. A fine day to go riding, she thought with longing, although that was no longer permitted.

Bishop Joscelin sat in an ornate carved chair with the light spilling onto him from the window embrasure. Even in today's heat he wore a woollen cloak edged with gold braid, and a cap crusted with embroidery. His ivory crosier rested in a socket at the side of the chair and a leather-bound book with jewelled clasps lay on the table at his right-hand side. His features, cadaverous with age, wore an expression of grim sorrow. Beside him sat another man, recently arrived to judge from the dust powdering the hem of his habit. Alienor recognised Thomas Agnell, Archdeacon of Wells.

Alienor approached the men and knelt to kiss the amethyst ring on the Bishop's right hand. His skin was shiny, almost translucent, with purple and brown mottles like an autumn leaf. 'Father,' she said, before turning to acknowledge the Archdeacon.

'Daughter.' The Bishop's voice trembled. 'Will you be seated?' He indicated the stool at his left-hand side.

Alienor would rather have remained standing, but did as courtesy required. She settled her skirts and folded her hands, making a conscious effort not to clench them.

The Bishop's own hands shook with palsy. 'Daughter, the Archdeacon comes to us with grave news.'

Alienor turned to Agnell. He was younger than the Bishop by twenty years, still robust and of the world, although just now he too looked deeply burdened.

'Madam, it has fallen to me to bring you these tidings and I am sorry to be the one to bear them.' He drew a deep breath. 'It grieves me to tell you that your son Henry, the Young King, has gone to be with God in heaven.'

The words sat on the surface of her mind like raindrops on waxed leather. Her lips formed the words, but they were meaningless.

'I am sorry to say he contracted the bloody flux after robbing the holy shrine of Our Lady of Rocamadour. Some say that God's wrath has been visited on him for this deed of sacrilege and that the gates of heaven have been barred to him, but I am not one of them. He made full confession and repented his sins before death took him from the world, and I know he is with God and His angels.'

It was as if he had snapped shut a book under her nose, and the dust from it had come up in a cloud. She could feel the hardness of the stool beneath her, the tightening pressure of her fingers against each other until she touched bone. It wasn't true. It was a story concocted to torment her. How could he be dead and beyond her help? And yet evidently something had happened. 'I must go to him.' She tried to stand up, but there was no strength in her legs. She had heard the words clearly with one part of her mind, but her emotions had not caught up, and all she could think of was her son hurting and in desperate need of his mother. 'It is not true,' she said. Clutching at straws. 'Where is your proof?'

Agnell held out a piece of parchment. 'Madam, I have a letter sent under the King's own seal. I have no reason to doubt what is written. The Young King died at Martel in the Limousin on the eve of the tenth of June, God have mercy on his soul. Truly, madam, I wish I did not have to bring you these terrible tidings.'

Alienor's breath caught as if he had struck her. She thought of the vivid vision she had experienced of Harry seated upon a throne and wearing both a royal crown and a diadem above his head, blazing with light. Not an earthly throne, but a heavenly one. Dear God. The nausea and pain returned too and she put her hand to her belly and gasped.

'Madam, you are distraught,' said the Bishop. 'Will it help you to pray for him now and take time for contemplation?'

Alienor gave the concerned prelate a blank stare. 'Why should I pray?' she said bitterly. 'God is not listening.'

The Bishop made a sound of protest, and raised one of his palsied hands. Agnell leaned forward. 'God always hears our prayers,' he replied gently. 'It is not our place to question Him, but only to yield ourselves to His mercy.'

'Mercy?' Alienor shuddered. 'If this is God's mercy, then I am finished with God.'

Once more she tried to rise and this time succeeded. The soldiers who had escorted her to this terrible meeting stood ready to catch her, but she warned them off with a hard look.

'Oh, madam,' Amiria said, her eyes liquid, 'I am so sorry.'

'What good is that to anyone?' Alienor snapped and swept from the room. At first she walked with her head up, but as she traversed the cloister, her pace quickened until she was running and stumbling, half blinded by tears.

Once in her chamber she began plucking clothes off the poles and hurling them into a coffer. 'I cannot stay here, I must go to him. It is my duty above all duties as a mother to be with him.' She tipped her jewel casket into the coffer and watched the rings and brooches tumble over the wool and linen like glistening entrails.

The guards exchanged glances and left the chamber, closing the door firmly behind them. Belbel gazed at Alienor with shock and consternation.

'It is the Young King,' Amiria told her, tears rolling down her face. 'He is dead and the news has overset my lady.'

'Dead?' Belbel covered her mouth with her hand.

'Of the bloody flux in the Limousin . . . the Bishop has just told her.'

'Don't just stand there,' Alienor commanded. 'Help me pack.'

'Madam, they will not let you leave,' Amiria said gently. 'Even for this. And the Young King . . . as the Archdeacon says, surely he is with God in heaven. Let Him care for him now.'

Alienor ignored her and continued to toss her belongings into the baggage chest. 'He needs me,' she repeated.

'Madam, he is beyond earthly cares.' Amiria moved to stand in Alienor's way. Her quiet steadiness and inner core of spiritual strength made her better able to deal with Alienor now than the more forthright Belbel. 'They will not let you leave; you must pray for his soul where you are. I will come with you and light candles and keep vigil.' She gently tugged at the cloak Alienor was clutching.

Alienor resisted her for a moment, and then let go and slumped to the floor, putting her face in her hands. 'He hated to be alone,' she wept. 'He needed people around him and he shone for them. What will he do alone in the dark?'

'He is not alone, madam, he is with God and His angels.'

'Are you so sure of that? After what the Bishop said about robbing the shrine at Rocamadour?'

'The Bishop said he had done penance and been confessed, madam.'

'But that some still reckoned him damned.'

'No, madam, never that.'

Alienor thought of Harry as she had seen him seated in glory with his twin crowns. Surely that meant salvation, but she had to be certain he was safe and as always she felt so impotent, trapped here in this stultifying small corridor between Sarum and Winchester. She had not been there, not been able to sustain him and provide the help he needed as he destroyed himself. Those she had trusted in her stead had let her down.

Amiria sat down with her on the floor, enfolding and rocking her. Alienor wanted to crawl into darkness, to hide her wounds and never emerge, but Harry needed her prayers.

Wiping her eyes on the soft cloth Belbel handed to her, she stood up and smoothed her gown. The guards outside the door allowed her and Amiria to pass through to the small private chapel of St Nicholas beyond the hall, and here she prostrated herself before the altar and prayed for the soul of her eldest son. She desperately desired to see that vision of him again, but all that came was darkness welling from a bottomless pit of grief.

In the following weeks, Alienor slowly came to terms with the fact that Harry had died of the bloody flux in squalid circumstances less than a fortnight after robbing the holy shrine of St Amadour to pay his expenses. She learned that he had expired on the floor of a fortified lodging house in Martel, repenting in his last hours on a bed of ashes with a rope tied around his neck. His coffers had been empty; there had been no money for alms to distribute as the funeral cortège wound its way north.

The procession to Rouen had been met along the road with wailing and outpourings of grief, but had turned into a debacle when the people of Le Mans had seized Harry's body and insisted on burying him in their city, where his father had been born and his grandfather lay entombed. A deputation from Rouen had arrived to reclaim him, since he had requested on his deathbed to be buried in their city. After much heated negotiation and discussion, Harry had been disinterred and taken on to Rouen.

When Alienor first heard the news, she had been sickened that men should use her son's corpse for their own pecuniary interests. Perhaps it would have amused Harry – he had always possessed an irreverent sense of humour – but it only served to make her grief more raw. Beyond those details, other considerations were slowly coming home to roost. With Harry gone she had lost another champion to her cause – one less person to stand up to Henry. Her son had constantly campaigned for her release and now that intercession was lost. Harry's death had drastically changed the path of the future because eventually he would have ruled England and Normandy, and she could have retired to Aquitaine with Richard and lived out her days in Poitiers. All that was swept away, tumbled and torn like shipwrecked timbers.

On a sultry morning in July Alienor returned from mass in the cathedral and saw horses in the courtyard, including a fine dark bay stallion that she instantly recognised. The dull grey feeling at her core lifted and kindled, not with joy but with a fire of grief and anticipation that sparked with rage. William the Marshal was here and she would have the truth from him, every last drop, even if she had to cut him open to get it, and she did not care if she did. She sent a servant ahead with orders to bring William to her private chamber, not the public space of the hall. Her heart was hammering in her chest and her breath was so short that she had to pause in the vestibule at the top of the stairs and compose herself before she continued through the hall and into the chamber beyond.

He stood in the middle of the room, dressed in serviceable travelling clothes that had seen hard wear but were brushed and cared for, and he had wiped the dust of the road from his boots. His sword was propped near the door, his cloak and satchel beside it. The sun's strength had browned his face and burnished his dark brown hair with strands of deep gold and amber. Fine lines fanned from his eye corners, laughter lines, but there was no laughter in him now, only apprehension, misery, and the look of a man on a battlefield facing his downfall but prepared to stand until the final blow cut him down.

'William, dear God, William!' Alienor's voice broke. She flew at him and hugged him as if by feeling his living

137

masculine strength she could feel Harry too. The sight of him was a vent for emotions she had been holding back for far too long. 'How could you!' she wept. 'How could you let this happen! Why could you not keep him safe!' She struck his chest with her clenched fist. 'That is all I ever asked of you. I trusted you and you failed!' She struck him again and again, pounding against his solid bulk, and he took each blow gladly, welcoming the punishment.

'Madam, I would have given my life if it would have saved his.' William's voice was raw with pain. 'I know I failed. It is my fault. I should have protected him better. I did all I could to dissuade him from the courses that led to his demise, but it was not enough; he would not listen. Strike me to the heart and kill me for failing you and him.'

'I should do.' She raised her fist again, but then opened her hand to grip a fistful of his tunic and clench around that. 'But it will not bring him back. Nothing will ever do that.'

'I am so sorry.' William's voice fell to a hoarse whisper and she felt the catch in his chest. 'He . . . he desired me to go to Jerusalem, to the Holy Sepulchre, and fulfil his vow to lay his cloak upon the tomb of Christ. I promised him I would, and it is my sworn intention. If I can no longer serve his earthly body, then may I serve by advancing the state of his soul.'

Alienor swallowed and slowly released his tunic. Others had written to her, expressing their condolences, absolving themselves of blame. And here was William taking that blame, offering himself to keep on walking down that path. It did not exonerate him; but it softened something within her that he was prepared to stand at the gates of hell as a shield and boost Harry's soul towards heaven.

'Sit.' She gestured with a trembling hand to the benches set either side of the hearth, bereft of fire in the summer heat.

William sat down heavily while Alienor poured wine for both of them. For a while they sat staring into the blackened cavity as if watching imaginary flames. And then William shuddered and brought his palm down over his face.

'Tell me,' Alienor said. 'Tell me everything.'

Haltingly, but without sparing himself, William related the details of his young lord's demise. 'He was never more true or brave than in the courage with which he faced his death,' William said. 'When he knew the end was close, he asked for my hand. He said he wanted to do right, but could no longer fulfil his obligations or make amends because he knew he was dying. He said . . .' William paused to swallow emotion. 'He said he wanted to build a great cathedral to the honour and glory of God but could no longer accomplish that deed. And then he asked me to do one thing for him beyond all others. He begged me to intercede at God's throne, because he did not want to burn in hell for his sins; he asked me to go to Jerusalem on his behalf and ask God's forgiveness.'

Tears pouring down her face, Alienor took his hands between hers and gripped them, remembering her dream, of Harry upon his throne, twice-crowned.

William bowed his head. 'I have sinned greatly in my life, and this is one of my greatest. I promised you I would protect him, and I did not, and for that I beg your forgiveness. I do not deserve to receive it, but if of your mercy you would show it, then I will go in peace and meet my maker. If God so desires it, then let my end be in Jerusalem where I have promised your son and my lord to make my pilgrimage.'

Alienor continued to grip his fingers in hers, feeling the vital living flesh and bone where her son had none.

'It is more than a pledge, madam, it is my life's duty and nothing will stand in my way.'

'I believe you will do it,' she whispered. 'I forgive you without reserve. You have burdens enough to bear and I will not add to them. In truth, it was the plotting of your enemies at court that meant you were not there when you were needed, when you might have turned the tide.'

A look of disgust crossed William's face. 'I will not speak of those insinuations, madam. To think of them sickens me.'

'I know the truth of your honour and I do not doubt it.'

139

He gently reclaimed his hands. 'By your leave, madam.'

He went to his baggage, returning a moment later with a leather satchel from which he took a roll of plain grey cloth and unfastened the ties. Folded inside it was a brown woollen cloak, a cross of white linen stitched over the heart.

Alienor had never seen the garment before. William did not have to say it had been laid upon Harry's dying body. A strand of his hair like gold thread sparkled on the collar. 'Is this all I am to have of him? A solitary hair?' Her grief welled up.

William said nothing, his lips tight and his throat working. For a while Alienor could not speak. This small, inconsequential thread was as precious to her as a relic because it had been part of her boy when he was alive. If only she could conjure his whole body from this one tenuous strand. With tender care she threaded the hair onto one of her silver needles and pinned it securely to a piece of silk cloth in her sewing casket.

'When do you leave for Jerusalem?' she asked when she could speak again.

'As soon as I may, madam. First I must visit my family and make my farewells, and I have to prepare for the journey.'

She raised a warning forefinger. 'It will be long and arduous, I promise you that.' She had travelled the road to Jerusalem, had survived the vagaries of the pilgrim road, storm-tossed seas, hostile attacks by infidel tribes, Greek political dealing that made sewage seem clean by comparison, and a husband she had come to loathe beyond bearing.

'Even if the road was paved with thorns from Dover to Jerusalem and I had to go on my knees, I would not turn back. God willing I shall accomplish my task, and if I do not, it will be because I have died in the attempt.'

'My resources are limited,' she said, 'but I can provide you with horses and provisions for your journey. It is a long time since I took the pilgrim road, but I have friends upon whom you may call to aid you should you have need. I will help you in any way I can to reach the Sepulchre.'

He nodded stiffly. 'Thank you, madam. I am grateful, and it is more than I deserve.'

'I would move heaven and earth to get you there – for my son's sake.' She gestured to the cloak. 'Put it out of my sight, William. I cannot bear to look on it any more and at the same time I am so tempted to take it from you and keep it close that it is destroying me.'

In silence he set about folding the garment and returning it to its satchel, his moves careful and reverent.

'Have you talked to the King? Yes, of course, you must have.'

William latched the bag. 'Yes, madam. He grieves deeply even if he buries it before others. He said that although his son had cost him more money in life than it took to rule a country, he still wished he was alive to cost him more.'

Alienor closed her eyes. Harry would still be alive if Henry had given him land and responsibility instead of handing him money and empty promises.

William sat back on his heels and looked at her. 'He has buried the grief deep and shows nothing to the world. He has given me funds for the journey in exchange for two of my horses, and letters of safe conduct, and promised me a place in his service should I return from Jerusalem – although I do not believe he expects me to.'

'You must,' she said fiercely, 'because I need to know you have achieved your goal, and because of Harry. You say you will do or die; then I entrust you with "do", William, and if you let me down in this I shall seek you out in the afterlife and I swear I will kill you again.'

He knelt at her feet and taking her hand, pressed his lips to her fingers. She reached out her other one to lay a light benediction on his head. 'God be with you,' she said. 'And God keep you safe. My prayers are with you every step of the way.'

William departed the next morning, furnished with a barrel of silver for his expenses and the promise of more. Alienor had already set her scribes to writing letters of commendation.

She came to the courtyard to see him off with his small entourage. In the bright summer morning, the toll of recent weeks showed evidence in the gaunt hollows of his cheeks. There was a determined, almost grim set to his shoulders, and the familiar wide smile was gone from his lips.

'William, you have a sacred charge. I will see you again, swear it to me.'

'If God wills it, madam,' he replied, reminding her that her word was not the final one.

She watched him set his foot in the stirrup and mount his palfrey. The grace, the limber movements were still there. She remembered him as a young knight, riding at her side in Poitou, entertaining her on the road, and then putting himself in the path of her assailants, buying her time to escape. He had been captured and she had paid his ransom and taken him into her household because she could not allow such courage to escape her service. He was intelligent, courtly, honest and brave, and for those very qualities she had entrusted Harry's care to him – and it had not been enough. Watching him ride away now was like watching another part of her life that had been good and solid tear off and float away downriver and out of sight.

18

Rouen Cathedral, September 1183

Alienor came to Rouen Cathedral on a glorious September day that hung like a jewel on the end of summer. The sky was deep blue and the clouds puffy white without obscuring the sun which was still strong enough to be hot, and yet the shadow cast by the cathedral was dense – palpably black and damp.

She had arrived late yesterday, crossing the Narrow Sea for

the first time in more than ten years of being held prisoner at Henry's whim. Nothing had changed save that he had lengthened her leash. It was not because of compassion following Harry's death. He did not care whether she mourned at his tomb or not, but there was the matter of inheritance to be decided and he needed her presence for that since she was Duchess of Aquitaine.

She had been dreading this moment ever since receiving Henry's summons at Sarum. To know her son was dead was difficult enough, but to confront his tomb and face the evidence of finality was beyond endurance, yet endure it she must. She was like an effigy, hard and regal, her face taut with effort as she swallowed her grief and felt it lodge like a stone at her core.

Henry paced at her side, his jaw set and his posture stiff. He had not looked at her once since they had arrived under separate escort at the cathedral doors. He had visited his son's tomb before, and this for him was a matter of formality, of escorting her as his consort, and presenting to the world an image of parents mourning a son.

Harry had been interred before the cathedral's high altar, and a blaze of candles surrounded the tomb. The effigy had yet to be carved and his resting place was marked by a plinth of pale marble, covered with an embellished silk cloth. Offerings surrounded the tomb – coins and trinkets, candles, and the wax image of a hand and arm presented by the grateful recipient of a cure. In death her son was loved and esteemed a miracle worker, a hundred times more powerful than he had been in life. That was why Le Mans had wanted him and Rouen had fought back. Canterbury had the martyr Thomas Becket who had died because of Henry. Rouen had Henry's son, dead of the same source cause.

Wreathed in coils of incense, Alienor stood upright before the tomb and resisted the urge to fall across it and wail. The effort made her movements jerky. Her expression rigid and fierce, she gave a single sharp nod, and turning to Robert de Neubourg, Dean of Rouen, gave him a soft pouch of red silk containing a mark of gold, acknowledging his part in settling Harry to rest and making all seemly.

De Neubourg bowed and accepted the pouch with gravitas. Alienor returned his bow and went to pray alone in the side chapel dedicated to the Virgin Mary. A blaze of candles surrounded a carved statue of the Mother of God painted in crimson, blue and gold, the baby Jesus perched on her knee. On another wall hung an image of Christ on the cross, his face contorted with suffering.

Alienor knelt, signed her breast and bent her head. As she prayed, she thought of Mary, holding her infant son in her lap, nurturing and sustaining him through his childhood, and then watching all that love and care dying tortured on the cross. But in dying, the Blessed Virgin's son had granted eternal life to all.

'Of your great compassion, Lord Jesus Christ,' she whispered, 'have mercy on my soul for all my wrongdoings, no matter what they are. And have mercy on my son's soul and grant that we may meet again in the next life, and may that meeting be swift.' She crossed herself and gazed at the windows, shedding rainbow colours on the chapel's stone floor. The light from these windows shone just the same as it had when Harry was alive; that had not changed. And she must go on the same too, unchanging, for even when the sun did not shine the colours in the glass still existed.

Alienor knew well the chamber she had been allotted in the Tower of Rouen for she had stayed here many years ago when the children were small. It was well maintained and pleasantly appointed with colourful wall hangings and a good fire burning in the hearth.

Henry had followed her into the room to see her bestowed there following their visit to the cathedral but was already poised to depart. However, she would not let him go, and stood before him, blocking his way as she looked him in the eyes.

'This is all your fault. If you had given him the funds and

the lands, he would have had no business to go marauding about making trouble and plundering his brothers' estates. He would still be alive had you not forced him into a corner.'

'I forced him nowhere,' Henry retorted, grey eyes glittering with anger. 'His end was of his own doing.'

'Which would not have happened if you had had sufficient fatherly concern to heed his complaints and let him live as a man.'

'I emptied my treasury for him, how dare you say that.'

'Yes,' she said with contempt. 'Money, Henry. You made a beggar of him by giving him money. Small wonder he was driven to do what he did.'

He ground his jaw. 'I do not need a lecture from you on the matter of my sons, madam. You have done quite enough in that department already, little of it commendable. You know nothing.' He made a grasping motion with his hands as if he wanted to set them around her throat, then turned on his heel and slammed from the room.

Alienor stood alone, one fist pressed to her heart, and wondered why she had bothered to speak at all and feeling empty and powerless now that her outburst was over.

'Mama?'

She turned her gaze to the young woman standing on the threshold of the chamber. She was tall with wide grey eyes like Henry's, strong cheekbones and a natural upward curve to her lips that was almost a smile.

'Matilda,' Alienor breathed. 'Daughter . . .'

The young woman came forward and knelt at her feet, the scarlet hem of her gown puddling around her knees.

Her formal greeting gave Alienor a vital moment to recover. Her last view of Matilda had been of a little girl of ten years old, waving from the deck of a ship as it receded to the horizon, carrying her to her marriage to Heinrich, Duke of Saxony.

She looked down at the fine weave on Matilda's headdress and a shiny strand of hair that had slipped loose. Golden-brown,

145

tinged with copper. Harry's hair had been like that but a shade lighter. So much joy, so much sorrow. How was she supposed to navigate a course through such jagged straits?

'I am so pleased to see you,' she said, and then the formality shattered and she flung her arms around Matilda with joy and tears. 'It lights my darkness to set eyes on you again, for I thought I never would. Let me look at you.' She held her away. 'My child has become a beautiful woman!'

A pink flush coloured Matilda's cheeks. 'She has become a mother too, several times over.' She placed her hand on her belly which was the softly rounded one of a fertile matron. 'If you have the strength, I will summon your grandchildren and present them to you.'

Alienor's smile was starry with tears. 'Indeed, bring them to me. They give me strength to go on. They are my hope for the future.'

Matilda went to the door. A few words, a swift summons, and a pleasant-faced woman ushered three children into the room – a girl and two boys, in perfectly stepped ages. 'Come,' Matilda said. 'Greet your grandmother and kneel to her.'

The children obeyed their mother swiftly, glancing at each other in a way that told Alienor they had been practising their manners.

'This is Richenza,' Matilda said, as Alienor bade the children stand. She set a light hand on her daughter's shoulder. The girl was just starting to bud into womanhood. She had a curly mane of red-gold hair and serious deep blue eyes. A child who knew her worth but was very conscious of her duty.

'Save for the hair, she looks so much like you,' Alienor said. 'I thought my heart would break when I had to bid you farewell.'

Matilda nodded. 'My heart too, Mama, but we have both survived have we not?'

'After a fashion,' Alienor said, grimacing.

Matilda indicated the two boys. 'Heinri and Otto,' she said. 'Lothar we had to leave behind as a pledge.' A look of pain flashed across her face. 'But we shall see him again soon enough.'

The boys swept her more flourishes. Otto the younger one had an auburn tint to his dark hair, and a dusting of freckles across his nose. His impish expression made Alienor want to laugh and the hard lump of endurance at her core dissolved a little. Heinri was upright and proper, very much the heir. 'What fine men you have brought me,' she declared. 'Brave young knights to defend and protect their grandmother.'

The boys preened and puffed out their chests, especially Otto.

'I have something for you,' Alienor told the children and directed them to a large wooden chest near the window, holding toys that had belonged to her sons and which she had had brought from Winchester with the baggage. She had been unable to bear looking inside it herself, but a new generation of children would bring joy to the moment and diminish the shadows. She watched them fall on the contents with the eagerness of wolves upon a fresh kill in winter, and felt a pang when they exchanged excited chatter in German of which she understood only a smattering.

'Heinrich hopes to reconcile with the Emperor so that we may go home soon, and Papa is interceding on our behalf too,' said Matilda. 'At least for now we have a home, and it will be so good to see my brothers when they arrive.' Her face fell as she realised what she had said. 'I grieve for Harry. I am glad I have been able to mourn at his tomb instead of from afar, but he should not be dead – not Harry.'

Tears stung Alienor's eyes. 'No,' she said, 'he should not.'

'I remember sitting on the rump of his horse and holding on to him tightly because he wanted to gallop.' Matilda's voice quivered. 'I didn't scream, I just gripped him for dear life, and I could feel the laughter in him going through the palms of my hands and into my heart. That is the memory I will hold of him in the same way I held him on that day.'

Alienor had to swallow before she could speak. 'You are right to do so; no one can take it from you, even if they take everything else. I have often wished I had never wed your father for then I would have had none of this great grief, but then I see you, my daughter, and I see my grandchildren at play and I can never regret such blessings. You are my greatest consolation.'

She glanced at the boys who had found a pair of wooden hobby horses with red leather reins and some toy lances and were already intent on conducting an indoor tourney. Richenza had discovered four brightly coloured juggling balls and was throwing and catching them with aplomb.

'You have the skills of a proper tumbler,' Alienor said, forcing her way through her sorrow.

'Grandpa taught me,' Richenza said.

Alienor raised her brows. 'Did he indeed?'

Richenza threw one higher than the rest and deftly caught it. 'Yes, but he can throw and catch a lot more balls at once.'

'That's because he has had longer to practise, and he does it all the time, but I will tell you something – sometimes he drops them.' *And then he stands on them and grinds them into the dirt.*

Richenza eyed her quizzically. 'I haven't seen him do that.'

'I hope you never do.'

Exchanging a swift glance with Matilda, Alienor swallowed her bitterness.

'He is a good grandfather.' Matilda's tone was conciliatory. 'He treats us well and is doing his best for our situation.'

'Then that is all to the good,' Alienor said neutrally.

'Do you remember when I pretended I was a shoemaker and took away Papa's good kid slippers and put big green stitches in them with woollen thread?'

Alienor gave a reluctant smile. 'Indeed I do.' Such occasions had been infrequent because Henry had usually been off somewhere on matters of government, but in the rare moments they had come together as a family he had always had time for his children when they were small. It was only as they matured and became old enough to send away in marriage or to challenge his will that he had changed.

148

'He never complained or told me off. He played along with my childish whim – and I loved him for that. He was the best father in the world – so I thought then.' She flicked her mother a defensive glance. 'You were the one who set down the rules and educated me in what it would mean to be a great lady and a consort for a man of high standing. I used to think you were too strict – until I had a daughter of my own.' She blinked hard. 'I have memories of him that are like jewels, and others that are stones, but my memories of you are always consistent, Mama.'

'And are they jewels or stones?' Alienor asked with a strained smile.

'Neither,' Matilda answered. 'They are pure gold.'

Alienor patted Matilda's hand, touched to tears but experiencing a small moment of humour at the pun on her own name. She had been christened Alienor after her mother Aenor for the meaning was 'another Aenor', but her name also meant 'Pure Gold'. 'I have kept you in my prayers every day,' she said. 'I tried to instil duty to your family within you, but I admit that when I knew you were to wed a man thirty years older than you were, I was apprehensive.'

Matilda smiled and shook her head. 'You have no cause to worry, Mama. Heinrich treats me very well.' Her expression grew fond. 'He can be irritable when he's tired or upset, but he cares for me and he sees beyond my role to who I am. Papa chose well when he chose Heinrich, even if it was for his own political purpose.'

The boys had abandoned their tourney and were now crawling about the floor, busy with some painted wooden knights once owned by Harry who, as a laughing child, had done the same with his brother Richard. Once more Alienor's eyes filled with tears.

'I am sorry,' she said. 'This comes upon me without my will.'

'Harry loved those knights, didn't he?' Matilda's chin wobbled too. 'I knew I might never see him again when I went to Germany, but it was comfortable to know he was still in the world. Now . . .' She broke off, and the women embraced, hugging each other, sharing their grief.

Eventually Alienor drew back and wiped her eyes. 'Ah enough. I have wept an ocean already. Has your father spoken of Harry to you?'

Matilda frowned. 'No, Mama. His grief is buried deep. It is like a thorn in his flesh that works its way in and festers, but on the surface is nothing but a dark shadow. I pity him.'

'Then you are more charitable than I am,' Alienor replied. 'The place in my heart where such feelings once dwelt has withered and will never grow green again.'

Matilda said nothing and by mutual consent the women turned their attention to the children, because there was nothing more to say, and Alienor did not want to become the focus of her daughter's pity too.

Alienor had retired to her chamber for the night when Richard came to see her, having ridden in long after dusk. When she started to send for food, he refused. 'I ate with my father – not that I especially wanted to, but I was obliged out of duty. If you have decent wine, though, I will drink it.'

'Decent wine in your father's house?' Alienor curled her lip. 'That would be taking miracles too far – but Belbel managed to find a barrel that wasn't completely vinegar and appropriate it for my use.'

Dismissing her women, she served him herself and, as she handed him the cup, experienced a moment of love and terror for him that was almost pain. Thus far he had lived a charmed life given how vigorously he threw himself into battles, but that could end on the single thrust of a spear and there was nothing she could do to protect him.

'Your brother . . .' Her voice broke.

He was on his feet in an instant and his arms were around her, drawing her close. She held him tightly and wept again for her lost son and the living one in her arms.

'We were young together all our lives,' Richard said in a

constricted voice. 'I know we argued; at times I hated him; but I loved him too and he was always there. Now there is a hole and I cannot bear to look at it, yet neither can I bear to cover it with earth.'

'I know, I know,' Alienor whispered, while tears rolled down her face.

'Things could have been so different.' His breathing was heavy with grief and anger.

Making a tremendous effort, she drew back from their embrace. 'Yes, they could, but it's done with; and nothing can ever bring him back.'

'I know, Mama.' His jaw muscles flickered with tension. 'I have to step into the breach. I have to be more than I was before because of those who depend on me.'

She understood his anxiety. Suddenly he was the one standing at the prow of the ship to receive the full onslaught. No longer could he go about his own business and have that layer of protection because his father was looking elsewhere. Standing at the mast was a lonely position.

'You will rise to it. I have taught you well, as has your father, and even if you can only rely on yourself, you have everything within you that you need.'

His jaw relaxed a little. 'Yes, Mama. It is not what I saw in my future, but I must change to face the weather.'

They sat down to drink their wine. Alienor looked at the firelight gleaming on his hair, turning it to ruddy flame. His face was handsome and firmly masculine. He was twenty-six years old and stood in his own light, but he was still her child, her precious, beloved son.

'Did your father speak to you of the inheritance this evening?'

'No. He wanted to know how I was dealing with matters in Poitou, and required an accounting of funds, but his talk was of general matters.' His mouth twisted. 'John was clinging to him like a spider as he always does.' His tone held a mingling of contempt and aggravation. 'God knows what goes on in that mind of his, because no one else does.'

151

'He is your brother, and you have one less now.'

Richard shrugged. 'He was always just a little boy clinging to his nurse's knees, or running after our father and being swatted away, and now suddenly here he is with a fledgling beard and a child in the cradle if what I hear is true – a child he has chosen to give my name.'

'Yes.' Alienor's voice was subdued. 'I am afraid it is true on both counts.'

'Then I hope the naming is from admiration, and a desire for that child to emulate his uncle when he grows up.' He waved his hand. 'I do not know John, and I need to. Harry was always closer to him than I was. Perhaps a few games of dice and flagons of wine are in order. I have no idea what he was saying to Papa when I arrived, but he's definitely been whispering in his ear. Certainly he looked very pleased with himself.'

'That is John's way. If it was about you, then at least you are aware of it, but knowing how clever he is, perhaps his timing was intended to discomfort you.' She set her wine aside and leaned forward to take his hand. 'I love you. I love all my sons, but you hold the greatest future in your hands. Forget John for the moment; let him play as he will and listen to me. It is for you to be strong, to wield your power with passion and desire. You must not allow your hurt and grief to betray you but to keep you focused on what it is you want. Do you understand me?'

His gaze narrowed and he became like a lion intent on the hunt. 'Yes,' he said. 'Yes, Mama, I do.'

'You must use your will and your power to obtain what is yours. Do not be dissuaded under any circumstances to compromise. Take what is your entitlement and let the crumbs fall that are not worth arguing over. In these negotiations concerning the future there will be issues to which you might not agree.'

'I am prepared to deal with that, Mama. I have done all that is asked of me and I am ready to fulfil my obligations. I refuse to wear Harry's shoes, but I will take his banner forward,

152

and face my father to discuss what is best for the future.' He raised his head proudly. 'I will be his son, I will be his heir, but I will not be his minion.'

Alienor's heart swelled and she gripped both of his hands. 'God grant all mothers such a son as you.'

19

Rouen, September 1183

Alienor stood straight and still while Amiria and Belbel robed her in gold brocade. The silk was Sicilian, a gift from Joanna that had been stitched by Belbel into a glorious court dress. Until now Alienor had lacked a fitting opportunity to wear the gown, but today was the gathering to discuss the succession. Henry was being highly circumspect and had told her nothing of his plans, nor had he spoken to Richard and Geoffrey. John knew more, she was certain; he had that look on his face and he had been avoiding her, which usually meant he was plotting something.

Belbel pushed the final pin into her veil, and with an ermine-lined cloak fastened around her shoulders Alienor was ready to go and discover just what Henry had in store.

When she arrived, Henry was pacing the chamber impatiently. Several clerics sat at lecterns in the light from the window arch, toiling away over sheets of parchment, the scratching of their quills a constant noise in the background. Richard, Geoffrey and John were already seated at a trestle table with documents piled in the centre.

'At last,' Henry said. 'I thought we might have to begin without you.'

'I commend your restraint.' She took the empty seat at his side. 'Yet you could hardly do so and be legal, could you?'

She settled in the chair, keeping her spine erect, and folding her hands in her lap, each movement measured and stately. Catching Richard's eye she recognised his unease, although he was affecting loose-limbed nonchalance. He was already Count of Poitou and acting Duke of Aquitaine. Now came the moment when England and Normandy should be added to his inheritance – although nothing was ever a certainty with Henry.

'Mama.' Geoffrey bowed courteously. 'That is a beautiful gown.'

She thanked him warmly and ignored Henry's impatient rumble. John murmured a greeting, his gaze slipping over hers and away as he bowed his head.

Henry seated himself beside Alienor and, clasping his hands, leaned over them, his manner brisk and pugilistic. 'We are here to attend to matters of your inheritance,' he announced, looking round at their sons. 'I have had to make adjustments because of your brother's loss, and this is what I have decided to do.'

He reached to the pile of documents in the middle of the table, and Alienor realised that they had in fact been divided into three piles. Henry took each one and handed it to the relevant son, the parchments trailing cords and seals.

'This is your inheritance,' he said. 'I want to make it very clear so there are no arguments about what it will be, and no one claiming I have disinherited them. Is that understood?'

Alienor's stomach clenched. Henry's laying down of the law did not bode well.

'Is it?' Henry gathered his sons in a single fierce glare.

Richard leaned back in his chair. 'Perfectly, sire.' His right fist clenched on the table. Against his knuckles, the ring of St Valerie, symbol of his position as Count of Poitou, gleamed in the September light slanting through the open shutters.

His brothers nodded agreement, and exchanged glances, like men about to engage in a swordfight.

'Good.' Henry nodded stiffly. 'I expect your compliance.

You must move into the breach your brother has left in his dying and you must not flinch from the responsibilities placed on you to do greater things with your lives. I expect you to acquit yourself outstandingly because you are my sons and your duty is to uphold the family honour and pride. Whatever you do reflects on me, remember this. You stand in my stead in these positions while I am alive, and you must under no circumstances overstep that mark of being in my stead. The policies we pursue are family ones – mine while I live since I am head of this family. I expect your obedience.'

Alienor almost winced. It was like being threatened by a giant with a nail club. Did he think to win them over like this? She remembered the boyish charm he had once possessed and wondered where it had gone. Perhaps like a bag of gold dust with an open top, the winds of time had swirled it away in a glittering spiral until there was nothing left but an empty pouch.

'You must work with each other as one,' Henry continued, the words emerging from him, heavy as stones. 'You must not overstep the bounds with each other or indulge in deliberate provocation. That is ultimately what led to your brother's death. If any one of you dares to step out of line, the whole weight of my hand will come upon you.' His fist struck the table, causing the goblets to jump, and the dark wine to ripple across the surface. 'Where you are does not matter, what you do is imperative, and you shall do my will. You are my sons and I love you dearly. I have bestowed great wealth upon you and I know you will acquit yourselves well for you have my blood running through your veins. Remember that when you seek to make war on each other. When you fight your brother or me, you only make yourselves bleed. We are all one, and for the sake of our house we must remember that. We are one and we move forward as one to quell and dispel pretenders to our authority and only in this way shall we survive and excel.' He leaned back and waved his hand. 'What I have done is fair and just and I will brook no argument.'

Richard picked up the parchment before him and began to read, and as he did so his guarded expression turned to one of utter disbelief, closely followed by fury. Surging to his feet he glared across the table at Henry, who was watching him with hard eyes and set lips. Without a word, Richard crumpled the document, threw it across the table at him and stormed out.

Alienor stared at her husband. 'What have you done?'

'What needed to be done,' he replied shortly. 'The best for everyone, and if Richard does not see it, then he is a fool and he will take the consequences. It is my rule and my will.'

Alienor shot a swift glance at her other sons. Geoffrey's expression was shocked and astonished. John, in contrast, looked as if he was sucking on a particularly juicy oyster.

Alienor rose to go after Richard, but a swift gesture from Henry sent two guards to bar her exit. 'I pray you be seated, madam,' he said. 'I will deal with the matter myself in good time.'

Alienor felt sick. 'I ask you again, what have you done? Why has Richard walked out?'

Henry shrugged. 'Because he has not listened to a word I have said.'

'Or perhaps he heard you quite clearly.' She thought back over Henry's diatribe; the remark about disinheritance and compliance and about not arguing between themselves.

Henry drew an impatient breath. 'As my oldest surviving son, Richard is now to have England and Normandy. Geoffrey is to keep Brittany and be granted the earldom of Richmond in right of that title.' His gaze flicked to his smiling youngest son. 'And John is to do homage to Richard and govern Aquitaine.'

Alienor felt as if she had been thrown against a wall. She stared at Henry in appalled disbelief. 'Have you run utterly mad?'

'My reasoning is sound,' Henry snapped. 'John will do well for Aquitaine and Richard can concentrate his efforts on other dominions. That is my will and he has no choice.'

She shook her head and bit down on words that she would not speak in front of her other sons. That Henry could do this and not see how wrong it was, and how untenable, was beyond belief. Richard would never agree to give up Aquitaine. He had fought too long and too hard to hand it over to John, a youth not yet seventeen with no experience of governing. Aquitaine was in Richard's blood and bones and he did have a choice – the same one that had killed his brother.

Without a word she turned to the door again, and this time Henry let her go, but guards accompanied her to her chamber and then took up their posts outside her door, denying her any opportunity to have contact with Richard.

Richard raged around his chamber like a whirlwind, over-turning a trestle table, throwing stools, kicking over a heavy barrel chair, swearing he would never give up Aquitaine to his runt of a little brother. He did not care what his father said; his father wasn't God and he had no right to dictate such terms of inheritance. He would fight until he was the last man standing.

He was snarling at his servants to pack the baggage chests when John sauntered into the room, swaggering a little, one hand resting on the dagger sheath at his hip. 'Do you want me to do homage to you for Aquitaine now?' he enquired.

Incandescent with rage, Richard strode to him and seized him by the throat of his tunic. 'You dare to come in here . . .' he spluttered.

'If you touch me, you will have to deal with Papa,' John said almost gleefully, although his gaze flickered with sudden fear.

'You think that would be a problem?' Richard scoffed. 'You'll have Aquitaine over my dead body. And as to touching you . . .' He flung him to the floor. 'I wouldn't foul my sword. Get out, you worm!' He picked up a bowl of sops in wine from a small table that had survived the first onslaught of his fury and dumped it over his brother's head. 'There, let that be your anointing, you conniving brat. You are no more fit to rule

Aquitaine than a carbuncle on a beggar's arse. I will never accept your homage, never! Aquitaine is not our father's to give.'

John stumbled to his feet, pieces of soggy bread clinging to his tunic like drowned mice. His expression was contorted with malice. 'You heard what he said – that we had to obey his will and he would strike down anyone who opposed it.'

'Let him try' – Richard bared his teeth – 'and let us see who wins. It won't be you, no matter how you wheedle and plot.'

'Don't be so certain of that,' John retorted, but finally made discretion the better part of valour by taking swift leave of the room. 'I'll win, you'll see!' he called over his shoulder before banging the door shut.

Standing at her narrow chamber window, Alienor watched Richard make final preparations to leave Rouen. He glanced up in her direction, and as a groom brought his palfrey, bridled and saddled, he ran up the outer wooden staircase until he was close enough to speak to her through the window opening.

'I will return for you,' he said fiercely. 'Mama, I promise.'

Seeing the taut, angry lines on his face, put there far too young by his father, Alienor shook her head. 'Godspeed you on your journey. Do not worry about me and do not give into him however he threatens you, even if it is through me. But think before you move. What he has suggested is untenable, but do not burn every bridge.'

Richard's expression twisted. 'I have told him I need time to digest what he has said and to consult with others, but I tell you now, Mama, I will never yield Aquitaine to John. I will fight until I fall before I let that happen.'

'I promise you it won't. Go now, my son, and swiftly.'

Barely had Richard left in a cloud of dust when Henry walked into the chamber, John and Geoffrey a few paces behind. John had changed his clothes since the morning and his hair was combed back and darkly damp. A faint herbal scent hung around him as if he had just taken a bath.

'I suppose you cooked this up between you,' she said with cold fury. 'Well be damned to you because it is not your heritage to decide.'

'I have to do what is for the best,' Henry answered. 'It makes sense that John should have Aquitaine. If he pays homage to Richard for it, then I see no reason to baulk.'

'Then you are blind. You would set a child in the place of a proven man.'

'I am not a child,' John protested indignantly. 'Papa was Duke of Normandy when he was my age.'

'You are not your father either, and heaven help you with him as an example,' Alienor retorted. 'Begetting a child on your cousin and scheming behind your brother's back makes you neither a man nor a good ruler. It makes you someone who does not know the boundaries. It makes you someone who cannot be trusted to keep his word.' Her anger was hard and bitter. 'You are not ready to govern Aquitaine and Richard will never be manipulated into the same position that Harry was.'

John reddened. 'I am more than ready, Mama; you just do not see it because you only have eyes for Richard.'

'That is not true. I am concerned that all my sons should be employed in the roles that best suit their skills.'

Henry had been silent during the exchange, although his eyes had narrowed as he watched the repartee. 'Richard will do as I command or face the consequences,' he said curtly. 'He has too many responsibilities. Some of them must be shouldered elsewhere.'

'Too much potential power you mean,' she retorted. 'There are better ways of dealing with this. Tell me, how many of your own responsibilities have you been willing to place elsewhere?'

'I do not know why I bother speaking with you, madam,' Henry said and stalked from the room. John gave her a similar look and followed his father out. Geoffrey made to go after them and then hesitated.

'You know he won't let it rest, Mama.'

'Neither will Richard,' she said tightly.

159

'Then there will be war again.'

She noted her middle son's air of guarded reserve. She did not know where Geoffrey's loyalties lay because he was reticent. He did not try to ingratiate himself with Henry as John did, but held more aloof. There was a strong rivalry between Geoffrey and Richard; they were not comfortable in each other's company. If she imagined scales with Henry and John on one side and herself and Richard on the other, then Geoffrey held the balance, and he would play whichever side was to his own advantage.

'Yes, there will, but what part will you take, and on whose side will you stand, my son?'

'My own. I have the responsibility for Brittany and for Richmond and I must do what is best for them and for my heirs.' He drew a pattern on the floor with the toe of his boot. 'Constance is with child. She told me just before I set out for this meeting. Come late spring we shall have a son or daughter.'

Alienor was thrown by the change of nuance, from talk of political manoeuvring to an announcement of family news, but she adjusted swiftly. 'Oh, I am so pleased for you. Constance is well?'

'A little sick in the mornings, but nothing untoward.'

'It will change your world,' she said.

Geoffrey nodded, and behind his smile his eyes were shrewd and thoughtful. 'Indeed. It behoves me to think even more carefully about the future.' He bowed to her, took both her hands and kissed them. 'I honour you, Mama, I always will.' And then he left to follow his father and John.

Frowning, she went to sit in the window seat and stare out. Her grandchildren were playing with some other youngsters in the courtyard where Richard had so recently set spurs to his palfrey. Heinri was giving little Otto a piggy back and the latter was shouting instructions in his native German and waving a stick in his hand as they jousted with a rival pair of boys. The sound of their shouts floated up to her, high-pitched with glee. Her sons had once played like that too, but it had

160

all changed as the rivalry grew too strong. She suspected that Geoffrey's careful thought about the future was likely to lead to yet more difficulties rather than a solution.

20

Winchester Castle, July 1184

Alienor took her newborn grandson, fresh from his first bath, and cradling him tenderly in her arms brought him to her daughter. Matilda lay in bed, supported by pillows and bolsters, her face drained of colour and her eyes heavy with exhaustion. However a joyful smile lit her face as she held out her arms for the baby. He had not yet been swaddled and she counted his miniature fingers and toes and kissed his soft skin. Fine glints of red gold sparkled where the light caught the top of his head.

'You have done well,' Alienor said proudly. 'What a beautiful child. I am so glad you came to Winchester for your confinement.' She brushed tears from her eyes. After the heartache of losing Harry, and amid the continuing strife and troubles that set father against son and brother against brother, the miracle of this snuffling, squawking little scrap of life was a treasure beyond value.

'I am glad too, Mama.' Matilda kissed the baby again and returned him to Alienor. 'Will you take him and show him to everyone?'

'You could not stop me!' Smiling, Alienor tucked the blanket around her new grandson to keep him warm and protected. Once returned to the confinement chamber he would be wrapped in swaddling to keep his limbs straight and true, but first he had to be shown and acknowledged. He was to be christened Wilhelm; his parents had agreed upon the name while he was still in the womb. 'Rest. I will return in a short while.' Having kissed her daughter's damp brow, she went out to show him to his waiting family.

Heinrich was elated to greet his son. Clearly used to handling small babies he cradled him in his arms with confidence, and pride. The other children crowded round to look at their new sibling. Richenza was fascinated, her brothers slightly less so and they soon returned to their play, but she stayed and put her finger in the baby's hand and smiled as he tightened his grip around it.

Alienor liked Heinrich, although she had been cautious at first. He was not much younger than she was, but still hale and vigorous, as attested by the offspring he had sired, and by his ability to continue begetting them. He loved them dearly, and was plainly very fond of Matilda. Their household was busy and boisterous, filled with loud voices and laughter, and even if it was wearing at times, there was much to be said for that kind of treasure.

Henry arrived to inspect his new grandson, although did not offer to hold him. 'A fine child,' he opined, and tickled the baby under the chin, making him screw up his little face and mew. His air was preoccupied. With Richard still refusing to cooperate over the matter of Aquitaine, he had given John and Geoffrey free rein to invade Poitou and bring him to heel by force. However, it was proving to be unfruitful. The brothers had taken to raiding each other's border lands in what amounted to no more than tit-for-tat squabbles and Henry's ill-conceived instruction had stirred further bitterness into the brew. Having received news of yet another abortive, expensive skirmish that morning, his mood was as sour as a windfall apple.

Alienor said nothing to him about the situation. The results were evident; sooner or later he would have to accept that Richard would not budge over the matter of Aquitaine. Henry would have to find an alternative for John and mollify Geoffrey, who held Brittany and Richmond, in right of his wife, but had precious little from his parental inheritance.

She was about to return the baby to his mother when more

children trooped into the bower to greet the newcomer. One was Henry's son by his former mistress Ida de Tosney, an engaging, fastidious little boy with his mother's dark hair and melting brown eyes. Alienor did not blame the child for the circumstances of his birth; they were not his fault, and although only four years old, he had beautiful manners. His small companion had soft brown hair and blue eyes very like her own. He was barely more than a toddler but he had his first words and was already steady on his feet. John's son born of Belle de Warenne was a sunny, uncomplicated little boy, his nature the complete opposite of his mercurial, dissatisfied father. Sit him down with a toy, tell him a story, cuddle him, and he was blissfully content. Belle had married the middle-aged Robert de Lacy last year, but Alienor knew nothing beyond that, nor did she particularly wish to.

Richard gave his new baby cousin a kiss on the cheek, and then for good measure kissed his four-year-old uncle too. His simple affection made Alienor smile and think that perhaps there was hope for future generations after all.

Matilda's recuperation from Wilhelm's birth was slow but steady and by the time she was churched in August she had almost recovered. She had new robes for the occasion and Heinrich gave her a belt sewn with pearls and sapphires.

Alienor's apartments were in a state of constant activity, busy with ladies, children, dogs, and the coming and going of numerous servants. She had grown close to Matilda during their time together and it was delightful to have company and conversation in her life again. Her daughter was warm and merry and her presence lightened Alienor's days, as did the children with their amusing antics. She was closely watched by Henry's guards, but her bonds were looser, and if she did not think too hard, she could almost imagine she had a degree of freedom.

One September afternoon she was sitting with Matilda, watching over the baby and playing a finger counting game with her grandson Richard, when Henry hobbled into the chamber, a fearsome scowl on his face. His limp was caused not by the old leg wound that so often pained him but by a sorely inflamed toenail. A piece of parchment was clenched in his fist.

'Enough,' he said abruptly. 'This has to end.'

'Two, fee, six!' Richard cried triumphantly. 'Seven, nine, ten!'

Alienor hugged him and signalled to his nurse, Agatha, to take charge of him. 'What has to end?'

'Richard.' He shook the letter at her. 'He has invaded Brittany. I tell you I will not stand for any more of his warmongering.'

'As I recall, he did not start this fight. It was you who sent Geoffrey and John into Poitou with sanction to make war on him. What was he supposed to do? Open the door wide and invite them in with a bow? I agree with you that enough is enough. Arrange a truce and think again about the division of the inheritance.'

'I will not have Richard flouting my will, do you hear me?'

'Then treat him fairly. The sword has two edges. You should never have agreed to give John Aquitaine. Let him have Ireland as you originally planned.'

Henry leaned against a trestle to take the weight off his feet. 'I have a nest full of eaglets, and they strive to tear me to pieces.' His mouth twisted. 'They would devour me to the last bloody morsel given the chance.'

'You devour yourself,' she retorted. 'You turn on them and you pluck the feathers from their wings so they cannot fly the nest but have to fight you for their place.'

'What are you going to do, Papa?' Matilda hastily intervened between her parents to move the situation forward before it became entrenched.

He exhaled heavily. 'Recall them. Let them come to me here and I will listen to what they have to say, and in their turn, they will listen to me – and then do my will.'

'Do you truly believe that will happen?' Alienor was astounded at his blindness. 'You do not know your sons, any of them, and yet they are so like you. Their will is a mirror of yours, and that is why they will not listen.'

'I begot them.' Henry's eyes were bright with anger. 'I own them. They do not own me, and therein lies the difference.' He shot her a warning look. 'You will support me in this, madam.'

Alienor inclined her head. 'I will do all I can because I have no desire to see my sons destroy themselves fighting each other – look what happened to Harry. But I will not condone you giving Aquitaine to John. He is not my heir, and he is much too young.'

Henry's jaw worked, but he said nothing and in his gaze, behind the anger, was something more – a spark of calculation that made Alienor wary.

'For now, I will recall them,' he said. 'And then we shall see.' He pushed himself off the trestle and limped off about his business.

'He is planning something,' Alienor said, narrow-eyed. 'I do not know what, but I could almost see the ideas turning in his mind.'

Matilda gave an impatient shrug. 'Papa is always planning something, and I cannot remember a time when my brothers were not fighting each other, and it was always over possessions.'

Alienor heaved a weary sigh. 'What can I do? Even if I talk to them, I will never tell Richard to give up Aquitaine. He has been my chosen heir from the moment he left my womb and entered the world. Ah, I don't know.' She waved an exasperated hand. 'God grant you have no such troubles with your own little ones.'

Now it was Matilda's turn to sigh. 'I pray that our petition to the Pope is successful and that eventually we can return to Saxony. I am happy to be here, Mama, and to have your succour, but I am Heinrich's loyal wife and this is not where he belongs.' She slid her mother an anxious look.

Alienor hugged her in reassurance. 'Your father is doing everything in his power to mediate with the Pope and the

Emperor. He may not deal fairly with his own sons, but when matters are a step removed he sees more clearly, and he has considerable skill. He will succeed for you and Heinrich, I promise – and I do not make promises lightly, especially when your father is involved.' A sudden, unexpected feeling of warmth stabbed her heart. Time and again when she thought all feelings but hate for Henry were dead, something would snag her like a thorn on the stem of a living rose and she would bleed anew.

Entering the chamber, John's gaze was immediately drawn to the small boy sitting on Dame Agatha's knee chattering happily to her as she cuddled him. John experienced an unfamiliar feeling of tenderness. A sense of possession was present too, but with a gentler awareness. And pride, because although his sisters had borne boys, he was the only one of his brothers to have sired a son. Geoffrey's wife Constance had birthed a daughter earlier in the year, revealing to everyone that Geoffrey's seed had not been strong enough to make a male child. But this little boy was living proof of his own superior virility.

Agatha hastily rose to curtsey. 'Sire,' she said, 'I did not see you.'

John was pleased. He enjoyed walking quietly round the edges and going unnoticed until he was ready. For a time Agatha had been his own nurse and he had sought her out to care for his precious son. Gesturing her to sit, he crouched to tousle Richard's sunny-brown hair. He was determined to be a good father, better than his own was to him. Despite the hand-wringing of others over the circumstances of his birth, John did not have an instant's remorse or regret.

'I am your papa,' he said. 'Can you say that word?'

The little boy nodded and swung his legs. 'Papa,' he repeated.

'That's right.' As John scooped him up in his arms, his sense of possession intensified. He had created him, and Richard belonged to him as nothing and no one else did. The child didn't cry or wriggle to get away, but eyed him fearlessly, without subterfuge. 'You are mine; I own you.' The last words were said with a double meaning of acknowledgement, and possession. 'I am well pleased with him,' he told Agatha.

'Indeed, sire,' she replied fondly. 'Everyone falls under the spell of his charm.'

'Ah then, he takes after his father.'

There was a sound behind the door, a soft footfall of someone else who was acting in stealth, and John was suddenly alert. 'Come forward,' he commanded, angry and a little fearful that he was now the one being stalked and observed.

In a swirl of red skirts and a glint of gold embroidery, Belle stepped into the light. A tight-fitting court dress revealed the curves of her figure, but she wore the full linen veil of a married woman, and it framed a face where the softness of girlhood had been replaced by the taut bone structure of an adult woman – one who had learned some difficult lessons. The hand that lifted the hem of her gown above her gilded shoes was adorned by a wedding ring.

He stared at her and she stared back defiantly.

'I will not ask what you are doing here.' He tightened his arms around his son. 'That much is obvious.'

'Papa!' Richard wriggled.

'I would not expect you to. In truth, I only came to look because when you have been wounded beyond healing, you cannot ignore the pain.' Belle's tone was bitter and dark. 'You took many things from me on that day and what you gave in return will burden me for the rest of my life.'

'You may see him as and when you choose,' John said. 'I will not prevent you.'

She shook her head. 'That would not be wise, because it would only deepen the wound. Last time I saw him was when I bid him farewell at Shaftesbury's gates when he was still suckling from the wet nurse. Now I am looking at a little boy. Then it will be a bigger boy and then a man, and all the voids of the years in between. It is too much, I see that now.' She walked to the door but on the threshold she turned. 'I ought

167

to curse you for what you did to me, but you are the father of my child, and I would not do that to our son.' She went out, closing the door behind her with dignity.

John returned the infant to Agatha. He considered going after Belle, seizing her in his arms and stealing her breath in violent kisses until he vanquished her, but that would be unwise with her husband and her parents at court. Her husband was an ageing man, grey above, probably limp as a dead eel below, but he was more wary of Hamelin, with good cause.

'Not a word,' he warned Agatha.

'I know when to seal my lips, sire,' she answered with dignity, 'but as once your wet nurse, I venture to say you should be careful.'

'I intend to,' he replied. 'Very careful indeed.'

'Mama?'

Alienor looked up to watch her middle son cross her chamber, his chestnut and white spaniel Moysi trotting at his heels. The dog had been a wedding gift from Constance and accompanied him everywhere. He came to Alienor and kissed her cheek. His lips were as cold as stone and his cloak was starred with melting snowflakes. There was a loud flapping noise as the dog shook itself from its folded ears to feathery tail and almost fell off its paws.

'The snow will be knee deep by morning,' he said.

Alienor put down her sewing. She was warm by the fire, hot wine to hand and a fur-lined cloak draped over her waist and legs. Matilda sat at her side, working with a single needle on an elaborate pair of socks for her husband.

'It will not please your father if he is unable to ride out to hunt,' Alienor said. 'I suppose everyone will have to stay within and argue instead.'

'I suppose so,' Geoffrey said wryly, 'although as soon as it clears, I shall leave.' He sat down beside his sister and held out his hands to the fire. 'Constance writes that she is with child again and perhaps this time it will be a son.'

'Indeed, that is good news. I am pleased for you.' Alienor embraced him.

Matilda hugged him too and went to pour wine so they could raise a toast.

Geoffrey took the cup, and after the salutation rested it on his knee and cleared his throat. 'That is not the only news I received this morning.'

Immediately Alienor was on her guard. Henry had managed to patch up a truce between his sons, but it was more fragile than a spider's web. He had promised to think more upon the matter of the inheritance and come to a better settlement for all. That for him was an enormous compromise, but Alienor knew his propensity for procrastination and going back on his word. So did his sons. There couldn't be a better settlement for all, because whatever was given to one, the others would see as an unfair advantage or threat, and Henry would still play them off against one another.

'Papa is sending me into Normandy to be his governor there, as soon as I may.'

'Normandy?' She narrowed her eyes. Geoffrey was now Richard's heir, and his ambition had grown both with his change in status and with his fruitful marriage to Constance. He was the one begetting a new dynasty, and not of bastards. She suspected it was why he had agreed to invade Poitou with John when Henry had encouraged him to do so. There was only a year between him and Richard and the rivalry between them had intensified since Harry's death. In giving Geoffrey Normandy to govern, Henry was sending out a warning to Richard, that the succession in Normandy and Anjou was not set in stone.

'Well Richard is too busy with Poitou, and Papa knows I am competent and will do as he asks.' He gave her a sidelong glance and dug his hands through the thick ruff of fur round the dog's throat. 'Richard will not be pleased, but he cannot sit on everything like a treasure chest.'

Alienor eyed him shrewdly. The defensive set of his shoulders told her he had not come to apologise or make amends for the quarrels between him and Richard, but he did want her approval for this latest scheme.

'You are grown men. You have the wits God gave you, but it is up to you to use them wisely. It would be better to make allies of your brothers and not allow your father to drive a wedge between you.'

'No, Mama.' He hesitated. 'Will you give me your blessing?'

'You are my son, of course I will. You will always have it, the same as any of my sons and daughters; I love you all dearly. All that I ask is that you consider well and do not squander the opportunities you have been given by God and the privilege of your birth.'

He gave her one of his steady, inscrutable looks. 'No, Mama, I won't.'

He knelt again, and she touched his hair tenderly. Perhaps it was not so foolish of Henry to give him Normandy, but it would cause tension, and she could only pray that her sons would not allow themselves to be manipulated by either their father or the wily Young King Philippe of France who was proving to be a player of skill and subterfuge. She could cajole, advise and chivvy all she chose, but ultimately the choice to listen was theirs.

21

Windsor Castle, January 1185

It had snowed overnight and the drifts were deep, but the morning had dawned cold and bright. In the ward the children pelted each other with snowballs, building powdery white fortresses and yelling at the top of their lungs. Alienor and Matilda preferred to sit by the fire and sew but had barely established a rhythm of needlework and conversation when

170

Heinrich arrived from Winchester, his broad face scarlet with cold, his hands stiff inside his gloves from clutching the reins, and his whole demeanour one of excited enthusiasm that almost outdid the children clamouring around him like a pack of frantic small dogs.

His boots were dark at the toes from melting snow, and powdery circles decorated his cloak where his offspring had pelted him. Going straight to Matilda, he picked her up and swung her round.

'Put me down!' she cried, gasping and laughing at the same time. 'What is this?'

His cold-reddened cheeks brightened further. '*Liebling*, I had to bring you this news myself. Your father's envoys have returned from the papal court. The Emperor has agreed to a reconciliation. Come spring we can return home. Our exile is over!' He spoke in French as a courtesy to Alienor, but his German accent was heavy and she could still barely understand him. However, his joy made the content evident.

Matilda's eyes began to sparkle. 'Praise be to God! I hoped and I prayed, but I was not certain it would happen.' She kissed him soundly.

'Your father is a miracle worker, that is for sure,' Heinrich said. 'It is his diplomacy that has triumphed.' Belatedly he bowed to Alienor. 'I am sorry for bursting in upon you, but the news means so much to me, and my family.'

Alienor smiled graciously. 'And it's understandable.' If only Henry was half as skilled in diplomacy where his sons were concerned.

'I am to escort you to Winchester,' Heinrich said. 'All of you, and a formal announcement will be made in full court.' He waved his arm. 'I could have entrusted a messenger, but I wanted to bring the news myself.'

Alienor embraced both of them warmly. 'It is indeed wonderful news, but I am going to miss you,' she said, and turned to Matilda. 'If anything good has come out of your exile, it is the opportunity we have had to see each other again.'

In the midst of her joy, tears brimmed in Matilda's eyes. 'Mama, I would bring you back with me if I could.'

'I know you would, but it cannot be. Be thankful for what we have had.'

Alienor called for food and wine, and made Heinrich comfortable by the fire. The children crowded around him, and he set the baby on one knee and little Otto on the other. Richenza stood at one shoulder, playing with the silver curls at his nape, and Lothar leaned against his other side.

'There are still arrangements to make and safeguards to put in place.' Heinrich gave Alienor a meaningful look. 'A prudent farmer does not put all of his chicks in one basket. For now I think it safer to leave the children with you and send for them when we are sure of our ground. I do not expect trouble, but it is best to be safe.'

'You are wise,' Alienor said. 'They will be well cared for here and I will enjoy having them for a little longer.'

Matilda bit her lip but she kept her head up. She had gone to her marriage in Saxony when she was just ten years old, slightly younger than Richenza now. Her children were better off than many. They were not going to foreign lands and marriage with strangers but would be with their grandmother.

'You are right.' Her voice was tight but steady. 'It must be done for their safety.'

'It will not be for long, I promise you, *liebling*,' Heinrich said and kissed her in reassurance. Observing their closeness, Alienor was both pleased and wistful because she had not been able to call upon that kind of support in either of her marriages.

On a mild evening several months later, Alienor was preparing for bed when Henry arrived to see her. Belbel had been combing a scented lotion of nutmeg and rose water through Alienor's tresses which were still thick, falling to her waist in a blended waterfall of grey and silver. Henry had not seen her hair loose for a long time and his expression filled with surprise and even a hint of admiration.

'I thought you were still at Westminster,' she said. 'It is late for travel.'

He shrugged. 'There was enough light when we set out, and a good moon. Why waste time?'

She ought to have known. Henry's determination to squeeze every single drop from the day was a constant.

She had stayed at Windsor with Matilda and the children as winter thawed into spring. Matilda and Heinrich had been busy and preoccupied, preparing for their return to Germany. In February Heraclius, the Patriarch of Jerusalem had arrived to lay the keys of the tower of David at Henry's feet and offer him the throne of his cousin King Baldwin of Jerusalem who was dying of leprosy. Someone was needed to take command and the Patriarch had come to England, seeking funds, seeking support – seeking a king.

Henry had sworn to go on crusade in atonement for his role in the death of Archbishop Thomas Becket, but had no intention of taking up the Patriarch's request. In the interests of diplomacy he had said he would yield his kingdom and depart for Jerusalem if his barons agreed that he should go. He had ensured that their reply was a refusal but had been most accommodating to the disappointed Patriarch, giving him leave to recruit funding and men wherever he could.

'To what do I owe the pleasure of this visit?' Alienor dismissed Belbel and poured Henry wine herself. 'Did you decide to check up on my activities late at night to see if I had taken a lover?' She gave him a sardonic smile. 'Or are you here to complain to me of Richard again?'

'Oh, both of those,' he replied in the same tone she had used to him and sat down on her bed, rubbing his leg.

Alienor eyed him covertly. If he needed bodily comfort there were accommodating women at court, so this was something more. She brought him wine and refreshed her own cup. 'Here,' she said. 'At least the wine in my chamber is decent.'

He made a derisive sound, but took a long drink before resting the goblet on his good leg and scrubbing his other hand over his face. 'John is begging me to let him go to Outremer and take up the crown of Jerusalem. He went to see the Patriarch behind my back and announced to him that he was ready to serve.'

Alienor was astonished. 'John go to Jerusalem?' The notion of their eighteen-year-old son ruling the holiest land in Christendom from the centre of the world itself was preposterous. She understood now why Henry had come to her. There was ambition, and then there was desperate ambition – anything to soar above his brothers. 'What did the Patriarch say?'

Henry's mouth twisted. 'That it was good to see at least one of the family had a conscience and a sense of responsibility, and that he would think seriously about accepting him. Which goes to show that either he is completely desperate or an idiot.'

'Or trying to force your hand.'

'If so he is trifling with the wrong man. I told him it was impossible, but I would help him financially where I could, and that is all he will have from me.'

'And John – have you told him your decision?'

Henry rubbed his beard. 'Yes, and dealt with the tears and recriminations, but he saw reason in the end. I suspect he never really thought I would agree. Give him ten years and he might be up to the task, but he still has too much to learn and he is not sufficiently mature.'

'And yet you would have him govern Aquitaine?' Alienor said acidly.

'That would have been different. He would have had my skill and advice to call upon. In Jerusalem he would be on his own and out of reach.'

'Would have been?' Alienor asked sharply. 'Are you then considering removing him from the rule of Aquitaine? Have you seen the folly of your ways at last?'

Henry scowled at her, but more from habit than serious intent. 'No,' he said. 'I have seen the folly of Richard's and

I will have no more of it. We must come to terms with each other; this cannot continue.'

'The remedy lies in your hands. Only you can put a stop to it.'

'That's why I came to talk to you tonight.'

Alienor sat down facing him. She tucked her hair behind her ears and saw him follow the gesture with a glint in his eye – perhaps remembering distant times when they had been allies and lovers. Long ago in a very different place. 'Well then, tell me.'

'I am giving John the opportunity to prove himself worthy of government without recourse to battling with Richard or wading out of his depth in Outremer. I am sending him to Ireland where he may test his wings without doing too much damage. It is far enough removed to give him autonomy, but sufficiently close for me to keep an eye on him. I will knight him at Easter, and then he will go. I shall make sure he is accompanied by some good men and we shall see.'

Alienor was thoughtful. It seemed a good solution in many ways, and she was relieved that her sons would no longer be squabbling over Aquitaine, yet she was uneasy. 'What does John say?'

Henry shrugged. 'He would rather Jerusalem and he would rather Aquitaine, but I told him that with Ireland he has a chance to prove himself. It may well be the making of him, and it will keep him out of mischief. He can settle down and not be in competition with his brothers.'

'There is that.' Alienor sipped her wine. 'So you will let Richard govern Aquitaine in peace, and see that he and Geoffrey are reconciled.'

'I did not say that.' Henry plucked at his beard. 'Richard has overstepped all bounds. He disobeys me and constantly rebels against my will. I cannot allow it to continue so I am recalling him.'

His face had set in an expression Alienor knew well. Pugilistic, brooking no challenge.

175

'And then what? Do you truly think he will come?'

'Oh yes.' A tight smile pushed his cheeks upwards. 'He will have no choice, because you are going to demand that he returns Aquitaine to you forthwith. You shall have all your rights in your duchy restored. If Richard declines, you will have no choice but to take it from him by force.' His grey eyes were flinty. 'If he yields, his succession to Aquitaine is immediately confirmed, and he can rest secure in the knowledge that his beloved mother has had her just rights restored. Naturally as her husband, it is my duty to administer them, and meanwhile John will be occupied in Ireland and no longer a threat.'

'You snake!' She wanted to gag with revulsion.

'And you, madam, are a viper, so that makes us a match. You will cooperate. I am not removing Richard's rule. He will still deputise in Aquitaine, but on a much tighter rein. I will have obedience from my sons and from my wife.'

'Obedience perhaps,' she retorted, 'but never respect and never love. I do not say this to be perverse, even though you think it of me. You breed hate and envy in your sons. You give John Aquitaine and then take it from him. How does he truly feel about that even if he smiles and obeys you to your face? You dishonour all Richard's striving in Aquitaine and try to hand it to your youngest son who is not yet knighted. Now though you withdraw it, the damage is done. This new ploy of yours – yes, it will bring Richard to kneel at your feet, but by force not filial devotion. And having fettered him you will threaten him with Geoffrey, thinking to keep both in hand, but they will curse you for it.'

Henry drained his wine. 'Richard will come and he will yield his rights to you.' He bit the words out. 'And John shall go to Ireland. Geoffrey will devote himself to Brittany and Normandy as my governor.'

'And as Duchess of Aquitaine am I free to come and go as I choose?' Alienor shook her head before he could reply. 'No. You will let me sanction a few charters, grant favours here and there, make donations to a few monasteries and convents, but hoard the rest to yourself. Am I allowed to return to Poitiers? I think not.'

'You know why I cannot do that – as you know everything else.' He stood up and so did she, so that she faced him, close enough to touch. 'You may continue to live your life within the parameters you already have. You shall have money to buy what you require for daily comfort and to do good works that befit a queen. You shall have visitors to enliven your life—'

'Of your choosing.'

'That goes without saying, but within my tolerance you shall have room to breathe.'

'Henry, whatever you do, you stifle the breath in my body,' Alienor said with weary contempt. 'Do you have any more to say to me, or have you finished? Doubtless your latest mistress awaits. How old is she this time?'

He returned her smile and leaned over to brush her cheek with his lips. 'Younger than you,' he murmured, 'and a thousand times more amenable.'

'That is because she has everything to gain and I have nothing left to lose,' Alienor retorted.

'Oh, I wouldn't say that.' He bowed to her and departed, limping on his bad leg, but his step was still forceful.

'Mama.'

Alienor extended her hand and Richard knelt to kiss the ducal ring that had belonged to their forefathers for generations. Earlier he had surrendered both it and Aquitaine to his mother in a formal ceremony before the whole court, but now he had come to her to speak informally. They both still wore their full regalia. Richard's tunic of green cendal sparkled with gold thread and Alienor's damask gown caught the light each time she moved.

She stooped to give him the kiss of peace, and having twisted the ring from her finger, presented it to him. 'All that has changed are the formalities. When you return to Poitiers, I command you to wear this as your right.'

He rose and bowed before slipping the ring into the pouch at his belt. 'At least my father has changed his mind about giving Aquitaine to John, but God help the brat in Ireland – or perhaps God help the Irish.'

'Now,' she admonished gently. 'Whatever happens, John will learn valuable lessons.' She rested her hand on his arm. 'I am sorry to lose you, but you must hasten to Poitou.'

'I intend to, Mama. Only my concern for your well-being would hold me here.' His lips curled. 'I do not choose to be his dog on a leash.'

'Do not worry about me,' she said. 'I have weathered much worse. Since your father has restored Aquitaine to me, it is in his interests to keep me in good health and well provided for, because it is not his desire to have you Duke of Aquitaine in your own right.'

He nodded in wry acknowledgement. 'You know that Philippe is pushing for me to marry Alais.'

'Yes, I have heard, but it will not happen. Your father excels at procrastinating and making promises he has no intention of honouring. It does not suit his policies to have you marry Alais, no matter how much Philippe cavils. Let him bear that weight.'

Richard rubbed the back of his neck. 'There are new rumours about my father and Alais.' He looked away, watching Amiria and Belbel who were quietly lighting the candles and closing the shutters as the spring light faded to dusk.

'Yes, and I do not wish to know if they are true; but their existence plays into your hands. Should it come to the point where you are forced to wed, you have a perfect reason to refuse. To use it now would be a waste. It is a last resort, but you know you have it.'

His gaze returned to her, his blue eyes guarded. 'You are wise, Mama.'

'The price of experience,' she said. 'I wish I had been wiser when I was younger.'

* * *

In the morning, Richard departed for Poitiers, the ducal ring tucked under his shirt on a silk cord. He had already made his personal farewells to Alienor, and in the courtyard under the scrutiny of all, their leave-taking was formal and circumspect. The farewell between Richard and his father was cool and a matter of business with courtesy on both sides, but challenge and tension surging beneath.

Matilda and Heinrich were leaving too, and were travelling with Richard until they were beyond Alençon's city walls. Alienor bade farewell to her daughter with tears in her eyes; she had grown accustomed to her dear company and she suspected they would not meet again. Twenty years ago she had said goodbye to a brave little girl going to her match with Heinrich of Saxony. Alienor had not thought to see her again in this lifetime and in a way that expectation had been fulfilled because the child was now a grown woman with offspring of her own, a woman who spoke German more easily than French and had her own opinions and ways. But a new knowing had grown, together with a different love, deep and appreciative.

Alienor strove to remain regal and calm despite the painful intensity of this parting but inside she was weeping. Richenza stood pale and solemn at Alienor's side with her brother Otto while a nurse jiggled little Wilhelm in her arms. Matilda and Heinrich had decided that Richenza would remain behind with her grandmother; she was already of marriageable age and a suitable alliance would be found for her at the Angevin court. Her brother Heinri was returning with them, but Otto, Lothar and Wilhelm would remain here until the situation in Germany became better known.

'Be good for your grandmother,' Matilda instructed the children, and swallowed painfully. 'Remember your manners, attend to your lessons, and write to me often.'

'Yes, Mama, I promise,' Richenza curtseyed, while Otto and Lothar bowed most properly.

Matilda's chin dimpled. 'Be brave. I trust you, and you have my love always, remember that.' Abruptly she turned her mount and rode towards the gate.

Alienor's heart bled for her daughter because she knew precisely how she felt.

Heinrich smiled at the children, spoke to them swiftly in German, and gruffly clearing his throat, reined away to join Richard who was waiting for him. Heinri, buoyant with a sense of adventure, waved cheerfully over his shoulder to his siblings.

Once they were gone, Alienor retired to her chamber with the children and pursued her normal routine, as if it was just another day. The nurse dealt with Wilhelm, while Otto and Lothar went off to their lessons with some other boys, leaving Richenza and Alienor to work on an altar front they were sewing.

'Some of these stitches are Mama's.' Richenza touched them with a light forefinger. A solitary tear rolled down her cheek.

Alienor hugged her. 'And they will always be there as a reminder, but it is for us to finish now.' She indicated a wall hanging covering the shutters. 'Your mother's stitches are in that one also, made when she was just a little girl before she left England to marry your father. I thought on them often after she went to Saxony.' She stroked her granddaughter's damp cheek. 'There is much of her in you, and I know all will be well.'

She lowered her hand, picked up a needle and began to sew. After a moment, Richenza followed suit.

22

Fortress of Domfront, Christmas 1185

The December morning dawned bitterly cold, and the early sun that rose in silvery light from a bed of misty oyster-shell gradually disappeared behind a bank of thickening cloud.

Snow flurried in the wind, making Alienor glad she had decided not to go riding; however she did not feel like sitting by the fire. Cooped up within the keep at Domfront where the court was spending Christmas, she felt restless and apprehensive. The enclosing walls and long, gloomy days reminded her of her confinement at Sarum and the cold, comfortless stretches of time when she had dwelt in darkness interspersed by short grey moments of winter daylight.

Uttering a short huff of impatience, she wrapped herself in her fur-lined cloak and, after leaving the chamber, climbed the twisting stairs to the battlements.

The air was so cold that it hurt to breathe, but she inhaled strongly all the same, because it was better than the smell of smoke and sickness within. They should have returned to England for Christmas; indeed the ships had arrived to bear them across the Narrow Sea, but Henry's old leg wound had flared up, leaving him febrile, weak and unable to travel. The ships had returned to England bearing orders and messages, and Henry was recuperating here at Domfront, planning to sail as soon as he was well. He had been so sick that for a time Alienor had wondered if he was going to survive, but he had rallied on Christmas Eve, and improved steadily since then.

Richenza arrived at her side, slightly breathless from her climb. Her dark green cloak was lined with rich auburn squirrel fur that matched the colour of her hair. Her face was rapidly losing its puppy flesh, exposing wide, high cheekbones, a delicate nose, and a determined jaw. She had grown too, and Alienor no longer had to look down to speak to her. Earlier in the summer she had experienced the first bleed of her womanhood.

'I saw you climbing the stairs, Grandmère, and I wondered if you were all right.'

Alienor smiled. 'Indeed, that was thoughtful of you. Perhaps you were also a little curious to wonder what an old lady was doing climbing the steps to the battlements?'

Richenza looked scandalised. 'You are not old, Grandmère!'

Alienor laughed. 'No, but I have still lived a long time compared with your tender years. When I was your age I was Queen of France and living in Paris. I would often climb to the top of the Grand Tower to escape from my husband and my mother-in-law.' She gave a faraway smile. 'Of course the view was very different – a great city, heaving with people, and the river coiling around us like a silver snake.'

'Who were you escaping from this time?' Richenza's gaze was perceptive, for a girl of her years.

'I was avoiding my thoughts,' Alienor said. 'I know we carry them with us always, but some things revive memories best forgotten and make them intense. I needed to breathe fresh air for a little while.'

Glancing down on the courtyard she saw that Henry too had left his chamber and was hobbling around the ward using a walking stick. Otto and Lothar, cloaked and hooded, were accompanying him on his perambulation, and so were a couple of dogs. Every so often the boys would throw a ball for the dogs to chase, all the time chattering to their grandsire. At one point she heard Henry's laugh ring out, clear and strong above the children's fluting voices. Henry related so well to small children, she thought, but the moment they began to turn into adults he perceived them as a challenge to his authority. He clearly doted on his grandsons and they on him. The same went for his bastard son William, and John's boy Richard, and it saddened her to know through his own actions he would eventually lose those fond attachments.

The snow started to fall harder. Henry took a turn around the courtyard and then hobbled back inside, giving his grandsons into the care of an attendant. Bitter air knifed through a gap in Alienor's cloak and she shivered. Glancing at Richenza, she noticed how pale she had become although her lips were startlingly red. 'Come, it is too cold. We should go back to the fire.'

As they turned from the battlements, Alienor glimpsed several riders arriving at the gate, their cloaks colourful against the bleached hues of the winter day. There were soldiers among them clad in the gleam of mail shirts. Alienor narrowed her eyes, wondering who was paying a visit, and thinking that at least they had outridden the snowstorm flurrying at their heels.

The women lost sight of the party as the men entered the outer defences, but an instant later the riders reappeared on the other side. She gazed at the young man dismounting from an iron-grey palfrey. His cloak was of a blue so dark it was almost black. 'John.' Her whisper was scarcely louder than her breath. He was supposed to be in Ireland, and the sight of him here at Domfront filled her with surprise and trepidation. 'It's your uncle John,' she told Richenza. 'We had better go and find out why he is here.'

Alienor entered Henry's chamber and crossed to the fireside where her husband sat with his bad leg propped upon a footstool. Fine beads of sweat dewed his forehead and he was clearly suffering. John, who had just risen from paying his respects to him, turned and knelt to her.

'My lady mother.'

Alienor stooped and kissed his icy cheek. 'This is a surprise. I thought you were keeping Christmas in Dublin.'

Henry made a harsh sound of disgust and struck his fist on his good thigh. 'And so he would have, had he not squandered his opportunities and behaved like an errant child.'

Alienor was jolted by surprise; it was highly unusual for Henry to castigate John. She noticed he was clutching a piece of parchment, its edges trembling as his hand shook.

'It was not my fault,' John answered, flushing. 'I did not have enough resources, and the men you entrusted to serve me gave me bad advice and let me down. I had no choice but to return.'

'And did they also advise you to scorn the Irish chieftains?' Henry demanded. 'To pull their beards and behave in the manner of a foolish drunken boy if I am to believe this?' He raised the crumpled parchment in his fist. 'At whose feet does that blame lie, my son?'

'The Irish are heathen savages,' John said with a sulky scowl. 'They worship stones and eat horse flesh and live like beasts. They had no respect for me. You do not know what it was like.'

'Hah, I know perfectly well what it was like,' Henry retorted. 'I was there ten years ago, and I comported myself like a king, which is what I expected of you, not this childish folly. You seriously disappoint me.'

'Do I have your leave to go?' John asked mutinously.

Henry wiped his brow. 'No,' he snapped, 'I have not finished. I know you, John. You are the one most like me, the son dearest to my heart, and that makes my disappointment keener because I know you can do better.' He picked up his wine with a shaky hand. 'I know you wanted Aquitaine. I know you wanted Jerusalem and had to make do with Ireland instead. But it was a testing ground. I never intended to dump you there and forget you – I hope you know that, and I hope you understand why I could not give you the other things.'

John stared at his father like a young wolf eyeing a mangy pack leader and debating whether to dare a challenge or back down.

'If you thought by your behaviour to express your displeasure, then you have misjudged me. As soon as the weather improves, you will return to Ireland with what you need to finish the task. I can forgive you the one mistake, but you must make good on the rest. Do I make myself clear?'

John clenched his jaw. 'Yes, Papa.'

'Good. Then come kiss me and go and settle yourself and we shall speak again later.'

John dutifully kissed his father's cheek and Henry slid his arm around John's neck for a moment, drawing him close.

'I want to be proud of you,' he said.

'And I swear I will make you proud, Papa,' John replied. His attitude had changed on the moment from defensive to dutiful, but Alienor wondered how much was a front.

When he had gone, Henry slumped in the chair and closed his eyes.

'I will send for your physician,' Alienor said.

'No.' Henry forced his lids open. 'There is no need. I am tired, that is all.'

'Perhaps now you can see why it was not a good idea to give John Aquitaine.'

Henry struggled upright against the chair cushions. 'And perhaps one of the reasons John did not do so well in Ireland was that his heart was not in it.'

'Or that he was far enough away from home to do as he pleased.'

'Well he knows now that he may not,' Henry said testily. He gathered himself and rose to his feet, but the effort left him grey and shaking, and Alienor summoned his physician anyway, deriving a certain satisfaction from overriding him, and for all that he complained that she was meddling, for once she had the full support of the courtiers.

Henry's relapse further delayed their return to England, and he spent the rest of the winter and early spring in Normandy. As he clawed his way to recovery, he found time to meet with Philippe, the Young King of France, and promised him that he would make the marriage of Richard and Alais his first priority the instant he returned from his delayed visit to England.

By April, Henry was well enough to make plans to take ship at the end of the month. But first he embarked on a hunting expedition with his barons at his park of Lyons la Forêt in north Normandy, his first such excursion since the late autumn.

Alienor was sewing in her chamber with her women when a squire brought her news that William Marshal had ridden in and was requesting an audience. Her heart leaped and she commanded the youth to bring William to her immediately. Another squire was sent for fresh wine and a platter of pastries and wafers.

She waited, a strange mingling of anxiety and anticipation settling upon her after her initial spark of joy. She had often thought of William on his journey and prayed that he would accomplish his mission, but she had not known if he would return. Indeed she had even thought that if he survived, he might choose to remain in Outremer.

'Who is William Marshal?' Richenza asked curiously.

Alienor turned to her granddaughter. Of course she would not know. 'Many years ago when he was a young knight in the service of the Earl of Salisbury, he saved me from ambush, perhaps even death, when I was in Poitou. He was captured during the attack and later I paid his ransom and took him into my household. He became marshal to your uncle Henry, and when he died, undertook to lay his cloak on the tomb of Christ's Sepulchre in Jerusalem – that is where he returns from now. He has my trust and friendship, and you know I do not give those things lightly.'

The squire returned, William following in his wake, and Alienor went forward to greet him, one hand extended.

'Madam.' William Marshal dropped to his knees. Taking her hand, he pressed his lips to her ring. 'My liege lady.'

His deep brown hair was tipped with the gold of hotter climes and his skin wore the Outremer tint of a recently returned crusader. He had knelt to her smoothly – he was still lithe – and although there was a new gravitas about him, his former spark still glowed in the depths, even if it was tempered by exhaustion.

Pressure increased behind her eyes, almost tears, but her voice was firm and strong. 'William! Welcome back. It is so good to see you.'

'And you, madam, are a pleasing sight for travel-weary eyes,' he replied with the gallantry she remembered. 'Of all the fair women I saw between here and Jerusalem, there were none to match the Queen of England.'

'Ever the flatterer.' She gestured him to his feet before directing a squire to pour him wine.

'Madam, it is the truth. You will only ever receive truth from me.'

'Then I must believe you, for even the King says that William Marshal does not know how to tell a lie.'

He took the wine, and stared into it as if it were an unfamiliar object.

'You may drink it and not be worried; it is for my personal use. I refuse to touch the vinegar that my husband forces everyone else to swallow.'

'Then in that case, to your health, madam,' he toasted with a forced smile.

Alienor resumed her seat behind her tapestry frame and gestured him to a cushioned stool facing her. 'I truly wondered if I would see you again.' Her throat tightened. 'I thought you might be like all the other people in my life who have died or gone away – who live in my memory and nowhere else.'

'Never that, madam,' he said ruefully. 'There were times when I did indeed think I would die, there were many perilous hardships, but with God's help I won through.'

She fell silent while she composed herself. 'Jerusalem,' she said eventually. 'Tell me about it.'

He took another swallow of wine, cleared his throat and began to recount his journey. She could sense he was not telling her everything and that there were difficult personal areas he was keeping to himself, but she did not press him.

'My young lord has been acknowledged by the keepers of the Sepulchre and his cloak accepted,' he said. 'They pray for him daily, as do I. I have done my utmost for his soul's release, and I pray that he is with God and Our Lord Jesus Christ in heaven and that it is as you would wish.' The look he gave her shone with tears but was direct and powerful. 'I have done what I strove to do. Amen.'

'Your service will never be requited.' Her own eyes were full. 'But I love you for it, and I will do all in my power to help and advance you now you have returned.'

He inclined his head, thanking her without words because he had reached the end of speech. With a quick motion he wiped his eyes.

'Have you spoken to the King?'

'No, madam. I am told he is still out with the hunt, but when he returns I shall go to him too and make my report.'

'I will speak with him and make sure he gives you due acknowledgement for what you have done.' She saw the exhaustion in him, even though he was bearing up well. The moment he stopped he would collapse, she was certain. 'The King plans to return to England very soon. You shall stay at court and travel with us as our guest before you resume your duties.'

He smiled, and his expression relaxed. 'Indeed madam, it will be a pleasure.'

When William had gone, she looked at the gifts he had brought her. There was a rock crystal phial containing water from the River Jordan, a spindle weight made from the clay of the Garden of Eden, and a marvellous little object fashioned from a piece of exquisitely carved ivory. It looked like a needle case, but there was a slit in it and inside, wrapped around a spindle, was a length of silk ribbon that told the story of the raising of Lazarus from the dead. Richenza was awestruck and thought it the most remarkable thing she had ever seen, and Alienor's heart overflowed with warmth towards William for his thoughtfulness.

Henry arrived as she was putting the items away in her personal coffer. There was little evidence of his limp now, just a hint as he crossed the room to her. She wondered if William had brought him anything from Jerusalem.

'So,' he said. 'I understand that the Marshal has already paid his respects to you.'

'You were away at the hunt when he arrived. I offered him our hospitality and he spoke to me of our son and what he had done for him at the Sepulchre.'

Henry grunted and turned to pace the room, clear evidence that his energy was almost back to normal.

'I hope you intend to reward him for his service.'

'I have already done so,' he replied. 'I never expected to

see him again, but since he has returned, he should indeed be acknowledged for his diligence and loyalty. I have given him custody of Heloise of Kendal. She will make him a good wife should he choose to marry her, and bring him enough land on which to live. I've given him the wardship of William of Earley's boy too. That will bring him more revenue and give him a youngster to train up to manhood.'

Alienor eyed him with surprise bordering on disbelief. 'I would have thought you would give him more, and not so far away from the court.'

Henry shrugged. 'He has not been at court for many years and I have managed without him. I may need him in the future but this will keep him occupied for now. Let him settle to ordinary toil and then we shall see.'

'You have greater heiresses in your wardship. Does he not merit one of them?'

Henry snorted. 'I have no intention of handing one of them over to an adventurer newly returned from pilgrimage.' He wagged his finger at her. 'I do not want you interfering, is that understood? I know he is one of your pets.'

'You disparage him, ' she said angrily. 'There are very few men of his calibre; you should do your utmost to bring him into your affinity, never mind mine, especially after what he did for our son in Jerusalem. You could have been more generous, but perhaps it is not within you.'

'Good Christ, woman!' he snapped. 'I have given him land of his own, the wherewithal to make a family and a profitable wardship. I do not call that ungenerous. He could have returned to nothing. Indeed, I could make him nothing just like this.' He clapped his hands together, making a loud report.

Alienor lifted her chin. 'Indeed, as you see fit – sire.' Argument was pointless and might lead to difficulties for William. At least he had returned from the dangers of Outremer to tell his tale, and Henry had given him a reward of sorts. It would have to suffice.

23

Woodstock, August 1186

The court spent the long, hot days of summer at the Royal Palace of Woodstock. Henry had allowed Alienor to remain with the domestic household and had not mentioned a return to Sarum. Every letter she sent, every charter she witnessed was vetted either by him or one of his representatives, but she had some leeway in domestic areas. She had grandchildren to instruct, clergy to entertain, and visiting baronial wives for company. Henry had loosened her fetters, but she was well aware that the slightest move in a political direction would immediately curtail her liberties.

One afternoon she went to take her leisure in the garden with her women and enjoy the blooms. Her daughter Joanna had sent roses from Sicily, bearing flowers of rich, deep red striated with cream and gold – bounteous, sensuous blooms that reminded Alienor of the southern courts of her youth but set amid moist English greenery. A clear stream rippled through the garden from its natural spring source, and the children played in it, splashing each other and squealing.

Sitting at Alienor's side, Isabel de Warenne watched one particular small boy, a haunted look in her eyes. Alienor followed the direction of her gaze to young Richard FitzJohn who was deeply absorbed in sailing a toy ship on the water while telling himself a long, involved story about the people voyaging on her.

'Our grandson is a fine little boy,' Alienor remarked.

'Indeed he is,' Isabel replied stiffly.

Alienor had not seen Isabel for a while and there was constraint between them. The child had united them in blood, but driven them apart in other ways. Isabel would always hold John culpable for what had happened to Belle, and Alienor thought Belle less of an innocent led astray than her parents wanted to believe. There was guilt and there was blame, coupled with a deep sadness that they could never go back to how it was before.

Richard was joined by Will, Henry's bastard son. He too had a small boat to sail down the stream, and soon the boys were engrossed in their play.

'How is Belle?' Alienor asked. 'Has she settled into marriage?'

'Her husband is good to her and she is a dutiful wife,' Isabel replied neutrally.

'And Hamelin?'

Isabel gave a small shrug. 'It is hard to tell. He speaks to Belle now, but he has lost his trust in her, and that, as you say about the past, can never be restored. He has lost his trust in me too . . .' She bit her lip and turned her head.

Alienor watched Hamelin pick his way across the garden towards their seat. As he and Henry had aged, they had come to resemble each other more closely, and for an instant she had thought the stocky man with dusty gold hair and green tunic was her husband. Certainly his dour expression was reminiscent of Henry.

'Madam, the King seeks you,' he said without preamble. 'There is news from Paris.'

Alienor's heart plummeted. For Hamelin to fetch her it was important, and not good to judge from his expression. Feeling cold despite the intense heat of the day, she set her sewing aside and stood up, beckoning Isabel to accompany her.

The women followed Hamelin back through the garden, the scent of roses cloying now in the hot air and the chatter of the courtiers no more than the meaningless twitter of sparrows.

Henry was in his chamber, sitting in the chair from which he conducted business, but he was hunched over, as if someone had knocked half the life from his body. One hand covered his brow and eyes, the other gripped his midriff. A dark-robed priest stood at the side of his chair, and beyond him stood a messenger holding a chestnut and white spaniel on a short leash – Moysi.

'What has happened?' Alienor demanded.

Henry slowly lowered his hand and fixed her with a dull, red-rimmed stare. 'Geoffrey is dead.' The words fell like stones. 'Trampled to death at a tourney in Paris.'

Alienor stared. 'No,' she said. 'No.' Her gaze flicked to the others in the room and she saw the grim faces, the looks that dared not convey pity. 'How?'

'A blow to the head, madam, from a rearing horse,' said the priest. 'He was only wearing his coif at the time. The King of France was distraught – such a tragedy. I am deeply sorry.'

The words entered her brain like echoes in a cavern. 'He can't be dead, it is impossible. What was he doing in Paris? Why would he go there?'

'What my sons usually do when left to their own devices,' Henry said in a rusty voice. 'Plotting. Why would he go there for any other reason?'

'Madam, he has been buried with all honour in the new cathedral in Notre Dame,' the priest added. 'Before the high altar, and honoured by King Philippe who has granted four chaplains to the cathedral for the sake of the Count of Brittany's soul.'

Henry jerked to his feet and strode into the shaft of light streaming through the window, but with no more purpose than movement itself. 'And since the souls of those who tourney are damned, is it likely that he was there in Paris to joust at all? Why is he buried before the high altar if that was how he met his end? There is more to this than a simple tale of sport gone awry. I have no doubt he was in Paris for reasons far more nefarious than a tourney. Perhaps I should rejoice – do you think?' He swung round, and now his eyes were no longer dull but piercingly bright and raw with pain.

The hollow feeling inside Alienor became a cavern. The

ground rushed up to meet her, and as her knees buckled she heard Isabel's cry of consternation and felt Hamelin grab her and take her weight. Together they helped her to a bench and Isabel put her arms around her.

'Oh, my dear, I am so, so sorry,' she whispered. 'So very sorry.'

Alienor shuddered. 'Is there nothing I can do?' she whispered. 'One by one I have borne them, and one by one they die. How am I to bear this?'

'Lean on God,' Isabel attempted, to comfort her. 'Pray to Him and He will succour you.'

'After He has wrought this on me?'

Alienor tried to shrug herself free, but Isabel held her tightly.

'God is not to blame. There are moments when I have grieved to the limit of my endurance, but always there has been an answer, or a branch to grasp. Truly. Come, I will pray with you in vigil.'

The next hours passed in dark limbo for Alienor. She went with Isabel to pray because it was the path of least resistance, and in a way the chapel was a sanctuary, a comforting blanket around her. She could bow her head, say prayers for Geoffrey's soul, and not have to interact with anyone.

Isabel knelt at her side, praying quietly without intruding, and whatever the differences that had crept up between them in the last few years, Alienor was glad of her presence now. She had once snapped at Isabel that she would never understand the role of a queen, and that still held true, but Isabel did understand the riptide of grief for beloved family members taken untimely and would genuinely share her grief. Henry would not come near, she knew, because to him death was a devouring monster he could not defeat, and thus to be ignored, as if by doing so he could negate its power. Yet to ignore it was to acknowledge its existence, and one day it would come for him.

* * *

Hamelin left Henry in the first light of a summer dawn and stumbled through the palace towards his own chamber. The light was muted grey in the moment before sunrise and the birdsong was a hymn to the new day and all the glorious business of living in the moment. The night had been one of black and bitter rage as Henry paced his room in a fury like the demon from whom he was reputed to be descended, or else sat on a stool with his head in his hands, the silence so thick that it could be cut with a knife. That had been his vigil for Geoffrey while all the sordid details had been dragged out in the open like entrails from a corpse.

Geoffrey and Philippe of France had been secretly planning an uprising against Henry. Geoffrey wanted his share of the family patrimony and felt he had been dismissed in favour of Richard and John. The astute young French king had carefully nurtured Geoffrey's grudges until the sore spot had become a swollen abscess, which would have erupted full blown had not Geoffrey died on an airless Paris night – either of tourney wounds or sickness it mattered not now because the truth was out.

Henry had still been awake when Hamelin left, lying on his back staring at the rafters as the room filled with the dawn. He had dismissed his brother, telling him to get some rest, but first he wanted him to send a messenger to recall John from the coast where he was awaiting a fair wind to return to Ireland.

'Bring him back,' he said. 'I have few sons left to me, and I would not see my last hope drown.'

Having roused and instructed the scribes, Hamelin had turned towards his own chamber and suddenly checked as he encountered a small, spindle-legged wraith wearing a linen shirt and braies and trailing a well-worn square of blanket behind him. Hamelin stared at his grandson, Richard, a child he had tried to ignore, but it was difficult when the boy was constantly under his nose at Woodstock. He was aware of Isabel's silent, wounded reproach, but she did not appreciate how difficult it was for him to accept this child whose existence had ruined his notion of a perfect family. He looked round but there was no sign of a nursemaid.

'What are you doing out here, child?' he demanded brusquely. 'Where's your nurse?'

'Sleeping, sire.' Richard looked up at him out of wide blue eyes. 'The door was open and I was hungry.' He hitched his blanket scrap under his arm and tickled his nose with the end of it.

Hamelin gripped his belt and looked stern. 'So you thought you'd find your way to the kitchens unaided, hmm?'

'I know where they are.'

Hamelin thought of Henry, lying in bed, staring at the ceiling, unable to process the grief that another son was dead but with the knowledge lying on him like a crushing weight. Meeting the fearless stare of this small boy, their joint grandson, something tore in his heart.

'Perhaps you do, but you should not be walking the corridors on your own when everyone else is asleep.' He extended his hand. 'Come, there is food in my chamber. I will send a squire to tell the women where you are.' Later he would have words with whoever had been lax enough to leave the nursery door open.

As the little hand folded around his, the tender pain in Hamelin's heart became almost unbearable. He remembered Belle's hand similarly clasped and how he had sworn to protect her from everything. He had failed, and this child was the result. Until now he had seen him as evidence of shame, but suddenly, with a different slant on the world, what he had seen as a blight on his family's life was actually a blessing.

He opened his chamber door and quietly entered. His chamberlain looked at him askance. Isabel emerged from the curtained-off sleeping area, robed in her chemise with a cloak draped over. Her hair hung to her waist in a dark and silver waterfall ready for plaiting. He saw the surprised, almost shocked expression on her face.

195

'Do we have anything for this little one to eat?' he asked. 'He says he's hungry.'

Isabel gestured distractedly to a white linen cloth mounded over a trestle. 'There is bread, cheese and meat. I had it brought not long ago.'

Hamelin lifted the cloth to reveal thick slices of cold bacon with a satisfying rim of fat, a goats' cheese the size of his clenched fist, two small loaves of bread and a jug of wine.

'I have honey water.' Isabel fetched a jug from the bedside. She poured a cup for the child, who bowed with very proper manners and thanked her.

'I found him wandering in search of food,' Hamelin told her. 'Someone had left the nursery door open. I suppose with the recent news matters are bound not to run to order.' He turned to his grandson. 'Come, what would you like?'

Richard decided on a portion of everything, and Hamelin sat down with him before the hearth, bare in the height of summer but still a focal point. He watched the little boy eat with gusto but with schooled manners, and realised how long it was since he had taken any notice of the everyday things that underpinned the great matters, and in truth made those great matters very small in comparison. He glanced at Isabel. In a moment she would realise her state of dishabille and retire to don all the trappings of a countess.

He gestured her to join them. 'Stay – if you will.'

She hesitated, and then inclined her head and sat down. With his new eyes he saw her lowered gaze and set lips. The silences between them were no longer companionable.

'I have already eaten,' she said, but poured herself a cup of honey water. 'You have not roused me, but caught me on my way to bed. I have just come from vigil with the Queen.'

'Ah, I had assumed . . .' He waved his hand. He had been so taken with his own concern that he had forgotten she would be with Alienor. 'How is she?'

'Grieving deeply.' Isabel's expression filled with pity. 'I do not know how she endures without going mad. I know I would.

196

Even to think . . .' She broke off and gently smoothed their grandson's dark golden hair. 'Every life is precious.' Her eyes met Hamelin's across Richard's head. 'What about Henry?'

'The same as Alienor, but you will not see it in him. Tomorrow it will be as though it has not happened because that is how he deals with these matters.'

'But there is a price to pay.'

'Yes, indeed,' Hamelin said bleakly. 'It leaves its mark on him. He is recalling John to his side; he is not to sail for Ireland now because of the changes.'

Her eyes lit up. 'That means William will be coming with him?'

'Yes.' Their son had been bound for Ireland with John and Hamelin knew the sea crossing had been preying on Isabel's mind. She found it hard to let Will go, although to her credit she tried to rein herself back. But still, the return of a son into the bosom of his family at a time like this was a powerful thing. As to John himself: time had dulled the edge of Hamelin's anger, and today's news had left him philosophical.

'Come,' he said to Richard who had cleared every morsel, even to dabbing up the crumbs on his forefinger. 'I need to sleep; so does your grandmother. It is time you returned to your nurse.'

'May I come again?' Richard asked.

Hamelin drew a deep breath, aware of Isabel's gaze fixed on him in hope. 'Yes,' he said to the child. 'You may visit as often as your grandmother desires. But bid her farewell for now.'

Richard flourished a perfect bow in Isabel's direction, thanked her for the food, and then turned to Hamelin. Taking his grandfather's hand, his gravitas was enlivened by a little hop and a skip.

Hamelin restored Richard to the women, admonished them about the open door, and made his way back to his chamber to snatch some sleep before Henry woke and asked for him.

'Did you mean that about him being permitted to come as often as he wanted?' Isabel asked as he removed his shoes.

'I would not have said so otherwise,' Hamelin said gruffly. 'He is a fine little boy, even if I cannot reconcile the circumstances of his birth, and I have been blind of late to other considerations.'

'And our daughter?'

He frowned and paused, unfastening his belt. 'Do not push me. I will come to it in my own time.'

'But if she were to visit on occasion?' Isabel bit her lip. 'You need not even be there.'

He hesitated, balanced on a precipice between still being angry and hurt enough to turn Belle away, but on the other hand having the courage to widen the tear in his heart and allow her to step inside it as the child had done. He could never trust as before; that part of him was bled out, but there were other areas that would heal – if he let them. There was a dark satisfaction in choosing to remain wounded; yet he had seen what happened to Henry when he cut himself off from love.

'Write to her. Tell her she may visit you at Conisbrough or Sandal or Acre, and I will not shun her.'

Isabel made a small sound, and then put one hand over her face. Her shoulders shook and she began to sob.

Hamelin felt a spurt of impatience, but mingled with it was guilty concern. 'Here now, I have given you what you asked for, no need for tears.' He put his arm around her and she leaned into him and wept.

Eventually Hamelin took her to the bed and lay down with her, folding himself around her as he had not done for a long time.

At last her crying eased and she lifted her head. 'It has been inside me for too long and all dammed up,' she sniffed. 'I had to let it go.'

He stroked her hair. 'I know, I know. Hush now, go to sleep. All is well.'

'Stay with me?'

Hamelin kissed her temple, her damp, salty cheek and lips. 'I am not going anywhere,' he said. 'Sleep.' He held and stroked her. Things could never be the same, but to be shown the light in the darkness was a wondrous gift from God and he was determined to follow it and find the path again.

24

Winchester Castle, April 1187

Eyes fixed intently on the piece of chicken Richenza was holding between her finger and thumb, Geoffrey's chestnut and white spaniel Moysi sat as he had been bade to do and licked his lips in anticipation.

'Paw,' commanded Richenza. The dog immediately proffered his foreleg, and whined. 'Good boy.' She tossed the meat and with an adept leap he caught it, gulped, and looked for more.

'You will make him fat,' Alienor warned, shaking her head but smiling. Richenza and Moysi had become inseparable ever since Alienor had brought him into her household. He went everywhere with the girl. When she rode out he shared her saddle and he slept at the foot of her bed, sprawled on his back in abandon, exposing his furry masculinity to the world.

'I won't. I'll take him for a long walk later I promise.' Richenza reached for another sliver of chicken.

Alienor looked fondly at her granddaughter who was almost sixteen years old. She was robust and active, with a mane of fox-red ringlets and alluring sea-blue eyes. Her features were even and regular and her smile lit up her entire face. Several nobles were vying for her hand, the forerunner being Geoffrey, heir to Rotrou, Count of Perche, but negotiations were at a delicate stage and might yet come to nothing.

Alienor was about to go and see if her scribe had finished writing out a charter gifting a monastery with several fields and a mill when a messenger arrived. As usual Moysi rushed to greet him, making himself into a much bigger dog by stretching on his hind legs and taking the opportunity to sniff the man's satchel in hope. Richenza hastened to pull her pet away by his red leather collar. Thus far his training had not developed further than begging for food.

'Madam, there is news from Brittany.' The messenger bent his knee and handed her a letter. 'The Duchess Constance has been safely delivered of a son.'

Alienor took the letter and looked at the seal, which was Henry's; the news had come first to him. She opened the parchment and unfolded it, but the writing was too small and she gave it to Richenza to read.

The wording was formal and contained the basic bones of detail. When Geoffrey had died last August, his young wife had been newly with child, and that child now born was a son.

'He's been christened Arthur,' Richenza said, glancing up from the letter.

An emotive name with strong connotations of Breton individuality. A male heir for Brittany also meant another male player in the line of succession. The lawyers would argue whether he should follow Richard or John, but it still put this newborn boy very close to the throne.

Alienor commanded Belbel to bring a flagon of the best Gascon wine. 'We should toast your new cousin's birth.'

'And your new grandchild,' Richenza said with wary eyes as she tried to gauge Alienor's response to the news.

'Yes.' Alienor's smile masked her pain. 'It grieves me deeply that his father is not here to welcome him into the world, but at least a part of him survives. We must give thanks to God, and you can help me choose gifts to send to Constance and the little one.' She tested his name in her mind again. Arthur. It felt uncomfortable – a challenge, although she understood why the baby had not been called Henry or William or Richard.

* * *

Alienor settled her new gyrfalcon on her wrist. The young bird was still fresh to her training and she danced on Alienor's glove, bating her wings and crying harshly. Her name was English – Snowit, and her breast feathers did indeed gleam like freshly fallen snow, while her wings were mottled with flint-grey speckles like winter granite, and her eyes were obsidian mirrors.

'Are you ready?' she asked Richenza, who was reining her chestnut palfrey around with an accomplished hand.

'Yes, Grandmère.' Richenza smiled and patted Moysi, who was perched on her saddle.

They rode out over the Downs with their escort, and Alienor enjoyed the breeze in her face, fresh and invigorating. The September day was fine and crisp and even though the nights were shortening and autumn lay close, the world still clung to the last of summer.

Alienor flung Snowit from her grip and watched her spread her wings and fly low, hugging the contours of the grasses, her flecked mantle a camouflage as she sought the soft grey partridge amid the windswept grasses.

'Your grandsire's gyrfalcon once took a crane,' Alienor told Richenza. 'They fought in mid-air for all to see and fell to the ground together, and when the riding party came upon them, they discovered that the falcon had killed the crane with her talons, but the crane had stabbed the falcon in her breast with her long beak and both were dead. Everyone marvelled at the sight, but grieved the loss of the falcon.'

Snowit startled a small flock of partridge into flight, chose her prey, and brought the bird down in a clean strike. Alienor's falconer ran forward to remove the kill that the gyrfalcon was mantling with her spread wings. Tying the dead partridge to his belt, he returned Snowit to Alienor's glove. She stroked her, crooned her praise and once again launched her aloft.

'Would you ever pit her against a crane?' Richenza asked.

'I would,' Alienor replied, 'but not until she has gained experience. She has youth and strength, but judgement and wisdom still await.'

'Perhaps people are like that too, Grandmère.'

Alienor chuckled. 'You may be right, my dear. I have often thought how much more I could have accomplished if I could have had wisdom and judgement at the same time as my youth and beauty.'

'But you still have your beauty, Grandmère, and you are strong.'

Snowit made another kill, blood spattering her pristine feathers.

'Beauty of the flesh is fleeting – like springtime it is gone in a season.'

'But autumn is beautiful too, and winter – the season doesn't matter,' Richenza argued, her face rosy and earnest.

'Ah, you are indeed sage beyond your years.' Alienor's smile was wry. 'I was going to add that indeed I am strong. Adversity has pared me down to the very bones of my soul. Sometimes all I have had is the strength to endure each minute and bide my time. But not today. Today is for replenishment and putting a little flesh on those bones, hmm?'

On their return to Winchester Alienor found a messenger from Richard waiting for her. He was one of Richard's trusted mercenaries, Amalric de Lavoux, distant kin to Richard's captain Mercadier. Entering Alienor's chamber, he dropped to his knees in salutation and bent his head.

'What news?' She gestured him to stand up. 'Tell me.'

He struggled to his feet. He had washed, for his hands were clean and the ends of his hair damp, but he wore an unmistakeable aroma of hot horse. 'Madam, there is much you need to know.'

Alienor sat down before the hearth. Tired out from the hunt, Moysi flopped across her feet and closed his eyes. 'I suppose the Count of Poitou is still locking horns with the King.' She spoke with resignation, because she could do nothing about the state of affairs. She had the freedom to hunt, to entertain guests, to perform charitable and religious work, but she was excluded from any kind of power in Henry's political arena.

'Madam, that is indeed the case, but there is more to the matter.'

She raised her brows. 'Go on.'

'The King summoned the Count of Poitou to court but he refused to attend and rode to Chinon and forced the constable to open the treasury. And then he went into Poitou and began fortifying his . . . your castles.' The mercenary rubbed his face. 'But the King sought a reconciliation and they have agreed terms.' He moved his shoulders as if shifting an uncomfortable weight. 'Madam, the Count of Poitou has been much concerned over the crisis in Outremer and the plight of Jerusalem.'

'As have we all.' News had arrived a month ago of a disastrous battle fought outside Jerusalem. The Christian army had been decimated and Jerusalem's king, Guy de Lusignan, taken prisoner together with the reliquary banner of the kingdom that contained a sacred piece of the true cross. The catastrophe had sent ripples of shock throughout Europe.

'Madam, I have to tell you that the Count of Poitou made a vow before the Archbishop of Tours to relieve the plight of Jerusalem and that he will go as soon as he can raise the men and resources to do so.'

Alienor's heart turned to ice.

'He is determined on the matter, madam – nothing will dissuade him. He says that if his father the King will not vouchsafe him his inheritance, then what point is there in remaining here?'

She should have known this would happen. What else did she expect of a warrior son who had been pushed to the edge by his accursed father? A son whose gift from God was the art of war. Why else had he been given that talent except to save Christ's city? She understood him all too well. Henry had been promising to take the cross for years; like all of his promises it was empty, but Richard would do it or die.

'Madam, you are unwell?'

She shook her head and held out her hand to keep him back. Picking up her wine she took a few small sips. 'Shocked, but not surprised. What does the King say?'

'Very little, madam, but it is plain to all that he does not wish him to go and believes he is doing it to be difficult. The King of France is angry too, for if the Count of Poitou goes to the Holy Land, it will delay his marriage even longer.'

'I doubt that avoiding espousal was the first notion in Richard's mind,' Alienor said grimly.

'No, madam, but the King of France says that if he does not wed the princess Alais, she and her dower must be returned, or there will be war in earnest.'

Henry would never return Alais. Her dowry of strategic lands was too valuable and Henry did not deal well with having terms dictated to him, especially by a younger man. He might agree to finalise the marriage, but Richard would refuse.

'Madam, you should also know that the King of France has an heir. His queen was delivered of a son baptised Louis, last week.'

She concealed a grimace. So unlike his father who had had to wait more than twenty years for his own son to arrive, Philippe had accomplished the task at the first try, making his position a lot more secure.

That was the end of his news. Alienor thanked and dismissed him, and when he had gone, her shoulders slumped.

'Grandmère?' Richenza said softly.

'Richard is not doing this to be difficult,' she said. 'He is doing it because it is what he was born to do. I knew it from the moment I saw him pick up a sword when he was still a very little boy in the nursery.' She lifted her gaze to her grand-daughter. 'My heart almost bursts from my pride for him, but you will discover when you have sons of your own that from the moment of their birth, fear goes with that pride – and that is what kills, but you must never show it.'

Wide-eyed, Richenza nodded. Alienor studied her. She was intelligent and swift to learn, but how could she understand without the experience? For the moment it was just words.

The messenger had brought a satchel of letters too, and Alienor had her scribe read them to her. Most concerned routine matters that were insignificant beside Richard's decision to take the cross, but she became alert when the clerk read out Henry's order that she send Richenza and Alais across the Narrow Sea to attend the Christmas court at Caen under the escort of the chancellor Ranulf de Glanville. Alienor was to remain in England and keep her own Christmas at Winchester.

Richenza, who had been quietly sewing, looked up, her expression a juxtaposition of anticipation and dismay. 'Christmas at Caen?'

'Why so surprised?' Alienor forced a smile. 'Your grandsire will be keen to see how you have grown and what you have learned. You are not a fool. I think you know very well why you have been summoned. You are a great marriage prize, and the time has come to display you in your rightful setting.'

Richenza blushed. 'What if I disappoint him?'

'You won't. I shall miss you because you have become dear to me, but you cannot remain my companion for the rest of your days. You have a different life to live.'

'But I will return to stay with you,' Richenza said anxiously.

'Indeed, I shall expect it. We have a little time before you leave. Enough to make some fine gowns to dazzle all your suitors.'

Richenza's blush deepened.

Alienor clapped her hands and summoned her musicians, determined not to fall into gloom, but instead to celebrate the moment, and she called for the keys to the fabric coffers.

'Green silk will suit you, and the blue wool with a vair-lined cloak.'

Richenza's eyes lit up despite her anxiety. She had a passion for beautiful fabric and fine jewels which Alienor had encouraged because it was part of a noble woman's duty to dress to fit her status; and indeed to know how to dress. Alienor saw so many women who thought that loading themselves with every gaud they possessed was an aid to enhancing their worth, which it might be, but it did nothing for their presence. She had taught Richenza to be selective in her choices and how to use clothes as an asset – as an act of seduction, as a shield, as an extension of who she was – a projection of her feminine power.

She immersed herself in the task because it was something practical she could accomplish, whereas there was nothing she could do to improve the situation between Richard and Henry.

25

Palace of Sarum, Autumn 1188

Dusk had fallen early on this chilly September evening. A rain-spattered wind hammered against the shutters like a fist on a sanctuary door, and Alienor was glad of the fire in her chamber, and the fresh batch of wax candles that had arrived earlier that day. Bored with her current sewing project, finding it difficult to concentrate on the fine stitches in the poor light, she was delighted for the excuse to set her work aside as her chamberlain announced the arrival of William Marshal.

She had not seen William since he had gone to Kendal two years ago, taking his little heiress with him, and although she had thought it a great pity that such talent should go to waste in the sheep-inhabited wilds of the North country, she had resigned herself to the fact she could do nothing about it, and at least he was safe.

When William was ushered into her presence she noted

that he had taken time to change his garments, for they were clean and dry and his hair bore the furrow marks of a comb. A close-cropped dark beard framed his jaw and there were fine smile lines at his eye corners.

He knelt to her and she swiftly raised him to his feet and kissed him. 'Ah William, it is so good to see you!'

'And you, madam. I thought I should find you at Winchester, but was told you were here.'

She made a face. 'I always know when things are not going well for Henry, because unless he needs me to resolve his difficulties, he sends me to Sarum and tells me nothing – although I am still allowed visitors, or you would not be here.'

She gestured him to sit by the fire. A servant arrived with wine and a laden tray of cheese wafers, fresh and hot off the irons.

'I remember how much you loved these when you were a squire,' Alienor said, smiling. 'You could devour an entire platter in the time it took a troubadour to sing three verses.'

'Nothing has changed there, madam, I assure you.' At her gesture, he took one in a napkin and began eating with relish.

'So then,' she said. 'Did you marry your little northern heiress?'

He chewed, swallowed, and shook his head. 'No, madam. She is a sweet girl, and I have kept her safe and seen to her welfare, but I shall not wed her.'

'I take it that you do not intend to make your life in Kendal?'

William started on his second wafer. 'Madam, it is a very beautiful country, and it is balm to my spirit. I intend founding a priory on the lands the King has given me at Cartmel, and eventually I shall furnish it with monks from Bradenstoke. My young lord will be forever remembered there and prayers said for his soul.'

'But while it satisfies you in spirit, it does not satisfy the part of you that desires to be in the world,' she said astutely. 'I am pleased that you choose to remember my son in your foundation.'

'Madam, that was always my intention.' He offered her the platter, but she shook her head.

'So what brings you away from the North?'

He stretched his legs towards the fire. 'The King has summoned me to join him and the Count of Poitou at Chateauroux. King Philippe has claimed jurisdiction, and there is war.' He gave her an assessing look. 'He has offered me Denise de Chateauroux in marriage if I will come to him bringing as many men as I can muster.'

Alienor sat back in her chair. Denise de Chateauroux was a great marriage prize, an heiress of a rank far higher on fortune's ladder than Heloise of Kendal. Henry had never indicated before that he valued William so highly. To make such an offer, he must be in dire need – or had chosen to change his strategy. 'And you have accepted?' She knew little of Denise de Chateauroux personally, but her lands were a vital zone of control and contention straddling French and Angevin interests. It would take a strong man of sound military abilities to hold such a fortress and William was ideally suited.

'Madam, I am his loyal vassal and I will go to him, but it is not my intention to accept the offer he has made to me.' He took a third wafer.

'Why not?' Alienor was astonished. 'You are turning down a great prize.'

'Indeed, madam, but one I will have to fight to obtain, and once I have obtained it, fight again and again in order to keep it. It would be the opposite of the peace I have now – and I would rather have balance in my life.'

Alienor frowned at him. 'So, what *do* you want, William? If not Heloise of Kendal, if not Denise de Chateauroux?'

The wind howled against the shutters and rattled the catches. She watched his chest expand as he drew a deep breath, and saw the colour flood his face. 'The heiress of Striguil is in wardship,' he said. 'I want Isabelle de Clare.'

'Ah.' Alienor gave a knowing nod. 'And that would be the balance in your life?'

'More so than Chateauroux, madam. The de Clare lands are in Normandy, the Welsh borders and Ireland.'

'Not easy to govern when so spread out, and dangerous in parts.'

'But not all in one basket either, and more accessible than Chateauroux.'

'And the lady?'

'Young and fair.'

Alienor raised her brows. 'You have met her?'

'In England as I set out for Jerusalem. It was a passing salute on my way to the coast from my sister's house. Not that I gained more than a fleeting impression, but were I to have a choice, I would thank God for that one.'

Alienor shook her head. 'I can do little to help you from where I stand, but should the opportunity arise, I will do what I can to see your wish fulfilled.'

'Thank you, madam.'

'Although you should be careful what you wish for,' she added.

'Indeed.' He took another wafer, eating more slowly now. 'I could easily have lived out my life comfortably in the North, begetting children, tending my estate and doing everything with one hand tied behind my back, but that would be neglecting my duty. God has spared me for more than this, and I say so with as much humility as ambition.'

Moved by his words, Alienor touched his sleeve. 'I believe that too, William. While I can imagine you growing paunchy and content in some distant small manor away from court, I know you were meant for more. Better the robes of a magnate and the hauberk of a warrior than to grow stale for want of challenges.'

'That is what I thought too, madam,' he said.

He rode out in the morning with gifts of food for the journey and a fat pouch of silver to cover some of his expenses. She had given him letters for Henry and for Richard, exhorting them to keep the peace with each other and not be divided – for what good it would do, but she had tried. There was a letter for Richenza too, who was dwelling at Fontevraud in the secular ladies' house. Negotiations for her betrothal to Geoffrey, Count of Perche, were continuing and Henry was procrastinating in order to encourage the suitor's family to offer more advantageous terms.

'Godspeed you,' she said. 'And may God answer your prayers.'

'And yours, madam.'

'Amen,' Alienor said, but while she was optimistic for William, the likelihood of her own being answered seemed as distant as Jerusalem itself.

Alienor spent another winter at Sarum, and once again her world closed in to a few rooms and a courtyard. As the snow fell and the dark days tightened their grip, she felt as if she was dwelling in the grip of oblivion.

Henry had apparently spent his own Christmas in Saumur, and from her scant gleanings she understood that Richard had demanded that his father confirm him as his heir. Henry had refused, saying he would not be pushed into a corner, so Richard had turned to Philippe and done him homage for Normandy instead, and now kept company with him and ignored his sire.

The days lengthened, and the grass began to grow, showing tender green tips through winter's brown. Not that Alienor was permitted to ride out and enjoy the changing season because Henry had ordered that she be kept closely confined as in the early days of her imprisonment. She deduced that matters were going badly for him, but without access to fuller information she could only speculate. She had learned from gossip that Alais, Richard's betrothed, had returned to Winchester after spending Christmas in Normandy, and Belbel heard a rumour that during Lent the princess had suffered a particularly severe flux of her womb and had bled so badly that she had had to take to her bed for two weeks. Speculation was rife. Privately Alienor determined that even if Alais' bleed was not the result of a miscarriage, she would see hell freeze over before Richard took that particular young woman to wife.

One April morning soon after Easter Day, Alienor paused before the hawk perch in her chamber and stooped to pick up two white tail feathers, furrowing in the breeze from the window. Snowit was moulting and for the moment Alienor was cosseting her more than usual. She tucked the feathers in her wimple band, donned her hawking gauntlet and coaxed the falcon onto her wrist. 'Soon,' she said. 'Soon you will fly high and free, I promise you.' She could be flown even now, but the falconer preferred to ground his birds during their moult. Alienor was hoping that by the time Snowit was ready to fly in full plumage, Henry would have relented his cruelty and permitted her to ride out again.

She began feeding Snowit morsels of chopped rabbit from a wooden bowl. Despite her lack of exercise, the gyrfalcon was ravenous and gulped them down as Alienor stroked her breast and crooned to her.

The door opened and a chestnut and white spaniel nosed into the room and gambolled up to Alienor, feathered tail wagging frantically, mouth open in a wide laugh. Scenting Snowit's meal, he stood on tip-toe at Alienor's skirts, snuffling the juice on her fingers. The gyrfalcon bated her wings and screeched.

'Moysi?'

Alienor stared at him in open surprise and then focused on the door as it opened further and Richenza entered with her father.

Alienor hastily restored Snowit to her perch and put the last of the rabbit scraps on the floor for Moysi to devour.

'Grandmère?' Richenza advanced into the room and started to kneel, but Alienor stopped her, and embraced her with a fierce hug.

'What a wonderful surprise, let me look at you!' She held her granddaughter at arm's length. 'What a beauty you are!'

211

Richenza's cloud of wiry red hair had been tamed and tidied into a thick braid woven with gold thread. A light veil covered the top of her head, secured by sturdy golden pins. Her gown of vibrant spring green was laced tightly to emphasise her figure, and her cloak was lined with squirrel furs the same auburn shade as her hair.

'Indeed, I am most proud of her,' Heinrich said in his heavily accented French as he followed her into the room. He bowed to Alienor. 'She is a credit to her family.'

If Richenza was blooming, Heinrich looked unwell. He was a heavy-set man who usually carried his weight with muscular vigour, but today his features were slack and doughy and he seemed tired.

Moysi, having cleaned the bowl, was busy shoving it around the room with his nose.

Alienor sent Amiria to bring wine, her initial delight at having visitors turning to caution as she started to realise the implications. 'What brings you to Sarum?'

'A visit,' Heinrich said with half a shrug. 'That is all.'

Alienor did not believe him. 'Then I am delighted to see you. My daughter is well?'

'Yes.' Avoiding her gaze, Heinrich went to look at Snowit. 'I see she is moulting.'

Alienor's sense of unease intensified. 'Yes, but she will go through it swiftly I think. Are you staying for the night?'

He inclined his head. 'Yes, and I have brought Richenza to you for a little while.' His gaze flicked to his daughter who was busy rescuing the bowl from the spaniel. 'The Emperor desires me to join the crusade, but I have no wish to go. Let younger men take those risks. Some of us must remain at home and govern but the Emperor would rather I was else-where in his absence, so once again I find myself an exile.' He folded his arms in a defensive gesture. 'It will not be for long, and this time I do not have to uproot my entire family. Matilda has stayed behind as chatelaine. She sends you her love and greeting.'

Alienor was not taken in by his platitudes. He was in exile again and biding his time until his overlord had departed on crusade. In the meantime, Matilda was left to weather matters as best she could.

'I have brought Richenza to you because she is safer here. She loves you dearly, as I know you love her.'

Alienor frowned. 'Indeed I do, but what do you mean when you say matters are not safe?'

Heinrich rubbed his fleshy palm over his face. 'Ach, I do not want to tell you this, but I must. The King's health is failing. Normandy and Anjou are being overrun by Richard and the King of France, and their demands on him increase daily. He is being pushed into a corner and soon he will stand at bay.'

'How is he failing?' Alienor demanded. Her stomach churned with a mingling of fear and dreadful anticipation.

'He is suffering from his old ailment – his thigh weeps constant pus, and he has another fissure higher up.' Heinrich indicated his buttock. 'He can barely sit a horse, but still he struggles to do so and he refuses to rest – although he could not even if he wished, because he is being pursued hard and driven back. Many have deserted him and sworn their fealty to Philippe, or to Richard.'

Alienor bit her lip. She ought to have been brimming with triumph; indeed she did feel a little of that emotion, but she felt sick too. That it should come to this when it need never have happened. 'Is John still with him? And William Marshal?'

'Yes.' Heinrich nodded slowly. 'I do not know what he would do without them. Baldwin de Bethune remains staunch too, and Gilbert FitzReinfred.' His mouth twisted. 'But it is not good – for anyone – and that is why I bring my girl to you.'

'To share my confinement?' Alienor sent Richenza a wry glance.

'For her to be safe,' Heinrich emphasised. 'She will keep you company and you will keep her from harm. It will not be for long as I say.'

He would not be further drawn, but his hints left her in no doubt about what he thought might be about to happen.

26

Palace of Sarum, July 1189

Alienor was returning from her devotions in the cathedral, Richenza at her side, when the messenger rode under the gatehouse arch at a reckless pace and flung himself from his sweating horse so swiftly that the beast was still in motion and he was almost trampled beneath its hooves. Tossing the reins to a startled groom, he stumbled over to the women, knelt in the dust at Alienor's feet and touched the hem of her gown.

'My liege lady,' he panted, 'I bear tidings of great import. The Kingdom is yours; you are the Dowager Queen. King Henry is dead!'

Richenza gasped and put her hand to her mouth. 'No!'

Alienor stood very still. There was a sensation within her of everything jolting to a stop, but not with dismay. It was like seeing a magnificent glow suddenly appear over her horizon, but not being sure what it meant and for the moment there was nothing beyond it. She had been expecting the news ever since Heinrich had brought Richenza to her for safe-keeping in April, but she was still unprepared for the moment when the hammer hit. Henry dead. No longer of the world. All that fierce pugilistic energy gone to nothing, like a sky cleared of clouds in the aftermath of a thunderstorm.

She looked around. Everything was still normal beyond the small ripples caused by the young man's hasty arrival, and no one knew the reason for that haste, only that it must be important news. The sun still burned in the heat-bleached sky. Three children played with Moysi, throwing a leather ball for him to chase, and a woman was flirting with one of the soldiers, flicking her hips at him. None of that would change for the sake of this piece of news.

'I cannot believe it!' Richenza's voice was tight with tears. 'It can't be true!'

Her declaration broke the moment and Alienor took a deep breath, and then another, drawing life into herself. What had been boxed in was now open space, wide with possibilities. 'Hush now.' Taking Richenza's arm, she addressed her firmly. 'You are of his lineage. Remember your position.'

Richenza raised her head and made a valiant effort although her face was flushed and her eyes brimming.

The messenger still knelt in the dust, his hat clenched in his fists and his head bowed almost to the ground. It was one of Richard's hearth knights, she realised, Robert de Saintonge, who had once served as a page in her household. Alienor tapped him smartly on the shoulder. 'Get up,' she said briskly.

He rose to his feet, sweat trickling down his sunburned face. A groom led the horse away to rub it down.

'When and where?' she demanded.

'At Chinon, madam, on the sixth day of July. I have letters for you, but news in more detail is following behind. I am but the harbinger.'

Something was developing within her, rising up like a fine swirl of dust, but gathering substance. She summoned a servant to take the young man and tend to his needs. 'Go and refresh yourself,' she commanded. 'I will send for you again in a short while.' She held out her hands for the letters, and as the knight departed she turned again to Richenza. 'When I went to mass I was a prisoner, and now I am free. Indeed, I was free last night and the night before and did not know it. I could ride out of here this very moment and no one would have authority to stop me – no one!' She envisaged doing exactly that. 'I shall order the cooks to prepare a feast.'

Richenza's eyes widened in shock and Alienor shook her head. 'No, not to celebrate,' she said impatiently, 'although I know God would forgive me for doing so. My reasons are practical. I will never return here, and before I leave, we should empty the larder.'

Glancing up, she saw her gaoler Robert Maudit hastening towards her. Plainly the ripples were flowing outwards as the news came to be known. She stood tall to face him, and felt life flowing back into her veins.

He bowed awkwardly. 'Madam, I grieve to hear the tidings of the King's death.'

'You will understand if I do not,' Alienor replied, 'although when I know more, I may mourn the circumstances. My command is that you prepare to move my household to Winchester on the morrow.'

'As you wish, madam.'

'You did what you had to do and your orders were the King's,' she said. 'Now your orders come at the behest of a new king, and since he is not present, from those who represent him. Let the rest of today be a time for reflection and prayer for the late King's soul. Let a requiem mass be said in the cathedral.'

When he had gone, Alienor returned to her chamber with Richenza. 'I knew he was dying ever since I saw your father in April. The question was only when, and how much more damage he would wreak on us all before he came to his end.' She bade Amiria leave the door open and the windows wide. In practical terms it created a breeze through the room that helped to freshen the summer heat, but it was also the taste of freedom. After tonight she would never set foot in this room again. 'So much wasted time,' she murmured.

The messenger returned, having spruced himself up and changed his garments. 'I am bidden by King Richard to escort you where you wish to go, madam, and remain to serve you in any way you judge fit.'

'I am certain I can find a use for your talents.' She smiled at him, and again felt a stirring within – of flirtatiousness and power. 'I know you were sent in haste, but what more can you tell me?'

He cleared his throat. 'I do not know how much you know, madam. In his last days the King was too ill to attend talks with Count Richard and the King of France and took to his bed at Chinon. I was in the company of Count Richard so I do not know the full details, but when news of the King's death was brought to us in the field, my lord sent me straight to England. I can tell you that as I departed King Henry was being borne to Fontevraud for burial.'

'Fontevraud?' She was surprised. 'Not Grandmont?'

He shook his head. 'It was too far in the summer heat.'

'Of course.' She banished the image conjured by his words. Fontevraud at least was a suitable alternative. Henry had told her he had dwelt at the abbey sometimes as a boy, and when they had visited early in their marriage he had been at peace there, so it was entirely fitting.

The young man could tell her no more because he had ridden in such haste. His sole duty had been to bring her the news and spring her from her prison. The only other detail he was able to impart was that Richard was in good health despite almost being killed by William Marshal.

Alienor stared at him. 'William Marshal tried to kill my son?'

'It was when King Henry was fleeing from Le Mans after the French had broken through, madam. The Count of Poitou gave chase and was almost upon him, but the Marshal turned back to protect the King's retreat. My lord was unarmed save for a padded tunic and light helm and the Marshal could have run him through.'

'But clearly he didn't.'

'No, madam. The Count cried out that he was unarmed and it would be a wicked thing to kill him. So the Marshal killed his horse instead and shouted that he would leave my lord to the devil. After that he got King Henry away to Chinon.'

Small wonder Henry had demanded William's services, Alienor thought. Thank Christ that William had had the bravery and intelligence to do as he had done. She only hoped Richard appreciated it too.

'My lord Richard was at his mercy,' the knight said. 'No one could have stopped the Marshal had he chosen to plunge his lance differently.'

'Then thank God he stayed his hand.' William Marshal had learned his lessons and knew just how far to take brinkmanship, but clearly Richard still had more to learn. 'And John? Was he not with the King?'

'Madam, I do not know. All we heard was that the King was dead and being borne to Fontevraud. As far as I know the lord John was not with him, because his presence was not mentioned, but I believe his son Jeoffrey was.'

That young man too would have to be dealt with, but all would have to wait until she saw Richard. For now she had to prepare as best she could and come to terms with the change in her circumstances while she waited for a new vista to fill that blank horizon.

Five days later William Marshal arrived in Winchester, where she was now residing, and at last she had her news.

His face twisted with pain as he limped into her chamber. 'Madam, forgive me if I do not kneel.'

'What have you done?' For a moment his action reminded her of the last time she had seen Henry and she experienced a jolt of fear. She gestured a chair to be brought for him and cushions plumped.

'The deck of the ship collapsed in Dieppe when I was boarding,' he said with a grimace. 'I managed to grab a strut and save myself but others were not so fortunate. Gilbert Pipart broke his arm.'

'Have you seen a physician?'

He snorted. 'Yes, he said I should rest it.'

Alienor took the letters he had for her. 'Well, you can do that while I read these and you tell me your news.'

Belbel provided an extra cushion for his back.

'I am about to go and claim a young bride,' he said, 'and here I am easing myself into a chair like an old man.'

Alienor eyed him with amusement. 'I doubt the parts that matter have lost their sap, William,' she said, and then laughed at his expression. 'Your spirit and the strength of your will!' She sat down opposite him. 'So Richard has given you Isabelle of Striguil despite you trying to kill him?'

William reddened. 'I had no intention of killing the King – he knows that well. But I had to stop him. I told him I was not so much in my dotage that I no longer had the strength to put a lance in its intended target. And indeed, he has granted me Isabelle of Striguil in marriage. Once I have delivered these letters to you, I am bound for London to marry her, although what a girl of eighteen will think of a grizzled old warhorse like me I do not know.'

'Either you are shamelessly angling for praise or you do not see yourself as women do,' Alienor said. 'You wear more years than when I first took you into my service but you were an untried boy then. Time has wrought experience, not lines. Isabelle de Clare will have no cause to complain of this match.'

'I pray not,' he said wryly.

Alienor looked at the letters in her lap. 'So,' she said after a moment, 'you were with the King when he died.'

A bleak look entered his eyes. 'Yes, but not at his deathbed, I am sorry to say, and it has troubled me deeply that he died alone.'

'Died alone?' she asked sharply. 'Was there no one keeping vigil at his side?'

'Madam, we were, but not at that moment, and it is to my deep regret. He had been delirious for a couple of days – burning up with fever and without control of his bodily functions.'

Alienor compressed her lips. Dear God, Henry. How many times had she thought he deserved to die alone and in agony, but now that this scenario was being presented to her, she was sickened. William faced her. Another man might have looked down or away, but his gaze was steady and level – as it had been when he told her about Harry.

'His bed linens and braies had to be changed and we left to take some respite from the sickroom while the servants dealt with the matter.' He hesitated, took a deep breath and plunged on. 'When we returned a short while later, the King was dead and the servants had fled leaving him naked on his unmade bed.' He clenched his fists on his knees. 'I find it very difficult to tell you this, madam. They had raided the chests, bundled all the movable goods of value into clean sheets and run away. One of our men covered the King's body with his own cloak. We caught a couple of the runaways and before they were hanged they told us the King had died while they were changing him, and they had panicked and run.' His eyes were fierce with chagrin and anger. 'It was no end for such a great king and I am ashamed. We should not have left him for any reason.'

'You were not to know,' she said unsteadily, 'but it is indeed a grievous end.'

'We did our best with what we had – found him raiment and clothing from among us, and from what we recovered from the servants we caught – but we had little to give the crowds lining the road when we bore him to Fontevraud.' He gave her a searching look. 'It was my decision to take him there because it was scarce twenty miles away and I knew he had a fondness for the place.'

'You did well.' Alienor's throat tightened. 'It was a good decision.' Her control was precarious, like walking on knives.

William made a small gesture of negation. 'We waited for my lord Richard to arrive and to decide what to do. You should know that the King was given a fitting burial.'

'I am glad of that. You did the best you could.'

William said nothing, clearly less forgiving of himself than she was.

'What of John?' she asked.

William's face was expressionless. 'My lord John did not see fit to stay with his father when it became plain that his death was upon him and enemies closing in. The King had asked for a list of those who had betrayed him, and was sorely distressed that his youngest son was numbered first among them. The Count of Mortain has since joined my lord Richard and sworn him fealty.'

It was so like John's nature, Alienor thought. He had never been able to stand in the storm even though he was attracted to power. She did not want to feel sorry for Henry, but the emotion came anyway, threatening to engulf her. 'It grieves me to hear such news, but I understand why John made that decision.' She defended him because he was her cub too. 'I am glad though that you remained with the King and saw to his dignity.'

'Jeoffrey FitzRoy was there also.'

Alienor narrowed her eyes. 'Indeed?'

'Yes, madam, and deeply concerned for his father's welfare – genuinely. He wept for him as not all did.'

Alienor nodded brusquely. She had a duty and responsibility to her husband's bastard, but she also had to protect her own sons. Henry had doted on his firstborn even if his mother had been a whore. He was an ambitious young man of proven ability and that made him both an asset and a danger. 'Thank you, William,' she said. 'You have told me what I wish to know.' She crossed herself. 'God rest the King's soul. Come now, let us talk of other matters – your wedding for one.'

When William had departed, limping but still with a buoyant tread, Alienor looked at the letters he had brought her. Matters of routine government. Instructions, requests, supplications. So much to do and so little time. The thought reminded her of Henry and how he had always been racing time until time had run out. Suddenly the emotion that had been gathering ever since she received the news of his death reared up and struck like a snake. A deep pain in her abdomen spread from there, tightening her chest, constricting her throat, burning her eyes. All the lost dreams, all the beautiful times between

221

them lay like a spring meadow over the soil of all the terrible things he had done to her, and to which she had retaliated in kind.

As the grief burgeoned, she uttered an anguished moan. She had been holding herself strong and defiant for so long against all the oppression, all that Henry had done to her, and now she had to let it go. All the rage and bitterness, all the regret and recrimination. She sought her bed, pulled the curtains around her and hugged the terrible pain of her grief. 'Henry, you were such a fool,' she raged, 'such a stupid, stupid man for all your wits. We could have had everything if you had dared to reach out.'

The feelings rushed over her in a torrent. And swirling on the flood was the love she had once felt for a vigorous, energetic red-haired youth who had had the temerity and tenacity to believe he could conquer the world. She had believed him then too, and gloried in his ambition, until she realised that she was just something else to be conquered along his way and then left in his wake. It did not make the love she had once felt any less real. Her hatred washed out of her on a wave of stinging tears, leaving behind a scoured shoreline, clean but bruised with pity for Henry – and what might have been.

'God have mercy on your soul,' she whispered. 'Be at peace, and let me have peace too.'

Pulling the coverlet over herself, she closed her eyes and slept properly for the first time since receiving the news.

She woke to the sound of her women whispering outside the bed curtains. Parting the hangings, she commanded them to bring her a bath, food, and clean raiment. She knew her face must bear signs of the raw emotions that had torn through her like a storm. Her hair was a sleep-tangled rats' nest, and her clothes rumpled, but she was aware of a change in herself, of a feeling that this was real. She was Alienor, Queen of England, and she had work to do.

27

Amesbury Priory, August 1189

Alienor stroked the palfrey's muscular shoulder, admiring the red-gold sheen of the coat, contrasting with the flaxen mane and tail. A leggy foal with a white blaze sniffed Alienor with fearless curiosity.

'She is a beauty,' she said to Joan, Abbess of Amesbury.

'Thank you, madam. We have good pasture here for horses and King Henry honoured us for several years.'

The nun's tone was bland, but Alienor saw through it. The handsome palfrey and her foal were just two of a dozen horses Henry had stabled here at Amesbury's expense. There were another five palfreys, three hackneys and two spirited chasers.

Alienor might have been standing in the Abbess's place had she taken vows as Henry had intended. Joan D'Osmont must know this, but she stood serenely with clasped hands, her manner deferential but not obsequious.

'I know how much cost you have incurred. The late King entrusted many houses of God with the care of his horses. I am of a mind to take the palfrey and foal off your hands as a wedding gift for my granddaughter and the Count of Perche, but I intend to freely grant you the others to do with as you wish – either to ride or to sell, and the same for every other abbey and priory in the land that currently stables the late King's horses.'

'Madam, that is generous indeed,' the Abbess replied with pleasure.

'Perhaps, but it is also fair. These animals have cost you dear and the new King recognises this.' Added to which Richard, once crowned, would be busy raising money for his crusade and what was given with one hand would balance what was taken with the other.

Before Richard could depart to the Holy Land, England had to be settled and peaceful with firm government, and that was for her to organise. She had sent out representatives far and wide to take oaths of fealty on Richard's behalf. She had seen to the regulation of weights and measures throughout the land so that they were uniform. Everywhere she had ridden she had projected her authority and made herself conspicuous, dressing in royal robes, a jewelled crown over her veil and Snowit perched on her wrist. Soon Richard would arrive, but for now Alienor, Dowager Queen and Queen Mother, held the reins of government in hands that had always been capable, though often denied. She was deriving great satisfaction and pleasure from her progress. It soothed the deep scars left by her imprisonment and she felt refreshed and invigorated.

'Madam, I have organised food and drink in my lodging.' The Abbess made an open gesture towards the convent buildings.

'That would be most welcome,' Alienor responded. 'I have to be in Winchester before nightfall, but there is time.'

Leaving the paddocks, she allowed the Abbess to escort her to her parlour. Earlier, she had knelt in the church to pray for Henry's soul and had given alms to the abbey for the same. And not just for Henry. Hard on the heels of the news of Henry's death, only two days later, a messenger had arrived from Brunswick bearing the tragic news that her daughter Matilda had died of fever and congestion of the lungs. Alienor had faced the news with numb disbelief and then dull acceptance because there was nothing she could do. The only succour was to keep her beloved daughter in her heart, give alms in her name and remember her every day in her prayers. Also to give extra love and tenderness to the children Matilda had left in her care – Richenza, Wilhelm, Lothar and Otto.

Although grief-stricken, Richenza had risen to a new maturity in dealing with her sorrow. She was her mother's daughter, and determined to do her justice. She had taken it upon herself to comfort her brothers and in so doing had found purpose and solace for herself. Alienor could not have been more proud of her.

'The King was keen for me to retire here,' Alienor said as she entered the Abbess's guest chamber, 'but I was not ready to lead a life of contemplation.'

'But one day you might, madam?' Abbess Joan asked with a quizzical smile.

'One day' – Alienor made a gesture that pushed the question aside – 'but not yet. I have too much to do in the world – although,' she added graciously, 'I know that any abbess of the house of Fontevraud holds a distinguished position.'

Servants arrived with dishes of salmon in green herb sauce accompanied by bread and clear wine of Auxerre. Alienor dined with pleasure; food tasted so much better for the salt of freedom. She was eager to gorge herself on life. She had a reason to rise early from her bed every morning. She was filling up with all the light and air she had been denied in captivity. Yet she was grounded too, because her life had purpose, and that purpose was her children, Richard in particular, and she would see him very soon.

'*Confinement is distasteful to mankind and it is a most delightful refreshment to the spirit to be liberated therefrom.*'

Listening to the scribe read the words back to her, Alienor felt their resonance at her core. She had ordered the release of all prisoners currently held in England's gaols. An amnesty; a new start for a new reign, not to be taken as a sign of weakness, but of a queen's clemency. She was truly embracing her role of peacemaker and healer of wounds. 'Yes,' she approved. 'Let copies be made under my seal and sent to every sheriff.'

The scribe bowed and set about the task. From the table at her side, Alienor picked up a small drawstring bag made from purple silk and tipped out the silver seal matrix it contained. She had commissioned it on the day she left Sarum and it depicted her wearing her three-pointed crown, a sceptre in her right hand and an orb in her left, topped with a cross and a dove – although in her private thoughts it was a gyrfalcon too. The wording around the outside of the seal proclaimed her title 'By the Grace of God'. Never before had that accolade adorned her seals, although Henry had used it on his. The phrase added authority to her letters and gave her a pleasurable frisson of power.

Once all had been delegated and each person knew his or her tasks, she withdrew to her chamber and had her ladies dress her in formal robes of silk and brocade, stitched with gold beads and pearls. Belbel had been earning her keep hand over fist during recent weeks, and seamstresses had been employed to make new garments fit not only for a queen, but for one who needed to travel far and wide conducting the business of the realm. There were clothes for great occasions, and then there were those that had to be practical for riding whatever the weather but still create a spectacle.

She had come across one of Henry's better cloaks in a coffer at Winchester – deep forest-green wool lined with squirrel furs and trimmed with red and gilt braid. There had still been a faint aroma of Henry in its folds, and it had struck a soft place in her heart and made her a little tearful. She had had it carefully brushed before being placed in a chest with scented herbs to repel moths.

Richard's herald arrived, bearing the news that his lord was at Winchester's gates and would imminently arrive at the castle. Alienor thanked him, summoned her ladies, smoothed her gown a final time, and set out to greet him. Her son, her king.

Isabelle de Clare, William Marshal's bride of a month, was a golden-haired, blue-eyed beauty, as tall as Alienor herself. She was respectful but not sumbissive and possessed a natural confidence and poise. Indeed, for a young woman of eighteen at her first court gathering she was remarkably calm and sensible. But then her father had been a courtly man who knew how to comport himself, and her mother was Irish royalty. Although her French held exotic cadences of Irish and Welsh, her voice was melodious and made a beautiful thing of the accent.

Alienor was pleased that Isabelle appeared highly satisfied with her marriage to William. His name came easily to her tongue, and colour heightened her cheeks when she spoke of him.

'I have known William since he was little older than you are now and he is dear to me,' Alienor said. 'I could wish no better match for him than he has with you, and you have my blessing.'

'Thank you, madam.' Isabelle's blush deepened. 'I count myself fortunate to have been matched with a man of such courtesy and prowess who will care for me and for my lands.'

The reply, while courtly, was heartfelt. Standing beside her, included in the conversation, was Richenza. Her marriage negotiations had been reconvened and agreement had been reached that she would wed Geoffrey of Perche at Westminster during Richard's coronation festivities. Geoffrey was tall, golden-haired and well-made, and Richenza was so consumed by excitement and tension at the thought of marrying him that she could barely stand still, although Isabelle de Clare's serenity was a calming influence and Richenza was trying hard to contain herself because she wanted to be seen as a mature young woman, not a flighty girl. Geoffrey was William's cousin and thus the young women would soon be kin by marriage.

Both William and Geoffrey were absent from the room. Alienor had noticed Isabelle and Richenza casting circumspect glances in search of their particular males. Richard too was missing.

'Men!' Alienor raised her eyes to heaven. 'They accuse women of huddling in gossip groups, but they are the real culprits.' Leaving Isabelle and Richenza, she went to find the absconders, and discovered them in the ante room that the scribes used for writing their letters where the light was good.

Richard was studying some sketches and maps that had been unrolled across a trestle table and together with William Marshal, Geoffrey of Perche, Rotrou his father and a few others was discussing routes and objectives concerned with the forthcoming campaign in Outremer. The atmosphere was of camaraderie, of men engaged in business, and Alienor once more experienced the feeling of being an outsider.

'So this is where you are, my lords,' she said. 'Shall I bring everyone to join you?'

She saw guilty looks dart, although not from Richard. He faced her, the clear autumn light burnishing his hair and beard like new copper. 'I wanted to show these gentlemen the proposed route and take advice,' he said.

'And it could not wait?'

His jaw tightened. 'Mama, this is important, not just a whim.'

More than being a king? she wanted to ask, but at the same time she understood his need. Richard saw fighting for God as a hallowed extension of his kingship.

'It is only for two years. I have every faith that those I leave behind will govern well.'

'I have every faith too, but two years is long enough.' Indeed too long.

'To govern?' Richard teased, since she was to oversee all.

'To endure the absence of a beloved son,' she answered sternly, 'even if you are putting actions in the place of words and fulfilling your oath. Come, there are people still waiting to talk with you and you should not neglect them.'

Richard sighed and straightened his shoulders. 'You are right, mother, of course.' He smiled an apology. 'I can finish this in a little while.'

The men left the room and Alienor paused to study the map that Richard had left out on the trestle, weighted down with stones. She was proud of him, but dreading the moment he left. Even with maps, people still got lost.

* * *

Later, when everyone had departed to their lodgings, Alienor sat down to speak with Richard properly for the first time in two years. Her feet were propped comfortably on a footstool and a jug of spiced wine was set to hand with a platter of candied fruits. Musicians played instruments in the background, but too far removed from the conversation to hear what was said; everyone else had been dismissed.

'John will meet us in London,' Richard said. 'His ship and entourage sailed to Dover. I wanted him to inspect the defences there for me and to make his presence known, but at my order, not his.' He hesitated. 'I suppose you heard he deserted our father when he knew there was no hope.'

'Yes,' Alienor said, 'but I do not blame him.'

Richard grimaced. 'He always thought ingratiating himself with Papa would reap benefits, especially after Geoffrey died, but when the likelihood of those benefits evaporated so did his loyalty. I know my little brother very well. He will take every opportunity to make mischief while I am gone but I do not fear for England and my domains with you at the helm, Mama. I know you are full capable of dealing with any crisis.'

Alienor raised her brows. 'I will not deny that, but in God's name do not go and get yourself killed, because I warn you now, I could not deal with that.' She experienced a pang within her, a cramping of her loins and womb and heart.

'God willing, you will not have to,' he replied with the assurance of a man in his full young prime.

Alienor dismissed the musicians with thanks and a couple of coins. It was best that no one be a party to their discussion now. Ensuring the door was firmly latched behind them, she returned to her seat.

Richard eyed her with guarded amusement and refreshed his goblet. 'A pity to dismiss them; I was enjoying the music and I am not sure I am going to like the next tune quite so much, even if I am interested to hear it. More wine?'

She held out her cup and he refilled it. 'Alais,' she said,

'and the succession. It is neither fitting nor politically meet that you marry her.'

'Unfortunately the King of France thinks it both.' Richard screwed up his face. 'It appears to be his life's ambition to see me wed to his sister. He is entrenched and nothing will move him.' Setting his cup aside, Richard gave her a direct stare. 'What is the truth about Alais and my father? Was she his concubine? Has she borne him children in secret?'

Alienor's mouth curled with distaste. 'From those at court who make it their business to know such things I understand that your father behaved inappropriately towards her – but how far he went in his behaviour no one is certain and Alais refuses to say. Her women report she has suffered two very heavy bleeds on different occasions, which could either be the purging of excess humours or the miscarriage of an unquick-ened child.'

'But grounds enough for annulment. Even if untrue, there will always be that taint attached to her.'

'Indeed, and whatever the truth, her reputation, as you say, is tarnished. No son of mine will take for his bride his father's leavings,' Alienor said forcefully. 'Furthermore, such signs of disturbed humours, whether caused by the loss of a child or the result of nature, do not bode well for her fruitfulness.' She reached for her wine. 'Philippe may be angry, but he cannot blame you when you have sound reason. You can negotiate to return her to him once you have settled terms that are mutually acceptable.'

'That resolves the situation,' Richard agreed, 'but not in an honourable way even if it plays to our advantage. It will be unwise to tell Philippe at this stage. I will put him off until we return from Outremer.'

She leaned forward. 'But if you are not to make Alais your bride, you must consider someone else because you have no heir of your body. You should set your mind to a beneficial alliance before you leave for Outremer.'

He drew back a little and set his jaw.

Alienor pressed her point. 'Philippe has already vouchsafed himself a son and for all I know will have a second child on the way before he departs. It behoves you to do the same.'

'As it happens I do have some thoughts, Mama. I have not been idle even if you think my mind revolves around nothing but war.'

She raised her brows. 'Who have you been considering?'

He left his chair to prowl the chamber and she clearly saw Henry's restlessness in him. Crossing to the window embrasure he picked up his lute. The instrument went everywhere with him; he had owned it since being invested as Count of Poitou at fifteen, and often played music for his own pleasure and peace of mind. The troubadour blood of Alienor's poet grand-sire, William, the ninth duke of Aquitaine, ran strongly in Richard's veins and the music was the other side of the soldier – the beauty and gentleness in his soul.

He adjusted the tuning and smoothed his long fingers over the curved belly of sycamore panels almost like a lover stroking his partner's fertile womb. 'I have a lady in mind.' He coaxed the first notes from the instrument like drops of honey. 'A princess of a warm southern kingdom who speaks a noble tongue.' He gave his mother a teasing smile across the lute. 'And who has a reputation for piety and wisdom.'

Alienor might have been shut away by Henry and kept from all sensitive information, but she was still aware of the wider connections. 'That would be a princess who is cousin by marriage to your sister in Castile,' she said.

'And who has an able father and brother who are not going to Outremer and who can watch my back while I am gone. I won't need to worry about encroachments from Toulouse. Philippe of France will be in Outremer too, so I can watch him myself.' He coaxed a delicate tune from the lute, plangent and haunting. 'I thought I would call this one "Berenguela",' he said with a mischievous smile.

'I think it an excellent notion,' she replied. 'And the sooner the better. Have you made approaches on the matter?'

'In general terms and with a positive response, but now I have to build the fortress on the foundations.'

She frowned. 'And little time to accomplish it.'

'No.' He picked out more notes. 'I will send envoys to Pamplona while I continue to make ready to leave. Once the negotiations are concluded the marriage can take place even if it must happen in the winter camp at Messina.' His gaze grew distant and she could tell he was dealing with logistics and tactics rather than dwelling on the fair graces of a future wife.

'I love all of my grandchildren,' she said softly, 'but I desire to see your sons around my feet most of all before I die. I want to see you continue in them.'

'That is in God's hands, Mama, but as much as it is in my power, I will give them to you.'

His words warmed her heart but filled her with anxiety too, because so much in practical terms had to be accomplished in order for that to happen, not least a wedding, and she was wary of the fickle hand of fate.

Alienor stood on the battlements of Marlborough Castle, taking a brief respite from the noisy festivities in the hall and enjoying the cooling breeze that had arrived with the onset of dusk.

All the matters of the realm were being settled in preparation for Richard's coronation in two weeks' time and that involved several appointments and marriages, including Richenza's to Geoffrey of Perche.

When Henry had been crowned, there had not been such a level of activity – or perhaps she had not noticed because she had been heavily pregnant and only involved on the periphery, whereas now she was almost joint head of state and every one of Richard's decisions was filtered through her opinion.

'Mama?'

She turned to face John as he sauntered over to join her. He had matured into a handsome man, not particularly tall but well-proportioned and with an aura of dangerous charm.

His expression was permanently inscrutable and he was always scheming, but it was up to others to guess at what.

He too had been celebrating his nuptials for he had wed heiress Hawise of Gloucester to whom he had been betrothed for several years. The match gave him land and influence but he had no affinity for the young woman, nor she for him; it was a business matter and they would continue to live their lives apart. Indeed, they were related within the proscribed degree, and had been married without a dispensation, which meant there might yet be an annulment.

John had arrived late the previous evening – indeed she had wondered if he was going to be in time for his own wedding – and there had been no opportunity to talk to him today because they had been hemmed around by ceremonies, rituals and other people.

'Are you also here to breathe fresh air for a moment?' she asked.

He gave her a half smile. 'Just taking stock, Mama.'

'Of what?'

He leaned against the crenel space between the merlons. 'Of my life – of its direction.' His cendal undertunic glimmered in the dusk like green fire. 'There is much to think about.'

'Now you are a married man?'

He slanted her an inscrutable look. 'Now I am many things that I was not only a few months ago.' He clasped his hands. A large emerald gleamed on his middle finger, reflecting the colour of the undertunic. 'My father,' he said. 'They all think I betrayed him. I see the way they look at me when they think I am off my guard, but I am never off my guard. I know – I can't not know.'

'You made your decision,' she said calmly. 'I will not condemn you.'

'But others do.' His eyes were bitter. 'But if I betrayed him, it was less than Richard did. My only mistake was leaving it until the end. I held firm for him for all that time . . . and yet he never held firm for me or for any of us if it did not suit his policy.'

'John . . .' Pity welled in her but she swallowed it down, knowing he would not thank her.

'Well, it did not suit mine to watch him take his last breath in front of me,' he said hoarsely. 'I knew there could be no other outcome. My only regret is the way he found out. Now Jeoffrey is ramming it down my throat that he is the only good son – the one who stayed. Hah – and where was he when the servants stripped my father's body and ran off with his cups and silver? Where was the Marshal? He died without dignity, and because of that everyone blames me.'

'They do not. You are seeing shadows where none exist.' That wasn't entirely true, but the shadows were less dark than he painted them. John had always been plagued by his insecurities; those shadows were inside him, not others. And perhaps he might give them full substance if he dwelt on them too hard.

'I grieved for him,' he said. 'More than Richard did. No one has accused Richard of being the cause of his death.'

'Nor should they,' Alienor said curtly. 'What happened was a long time in the making, and much of it your father's own doing. Not yours, not Richard's.'

John looked out into the distance. 'Let them say what they will; I care not. I should tell you, Mama, while I am opening my heart, that I have another child, a girl to bear my name – Joanna.'

Alienor steeled herself. 'And the mother?'

'Clemence le Boteler.'

'So she is of high birth again?' More smoothing of ruffled feathers to be done. She was hardly surprised though. John could be utterly charming when he chose; it had only been a matter of time.

John shrugged. 'I don't bed with whores, that's Richard's domain.' A sly look crossed his face. 'Of course he won't tell you about his own son, and with good reason.'

234

Alienor straightened up, her stomach churning. 'What do you mean "his own son"?' Even though the darkness was encroaching, making expressions more difficult to interpret, she could see John was enjoying this. She also noted that he had managed to deflect the focus from his own behaviour.

'A French whore came crying to Richard that she was with child and that it belonged to him. He gave her money to keep her and when the child was born he provided for a wet nurse and lodging.' He pursed his lips. 'He's called the brat Philippe for the King of France, and do you know why?'

Alienor shook her head. 'No, but I suspect you are going to tell me.'

'Because rumour has it that Richard and Philippe were sharing a bed and the woman. For all anyone knows, the child is Philippe's,' John said with relish. 'If Philippe had acknowledged it his, he might have named it Richard. I suppose they played dice to decide the paternity and, depending how you view it, Richard either won or lost.'

She wanted to slap him and disbelieve his words, but clearly he was well-informed. 'This is Richard's business.' She strove not to show how much the news had disturbed her. 'If he wishes to tell me then so be it, but otherwise I have no desire to hear tales. What of you and Clemence le Boteler?'

'She is at Bec with the infant. I have provided for them out of my income and set all to rights. I acknowledge the sin is mine, but at least she is not my cousin and I have been discreet.'

'And that is supposed to make it all right?' Alienor snapped.

'No, but I wanted to tell you rather than you find out of your own accord.'

'Well that makes a change.' And then she sighed. 'I suppose I should be glad you have done so. May that openness continue. While Richard is gone, we must all cooperate and pull in the same direction.'

'Indeed, Mama, I agree with all my heart.' The unfathomable look was back on his face, as guileless as his smile.

28

Westminster, September 1189

After this eventide, a new day star ascends and a new time of prosperity will come at sunrise. The age of gold returns, the world's reform draws nigh.

Listening to the harp-accompanied chant in the Queen's Hall at Westminster, Alienor's heart soared. Although it was September, the room was decked with greenery and flowers, reminiscent of springtime. The white linen cloths draping the tables were a perfect setting for the gilded cups and platters, the salt dishes and silver boats pooled with colourful sauces of tawny cameline and golden jaunce, sprinkled with sandalwood.

On the last occasion Alienor had presided over a banquet in the Queen's Hall she had been a young woman, most of her children unborn and her imprisonment at Sarum far in the future. Now she came again as Queen, and while she felt sadness for the lost years and time wasted, she was stirred up by triumph too. Before she had been the wife of the King; now she was the Queen Mother and the level of respect and power she commanded was beyond anything that had been hers in her young life.

A short while ago Richard had been crowned King of England in the cathedral church of Westminster Abbey. Baldwin, Archbishop of Canterbury, had anointed his head, chest and hands with holy oil, conferring on him the divine sanction of kingship. Richard had asserted his right by taking the crown from the altar with his own hands and presenting it to the Archbishop before mounting the throne, thus giving the moment a gesture of eloquent reciprocation that nevertheless conveyed the statement that the State came before the Church.

Sipping from her gem-studded goblet, Alienor gazed round the hall. Overlaying the music, a social percussion of chatter filled the air between table and roof. Knives clattered against dishes and spoons scraped the sides of bowls. A great sturgeon had been presented at the high table surrounded by glistening pearls of roe, displayed on a wider bed of seaweed with oysters and whelks. A strong but not unpleasant smell of the fresh seashore wafted to Alienor's nostrils. The diners were all women; following tradition the men's feast was taking place separately in the great hall, built a hundred years ago by William Rufus, son of the Conqueror. It had been the same at Henry's coronation and this was the second time she had presided over such a gathering. Some of the faces were the same albeit older, but many belonged to younger generations – women who had been small children or unborn the last time. How swiftly the years had passed and how few remained to achieve her goals; she wished that time would stand still in this golden moment of Richard's triumph.

Sitting at her right hand was Alais of France, Richard's betrothed, placed there out of necessity because her brother Philippe must remain convinced that Richard was going to wed her.

Alais was revelling in her new gown of green silk brocade trimmed with ermine, and her coronet of gold and pearls. With the wine flush on her cheeks she was pretty, and her smooth white hands were a perfect foil for the gold rings embellishing her fingers. Alienor had caught Alais studying her intently on several occasions during the feast and suspected she was eyeing up her chair and larger jewelled crown for size. The latter would be far too heavy for her to bear, Alienor thought with hidden scorn. She had no doubt Henry had bedded her. The whispers were too insidious – like smoke that crept from a fire even when it had been doused. She treated the young woman with cool formality and did not allow herself to feel sorry for Alais as Henry's victim. Her own loyalty and service were all for Richard.

When the formal feasting was over, Alienor mingled with the ladies who had not been in her immediate vicinity during the banquet. Isabel had travelled down from Conisbrough for the coronation and was resplendent in blue and gold, with a hemline and cuffs stylishly depicting the de Warenne chequers. A heart-shaped brooch twinkled, securing a pleat in her silk wimple.

'I am sorry for Henry's death, God rest his soul,' Isabel said as they embraced, 'but I am delighted for your release and for Richard, God grant him a long and fruitful reign, and success in all his undertakings. You must be so proud.'

'I am indeed,' Alienor replied. 'And I wish Hamelin consolation in his grieving for Henry. It must be difficult for him.'

'Naturally he mourns him,' Isabel said sombrely. 'Since he was the older by three years it reminds him of his own mortality, but he tries to be at peace with himself and to do God's will as best he can.'

'I have always respected Hamelin's ability to sail a straight course in stormy seas,' Alienor said. 'I shall value his counsel when Richard has gone, and I hope you will both keep me company at court sometimes – and bring me gingerbread,' she added to lighten the moment.

'Of course!' Isabel smiled for an instant and then bit her lip in a way Alienor remembered of old. 'Our daughters are married and settled to good men, so all is well in that part.' She glanced towards three young women who were talking in a group that included the newly wed Richenza and William Marshal's young wife.

'How is Belle?'

'She is a good wife to Robert de Lacy.' Isabel emphasised the 'good', and primly folded her hands, revealing that the wounds were still raw.

As if sensing their scrutiny, Belle raised her head and looked their way before dropping her gaze in what passed for deference.

'I am sure she is,' Alienor murmured courteously. 'Our mutual grandson is a delight.'

Isabel's expression softened. 'Truly he is. I hope he will visit me and Hamelin for a while in the spring or summer.' She regarded her clasped hands. 'It has been hard for Hamelin to accept, but he has come to terms with it better now. When Henry died, it made him reconsider the things that mattered. His first grandchild should not have been bastard-born, but he has come to love him dearly.'

'I am glad of that,' Alienor said. 'You should know that John loves him in a way I have seldom seen him have affection for anyone.'

'That is because he belongs to him,' Isabel said shrewdly. 'My daughter was a challenge and a means to an end, and that end was in proving his power over her and satisfying his lust. He did not think beyond that measure, but the moment there was a child – then it was different, because it belonged to him.'

Alienor opened her mouth to defend John, but thought better of it because Isabel was right and she did not want to begin another quarrel. Her friend had hardened, become less yielding, but at least she had learned to stand her ground instead of running off to weep and bemoan the way of the world. 'Richard will never suffer for the circumstances of his birth. I know it has been difficult for Belle and her path is not what you would have wished for her, but she has an honourable marriage.'

'Yes,' Isabel answered. 'We have all survived. I have retired from court life, and you have become what you were always meant to be.'

Alienor raised her brows but smiled. 'And what is that?'

'A woman with her hand on the reins.' Isabel touched Alienor's sleeve in a gesture of reconnection. 'A country without a strong ruler at the helm is a country in jeopardy. I remember with dread the time of the anarchy when I was a young woman. We were frightened all the time, and sometimes that fear became terror; I never want to live through such again. When Richard goes to Jerusalem, I am not afraid, because I know you will be here guiding us – and in that I put my greatest trust. We support you to the hilt, it goes without saying.'

Alienor's eyes prickled. 'We have had our differences, but I love you – you are my sister. I know you will hold firm for me even if—'

She stopped speaking at a sudden clamour from outside the hall doors – shouts and screams. The clash of weapons. Isabel met her gaze with fear-wide eyes and there were cries of consternation and alarm from the gathered women. Many of the older ones, like Isabel, remembered the strife between King Stephen and the Empress, and how moments of celebration like this could turn on the instant to wanton riot. Henry's mother had been forced to flee Westminster on the eve of her own coronation when a mob had taken against her. Surely that wasn't happening now? All had been joyful when Richard left the Abbey. The crowds had been cheering and lauding their red-haired Young King who was Christendom's greatest champion. He was their Lionheart, and if passions were running high, they were supportive ones.

The sounds surged closer and then faded, save for one male voice that rose to a shriek outside the hall doors, the sound followed by a loud thud.

Alienor commanded the ushers to find out what was happening. Walking regally, without haste, she returned to her chair on the dais, and directed the other women to be reseated.

Moments later two guards hauled a bleeding, battered man into the room and forced him to his knees at the foot of the dais steps. Blood streamed from a wound on his scalp, masking half his face and dripping into his greying beard. One forearm dangled at a twisted angle. The man wore robes of good wool edged with expensive braid.

'What is this?' Alienor demanded with cold fury. 'Who dares disturb the peace of this celebration?'

'Madam,' one of the guards spoke up, 'the Jews arrived to present gifts to the King and have caused grievous discontent and rioting among the crowds.' He wiped his bloody hand on

240

his surcoat with distaste. 'Why should good Christians have to stay outside while these infidels are granted access to the King?'

Alienor gave him a sharp look. 'Has the riot been contained?'

His expression contorted. 'The palace is safe, but I fear the unrest is spreading into the city.'

Alienor gazed at the blood-drenched man shaking at the foot of the dais steps. A Jew. Her instinct was to pull in her skirts and draw back, but she held her place. These people and their religion were anathema to Christians, but they were an essential element of royal fiscal policy and they were under Richard's protection. 'So this man came to present a gift to the King and this is what has become of him?'

'Yes, madam.'

'What is your name?' she addressed the Jew. 'Speak!'

'Manasser bar Jacob . . . madam,' he gasped through teeth bared with pain and stained red with the blood trickling from his cut lip. 'We came . . . present . . . gift of gold bezants to the King and Queen.' His eyes rolled, showing white under the lids.

She saw the looks on the faces of the guards; the mingling of anxiety, revulsion and dawning fear.

'Isaac . . . Isaac had the gold, but he . . . it was robbed from us by the mob. I didn't see the knife . . .' He slumped, close to losing awareness.

'Shall I throw some water on him, madam?'

'What good will that do?' Alienor snapped. 'You will either completely destroy his wits or kill him. Take him to safety and see that he is cared for so he can be questioned later. The King will be very displeased by this – as am I.'

Subdued and tight-lipped the guards obeyed, dragging the groaning Jew between them. Even as they reached the door, Richard slammed into the hall followed by a host of courtiers. He was still wearing his crown, the gold and gems shot with light as he stalked forward. He was every inch the King, and in a royal fury. Glaring at the Jew slumped between his knights he demanded an accounting of what had happened before brusquely dismissing them with an instruction to tend the man's injuries.

'It seems that the mob has turned on your Jews in righteous frenzy,' Alienor said, 'and the gift they were going to present to you has opportunely disappeared – a chest of gold bezants no less.' She clenched her fists on the finials of her chair. 'You must nip this in the bud before the riots spread, otherwise it won't just be Christian against Jew, it will be mayhem for all!'

'I shall deal with it,' he growled. 'The gold will be found and the ringleaders hanged.' His nostrils flared. 'Good Christ, I did not want my coronation to be decorated by a hanging tree, but I will raise one if I must in order to have peace. Anyone laying a finger on my Jews lays a finger on me – let it be known!' With that he flung round and stormed out, calling for the city officials to attend him.

Alienor was furious; a perfect moment had been ruined. If the Jews had had the sense to keep their distance and if the Londoners had been less drunk and volatile this would never have happened. Now, even if a stop was put to the rioting, a precedent had been set and a layer stripped back that would make it easier to riot next time.

'Perhaps Philippe of France was right, Mama,' said John silkily. He had not followed Richard outside, but was standing looking round the hall and eyeing up the women. 'He banished all his Jews at his coronation and took a percentage of all their goods before he let them go. Half of them are probably skulking here in London or up in Lincoln and York.'

'Richard is not Philippe of France,' Alienor snapped. 'He will deal with our Jews as he sees fit and we shall see that his will is done.'

'Yes, Mama,' John said blandly.

'You should go and help him. What are you still doing here?'

'I wanted to make sure my wife and my mother were both safe,' he replied with a disarming smile, 'but you are right. I should be about my business.' He flicked a perfunctory glance at his wife that suggested the opposite of his remark, and departed at a saunter.

Eyes narrowed, Alienor watched him leave, and then turned her attention to her guests. It was time to make an end of things and deal with this unfortunate business, but first she must return matters to normality and restore the focus to Richard. She sent the dapifers round to fill everyone's goblets and then raised hers on high. 'A toast!' she cried. 'A toast to Richard, King of England by the Grace of God!'

As the salute was shouted back to her from the women of England – the sisters, mothers and wives who would be governing their lands while their husbands fought in Outremer – she tasted both fear and triumph in her wine.

'I do not know what I am doing here,' Belle whispered. 'I swore I would never be alone with you again, especially not in a dark corner.'

John chuckled softly, and taking hold of the jewelled belt encircling her waist, pulled her close. 'Then you broke your vow,' he said. 'It is not such a big thing.'

'Not for you.' She made a half-hearted effort to free herself. 'I cannot be seen talking to you – my maid will be looking for me.' She cast a swift glance over her shoulder.

'We have a few moments.' He tugged her further into the shadows and pulled her against his lower body. 'I did not force you to come outside, did I?'

She pushed at him. 'I thought you wanted to speak to me in private.'

'I do. I have to go and help sort out this folly with the Jews – there are houses on fire in the city – but will you come to me later?'

'I can't, you know I can't.'

'But I want you . . . and that old husband of yours is no use to any woman on this earth. Find an excuse to get away.' He put his hand on her buttocks.

'You have your own wife for that.' She wriggled to escape. 'Indeed, I have yet to congratulate you on your marriage.'

'She's a means to an end, she doesn't warm my bed in any sense of the word.'

'I will not bear you another bastard.' Belle gripped his shoulders and pushed at him, both excited and appalled. Sick with desire.

'Who said anything about that? There are ways . . .'

'I hear you have another one now, in Normandy – Joanna is it?'

'That has nothing to do with us.' He looked round at the sound of voices. 'Do not say no. I'll be waiting.' He kissed her hard on the mouth, invading her with his tongue, and then he was gone, melting into the night, swift as a hunting cat.

Trembling, Belle hid in the shadows until two courtiers passed, too deep in conversation to notice her. She could not decide whether their appearance had spoiled her opportunity, or saved her from a fate worse than death.

29

Nonancourt, Normandy, March 1190

'How is your wife, my lord Earl?' Alienor asked William Marshal as she fell into step beside him, her tone slightly teasing as she addressed him by the latter title. She had arrived that morning at the great fortress of Nonancourt in north Normandy to attend a gathering where the government of Richard's lands was to be discussed and settled as he prepared to depart for Outremer.

'Isabelle is very well, madam, but resting at Longueville.'

'She must be near her time.'

'Late April.' He gave a self-deprecating smile. 'I have suddenly taken to looking in cradles and paying attention to women with babies in their arms, and thinking that soon it will be a routine part of my household.'

Alienor lightly touched his sleeve. 'Let me know when the child is born. In the meantime I shall write to Isabelle and offer prayers for her safe delivery. I am very fond of your wife.'

'Thank you, madam.' He inclined his head. 'She speaks often of you and with high regard.'

'I am pleased to hear it, although she must be cursing me too for the amount of time I take you away from her. I do not need to be a fortune teller to foresee how busy you are going to be in the months to come. You are going to earn that earldom of yours in every part.'

William grinned ruefully. 'When I was a young man they called me Gasteviande because I had such an enormous appetite. Now I must apply the same to matters other than food and hope I have not bitten off more than I can chew.'

His smile vanished as they were joined by Richard's chancellor, William Longchamp, Bishop of Ely, who had several rolls of parchment tucked under his arm. A clerk and a scribe followed in his wake bearing more parchments, quills and ink, and two more servants clad in the Bishop's livery.

'My lord Bishop,' William said with the bland courtesy of an accomplished courtier, 'I am sorry if I was walking too fast. Do you wish to rest for a moment?'

Longchamp suffered from swollen joints in hip and knee, and his body was twisted like a tree gnarled out of shape. He walked awkwardly with the aid of his crosier, and his lips were often bared in a grimace of pain. His eyes, however, were acquisitive and shrewd, and his mind was a razor, especially when it came to fiscal matters. He was one of the inner circle, the man Richard intended to set in a position of high administration to govern England during his absence.

'Thank you, my lord Marshal,' he answered curtly. 'I can

manage well enough.' *Without your help or solicitous gestures* his attitude said even though he was clearly in discomfort. 'It is not far.' He nodded at the open doors before them, leading into a chamber where a table and benches had been prepared for the council members.

Alienor had no love for Longchamp. He was cold and avaricious, and rebuffed all efforts at cordial relations, but he was also a precise and intelligent administrator and she could work with him, even if she did not welcome him in her social circle. Alienor suspected that Richard set great store by him because of Longchamp's ability to draw money into the coffers from all directions and formulate schemes for making more. He was intensely loyal to Richard and reminded her of a snappy small guard dog.

Others were arriving, but out of courtesy had to tailor their steps and await the slow progress of the Bishop with Alienor and William walking either side of him. Among the group Alienor noted Jeoffrey, Henry's eldest bastard son. Provision would have to be made for him, but it remained to be seen what, although by the end of this meeting matters would be clearer.

Alienor sat in her chamber, her feet propped on a stool, sipping wine while Amiria massaged them with rose-scented oil. It had been a long day and she was relieved to relax after the hard diplomatic negotiations over the plans for ruling Richard's lands during his absence. She had her doubts, but Richard was clear about what he wanted and she had to trust him.

She was to have regnal control and an overall hand on the reins, but the chief work in England had been divided between Richard's chancellor, William Longchamp, and Hugh le Puiset, Bishop of Durham. Both men were ambitious, capable administrators but had no experience of governing a country. Longchamp's scribes had been busy making notes on wax tablets and Longchamp had taken everything in with beady eyes, keen as a raptor on the wing.

Four co-justiciars had been appointed to help keep order

and implement decisions made by the senior ones, William Marshal among them, for which she was glad, for he was an ally and a man of sound reason.

John had been given control of six shires in England, the county of Mortain in Normandy, and confirmed as Lord of Ireland, all of which should have pleased him greatly, but all that power had been curtailed by a ban on his movements. Richard had forced him to swear an oath that he would not return to England for a minimum of three years. John had obeyed, but without good grace. Alienor had noted the faint twitch of Longchamp's lips. Not quite a smirk, but definitely satisfaction, and she suspected his fingers had been busy in that particular pie.

She was well aware that many saw her youngest son as an untrustworthy troublemaker, but to all intents and purposes he was Richard's heir. The only other claimant was Geoffrey's posthumously born son Arthur, who was a two-year-old. She had reservations about Richard's decision but was keeping her own counsel while she decided how to approach the matter.

And then there was Jeoffrey, Henry's bastard son, no longer a malleable youth but a grown man approaching his fortieth year. The story had come to Alienor's ears of how, when drunk at a feast, he had upturned a golden bowl on top of his head and asked if a crown suited him. The shard of bitterness in his heart at being the firstborn son of a king and denied regnal power because his mother had been a common whore had pushed its way ever deeper with time. Before his death Henry had promised Jeoffrey an archbishopric. He had been ordained following Richard's coronation and elected Archbishop of York in the autumn but was not consecrated. The Pope had yet to ratify the election, so Jeoffrey was an acting Archbishop, but in a kind of limbo. Having entered the priesthood under duress, his attitude was bellicose. If he upset people, then so be it, and that included Longchamp. The two men heartily disliked each other. Longchamp, who had his eye on Canterbury as a future prospect, was not overjoyed at having Richard's bastard half-brother as a rival archbishop. Longchamp had persuaded Richard to ban Jeoffrey from England for three years too. Alienor acknowledged fully that controlling all these petty power plays and keeping the peace would be difficult, not least because for part of the time she was not going to be there.

She took another sip of wine and looked round as her usher approached her and leaned down to murmur that John had arrived and was asking to see her.

'This late?' She gestured Amiria to cease rubbing and took her feet off the stool.

'Shall I send him away, madam?'

Alienor inwardly sighed, although she did not permit her exasperation to show. She could already guess what this was about. 'No, bid him enter. If it could wait until morning I am sure he would have done so.'

She dismissed Amiria, pushed her feet into a pair of soft sheepskin shoes, rose to her feet and faced the door.

John entered on a draught of cold air, his stride purposeful. 'Mama.' Kneeling at her feet he took a fold of her dress and kissed the heavy green damask.

She touched his hair and bade him rise. 'What brings you to me so late at night, my son?'

'I need to talk to you about Richard banning me from England,' he said. 'It is unfair.'

'It is Richard's decision to make. He has not left you destitute. You have funds.'

'Hah, just as my father handed out "funds" and kept us tied to his rope,' John sneered. 'He doesn't want me to help uphold his rule while he is away. He prefers to trust men who will bring everything to ruins. Longchamp shouldn't be left as justiciar. That is obvious even to a blind man. Someone needs to watch him.'

Alienor said nothing because in part she agreed with him, even while she understood Richard's reasoning. She was also wary of John's motives in this.

He put his hands together in a prayerful gesture. 'Mama, you have influence with Richard. Will you speak to him? He will listen to you.'

'Do you think so?' She shook her head. 'He may take my advice, but he is his own man.'

John lowered his hands and prowled over to the fire. This winter-born last son of hers had always had an affinity for flame and darkness. Practising for hell, some said. 'You are my last resort, Mama. You know I would not ask you unless there was no other way.'

She raised her brows. She suspected that coming to his mother for succour did not sit well with the image of manhood he preferred for himself. 'I do not know if that is a compliment or an insult, but I will take it as the first.'

He sat down on a stool before the fire and dug his hands through his hair. 'I never thought he would do this to me – banish me from England.'

'You are not banished – that is too harsh a word. Richard has given you revenues from your estates there and increased your standing.'

'But it is all as nothing if I cannot go there,' John retorted. 'In order to gain those concessions I had to swear I would not set foot in England for three years. Is that right or just, Mama? I do not know what to do.' His throat worked. 'I want to help Richard but it seems to me that he will never acknowledge me as having anything of value to give him.'

Alienor bit her lip. She felt desperately sorry for her youngest son, even while she wondered how much he was trying to manipulate her. He might have abandoned Henry on his deathbed but what else could he have done? He had always been the closest of her children to his father and she did feel almost a little guilty for loving Richard more.

Sighing, she rested her hand on top of his head. 'Richard may well not agree to do so, but for you I will speak to him.'

Immediately his expression brightened and the light returned to his eyes. 'Thank you, Mama!' He took her hands, and kissed them.

'Do not thank me yet; I may not succeed.' She withdrew from his grasp and wagged a warning forefinger. 'If I do this for you, I expect you in return to keep your word. If you do come to England, it must be for serious and peaceful purposes. I know your inclination to scheme and plot – I am not naive. You say you wish to help Richard, then make sure you do. Do not abuse my trust.'

He fixed her with a wide, melting gaze. 'Mama, I swear I would never do that.'

'There is no need to sell yourself with that stare,' Alienor said with annoyed amusement. 'Let your deeds be your bond, not your promises and cajolery. Heaven knows I had a surfeit of that from your father. Drink your wine and let me retire. It is late, and if I am to be about the matter of persuading Richard to change his mind, I need to sleep well and rise early.'

'Of course, Mama.' Contrite, eager to please, he set his goblet down, kissed her and left.

Shaking her head, Alienor sat down to finish her own wine, suspecting she had just allowed her heart to rule her head, something she had sworn never to do again.

Richard was busy examining a new sword, belt and scabbard when next day Alienor broached the subject of John's banishment from England. He showed little interest in what she had to say, remaining engrossed in the brass fittings and tactile rose-coloured leather of his recent acquisition, and she had to be forceful.

'Richard, leave that for a moment and listen to me.'

Puffing out an exaggerated breath, he laid the belt across his coffer and with laboured patience folded his arms. 'You have my attention, Mama.'

Alienor gave him a hard look. Since becoming King and with his focus firmly on Outremer, reaching him was increasingly difficult. 'Banishing John from England is going to cause a rift between you if you do not allow him to have a role there while you are gone.'

Richard raised one eyebrow. 'I have all the government I need firmly in hand, and I am not inclined to let John loose in England.'

'You may think that is fine at the moment,' Alienor countered, 'but what of the future? What of when you return? What of ten years' time? If you do not bring him into your sphere, you will create bad blood for certain, but if you encourage him he could be your staunchest supporter.'

'Has he been getting at you?' Richard enquired suspiciously. 'Asking you to intercede on his behalf?'

Alienor drew herself up. 'And have you, my son, been listening to all that Longchamp pours in your ears to the detriment of other voices? It is the role of a queen to intercede with the King on behalf of others. Yes there are risks, but you may be storing up trouble for yourself later by denying him now. You should give him the chance.'

Richard pursed his lips. 'But rather when I am here.'

'I believe you will be making a grave mistake if you do not in some form find the wherewithal to work together. It does not have to be close and intimate, but you should include him in your overall plan.' She saw his scowl deepen and was exasperated. 'He is my son as much as you are my son and I must support both your interests. See it for what it is – sound political advice for your good as well as his. Now you are men you must work together as men and put away childish things. You should be side by side, fighting the common foe. You will never know a similar relationship in your life. He is all you have left in terms of brotherhood and you should use him and appreciate him to the full and for your own good and for your mutual gain.'

Richard unfolded his arms. 'Did you say all these things to him as well?'

'In as many words. I am not taking sides and I can see your point clearly, but I understand his too and I am asking you to give him a little more leeway.'

'Enough rope to hang himself?' Richard gave a twisted smile but Alienor could see he had thawed a little towards the idea. 'I have already put the checks and balances in place for England, Mama. Everyone has their part. If I assigned something to John now it would destroy that balance and cause trouble. You know how much he likes to stir the brew – a bit of venomous seasoning here, a pinch of malice there. It is his nature.'

'I would step in to make sure it does not happen. He has much to learn, and he is not ready to rule, but he needs to do so for when he returns to Ireland or takes up a deputy's role once you are home.' She opened her hands. 'Even if he remains in Normandy, it will not prevent him from causing disruption. Better to content him in this and work together.'

Richard turned back to his sword belt but threw her a considering look. 'So that is your counsel – to permit John access to England if he so desires?' He pondered for a moment and then waved his hand in capitulation. 'Very well, Mama. Because you ask it of me and because, as you say, he is my only remaining brother in full blood.'

'Thank you,' Alienor said with a mingling of relief and anxiety. 'You have gladdened my heart.'

Richard looked wry. 'Let us hope you are not creating a world of trouble for both of us.'

Alienor gave a short laugh. 'By the very act of bearing sons I did that.' To further mollify him, she showed an interest in the belt and scabbard that had been occupying so much of his attention.

'It is for the sword of Arthur, for Caliburn.'

'I see.'

Richard collected swords with the same zeal that certain of his bishops collected holy relics. He couldn't resist them and had chests full of the things in his chamber. Several choice examples were always hung on his wall when he stayed anywhere for more than a night. He used only certain favourites in battle, but all were kept honed and ready, and all had names that invoked power. Joyeux Garde, Hauteclere,

Durendal, Caliburn. He was custodian of Juste, the sword of his great grandfather, the first Henry, and that blade in turn had belonged to William the Bastard, conqueror of England.

She admired the weapon he showed her, shining like silver fire. The hilt and pommel were inlaid with gold and garnets and the grip was of red cord bound with gold silk.

'It has been refurbished of course, but the core is the one of legend, drawn from the stone.'

Some swords had an aura of great mystique and power. She had felt it in the blade of William the Bastard when Henry had owned it, but although this one was a thing of beauty, the magic was absent. She suspected Richard was trying to convince himself that it was an original artefact. Of course, on the political front, announcing his ownership would immediately put the Welsh and Bretons in their places.

'Do you intend to take it with you to Outremer?' she asked.

'It will go in my baggage.'

Richard sheathed it as a messenger was brought to them by an usher.

'Sire, madam.' The man knelt and held out a letter. 'There has been more rioting against the Jews including a massacre in York. All the bonds they held of debts have been piled up in the middle of the town and burned to ashes.'

Richard stood very still and contained, that stillness increasing until he was as rigid as a stone. The messenger crouched lower, bending his head, trying to make himself disappear. Alienor took the letter from him and flicked her fingers in dismissal.

Richard drew a shuddering breath. 'They dare to do this to me,' he said hoarsely. 'By Christ who died on the cross I shall show them a King's wrath. I left strict orders that my Jews were not to be harmed. If all those bonds are lost, how much income owing to me has been destroyed? I will have the ringleaders strung up by their entrails!' Suddenly he was in motion, striding across the room, kicking over a stool, shouting for someone to bring Longchamp to him and John FitzJohn, who was constable of York. 'Do they think that because I am no longer in England my arm is not long enough? They were never more wrong!'

'What are you going to do?'

'Send Longchamp back early. He can deal with the fiscal details and stamp out the fire.'

Alienor nodded curtly. Longchamp was no diplomat but he did have the wherewithal to deal with finances and sort out the difficulties caused by the destroyed bonds. It would have to do for now.

'I cannot afford to become bogged down and distracted,' he said impatiently. 'Jerusalem cannot wait. Let others deal with the matter as I delegate. My will must be done in order that God's will be done.' He gave his mother a steady look, but it was one that sought reassurance too.

'I understand,' she said. 'Do what you must.'

A muscle ticked in his jaw above the line of his coppery beard. 'I am trying to leave my lands in a state of protected stability, but every time I seem to be making progress, I turn round and discover that another snake has reared its head. If I could put everything in a sack and hang it up out of reach of vermin until I return, I would be overjoyed.'

'Even your mother?' Alienor asked with a twitch of her lips.

He gave her a hard smile in reply. 'No,' he said. 'I need someone to watch the sack and hit it every now and again.' He made an exasperated sound, kissed her cheek and strode from the room in search of his chancellor.

Alienor walked over to where his hauberk was displayed on a purpose-made stand. It was the first thing anyone saw when they entered the room, the shining war-mesh of iron-dark mail, edged with brass rivets at the hem. At the foot of the stand was the leather sack in which it would be stored for transportation and it reminded her of what he had just said. The analogy was so apt concerning a sack of troubles, and she gave the thing a small kick with the embroidered toe of her shoe.

Chinon's castle bailey was crowded with onlookers, well-wishers, prelates and men of high secular authority. Baggage carts stood laden to the axles with barrels, chests and sacks. Burdened pack ponies champed in line. Soldiers awaited the command to move and the area sparkled in the June sunlight like a bulging fish net, for everyone wore their armour for this departure from Angevin territory to Vezelay on the first stage of the journey to win back Jerusalem. Once out of the town they would remove their arms for the rest of the ride, but for now, the parade was all.

Gazing from her chamber window at the great assembly, Alienor smoothed her gown of gold damask trimmed with silk of Tyrian purple. She wore her crown today over a head-dress of fluted linen, and stood on ceremony, not only the Queen Mother but Queen-Regent too. Soon she would leave this chamber, enter the public space and don that mantle to the full, but in these final private moments she was intensely aware of the man at her side, her beautiful son, and she was brimming with pride and trepidation.

His mail shirt gleamed like dark water – thirty thousand interlocked iron rings, topped by a surcoat of scarlet silk embroidered in gold with the lion device of his dynasty and his nickname. A cloak of forest-green wool was pinned high on his right shoulder and his hair was fiery against the contrasting fabric. She could see Henry in him clearly, but she could see herself too, like a mirror reflecting back to all their ancestors.

He turned to her now with a look in his eyes that told her his mind was already on the road. 'It is time, Mama,' he said. 'We shall meet again in Messina before Lent and celebrate a wedding, God willing.'

'God willing,' Alienor repeated, 'and flesh holding up.' It was a compliment that he took for granted that she was fully capable of journeying to Pamplona to fetch Berenguela, and then crossing the Alps to join him at his planned winter camp in Sicily.

'You are indomitable, Mama, I know you will succeed.'

'Rather I refuse to be daunted and I do what I must, but yes, until Messina.'

He dropped to one knee and bowed his head and she put her hands to his shining red-gold hair and for a moment gripped it between her fingers. 'God keep you safe,' she said, 'and go with my blessing. You are the light of my life, you know that.' She stooped and kissed him on the lips and then let him go and stepped back. It was the hardest thing she had ever had to do, giving away to others the thing she held most precious in the world.

He rose lithely to his feet, smiled at her, and went to the door.

Descending the stairs from her chamber, her jaw was tight with determination, but when she emerged into the hot sunlight and a great cheer surged towards her like a wave she raised her head and walked into it, with a smile fixed on her lips.

In the late afternoon the sunlight was golden, slanting through the high windows in the abbey church at Fontevraud and shimmering on the embroidered purple silk cloth covering the plinth of Henry's tomb. Alienor rested her hands on the cool fabric. It was difficult to believe that Henry's rotting corpse lay beneath this slab. All that vigour and energy dissipated into oblivion.

It was almost a year since his death and still she struggled to come to terms with it. She still expected him to burst into the room, cloak flying, eyes glowing with purpose, covered in scratches from his latest escapade in the hunting field. Waiting for that door to open kept her on edge because she feared that if he did come to her, it would be as a young man vibrant with laughter and all his unsquandered future before him, and that indeed would be too much grief to bear.

'Ah Henry,' she said softly, 'what might have been. Even in your tomb, you haunt me.' She stroked the silk and watched the sheen follow the motion of her fingers. 'I thought you would send me to my grave, but you are a prisoner of death and I am still of this world with so much to do after all the time you wasted.'

She eased to her feet, wincing as her knees and hips twinged, informing her that she was indeed still of this world.

'I shall visit you again,' she said. 'Now I am the one who comes and goes as I please.'

She departed the church with an almost defiant flourish and did not look round, but there was pressure at the back of her eyes, and when she drew a breath it caught on her larynx in a single involuntary sob.

30

Pamplona, Navarre, September 1190

Sancho, King of Navarre, regarded Alienor from heavy-lidded dark eyes. He was a handsome man, pleasant of manner, with a deliberate way of speaking that gave a first impression of a slow wit, but soon became apparent was the result of deep and measured intelligence. His eldest son and namesake, standing at the side of his chair, was quicker and lighter, but cut from the same cloth as his sire. He was also very tall, and Alienor wondered if she would have to crane her neck when it came to meeting Richard's proposed bride.

Alienor had arrived in Pamplona that morning and been shown to a richly furnished set of chambers in the magnificent Olite Palace where she had been able to rest and refresh herself and change out of travelling garments into a stylish silk gown and light cloak. Now she was meeting Sancho in his chamber prior to attending a banquet that had been prepared in her honour.

'It is a long journey you plan to bring my daughter to King Richard's winter camp in Messina,' Sancho said. Rather than Navarrese, he spoke the Lenga Romana of Alienor's most southerly dominions. Hearing its cadences, even with the Spanish inflection, took her back to her childhood when the troubadours and men of Bordeaux at her father's court had spoken and sung in that tongue.

'I would ask nothing of your daughter that I would not ask of myself. I am sure she has inherited the qualities of resilience and fortitude from her illustrious ancestors.'

'Indeed she has, and many others besides. Berenguela is a jewel amongst women, and I do not give her away lightly.'

'Your prudence is commendable,' Alienor murmured. The prospective bride was twenty-five years old, which was late for a woman of her standing to be unwed, but Sancho was clearly a fond and shrewd father, prepared to wait for the most advantageous match. 'Nor does my son choose his bride without deep consideration.'

Sancho directed a servant to refill Alienor's cup with watered wine. 'Your son is a great and famous king. Not for nothing is he honoured as the Lion-Hearted. He is Christendom's hope to take back Jerusalem from the infidel. Any father would be proud to see his daughter joined to such a one.'

Despite his words praising Richard, Alienor heard the reserve in his tone and knew that negotiations were far from over. Sitting up straight, she prepared to play. It was like a challenging game of chess – one she intended to win.

'One matter that does concern me,' Sancho said, 'is that your son still appears to be betrothed to the sister of the King of France. He has assured my envoys that this is not the case, but am I to take this purely on trust? As you have said, I am a prudent father, and I have the best interests of my daughter at heart.'

'Your concern and caution commend you,' Alienor replied

sincerely. 'If Richard has not yet informed the King of France about his change of mind in respect of his sister it is because the situation is delicate – as doubtless you know from your own envoys. I am willing to swear on holy relics that my son has no intention of marrying Princess Alais.'

'No, no.' Sancho made a small tutting sound and looked shocked. 'Madam, I would ask no such undertaking of the Queen of England. Your word and the very fact of your presence are proof of your sincerity, but a father's caution makes me anxious for my daughter.'

'Rest assured that should we reach mutual agreement, I will personally escort Berenguela to Richard and see the marriage solemnised,' she said. 'It is no light undertaking for me to cross the Alps in the middle of winter, and I hope my determination to do this thing will set your mind at rest. Berenguela and Richard will be married as soon as we arrive in Messina.'

'And if you arrive in Lent when no marriages may take place?'

'Then your daughter shall be well chaperoned by me and the Dowager Queen of Sicily and married when Lent is over. The sooner we can conclude negotiations and set out, the better.'

Sancho stroked his beard. 'Indeed, and I am eager for that to be the case.'

They settled down to haggle specific points and clauses of the marriage details, especially involving Berenguela's dowry. It was all very subtle, gracious and diplomatic, but still boiled down to a cross between playing chess for stakes and bargaining in the market place.

Eventually, the terms concluded to mutual satisfaction, Alienor leaned back in her chair and took a sip of the dark Navarrese wine. 'Perhaps I might be permitted to meet my son's prospective bride.' She put a light emphasis on the word 'prospective'. The final decision would depend upon the impression Berenguela made on her.

'Of course, madam, and I believe, even though I am a fond father, that you will look favourably on my daughter when you see her.' Sancho sent an attendant to fetch Berenguela.

Alienor inclined her head. It was a long way to come if expectations were not met, and she was filled with both curiosity and apprehension.

The young woman who entered the room, accompanied by a flock of attendants, was indeed tall like her father and brother, and well-developed. Her gown of dark blue wool revealed the generous curves of her figure but was modestly cut. She wore a plain white veil and a gold circlet over plaited ropes of wiry raven-black hair.

She sank in a graceful curtsey to her father, and then to Alienor, her head bowed, but her spine straight and firm. She remained in that position until Sancho raised her to her feet, kissed her cheek with affection, and presented her to Alienor.

Berenguela raised her lids and returned Alienor's gaze with measured steadiness. Her eyes were dark brown with thick black eyelashes and slight but not unattractive warm shadows on and beneath the lid. She had sharp cheekbones, a long, thin nose and a cleft chin. The entire effect was striking and handsome rather than being softly feminine.

'I am pleased to serve you, madam.' Berenguela's voice was quiet but assured.

'As I am to meet you,' Alienor replied. The young woman had an air of tranquillity about her – or perhaps calm reserve. She must be apprehensive about this meeting, yet her actions were measured – almost nun-like. 'I hope we shall come to know each other well.'

Berenguela dipped her head in acknowledgement and folded her hands modestly in front of her waist.

Alienor presented her with a small ivory casket that held a gold ring set with a large deep blue sapphire. 'The King of England gives you this as a mark of his esteem and prays you wear it in token of your future union.'

A flush mantled Berenguela's cheeks as she took the casket

with grave courtesy. 'I esteem him for this gift. Be assured I shall wear it with honour and to honour him – and hope that we shall meet very soon.'

What would Richard think of her? Alienor did not know her son when it came to women. She had never asked him, and he had never volunteered information. The only knowledge she did have had come from John with his tale of the whore-sharing with Philippe of France, and she had pushed it to one side because it was more difficult to contemplate than the notion of a single mistress or even rampant lechery. Yet this young woman would be the vessel on which Richard begot his heirs and they would have to come to agreement in the bedchamber.

'I hope so too, and to that end your father has agreed that we shall leave Pamplona in three days' time and begin the journey to Sicily.'

Berenguela's flush deepened and she curtseyed again to Alienor before departing with her gift and her ladies, her movements serene and graceful.

'You will find that my daughter has a well of deep and quiet strength,' Sancho said. 'She is a godly young woman who will do her duty, but there is more to her than that as those who know and love her come to find out. She will make a courageous and fitting queen for your son.'

'Yes,' Alienor said, 'I am certain she will.' But she was not certain at all, and could only trust in God that Berenguela would suit.

'You ride well,' Alienor said to Berenguela with approval.

Berenguela patted her palfrey's neck and smiled. 'My father insisted it was a necessary skill to learn. Often a wife has to travel between her husband's territories, and when a household is always on the move, it is easier if one has that ability.'

'Your father is wise. Mine was of the same opinion and I was taught to ride from the moment I could hold the reins. I have blessed him many a time for that forethought.'

They had set out that morning from Pamplona in a colourful array, silk banners snapping in the warm breeze and sunbursts flashing on helms and harness – a parade for the citizens and an ostentatious display of status and wealth. People had worn their finest silks and musicians had accompanied them along the route, playing and singing, beating the time on taut skin drums. The crowd had cheered, thrown flowers, and in their turn received showers of silver coins from the departing bridal party.

Berenguela had begun the journey perched sideways in a padded chair seat, her feet resting on a platform while a richly caparisoned attendant led the horse, small silver bells jingling on bridle and breastband. Two miles beyond Pamplona's gates, with the crowds gone, Berenguela had exchanged the chair saddle for a travel one in order to sit astride. Now it was mid-afternoon and they had at least another three hours of riding in front of them before they stopped for the night. Alienor was hoping they would reach Espinal, but if not they would pitch tents. The first leg of their journey was three hundred and fifty miles to Montpellier and the easier stretch. From there they faced an arduous journey over the Alps which would coincide with the harshest winter months.

'When my father told me I was to wed King Richard of England, I was pleased and honoured,' Berenguela said. 'Navarre is a small country, but important as a guardian of the pilgrim roads, and our alliance will be like a mail shirt, helping to protect Aquitaine's southern flank.'

Alienor eyed her with interest. 'Your father talks politics to you?'

'And my brother Sancho too,' Berenguela said, pink colour rising in her sallow cheeks. 'It is essential I understand these things so I can be useful to Navarre and to my family. Also to my husband – should he wish it of course.'

'And if he did not wish it? Would you keep to your sewing?' Alienor thought of Henry and her mistaken belief when she

262

married him that he would value her opinion and make her half of the whole.

Berenguela said thoughtfully, 'It would be his decision of course. I would find things to occupy my time. There are always opportunities to do good works in the world and prayer is a great solace to me. I would hope to bear my husband children and they too would occupy my time.'

'Indeed,' Alienor said. 'I am looking forward to that day, if God wills it.' It was the reason for this haste, so that Richard could marry and set about procreating an heir. He was a big, strong man, powerful as the lion of his nickname, but Geoffrey and Harry had been strong young men too and both lay in their graves. She was pinning her hopes on this pious but determined young woman.

'I hope I will please him.' Berenguela gnawed her lower lip. 'I will do my best, but I know so little about him. Madam, would you tell me what I should know that might be helpful?'

'I am his mother, I do not know what will be helpful to a wife,' Alienor said with a rueful smile. 'But since you ask, he is a great soldier, as is your brother. You must embrace the warrior in him and allow that part its free rein. I have not known you for long, but I can see already that you will not cling and be helpless, which is all to the good – Richard has no time for such people, be they male or female. I advise you to be practical in your dealings with him but beyond that I cannot advise you more save to say that your own nature will dictate his response. He is not unaccustomed to women, even if he lives a military life – he grew up with three sisters.'

Berenguela absorbed this like a conscientious diner absorbing nutrition. Alienor saw her glance covertly at her own brother, Sancho, who was escorting them part of the way, and suspected the young woman was taking him as her example of a man of military standing. Richard and Sancho of Navarre were friends with mutual politics and goals, but that did not make them alike as men.

'I am looking forward to meeting one of those sisters soon,' Berenguela said with a smile.

'So am I.' Alienor was pensive. 'Joanna's husband died a few months ago, and I need to know how she is faring – there has been so little detail.'

'I am sorry. Yes, we heard the news in Pamplona and were shocked. God rest his soul.'

'He was still a young man.' Alienor shook her head. 'And he and Joanna had no heir – their son died soon after he was born. I am concerned for my daughter, although I suppose there will be news once we cross into Italy. At least Richard will be able to take command of matters as her brother and head of the household while he is in Messina, but it means making new plans. Richard was counting on William and Joanna for aid, but now he will have to negotiate with William's successor – whoever that might turn out to be. Still, that is a bridge we cross when we come to it, and there are many of those to negotiate before we arrive. You and Joanna will be good company for each other.' She clicked her tongue and urged her palfrey to a swifter trot, her thoughts agitating her to increase the pace.

The women journeyed on towards Montpellier, skirting Toulouse which was hostile territory, but their well-guarded entourage, led by the ever-watchful mercenary captain Mercadier, was not approached and they passed through the landscape like a cavalcade of illuminated ghosts.

A fortnight into their journey they paused at midday by a glittering stream to let the horses drink, to fill their own water bottles, and eat. The sun still held warmth and the day had been mild. Clouds of midges danced above the grass at the water's edge, rising and falling like the notes of a song, and a few late bees blundered among the last of the alpine blossoms.

Alienor listened to the water rushing over the stones and watched the translucent patterns twist and change like silver ribbons rushing downstream. The sun warmed her spine and she drew a deep breath of life.

Belbel unfolded leather-seated stools from one of the baggage carts for Alienor and Berenguela to sit on while they ate and the rest of the entourage dismounted to stretch their legs and ease travel-tired limbs. On a sudden impulse Alienor removed her red silk hose and her shoes. She draped her cloak over the stool, hitched her gown through her belt peasant-fashion and, walking precariously on the stones and shingle, went to paddle in the water. The first contact was an icy shock, and took her breath, but filled her with exhilaration.

Berenguela stared at her open-mouthed, the piece of bread in her hand forgotten.

'Come,' Alienor beckoned. 'Refresh yourself.'

Berenguela hesitated and Alienor beckoned again, more peremptorily. 'Come, come. This is not an opportunity you will have every day. You too, Belbel.' She waded further into the stream, up to her ankles. The edge of her skirt began to wick up water, but she did not care because it would soon dry while the weather was warm and she loved the feel of the grit and pebbles between her toes.

Belbel needed no urging and, slipping off her shoes and stockings, splashed into the stream beside her mistress.

Berenguela hesitated, looking round. Sancho grinned and waved her on to the deed, while showing no inclination to do so himself, and Mercadier raised his brows, grunted, and champed his way through his bread and cheese, his expression stoical.

Somewhat reluctantly, Berenguela joined Alienor, raising her skirts in an effort not to wet the hem too much, while exposing as little of her legs as possible.

Alienor watched her face contort at the coldness of the water. 'When I was a young girl at court in Paris I was rebuked for dancing barefoot in the dew of the gardens by no less than the sainted Bernard of Clairvaux and then by my mother-in-law. It was behaviour inappropriate to a queen, they thought.'

Berenguela swished her foot and looked uncomfortable. Alienor suspected she would be on the side of obeying propriety.

'I was held prisoner for fifteen years by my husband,' Alienor continued. 'Even when I was not shut away and permitted to attend court gatherings I was unable to do anything save by his will. Now I am in a valley not far from Roncesvalles where Roland defended the pass against the Saracens, and I am refreshing my feet in a stream where perhaps he too stopped for a moment, and I am breathing the unsullied air of freedom. I may do as I choose. This stream has always run here – it ran when Roland was alive; it ran when I was a prisoner; and today I will bathe my feet in it and give praise to God.'

Berenguela looked chagrined. 'You must have had great strength and fortitude, madam,' she said. 'I think I understand.'

'I hope you do. I survived, but it comes at a price.'

Leaving the stream, Alienor sat down to eat while her feet dried and was not surprised when Berenguela immediately followed her. Belbel walked a little way upstream, stooping to collect coloured stones.

Alienor enjoyed the pungent goats' cheese, dried sausage and bread, strong and salty on her palate. 'The journey is going to grow more difficult,' she warned Berenguela. 'We should enjoy the moment. Perhaps the most important lesson I have learned is to embrace the small pleasures and turn them into lasting memories.'

31

The Alps, Winter 1190–1

Alienor and Berenguela pushed on with their journey, stopping at nightfall to claim hospitality at monasteries, castles and towns that were friendly. Between such accommodation, they camped under the sky in canvas tents. At Montpellier Berenguela's brother Sancho took a tender farewell of his sister and returned to Navarre, leaving the bridal party to continue on its way towards the Alps and Italy.

The season was advancing and the benign day in late October when they had bathed their feet in a stream and eaten bread and cheese with the sun warm on their backs faded into memory. After several days of cold, heavy rain, the gentle streams became rushing torrents of white water, intimidating to cross. Thick fog, as dense as a wet woollen blanket, followed the rain. Barely able to see ten yards in any direction, their progress slowed to a crawl for the best part of a week.

Alienor had still not gained a full impression of Berenguela. She was self-contained, pious and not given to any kind of frivolity, that much was obvious, but she was steadfast and no complainer. Richard would approve of those traits at least. The best to hope for was that she would be a sound, trustworthy wife who would fulfil her role of queen, bear children and provide a firm footing that would allow Richard to devote the time he needed to his affairs.

As they approached the Montegenevre Pass, the weather grew progressively colder. There rain turned to flurries of sleet and snow, and in between there were hard frosts and clear blue skies contrasting with the white dazzle of the mountain peaks, grey rocks thrusting through the white crumpled white coverings like the bones of giants. Everyone donned fur-lined gowns and cloaks, and stuffed their waxed riding boots with fleece, although the hard physical toil of the route often made them sweat inside their garments.

Alienor pushed on, fighting the weather, using every hour of daylight they had, and often the half twilight of the snowscape, determined to make as much distance as she could before the weather closed in. Despite all her efforts, the number of miles covered in a day continued to tumble with the temperature and the women slept together at night, bundled in their furs for warmth.

'It does not seem possible that there can be such extremes,' Alienor remarked to Berenguela, her breath frosting the air above the bedclothes. 'In Outremer, in Jordan and Jerusalem in the high summer, men long for this kind of cold.'

'At least there are no flies to ward off, and no weevils in the bread,' Berenguela said pragmatically. 'And no wasps and scorpions either.'

Alienor gave a rueful smile. 'That is true. We should indeed count our blessings.'

One morning in mid-December, Alienor was awake before the last stars had set and she immediately set about chivvying the servants and soldiers to build up the fire, heat water and food, and see to the horses. Fresh snowfall dusted the ground like sifted flour even if for now the sky was clear. Mercadier was awake too, bundled in his cloak, drinking steaming broth from a cup held in his mittened hands. She wondered if he ever slept. He had been talking to one of the guides they had picked up at Montpellier, and now he turned to Alienor.

'Madam, Jacques says there is more snow coming. Do not ask me how he knows these things, but I believe him.'

'How long?'

'This evening, he says.'

'Then we should make haste while it is clear. Tell the men to hurry.'

Mercadier gave her one of his looks, not insolent, but assessing and sharp. He put down his cup and served her with a cup of hot broth from the cauldron that had been standing in the night ashes of the fire. Taking it with a nod of thanks, Alienor returned to the tent.

Berenguela was awake and having her wiry black hair bound into plaits by her maid Zylda. Stamping snow from her shoes, Alienor gave Berenguela the news and that they must make haste. 'We must not be caught out on these mountains in a blizzard.'

Zylda pinned up Berenguela's braids and covered them with a linen cap and veil. Berenguela, already dressed in her fur-lined gown, pulled on her boots. 'What can I do to help?'

Together the women and their maids packed up the contents

of the tent and then took down the tent itself. Berenguela worked nimbly and willingly and Alienor noted her practicality with approval and thought that Richard would approve too.

By the time a red dawn rose out of the east, they were on their way. Last night's snow crunched under the horses' hooves and the frozen air was painful to breathe. The sun stained the peaks the pink of washed blood that gradually bleached out to become a dazzling white that burned the eyes. Alienor marvelled at the majesty of it all even while acknowledging how deadly it was. They were minute, insignificant creatures toiling through God's creation, their survival only made possible by His grace. She sent up prayers to St Bernard of Menthon and the Holy Virgin Mary to intercede with the Almighty and keep them safe, and heard Berenguela entreating God too, one hand on the reins, the other running her prayer beads through her fingers.

The path continued upwards in a series of sharp twists and snaking curves. On occasional straight patches they made better progress but even that was a careful plod with eyes peeled for landslides and tumbling snow or boulders. At midday they heard a crack, followed by a sound like thunder, and watched an avalanche of snow rumble down the steep slope of a peak to their left, tearing down trees and obliterating all in its path. Berenguela crossed herself. Their guide shook his head and kissed the crucifix around his neck. Alienor tried not to look at the snow-clad slopes lowering over their own path lest thinking about them precipitated a similar tumble. If that happened, their party would be covered and not found again until spring.

By noon the sun had grown hazy and snow clouds gathered, dense and tinged with yellow. Their guide hastened them on, whacking the horses on the rump with his staff, anxiously watching the thickening sky and muttering imprecations.

As the first flakes started from sky to ground, they came to a low stone shelter built for pilgrims and herders with stabling at one end of the low-roofed dwelling. Part of the end wall had fallen in and it was cramped and musty, but it was still sanctuary from the storm and they had wood and charcoal on two of the pack horses to build a small fire. Even before that was done, the snow had intensified to a curtain that obliterated anything else and the rising wind had developed a petulant whine. The travellers gathered around the gusting, smoky fire, ate their rations of hard bread and dried sausage, and said nothing, but all silently acknowledged that without the shelter of the hut, meagre though it was, many of them would have faced death this night.

By morning the storm had blown itself out and the sky was once again a sharp, brilliant blue. But so much snow had piled up in drifts that they had to dig their way out. Jacques had marked the boundaries of the road with two hammered stakes before the worst of the storm hit, so at least they knew where to begin, but it was hard and precarious work and beyond the stakes there were no boundaries, just mountains like jagged white teeth in a giant's mouth.

A mile further on their entourage came to a place where the track was partially blocked by snow, boulders and uprooted fir trees. There was just enough room to inch their way round it, but the route was hazardous and they had to ease along in single file. Alienor set her jaw and didn't look down as she led her horse along the slender margin of snowy path between the rock fall and the void.

The path narrowed further. Berenguela's maid began to whimper and was silenced by a terse command from her mistress to pray to God and get on with it. Alienor nodded approval and Berenguela rose further in her estimation.

A step, another step, and still the way was as thin as a pauper's ribbon, all tattered at the margins. The sun turned westwards and as the light shadowed blue in the hollows, a sudden clatter came from ahead, a scream, and several dull thuds. Alienor's horse tossed its head and jerked on the reins and she flattened her palm against its neck, soothing, and murmuring. Zylda's whimpers began again and Berenguela ordered her in a steely voice to be silent.

In front of them the line began moving again. Tentative, foot by foot. From somewhere Alienor found the courage to go on, but the first steps were terrifying, and she felt the same tension in her horse. *I refuse to die here. I will live to see tomorrow's dawn. One pace at a time, as God wills. One and then another. And never, never look down.*

At last, under a grey-blue sky illuminated by bitter moonrise, they arrived at a wider path and an open section of snow field where they could make camp and recover from their ordeal. One of the pack horses and its keeper had gone over the side into the ravine and were now food for the lammergeyers – as they could all have been. She shut off that thought with the vigour of bolting a door against the enemy. She would not let Richard down. Whatever happened she would bring Berenguela to him, whole and in one piece.

Berenguela's olive complexion was grey, and the brown shadows under her eyes were as pronounced as bruises, but she was coping; only the rapid fingering of her prayer beads revealed her agitation. Her maid shivered and sobbed under a blanket, and for now, Berenguela had left her to that indulgence.

'That poor man and beast,' she said to Alienor. 'I pray that his soul finds its way to heaven. It could have been any of us.'

'Indeed, God rest his soul, and we should give thanks to Him that we have been spared.' Alienor watched her breath frost the air. 'Once over these mountains, the journey will improve. This is the worst part.'

'I do not think it could worsen.' Berenguela gave a distorted smile. 'Besides, there is no way back.'

Alienor could not read the emotions in Berenguela's eyes, but the top layer was like her own – an indefatigable determination to see this through.

The next evening the party reached a proper pilgrim hostel, with welcome fire and torchlight, and good stabling for the weary horses. Eating hot vegetable pottage with shreds of smoked meat and hard, dry bread, Alienor thought she had never tasted anything so delicious. Even the raw red wine with an aftertaste of pine pitch matched for the moment anything she had drunk at court in Poitiers.

They were joined by a silk merchant with a fur-lined cap pulled down over his ears, and a bulbous red nose pitted like an orange. His name was Etienne and his journey was the reverse of theirs, for he was on his way home from Sicily to Montpellier, having been conducting business in Palermo.

Alienor would not usually have invited such a man to join them, but tonight she was mellow, and this kind of peril where one could be alive one moment and a corpse at the bottom of a ravine the next created a climate of camaraderie among those forced to travel. In winter there were few pilgrims but messengers, merchants and clergy still had to use these pathways and brave the elements.

'You should be on your guard on the roads beyond through Italy,' Etienne cautioned them. 'Bands of brigands roam at large and prey on the unwary – although perchance they will not trouble you when they see the strength of your escort.'

'If they trouble us, my sword entering their bodies will be the last thing they see on this earth,' Mercadier growled, hunching over his wine. 'But my thanks for the warning.'

'My party were threatened a couple of times,' the merchant said, 'but we stood up to intimidation.' He indicated a handful of dour, well-built soldiers sitting at another trestle. 'It pays to hire the best you can afford. I advise you to stock up on food when you can too, for the French army has been through and all but picked the land clean of supplies. Even if you think food will be available because you have the authority to command it, you cannot have what is not there.'

Alienor thanked him for the advice. She knew all about food shortages from her journey to Outremer with Louis. 'Since you have come from Sicily, do you have news of King Richard?' she asked. 'And of my daughter the Dowager Queen?'

He wiped his lips. 'Madam, I heard that King Richard was in dispute with Tancred the new king, about the Queen's dowry.'

Alienor's gaze sharpened. 'What is there to dispute?'

Etienne refilled his cup. 'King Tancred refused to release the gold and the ships promised by King William because he said that with King William's death that promise was null and void. He even kept the Queen hostage for a time, but was eventually persuaded to release her to your son.'

Alienor compressed her lips. She was not surprised at such perfidy, but she was angry.

Enjoying his tale, the merchant rested his cup on his rotund belly. 'The Lionheart swore that unless Tancred gave up the dowry and Queen Joanna, he would go to war against him . . . and he did. He took Messina and burned it. They came to an agreement after that. I do not know more because I left, but I heard a rumour that King Richard gave Tancred the sword of King Arthur to seal their pact.'

Alienor raised her brows as she remembered Richard's pride in Caliburn before he left for Outremer. Why had he given it to Tancred, and just what sort of pact had he made? She needed to know more, but this merchant couldn't tell her and it was impossible to find out anything in the middle of the Alps in these frozen winter months.

More wine arrived, hot from the fire and mulled with nutmeg and cinnamon from her coffers.

'The King of France refused to help King Richard take Messina, but insisted they share the spoils according to the treaty they had made,' Etienne added.

Alienor made a scornful sound. 'That comes as no surprise.' Philippe of France made Henry look like a saint as a political player. There was never a time when he was not manipulating the chess board, and making up the rules as he went along.

The merchant paused for effect before dropping his next nugget of information. 'Madam, it is also said that the French

King has been very taken with King Richard's sister, the Dowager Queen.'

Alienor coughed at the notion of Joanna married to Philippe of France. 'Oh, that is too preposterous to contemplate!' she spluttered. 'I sincerely doubt I will ever address the King of France as my son-in-law.'

Etienne nodded wisely, as if he spent every day of his life in the counsels of royalty. He spread his hands. 'I can tell you nothing more, madam, I am sorry.'

'I thank you for what you have been able to give, messire,' Alienor said. 'We are forewarned and forearmed – at least a little.'

It snowed again overnight, heavily, and they lost another four days sheltering in the pilgrim hostel playing dice, singing songs and telling stories until finally the weather improved sufficiently for them to set out on their way again. Bidding Etienne farewell and Godspeed, they ventured into the hostile white landscape. Another guide, Pieter, had joined Jacques and the men felt the way along the route using long wooden prods to probe the snow and make sure the ground underfoot was safe. Step by step, mile by slow mile they made their way through the mountain passes. Christmas was celebrated in yet another hostel, sheltering from the snow.

Berenguela wept as they attended mass on the day of the Christ child's birth, their surroundings not unlike a stable with people and animals crowded together. She gave precious frankincense resin from her own supplies to be burned in token of the wise men's gifts to the baby Jesus.

'I have knelt at the place of Christ's birth.' Alienor inhaled the scent of the sacred smoke. 'At the shrine in Bethlehem where the manger once stood. I have kissed the very place.'

'He was born just like us' – Berenguela had her hands clasped under her chin, her expression exalted – 'and he died to redeem our sins.'

'God willing you shall bear sons and raise them in Christ,'

Alienor said softly. She imagined dandling Richard's heir on her knee – a little boy with coppery hair, sea-blue eyes and a smile like the sun. But as yet that child was no more than seed in Richard's loins, and this earnest young woman praying at her side was the ground in which it must be planted.

Berenguela's colour heightened. 'God willing,' she repeated. 'It is my dearest wish.'

By mid-January they had reached Italy and, with the relief of mauled survivors, left the snow-clad mountain ramparts behind. Hostels became more frequent along the route, but they had to be on constant watch for roving parties of soldiers. The merchant Etienne had been right: food was indeed scarce. They had the money to obtain supplies but it was basic, subsistence fare and sometimes they went hungry. Mercadier slept little and kept a constant watch, his mood irritable as he shepherded the entourage on its way.

Arriving at the castle of Lodi just outside Milan one bitter evening they found themselves competing for accommodation and stable room with Emperor Heinrich of Germany who was on his way to Rome to be consecrated in that title, although he was already bandying it about. He had a claim to Sicily through his wife Constance and was intent on pursuing it against Tancred whom he considered had usurped his rightful throne.

Heinrich and Alienor were not allies, but since they were sharing accommodation on neutral ground they were courteous towards each other, albeit in the manner of two fighters circling, and not trusting to turn their backs. Heinrich was an ally of Philippe of France, and Alienor had no intention of revealing to him that she was bringing Berenguela to wed Richard. If he found out, he would send messengers at speed to Philippe, and that was the last thing Richard needed. Thus Berenguela remained in the background, as an unspecified lady of Alienor's chamber, and Alienor gave out the story that she herself was on her way to bring her widowed daughter home.

Among the young courtiers with the Emperor was Alienor's grandson Heinri, Richenza's brother. He acted as interpreter because he spoke fluent French as well as his native, paternal German. At seventeen years old he was tall and handsome, with a tumble of dark auburn curls and bright hazel eyes.

'How is your father?' Alienor asked when Heinri made a personal visit to her chamber.

'Well enough, madam,' he replied. 'His joints are stiff these days and his eyesight poor, but he continues as best he may. He misses my mother. He never thought she would die before he did because he was so much older.'

'Indeed, and I think of her every day, and pray for her. You have a look of her a little.'

Heinri smiled sadly. 'My father says that.'

Alienor told him how his siblings were faring in England and directed him to pour wine. He did so with a slight flush to his face at serving his grandmother and being under her scrutiny. She watched him with pride and a little sadness, wishing that Matilda could be here to see her eldest son on the cusp of manhood.

'The Emperor keeps you close?' she remarked. 'I suppose that is a mark of favour, and at the same time he can watch you and control your family.'

Heinri presented her with the cup. 'Indeed that is so, Grandmère, but at the same time I am learning from him and from the court. It is good training.'

At Alienor's grimace, Heinri shook his head. 'The sword cuts both ways,' he said with a pragmatic shrug. 'To know one's enemy one has to keep him close. I will not be banished as my father was.'

Alienor nodded approval and thought that this young man would do very well indeed. He had learned the political lessons swiftly and had a wise head on young shoulders.

Next day, as the women were breaking their fast, Heinri visited them again, but this time he was tense and agitated. 'A messenger has just arrived from Sicily in search of my lord,' he told them. 'He does not bring good news for him; I do not know whether it is good for you or not, Grandmère.'

Alienor bade him sit and directed a squire to pour him watered wine. She pushed a basket of bread and platter of cheese towards him. 'Tell me.'

He refused the food and took a token sip of the wine. 'Uncle Richard has made peace with Tancred of Sicily.'

'Yes,' Alienor replied, 'I knew that already.'

'My lord did not, and he is displeased that Uncle Richard has agreed to acknowledge and uphold Tancred as king there in exchange for ships and supplies.'

'Your uncle does what he must,' Alienor said.

Heinri brushed his thumb over the metallic sheen on the goblet. 'To seal the agreement, Uncle Richard swore an oath to Tancred. He has made Arthur of Brittany his heir and promised a marriage between him and Tancred's baby daughter. He sealed the pact by presenting him with the sword Caliburn.'

Alienor inhaled sharply. So this was the rest of the tale that Etienne the silk merchant had not known. It all made sense now, but she wasn't sure it added up to wisdom. From the German point of view the news was of treachery because Richard had thrown in his lot with Tancred. On the Angevin side, making his deceased brother's infant son his heir had the potential to destabilise all of Richard's lands, because John would not see it as political expedience, but as an act of betrayal. If Richard died in the Holy Land there would be strife throughout his dominions.

Heinri said unhappily, 'The Emperor will not forgive Richard for this. He was raging when he received the news.'

'Then he will just have to rage. Your uncle would not have done this without good reason.' She defended him knowing he had had to make that choice, but nevertheless her stomach was churning.

'I must go.' Heinri rose from the table, his wine barely drunk. 'I need to keep my head down for a while.'

'Have a care.' Rising, she embraced him with tender concern. 'And you also, Grandmère.'

He took his leave and Alienor prepared to move on, her mouth set in a determined line. Richard had made an enemy; it could not be helped but it was yet another difficulty to negotiate. And if John heard about the decision in Sicily before she could arrive home and smooth troubled waters, the seas would be stormy indeed.

32

Reggio, Italy, March 1191

As the women travelled south, the weather warmed, and by the time they reached Reggio and the point of crossing to Messina a soft breeze was blowing down the peninsula, fragrant with the green scents of spring. They had tried to take ship further north in Naples but had been detained because of continued political wrangling between Tancred, Richard and Philippe of France. Truces finally agreed, they had arrived at the tip of Italy from where they could see clear across to the Sicilian coast less than two miles away.

Berenguela had become quiet and withdrawn as they approached their destination, and had spent much time praying at her small, portable altar. The more unsettling a situation, the more she turned to God for support and solace. There would be no immediate wedding. Their delayed arrival had taken them into Lent and the marriage would have to be conducted en route to Jerusalem.

This morning Berenguela wore a gown of dark blue wool, brushed out and smoothed of creases. Her masses of black hair were coiled in thick plaits around her head and dressed with a white silk veil. The effect was one of quiet grace rather than lustre and fire. For the first time since leaving Pamplona, she wore her betrothal ring.

Alienor gazed out of their lodging window across the straits of Messina. The water in the channel was deepest blue but choppy with whitecaps. She was disappointed at the lost opportunity. Had they not been delayed by difficult weather and petty politics they would have arrived in time for Berenguela and Richard to be wed, and perhaps by now Berenguela would already be with child.

A messenger had recently arrived with letters from England and Alienor held several travel-stained packets in her hands, tagged with various seals including those of William Marshal, Geoffrey Fitzpeter and the other justiciars.

Leaving the window, she took the documents to a sun-splashed table in the corner, sat down, and began to read. A thin spotted cat twined around her legs, and then leaped onto the table and paraded in front of her on its tip-toes, a leonine purr rumbling from its chest.

Berenguela came over and started feeding the cat small morsels of dried sausage, talking to it in Navarrese like a mother to a small child.

As Alienor read what was written in the letters an exasperated sigh escaped her lips. 'While I am attending to the cauldron in front of me, the one behind my back is boiling over,' she said. 'There is no respite.'

Berenguela stopped talking to the cat. 'What is wrong?'

'The justiciars are complaining about the high-handed behaviour of Richard's chancellor William Longchamp, and Richard's brother has crossed to England to "help" – and that will only foment unrest, not calm it down.' She tossed the letters on the table. 'Longchamp was a mistake, I always thought so, but Richard would have his way.'

'What is wrong with him?' Berenguela asked curiously.

'He is intensely loyal to my son, I cannot fault him for that, and he is an excellent administrator. But he has no diplomacy and the English barons dislike him. He forces through his policies when sometimes it would be better to ease them with a little honey. He can raise money out of dust, but he has no ability when it comes to dealing with those he should cultivate.'

'I know men like that at my father's court.' Berenguela went to the window and glanced out. 'There's a galley,' she said.

Joining her, Alienor saw a vessel with a striped sail ploughing through the waves towards the wharf. The ship was still a way off but making good headway. A silk flag bearing the leopards of Normandy and England flew from the top of the mast, and the anxiety in her heart was overlaid by a quickening of joy. 'My dear,' she said to Berenguela who had stooped to pick up the cat and was cuddling it to her bosom, 'prepare to greet your future husband.'

A rosy glow coloured Berenguela's cheeks. 'I did not know he would come himself.'

'I suspect nothing would stop him,' Alienor replied with a smile.

Berenguela bit her lip. She put down the cat and brushed pale hair from her dark dress.

'Do not worry, he will know we are travel-weary and will not be expecting us in full court array for this meeting. You have crossed the Alps in the middle of winter; you have the courage for this.'

Richard arrived in a flurry of fresh air and sunshine and it seemed to Alienor that the room lit up the moment he entered it. She sank in a curtsey and Berenguela followed, bowing her head.

'Madam my mother.' Richard took Alienor's hands and, raising her to her feet, kissed her on the lips, and then, turning to Berenguela, greeted her in a similar fashion, although his kiss was to her cheeks. 'And my future lady wife. I am pleased to greet you both after your arduous journey.'

'Indeed,' Alienor said wryly. 'Only for you would I cross mountains in the depths of winter. I will not regale you with our trials, but I will tell you that Berenguela has been a courageous and uncomplaining companion.'

'Complaining would have made no difference to our circumstances save to make them more of a trial,' Berenguela said with quiet dignity.

'I would expect no less of a lady of the house of Navarre,' Richard replied with a bow. 'I trust that trait will stand you in further good stead in the days to come.'

'I trust so too sire,' Berenguela replied. 'Now that God has delivered us to a safe and honourable harbour, I will endeavour to fulfil my part of the bargain.'

'And I mine.' Taking her hand, he looked at the large sapphire betrothal ring then raised it to his lips and kissed the stone. 'You must tell me about your adventures when we dine in Messina.'

'Will you take wine while our baggage is loaded?' Alienor asked.

'Why not?'

Richard proceeded to introduce Berenguela to the lords who had accompanied him – Robert, Earl of Leicester, Hubert Walter, Bishop of Salisbury, and John, Bishop of Evreux, who was to solemnise the marriage once Lent was over.

Alienor watched Richard being polite and urbane. He could be as crude as the next soldier and doubtless would be when it came time to talk with Mercadier and the troops, but he possessed a courtier's polish and an innate sense of graceful etiquette. When he exerted himself he could dazzle anyone.

Sitting down at the sunny trestle with his cup, he looked at the cat. 'I see you have been collecting waifs and strays, Mama.'

'He found us,' Alienor said with a wave of her hand. She was not interested in small talk. 'I doubt he will add himself to anyone's collection. Tell me, are we to greet the King of France when we arrive in Messina?'

Richard's eyes glinted. 'No, Mama, sadly not. He left at first light this morning. If you had longer sight in your eyes, you might have seen his sails vanishing over the horizon.

Naturally he extends his regrets that he could not stay to greet you and my new bride, but he felt a sudden necessity to move on.'

'Naturally.' Alienor lifted a sardonic brow. 'What did he have to say about Alais?'

'All winter he has been insisting I marry her the moment I return home. But last month he got to hear you were on your way with Berenguela – such things can only be kept secret for so long. He confronted me to demand I keep my promise.' He shot her a meaningful look. 'So I told him the reason I could not.' His glance flicked to Berenguela.

'I know that reason, sire,' Berenguela said with dignity. 'My father would not have entrusted me to come all this way without being aware of all the details. I know when to be silent.'

Richard eyed her with interested amusement. 'Well that is a fine thing in a wife,' he commented.

'What did Philippe say?'

'He refused to believe it at first,' Richard said, 'although I think he knew. What king does not have spies at foreign courts? He said that I would make up any kind of filth to escape from the match and I told him if I was going to make it up, I would not tarnish my dynasty by citing my own father. I would just have said that Alais had been sullied by someone at court. I offered to provide the witnesses if he wanted them but unsurprisingly he declined.'

'I can see why. Have you reached an agreement about Alais' dowry?'

Richard finished the wine and set the goblet aside. 'I have to pay him two thousand marks to end the agreement, but the Vexin territory and Gisors will remain to me and my male heirs. Should I die without an heir, then the lands will go to Philippe.' He smiled at Berenguela. 'So it behoves me to wed and sire a son.'

Berenguela looked down and clasped her hands prayerfully. 'I will do my best, sire, God willing.'

'Unfortunately the wedding cannot take place until after Lent,' Richard said. 'I have no doubt Philippe is hoping I choke on my dinner or drown at sea, but I intend not to give him that satisfaction if I can help it.'

A squire arrived to say that the baggage had been stowed and the ship was ready. Richard pushed to his feet and glanced at the letters on the trestle.

'We have matters from England to discuss,' Alienor said, 'but they can wait until we are in Messina.'

He nodded brusquely and a look of annoyance crossed his face. He was being defensive, Alienor thought, but this was not the time to push him.

Waiting to greet them as their ship moored on the Sicilian side were more of Richard's officers, various Sicilian nobles and dignitaries, and a tall young woman wearing a gown of amber silk brocade, a gold veil fluttering over her long bronze-brown braids. Alienor stared with hunger and curiosity at this daughter she had last seen as a twelve-year-old caught in the moment between child and woman. Alienor's farewells had been made from a cage. Now she was free and her daughter was a grown woman of twenty-six, a widow who had borne and lost a child. She had her father's broad cheekbones and wide grey eyes blended with Alienor's fine nose and sensuous mouth.

'My lady mother.' Joanna started to give Alienor a formal curtsey but it broke down as Alienor pulled her to her feet and embraced her tightly, hot tears prickling her eyelids.

'Let me look at you!' Her voice quivered with emotion. 'So beautiful, so grown up.' She swallowed. 'You have been on my mind so much over the years. All the way here I have been thinking about you and wondering what we would say to each other, and now I have no words, only tears!' Laughing, she hugged her again.

Joanna returned the hug, her own eyes brimming. 'Mama, I never thought to see any of my family again; yet here you are . . . and my brother's wife-to-be.' She turned to Berenguela

283

who had been waiting quietly at Alienor's side. 'I am so glad to meet you. Richard told me about you, but I was sworn to secrecy because of the situation with the French. I am so glad it can be in the open now.'

'And I am pleased to greet my new sister,' Berenguela answered gracefully. 'I heard much about you on our journey and I am looking forward to knowing you.'

Formalities accomplished, the company withdrew into the palace where a welcoming banquet had been prepared. Because it was Lent, meat was absent, but there was an abundance of fresh fish and shellfish from the surrounding seas, plentiful bread, jewel-green olive oil, and flinty Sicilian wine.

As Alienor dined, she glanced often at Richard, trying to impress his image on her mind like a coin in wax, so she would always have the memory. He was wearing his crown for this feast and sunbursts of light sparked on the rubies, emeralds and amethysts jewelling the band and finials. When he spoke, he accompanied his words with elegant gestures of his long, finely shaped hands and it was difficult to imagine them wielding a sword, even though she knew his capabilities.

She watched him with Berenguela, and was anxious, because she could tell from the courteous expression on his face that Berenguela's quiet modesty was not engaging his interest in any depth. Berenguela murmured sensible responses to the questions he asked but they lacked wit and sparkle, even if spoken with genuine thought and sincerity. There was no lightness in her being; she was clearly projecting herself as a model of demure, noble womanhood. She made Alienor think of a saintly wooden image – the kind that folk paraded around the town on holy days.

Following the feast there was an informal gathering for the most important guests, with jugs of sweet wine and bowls of dried fruit and sugared sweetmeats. Outside the sun was setting over the Tyrrhenian Sea in a banner blaze of orange-gold, hemmed by a cloud-line of royal purple, and the breeze was warm with spring. Richard escorted Berenguela onto the balcony area and stood alone with her to talk, so that they were chaperoned, but private.

Seated on a curved chair, her feet propped on a footstool, Alienor covertly studied them. She knew Richard was giving her a ring, one that he had chosen informally and that was for her alone rather than part of the royal regalia. Perhaps this would unravel the knot of reserve between them.

Joanna joined her, arranging her silk skirts in a wide fan around her feet. 'I do not know what to make of her, Mama.'

'In what way?'

Joanna pursed her lips, considering. 'Well, she is reserved. She holds herself back, but not because she is shy or witless – indeed far from it.'

'I think that too.' Alienor was interested that Joanna had reached the same conclusion. 'She is deep like still water.'

'And we are all variations of fire, Mama.' Joanna smiled. 'Do you think he will burn her up or that she will quench him?'

'I hope they will balance each other.' Alienor sent her daughter an amused but reprimanding glance. 'And that she will provide tranquillity in his life.'

'But you do not want her having too great an influence,' Joanna said shrewdly. 'You do not want a wife for Richard who will be your rival.' She tilted her head to one side. 'Indeed, I do not believe any woman could be, because there is no other in the world to match you – certainly not in Richard's eyes.'

Alienor accepted the assessment with a judicious nod. Joanna was perceptive and astute, perhaps even a little cynical. 'That is probably true except that neither Berenguela nor I will ever rule your brother's life because he is a man and goes his own way.'

'But you have influence over him, Mama, I know you do.'

'Not over him,' Alienor corrected. 'I have his ear, which is an entirely different matter. He will listen to my advice but it does not mean he will take it. Berenguela has no share in our family's history. She has not had to survive your father for a start, and her own influence on Richard will be very different.' She looked at Joanna. 'I do not think I will have a close bond with Berenguela, but I admire her fortitude and respect her strength – and I believe that it is a mutual thing.' She paused to take a drink of the sweet raisin wine and changed the subject. 'I am sorry for the loss of your husband and the difficulties with Tancred afterwards.'

Joanna twisted the wedding ring she still wore on her finger. 'I was fond of William. He had mistresses, I know that, I am not naive, but he was never unkind and he treated me well. I could have anything I desired for the asking – except the heir we both wanted. Even though he had other women, he still came to my bed. I lost one baby scarcely before he had made an impression in his cradle clothes, and I miscarried another child just two months before William died – and so I have nothing.' Her chin wobbled.

'I understand.' Alienor grasped her hand. 'I am sorry.'

Joanna raised her other hand to swipe away tears. 'And then all this wrangling over the inheritance because there was no heir and I was powerless, and only saved because my brother arrived and dealt with Tancred's claim on men's terms.'

'It has always been thus for women. But without us men cannot make their alliances, and forge their links.'

'But it is still their world.'

Alienor gestured acknowledgement. 'We have our own worlds to rule within it and they are no less complex, and again, without them the bigger worlds cannot function.'

Joanna sniffed. 'I remember when my father sent you to Sarum – I learned a great deal then about the position of men and women.'

'It is in the past,' Alienor said bleakly.

'Do you still hate him?'

Alienor shook her head. 'No. All that remains is regret for what might have been. It is like standing in the ashes of a fire you once approached to warm your body a little, but which burned you to the bone instead. Now the ashes are cold, and sometimes you remember that even when your hand was in the flames, you still had a terrible need to thrust it deeper.'

Joanna swallowed. 'Mama, don't. You will make me weep.'

Alienor gave a self-deprecating laugh. 'I will make myself weep too. I do not dwell on it often for that very reason because I realise it is not in the past at all.'

Richard returned from his moment alone with Berenguela. The sun had set and the horizon sky was turquoise in the west, pricked with diamonds of starlight. Berenguela's rosy complexion and the coy smile tucked into the corners of her mouth told a story of approval. The ring Richard had given her was set with three rubies and she kept touching it with the fingers of her other hand, clearly moved and proud. Richard was smiling too, but his expression was less readable as he sat on a settle opposite Alienor and drew Berenguela down beside him.

'England,' Alienor said after a moment. 'Richard, what are you going to do?'

Berenguela sent Alienor a startled look, and Joanna a sharp one, because suddenly politics had come into play and, like the difference between sunset and dark, the vista had completely changed.

Richard replied calmly. 'I have already sent letters to Longchamp and the justiciars with instructions to deal with those matters. Longchamp has my authority to do as he must to keep a tight rein.'

Alienor was not to be put off. 'He is over-zealous in his dealings and the barons are turning to your brother.'

'Who I wanted to keep out of England,' Richard said with a flare of irritation. 'But you pleaded with me to give him permission to go there.'

'Yes, because in constraining him you would have made a rod for your own back, even more so than now. You have unbalanced the situation and made it dangerous by declaring Arthur your heir. From where you stand you might see it as political necessity, but John will view your making a child of four heir to your lands while ignoring him as a grave insult.'

Richard waved an impatient hand. 'It was necessary in order to secure Tancred's support. I needed those ships and I needed Joanna's dowry. As it is, Tancred is still being difficult because he knows you met his rival for the throne in Lodi.'

'That was unfortunate,' Alienor said irascibly, 'but not deliberate. It could not be helped. Heinrich received the news about your pact with Tancred while we were there and you have made yourself a bad enemy.'

'I had no choice. I had to make the decision for my situation here and now.' He clenched his fist and gazed at his bunched knuckles. 'It would be too easy to become buried in all the fine grains of sand and never walk on the beach. Jerusalem is the objective. Everything else can wait until the tomb of Christ is free. For now I entrust my concerns at home to my more than able deputies.'

'You are on a path to ruin with Longchamp,' Alienor said, holding to her point. 'These letters tell you that. You must do something about it.'

'Then what do you suggest, Mama?'

'Whether you like it or not, you must curb Longchamp. If you do not, your barons will look for ways to unseat him and your brother will make the most of it. My advice is that you appoint someone else to be justiciar in England, someone who will work with your lords.'

Richard tightened his lips, revealing his opposition to her suggestion, although he did not refuse. 'Did you have anyone in mind?'

'As a matter of fact, yes. The Archbishop of Rouen will do very well indeed. I have every faith in Walter of Coutances and he is better suited to being in England and Normandy than here with you. You have plenty of accomplished advisers.'

He thrust out his jaw, resisting.

'I shall need an escort to return to England and the Archbishop and his knights will be perfect. We can brief each other on the way so that we are agreed on a mutual purpose. He will be useful in Rome too, to assist in your half-brother's ratification as Archbishop of York. Once that happens it will be an additional tie on Longchamp's ambitions.'

Richard raised his brows. 'So you are advocating that Jeoffrey also returns to England?'

'As clergy, yes, not in a secular context. He will be a balance to Longchamp and he has good administrative skills.'

Richard continued to stroke his beard, but eventually nodded. 'Very well, let it be as you say, but I do not want to act in haste. The situation may yet resolve itself without resorting to a heavy hand.'

'If Longchamp proves too much of a problem, you must give me the power to remove him if necessary,' she said adamantly. 'That is not negotiable.'

She rose to her feet and walked out onto the balcony where Richard had recently been standing with Berenguela. The air was cool now, and the light in the west had blended with the rest of the sky to dark sapphire-blue. The sound of the waves shushing to shore failed to soothe her. She was breathing too swiftly and she felt faint and sick.

Richard joined her silently, and said nothing, although she could sense his exasperation.

'I cannot do this, my son.' Her voice shook. 'You give me responsibilities that seem never-ending, yet do not give me the tools to accomplish the task and at every turn I am blocked. I would come with you to Outremer and see you married, it is my dearest wish, but I must return to your lands for the sake of all of us, because if it is not sorted out it may turn to disaster.'

Richard exhaled and, putting his arm around her, drew her against him. 'Mama, I understand your concerns even if you think I do not. I would return if I could and deal with the situation but that is impossible for now.' He dug his free hand through his hair leaving deep finger tracks in the heavy red-gold. 'You may have as much support from me as you need – always, but I would rather you kept it to yourself. If news spreads of difficulties in my territories, there are those who will take advantage.'

'So you will give me authority to remove Longchamp if I must?' she pressed.

Richard's mouth twisted. 'You drive a hard bargain, but yes, Mama, I will. You and Walter of Coutances shall have letters of sanction to remove him from office should you find it necessary, and Walter will replace him in England. But that move is only to be implemented if there is no other way. Walter will also have power to clip John's wings if my brother is proving too friendly with the barons. Does that seem reasonable?'

Alienor composed herself. 'Yes,' she said. 'I can work with Walter of Coutances and the barons respect him. If we are to visit the Pontiff in Rome on our way home, we may need funds.'

'I shall put those in place for you, Mama, as much as you need.'

'Then it is settled.' She looked up at him and shook her head. 'I do not know why it had to be so difficult. You could have agreed with me in the first place.'

'But then it would not have been my idea and I would not have digested it in the same way,' he said. 'I am still uneasy, but I trust no one in the world as much as I trust you, Mama.'

Alienor made a face because while such words were gratifying to hear, they laid a heavy burden upon her. 'Well then, on the morrow I shall make ready. Joanna can chaperone Berenguela and be her companion until your wedding.' She glanced over her shoulder at the two young women. 'Both are good travellers and will be an asset to your household.'

'I know they will, Mama, although Joanna nags me just as much as you do.' His mouth twitched and the moment lightened a little.

'That is one of the roles assigned to mothers and sisters, as you should know by now. I hope you will be sincere and honest with Berenguela.'

'It seems to me that those are her own traits too,' he said, his tone slightly flat.

Alienor tapped his arm. 'Do not underestimate her or dismiss her as a means to an end. She will be useful to you if you are prepared to let her help. She would follow you into hell if you asked it of her – if not for love, then for loyal duty. Many wives would not do that for their husbands. I would certainly not have followed your father. Think of her as another weapon in your armoury.'

He looked wry. 'I will bear your words in mind, Mama.'

'Richard, I mean it.'

'So do I. You have my oath that I will honour her and treat her fittingly.' He kissed her cheek in reassurance, but also in finality, and Alienor knew she had taken all things as far as she could go.

After only three days' respite, Alienor set out again for Normandy and whatever she was going to find there. Walter of Coutances, Archbishop of Rouen, was her travelling companion, and the prospect was not unpleasant. He was an erudite and affable cleric, snowy-haired with a fresh complexion and a benign, cheerful manner. A mischievous twinkle enlivened his deep-set eyes and a natural upturn to his lips made him look as though he was smiling, but concealed just how wily, intelligent and ruthless he really was.

Alienor made her farewells to Joanna and Berenguela at the Messina wharfside on a warm but overcast day, with the sea a choppy grey at her back. She embraced both young women and gave an especially warm hug to Joanna. 'Have a care to yourselves,' she said. 'Look after each other, and look after Richard.'

'Inasmuch as he allows us to do so.' Joanna cast her glance heavenwards. 'Knowing my brother he will spend most of his time with his men – unless Berenguela can entice him away.'

Berenguela looked embarrassed but smiled.

Richard arrived and presented Alienor with a soft leather satchel holding the letters they had earlier written together concerning the matter of William Longchamp and his replacement should it prove necessary. Alienor's baggage was heavily guarded because it contained more than a thousand marks of silver, much of it destined for bribes in Rome. 'Saint Silver and Saint Gold,' Richard had said with a twist of his lip. 'That is the language that Rome knows best above all others.'

Richard knelt to her, and Alienor, with tears in her eyes, pressed her hand to his hair. 'Parting grows no easier. You would think I had had enough practice by now, but it becomes more difficult each time.' She raised him to his feet. 'Go and do great deeds, my son, and know you carry my heart and my pride with you.'

'I shall greet Jerusalem for you, Mama, and bring you a stone from the Holy Sepulchre when I return.'

'I know which will be the greater gift,' she said.

After a final embrace, she let him escort her onto the galley. She harboured a real fear that she would never see him again, that this was the final farewell, and hated that she was powerless to stem the flow but had to follow it downstream to whatever end.

As the ship surged out across the channel towards Italy, she gazed at the figures on the wharfside growing ever more distant, and sent her prayers and her love like invisible ropes across the widening gap, to bind in spirit, if not in flesh.

33

Bures, Normandy, Christmas 1191

Closing her eyes, Alienor inhaled the smoky perfume of frankincense rising from the braziers in her private chamber where she was warming herself before the fire. The scent always soothed her no matter her tensions.

Two musicians were playing a gentle duet on harp and

citole in the background, and that too eased her soul. She felt enclosed and protected. Outside a ferocious wind was slamming wintry rain against the shutters, and she welcomed the wild weather because it meant a respite. No messages would arrive from England while such a storm was in progress. Until this gale abated she had time to sip her wine and enjoy the fire, the music and the frankincense. So much had happened since Messina that she had had no time to catch her breath.

In Rome she had secured Jeoffrey's consecration as Archbishop of York but that success had cost her eight hundred marks. From the papal Curia she had ridden on to Normandy to watch and protect the duchy, leaving Walter of Coutances to cross to England with the letters from Richard and a mandate to deal with the hornets' nest of wrangling between the country's bishops and barons, with John stirring the mix while pretending to be utterly reasonable.

Henry's bastard son Jeoffrey had crossed the sea to take up his archbishopric and had promptly been seized and thrown into prison by Longchamp, who claimed he had no right to come to England. Eventually persuaded to disgorge Jeoffrey by deepening protests from the barons and Walter of Coutances, he had done so, and had the tables turned on him. In a desperate attempt to hold on to power he had tried to bribe John to side with him. John had gleefully refused and had Longchamp's underhand dealings cried far and wide until the latter had been forced to hand over the castles he commanded and leave the country. Walter of Coutances had stepped in as chief justiciar, put Longchamp's partisans out of office and replaced them with his own men. Longchamp had quit England and taken his grievance to Rome and for the moment was out of the dealings in person, although his hand was still stirring the brew from a distance. Coutances had also, under Alienor's direction, had John pronounced as Richard's heir, which had further calmed the situation.

She would have crossed to England herself, but Philippe of

France had reneged on his vow to liberate Jerusalem and, claiming ill health, had returned home, spreading the word that Richard was to blame for all the ills he had suffered on crusade, and that his sister had been disparaged and treated shamefully. Although he had sworn before the expedition not to encroach on Richard's lands, Alienor did not trust his word of honour and remained poised in Normandy, ready to counter any hostile move he made.

News from Outremer was sporadic and travel-worn. Richard and Berenguela had been married on the island of Cyprus, which Richard had subdued following an altercation with its ruler Isaac Comnenus. Acre had fallen to the Christians and Richard himself had been sick there but was recovering. All these pieces of information were a distant story and there was nothing Alienor could do but protect Richard's back. For the moment, this storm blessedly protected hers as well.

The fire snapped loudly, startling her, and a glowing ember coughed onto the edge of the hearth tiles and smoked as it turned from crimson to black. She finished her cup of wine, dismissed the musicians with thanks and a small purse of silver, and retired to bed.

A guest at Conisbrough, John donned a loose gown lined with the skins of northern squirrels and wandered back to bed, cup of wine in one hand and a letter in the other. Belle raised her head from the pillow and looked at him sleepily, her tangled hair a wild contrast from the neat braids with which she had come to his chamber. The orderly, demure young matron now looked like one of Southwark's best. Despite her protestations, he had always known he would get her back into his bed. Of course he was a lot more careful this time. Her elderly husband was impotent and while a blind eye might be turned to his bedding her because he was the King's brother and heir to the throne, it would not be turned if she got with child a second time.

'Well, my love, it seems that the game is afoot once more.'

Belle stirred and, yawning, sat up. 'What game would that be, my lord?' She bent one knee and eyed him provocatively.

John gave her an amused glance but did not take the bait. He had enough scratches on his back to last him a while.

'An offer of marriage – a very interesting offer of marriage indeed.'

She rolled onto her stomach. 'You are already married.'

'It's been disallowed by the Church. We're related within the proscribed degree.'

'I thought that was how you liked your women.' She stretched her arms above her head.

He snorted. 'Hawise was foisted on me because I had to take her in order to have her lands – as well you know.'

'And me?'

He raised one eyebrow. 'I haven't decided yet.'

'I am the mother of your son. You could have obtained a dispensation and had me.'

'I already have had you – twice last night. You should get dressed.'

She made a face at him but reached for her clothes. 'So who is the fortunate lady?'

John rolled his tongue around his mouth as if enjoying a choice morsel. 'The King of France is offering me his sister and all of the lands across the Narrow Sea for which Richard does him homage.'

'His sister?' Belle stared at him.

'Alais, you goose. Richard has cast her off and married Berenguela of Navarre. Such a move might keep his southern borders safe but the rest is ruined now that Philippe is back.'

'But Alais—'

'Is a princess of France,' he said with a hard smile. 'I know full well the reasons why my brother repudiated her but I care not if she is my father's leavings. A marriage is a business arrangement – a convenience. It would only be exchanging one convenience for another.'

Belle donned her hose, securing them above her knees with

daring red silk garters. 'You think you will be allowed to do that?'

He gave a dismissive shrug. 'Who is to gainsay me? Richard doesn't want her, and Philippe is willing to make me his brother by marriage. Why should I not take it?'

'You are a wolf,' Belle said, half in fascinated admiration, half in disapproval.

He grinned at her. 'Why thank you, my love.' He leaned over and chucked her under the chin. 'And you are a vixen.'

'You should be careful.' She pushed him off and reached for her chemise. 'You could be playing into the hands of a man with a wolf trap, and it is not good to face such a thing when there is an angry lion at your back.'

'But he's not at my back at the moment and I am the one with cause for anger. He betrayed me in Sicily when he named Arthur as his heir – a whining, snot-nosed four-year-old.' His eyes glittered dangerously.

'Perhaps it was necessary policy at the time, and if he is married now, he may soon have an heir of his own body.'

John's lip curled in a sneer. 'That may happen I grant you, Outremer is a land of miracles after all, but Richard is all bravado and little deed.'

'Oh come now, how do you know that?' Belle's gaze filled with greedy curiosity.

'I have my means.'

'But he has a son does he not?'

'So he claims and has acknowledged him as such, but I hear that the child resembles his namesake and the conception event had several players, including the King of France.'

Belle's eyes widened and she spluttered. 'Truly?'

'Of course it all goes unsaid, although I understand Richard has received absolution for his sexual excesses. It doesn't alter the fact that he has given that little Breton runt preference over me. Why should I be loyal? As soon as I have dealt with my remaining business here, I'm riding for France.'

'You mean it, don't you?'

'What do you not understand about what I have just been saying? Of course I mean it.'

'What about your mother?'

'What about her? She doesn't need to know. She would only side with Richard anyway because he is all that matters in her eyes.'

'You should be careful.'

John smiled and kissed her again. 'I intend to be. I learn by my mistakes – as do you, hmm?'

John made ready to depart for Howden, thirty miles away, where he was to spend Christmas with Hugh le Puiset, Bishop of Durham. Belle, by now tidy and modest, bade him farewell with everyone else as if she had not spent most of the night in his bed, indulging in all kinds of delicious, forbidden games. Her mother watched her with an anxious gaze and lined brow, and later, when the routine had returned to normal, and the women were about their duties, came to sit with her.

'You are playing a very dangerous game,' she said in a low voice, 'and moreover a dishonourable one.'

Belle looked up from her sewing. 'I do not know what you mean, Mama.' Feigning nonchalance, she threaded her needle.

'Yes you do,' Isabel said primly. 'You think you can go as silently as a wraith, but there are still eyes to see and ears to hear.'

Belle shrugged and thrust out her lower lip. 'He is gone now, and I doubt he will be back.'

Isabel was at a loss. Her daughter had a hard look about her, a mingling of defiance and misery. Lightly she touched her hand. 'I worry for you.'

'Then you waste your time.' Belle stabbed her needle into the fabric. 'He is going to France, and I shall probably never see him again.'

'France?' Isabel said sharply. 'Why is he going to France?'

Belle's expression closed. 'I suppose he has business there.'

Isabel wondered if John was going to visit Alienor. That would make sense, but why would he cross the Narrow Sea at this time of year unless he had to? But Belle hadn't said Normandy, she had said France. That meant Philippe. John was always intriguing. Isabel didn't like Longchamp and she had been glad of John's intervention, but her son was one of John's close companions and she disliked the idea of him being involved in his schemes. There was too much entanglement.

'What sort of business?'

Belle made no answer.

'Why do you say you might not see him for a long time?'

'Because if I am here in the North and he is across the Narrow Sea, how shall our paths cross?' Raising her head, she stared her mother in the eyes for the first time. 'I take what joy I can, Mama.'

'It does not seem like joy to me,' Isabel said bleakly.

'But I am not you, nor would I wish to be – ever.'

Isabel compressed her lips and turned away before she cried. She often wondered how she and Hamelin had begotten this troublesome daughter, so beautiful, so privileged, and yet so full of hostility and dissatisfaction. What had they ever done to foster this? Their other girls had given them no worry and their son made her proud with his manly ways, although at the same time she would not have him follow John to France without knowing what was afoot. Indeed John was the root cause of the difficulties she experienced with their children; but until Richard begot an heir, he was their future king, and so they must tread with caution and turn a blind eye to Belle's behaviour.

Later, she spoke to Hamelin. He had been busy about the demesne and was now relaxing in his favourite chair and toasting his feet before the fire. Sitting opposite him, she took out her embroidery and told him about John going to France. 'I am worried. We should prevent Will from going with him.'

Hamelin had not been overjoyed at hosting John under his roof, but he had been obliged, and given the current situation he was wary of crossing him. He spent a great deal of time looking elsewhere because he did not want to see the veiled glances cast between John and Belle. If they were duping him, he did not want to know any more because it was too painful. Isabel always fussed too much and had a tendency to coddle their son, but in this she was right. 'I will summon him home and find tasks to keep him occupied.' He sighed heavily. 'The sooner Richard returns the better. If John intends going to France, it can be for no good purpose.'

Hamelin and Isabel were breaking their fast when an usher approached to say that one of the foresters, Haregrim, desired to speak with him urgently, and that he had an injured man in the bailey.

Hamelin was settled and comfortable where he was, but the expression on his usher's face made him leave his meal and hurry outside.

A crowd clustered around a small cart, and lying upon it was a youngish man, grey in the face and fighting for breath, but still conscious and aware.

'What is this?' Hamelin demanded.

Haregrim stepped forward, a small, thin individual but wiry and tough, with intelligent blue eyes. Before becoming Hamelin's deer-keeper he had served as a serjeant in his lord's military household. 'Sire, I found him on the road; his horse had put its hoof in a pothole, broken its leg and rolled on him. I put the creature out of its misery and brought him here. The kennel-keeper has gone with his lad to bring the horse for dog meat.'

Hamelin recognised the injured man as a groom of John's household who had recently been promoted to the post of messenger. He was in his late twenties and far too young to be facing death. 'Bring the chaplain,' he commanded. 'Make haste.' He turned to Haregrim. 'Was he carrying any letters?'

'No, sire, nothing. All he had was his purse and his knife.'

Hamelin frowned. It was odd that he bore no message – unless of course it was a verbal one. Crouching, he spoke in the messenger's ear. 'You are sore wounded,' he said. 'We will care for your body and soul, but is there information you want me to pass to your lord? Where were you bound?'

The man's features contorted and he coughed, spraying blood from his mouth. 'I need to find the Count of Mortain,' he gasped.

'He is not here; he has gone to Howden, but I can send on your message.'

The messenger weakly shook his head. 'For my lord's ears alone.'

Hamelin's jaws tightened. 'Your loyalty commends you but you may tell me. Until yesterday he was a guest under my roof.'

'It is a sacred trust. Cannot . . .' He shuddered and his eyes rolled up in his head.

Father Hugh arrived in haste clutching the chrism box, his stole unevenly draped around his neck, and his hair sticking up around his tonsure. The gathering stepped aside to allow him to administer extreme unction. Moments later the young man died, clasping the cross Father Hugh had placed in his hands.

'Search him properly,' Hamelin commanded. 'Be respectful, but do it. Check the lining of his cloak and tunic.'

Giving a brusque nod, Haregrim patted the dead man's garments, checking for sewn-in pockets. He delicately searched inside the braies and leg bindings and also his shoes.

'Nothing, sire.'

'His hat,' Hamelin gestured.

Haregrim picked it up and looked inside. 'Lice,' he said, grimacing. He felt the braid surrounding the edge of the cap and suddenly stopped. Unsheathing his knife, he used the tip to rip the stitching, and plucked out a thin strip of parchment curled around a ring set with a Roman intaglio. Hamelin narrowed his eyes. The strip of parchment was a code strip and the only way to read it was to wrap it around a dowel that had been created to decipher the words. Such things could be broken, but it might take weeks of work, and there was no one here with sufficient experience or ability.

Turning on his heel he sought Belle, dragged her by the arm to his chamber and ordered the servants to leave.

'Tell me,' he said as the door closed. 'What business does John have in France? Do not say you do not know because you will be lying. Mark me, if you do not tell me, I shall consider it treason.'

'Why don't you ask my brother?' Belle pulled free and rubbed her arm. 'He is in John's entourage and a party to all he does.'

Hamelin gave her a hard look. 'Your brother is not here, even though he soon will be, but in the meantime you will answer me or face the consequences. Again, what business does John have in France?'

Belle flashed him a resentful look, but her sense of self-preservation led her to reply, albeit that she almost spat the words. 'Philippe of France has offered John his sister Alais in marriage and Richard's lands if he will come to him and do homage for them. John is considering whether to accept the offer since Richard has made it clear he would rather name the child Arthur as his heir and let John fend for himself.'

Hamelin felt as if she had punched him in the stomach. He should have expected something like this, but again had been too trusting. 'You would have kept this to yourself?'

'I saw no reason to speak. My brother knows it too, and he has not told you.'

'Do not use him as your excuse,' he growled. 'John has already ruined your life once, and he will do it again. Go now to your mother, and do not move from her chamber and the company of the women lest I see fit to confine you further than this – understood?'

'Yes, my father.' She swept him a deep curtsey which made him clench his teeth. In hindsight they should have found her a firmer husband than the elderly Robert de Lacy, but it only brought the blame back to him and Isabel and he had neither the time nor the inclination to go down that road.

Swallowing his fury, he called for his scribe and messengers because letters needed to be sent in haste to the justiciars and to the Queen. Whatever happened, John could not be allowed to sail for France.

A freezing February dusk had fallen as a saddle-sore Alienor rode into Windsor. She had pushed the horses and herself hard to reach the castle in two days from Portsmouth. The crossing from Normandy had been appalling and on several occasions she had thought the ship was going to capsize and make them all food for the fishes. She had weathered the battering because she did not suffer from sickness, but Belbel and Amiria were still groggy and nauseous.

As she drew rein in the courtyard, William Marshal emerged from a doorway and stood at her stirrup to help her dismount, and she was very glad of his assistance, for her hips and thighs had set like stone.

'Madam.' He bowed. 'I am glad to see you and sorry you have had to cross the sea in such difficult weather.'

His expression was serious and shadowed, but he retained his air of dependable strength.

'I am sorry too, but needs must.' She indicated her travel-spattered gown. 'Is John here?'

William inclined his head. 'Yes, madam, the Count of Mortain arrived a few hours ago.'

'Good, then at least he is prepared to talk.' She lowered her voice. 'But should he take thought to leave without greeting his mother I want you to prevent him – with courtesy.'

'It is already in hand, madam,' he replied. 'The Archbishop of Rouen issued the order the moment we received news from my lord de Warenne.'

'Good,' Alienor said with a brisk nod.

He escorted her to the chamber that had been prepared, matching his pace to hers but in such a way that it did not

302

seem as if he was deliberately slowing to make allowances for her stiffness, and his courtliness warmed her.

A fire glowed in the hearth, giving off welcome heat, and a clean linen cloth covered a platter of bread, cheese and cold meat. The bed was made up and piled with extra furs. As servants went round the room lighting candles and lamps and dealing with her baggage, she said to William, 'I understand you have added to your family since last we spoke.'

He smiled. 'Indeed, madam. My namesake will be two years old in the spring, and Richard was born in October. Not only the King's name, but he has red hair too.'

Alienor congratulated him, but then sighed. 'Sons,' she said. 'May yours make you proud and grow up not to give you sleepless nights, but I fear it is the way of the world.'

'They already give me sleepless nights,' he said ruefully.

'But not as much now as they will when they are older. Still, you need not worry about that for a while. I shall write to your wife and send a gift for your son. I shall talk to you more in a little while.'

William bowed and withdrew. Alienor sighed again, relieving tension and feeling lighter for that moment of banter with William. Warming herself at the fire, she ate some of the bread and cheese and drank a cup of wine. Amiria was still suffering from sickness, but Belbel had recovered sufficiently to help Alienor dress in a gown from her baggage, a favourite one of plain dark red wool with embroidered gold bands around the top of the sleeves.

Rested and refreshed, Alienor bade Amiria go to bed and, taking Belbel with her and a squire with a lantern, made her way to John's chamber.

Since he was not in the room, she made herself comfortable to wait. A chess set and gaming board stood in the embrasure, and there was a book seat, the lid raised to reveal several volumes, one with a jewelled clasp. A piece of parchment was curled on a coffer, writing scrawled on the shadowed underside. Knowing full well John would not leave anything important so exposed

303

unless by deliberate intent, she took a glance. It was a letter from his bastard son Richard, the writing unsteady and imperfect, but the heartfelt effort was obvious and there was an illustration of a characterful dappled horse in the margin that made her smile. Richard informed his father that he was studying hard and doing everything he was told. Alienor's feelings towards John softened as she read the words. Clearly he was doing the right thing by his son and the child loved him. It was a great pity that brotherly love was not so easily come by.

Sitting down, she helped herself to a cup of wine and a piece of preserved pear from a dish of candied fruits – a sweetmeat she had never been able to resist.

She had drunk half the wine before the door finally opened and John entered. He stopped abruptly for an instant and then advanced into the room. 'Mama, I did not know you had arrived.'

'Indeed?' Alienor raised her brows. 'It is very remiss of no one to tell you.'

He knelt to her, and she kissed him and bade him rise. The shadowy light made a dark gleam of his eyes. His expression was wary – as well it might be. It was the first time she had seen him since setting out for Navarre eighteen months ago and the last childhood softness had been subsumed in the harder features of the grown man. She could almost feel the danger emanating from him, like sparks in a thunderstorm.

'Shall I send for food?' he asked.

'I am not in need. I have had wine and sweetmeats to keep me company while I've been waiting.'

She resumed her seat and arranged the folds of her gown in a sweep of blood-red cloth. 'Sit.' She gestured him to the chair at her side. 'I wish to speak with you as a mother to a son and since I have crossed the sea in midwinter to do so, it behoves you to listen and give me a full answer.'

He hesitated, but after a moment poured himself some wine and sat down. 'What do you want to say, Mama? Whatever it is, I am not certain you will change my mind.'

'I understand why you might want to accept the offer Philippe of France has made to you. It is a great temptation, but you are mistaken if you believe he is doing it out of benevolence. His intention is to drive a wedge between you and Richard.'

John shrugged. 'Richard has driven in a wedge of his own. What am I to think when I hear he has disinherited me in favour of an infant? What message does that convey beyond contempt for my position?'

'That was expedience in a tight corner. When he returns he will reverse it, but not if you continue on this path. I cannot let you cross the Narrow Sea and go to Philippe.'

His lip curled with contempt. 'So first I am not permitted to set foot in England and then I am not allowed out of it. You play me both ways, and then wonder why I take the game into my own hands. Without me, the Bishop of Ely and his grand conniving for power would have brought England to its knees.'

'But he has been dealt with and replaced by the Archbishop of Rouen. You acted decisively in this and I am proud of you, but this other matter smacks not of high ideals but of grubby scheming. You know full well that Alais is soiled goods and yet you would make her your wife and bring her into our family?'

'Yes I would,' John answered in a hard voice. 'Why not when I have to make my own way in the world?'

Alienor controlled the urge to slap him. In naming Arthur his heir, Richard had done more damage than he knew, and she would only compound it by raging. 'You are born of my own body,' she said in a softer tone. 'I carried you in my womb for nine months even as I carried Richard. I love you dearly, but this discord cannot continue. You are all I have left in the world that I love. You and Richard must ride side by side instead of tilting against each other.'

'Richard should remember that too,' John said stiffly.

'I know that, and he has received the same words from me.

But for you, it is not seemly that you should jostle in a foreign court for attention. You must put your self-interest aside and work for the common good. That is what it is to be a prince or a king. You may think you are weaving a fine braid by including the King of France in your design, but in truth you are weaving with a dagger that will cut the threads as it goes in and out.'

John said nothing.

'As I love you, I take it that you love me, and for my sake I want you to put aside this intention of yours and seek a different path.' She reached across and touched his knee in a conciliatory gesture. 'Come, we can discuss this and see what benefits might accrue to you for your forbearance. Perhaps some new wardships and governmental duties.'

He shifted in his chair and she sensed an uncoiling within him and thought that she might have broken through. 'I might be willing to negotiate,' he said grudgingly. 'But what Philippe offers is worth a great deal to me.'

Alienor bit her tongue on asking him if Philippe's offer was worth more than his loyalty and integrity. Having castigated him she needed to soothe and repair. 'It is now, but it would not turn out to be a bargain in the future.'

'I will think on it,' he said.

Alienor stood up. 'I need your oath on this, my son.'

'Then I give you my oath that I will think on it, Mama,' he said, refusing to be moved. 'But I cannot give it now, and I am not a child to be offered sops of comfort in the place of true value.'

She clasped her hands around his. 'I know that. Promise me you will not suddenly ride out tonight and take ship for Normandy.'

His lips curved, but there was no humour in his eyes. 'Yes, I promise,' he said, and withdrew from her grasp.

Alienor recognised his attempt to control and manipulate the situation. 'Then I shall see you tomorrow in council.' She made to leave, but on her way, she turned. 'I saw your letter.'

His gaze sharpened with suspicion. 'What letter?'

'From your son . . . unless you have another?'

'Ah.' He went to pick up the piece of parchment from the coffer.

'He clearly loves you and wants to please you, and I think you are fond of him.' She spoke warmly, but still hinted how much he had to lose by going over to Philippe.

'It is said there is truth in wine, and the same can be applied to small children. For the rest we live on lies – all of us.'

Alienor crossed the space between them and kissed her son's cheek, over the softness of his beard. 'But there is always a deeper truth in our hearts.'

As she returned to her own chamber, she did not know if she had succeeded with him. He might still try to make the crossing and deal with Philippe, and that would be disastrous. John might think he was good at manipulation, but he was a child when it came to matching the King of France. Richard would be home by the end of the year and one of her few comforts was that each day that passed was a day closer to that time. She had to keep hold of John's leash until then, and after that, he was Richard's responsibility.

34

Palace of Westminster, Christmas 1192

The court children sat in a half circle before a tall wooden box draped with brightly coloured fabrics edging a stage. All were giggling at the antics of a puppet husband and wife who were arguing vigorously with a drunken bishop and a devil. Watching the entertainment with the children, Alienor was laughing too, but with a hollow ring at the centre of her mirth. Now and again she glanced towards the door, praying that Richard would stride in, whole and vibrant. But each time the door did open it was only to admit a guest or a servant, and when it closed she felt as if there was a cold draught at her back even though she wore an ermine cloak.

The devil offered the bishop a sack of gold. The latter took it, seized the devil round the neck and, climbing on his back, rode him back and forth across the stage, to gales of laughter from the children and amused chuckles from the courtiers, who well recognised the priest as Longchamp. A crowned figure arrived, knocked the priest off the devil, seized the sack of money and fled offstage.

Alienor raised her brows but was reluctantly amused, especially when a much larger crowned figure arrived wearing a white cross on his tunic. Having killed the devil in a vigorous sword fight, he dragged the other crowned figure on stage, seized the money from him while beating him soundly, and then gave the sack of money to the man and wife to loud cheers and applause.

The entertainment over, the children went off with their nurses and attendants. Alienor watched with amusement as William Marshal paused to play a moment of fisticuffs with some little boys before extricating himself.

'That was fine entertainment, madam,' he said to Alienor with a broad grin. 'It reminds me how much I used to love the players that came to Marlborough when I was a child.'

Alienor nodded. 'It is good to have such things for distraction and especially for children to remember.' After a hesitation she added, 'Another ship arrived today with soldiers on their way home from Outremer, but not one of them carried word of the King.'

'I heard, madam, and I am sorry.'

She frowned with anxiety. 'Berenguela and Joanna reached Rome in October and Richard was supposed to be following close behind. He should have been here weeks ago.'

'He cannot simply disappear,' William said. 'News will come. Perhaps he is waiting for a decent crossing even now. The weather has been bad in the Narrow Sea.'

Alienor waved her hand. 'You are right, and kind to offer me comfort. You would think I would have learned how to wait after all my years as Henry's prisoner, but in this matter my patience wears thin and I know that if he was on the other side of the Narrow Sea, nothing would prevent him from making the crossing.'

'He will come,' William reiterated.

'Yes,' she said with a wan smile. 'So I hope and pray.'

That night, unable to sleep, she kept vigil in her private chapel, alone save for Amiria. Bowing her head, Alienor prayed for Richard, imploring God to be merciful and keep him safe. He couldn't be dead; she would know in her heart. He had reached Brindisi, that was certain, so he could not be lost at sea. 'Where are you, my son?' she whispered into the shadowy darkness, her breath clouding the chilly air.

Soft footsteps padded behind her and she whirled round to see the glint of green silk, and inhaled the scent of incense, wafted by the movement of another presence. John crossed himself and, kneeling at her side, put his hands together. For a while there was silence, but eventually he raised his head and looked at her. 'I am praying for Richard,' he said, 'for his soul.'

Alienor drew a sharp breath.

'Mama, you have to face the possibility that he is dead.'

'Is that what you think or what you wish? Do you know what it does to me to hear you say that?'

'Well who else is to say it, Mama?' John answered in a reasonable tone and unclasped his hands. 'How much longer will you dwell in denial? He should have been home a month ago. No one is delayed that long. If he was sick, word would have been sent.'

'And the same if he was dead.' She clenched her jaw. 'I do not doubt that some sort of trouble has prevented him from reaching home, but he is not dead; I would know it in here.' She struck her breast. 'I do not dwell in denial; I dwell in hope.'

'As do I, Mama,' John said flatly. 'Why else would I come here to pray in the small hours of the night?'

'Yes, but in hope of what?' If her heart told her that Richard was not dead, then her heart also told her that John would make it bleed. 'Do not cut the ground from under my feet.'

He kissed her cheek. 'No, Mama. If it is your wish to believe Richard is still alive, I honour you for it – but I will not wait much longer.'

He left as silently as he had arrived and Alienor closed her eyes, two tears rolling down her face.

The weather in January turned bitterly cold with a brutal wind and despite blazing fires in every hearth, latched shutters and drawn curtains, everyone huddled in their cloaks and shivered. Ice frilled the edge of the Thames and the frozen layers in troughs and butts had to be hacked with picks to get at the water.

In her chamber, Alienor sat in council with the country's regents going over general matters of business. There was still no word of Richard and she was beginning to fear the worst even though she was trying desperately to keep her hopes alive. John was part of the group gathered round the fire, but separate from them at the moment and pacing as his father had been wont to do.

'How much longer must we wait?' he demanded. 'There has been no news and that tells me he must have taken a river crossing and drowned, or been caught in a storm and perished somewhere that his body will never be found.'

Alienor's throat constricted. 'No, I will not believe that.'

'I am sorry, Mama, but we must be practical and face the facts.' John came to crouch at her side, holding the arm of her chair. 'I am not the only one who sees it, even if I am the scapegoat who must use the words.' He glanced round at the silent, tight-lipped justiciars. 'We have to make plans based on the premise that Richard is not going to return.'

Alienor drew herself up. 'Indeed we do, and it is my advice

that we wait. I know time is passing, but it is not yet the moment to make these decisions. England is stable and well-governed. Another week or two will make no difference. If no news has come by Lent, then and only then shall I reconsider.'

'And when it comes to Lent, shall you then postpone it to Easter?' he demanded with impatience.

'Enough! You have your answer,' she snapped. 'We will wait.'

John made an exasperated sound through his teeth and stormed out.

The assembled counsellors prepared to leave, summoning their scribes and gathering their parchment and equipment together.

A clerk belonging to Walter of Coutances entered the room and hastened up to his master with a letter in his hand and a worried look on his face. The Archbishop took it from him, scanned the contents, and called out to the men leaving the chamber. Then he turned to Alienor.

'Madam, there is news. The King is alive, praise God.' There was little joy in his expression which was set and grim. 'But I am sorry to say he is a prisoner.'

Alienor stared at him while the words tumbled into place. 'What do you mean "a prisoner"?' She gestured at the parchment. 'What is this?' She had risen to see the men out, but her legs threatened to buckle and she had to sit down again.

Walter of Coutances grimaced. 'It appears to be a copy of a letter from the Emperor of Germany to the King of France.'

Alienor made a peremptory gesture. 'Read it.' Her heart was pounding so hard she thought it might lift straight out of her chest.

Coutances held the piece at arm's length and squinted a little, but his voice was firm as he began to speak.

'Because our Imperial Majesty has no doubt that your Royal Highness will take pleasure in all of those providences of God which exalt us

and our empire, we have thought it proper to inform you of what happened to Richard, King of England, the enemy of our empire and the disturber of your kingdom, as he was crossing the sea on his way back to his dominions.'

Alienor dug her nails into her palms and held her breath.

'His ship was storm-driven onto the Istrian coast and wrecked. By God's will, he and a few others escaped. A loyal subject of ours, Count Meinhard of Gorz, hearing that Richard was in his territory and calling to mind the treason, treachery and mischief of which he had been guilty in Outremer, went to arrest him. He captured eight knights from his retinue but Richard escaped. He reached a town called Friesach in the archbishopric of Salzburg, where six more of his knights were arrested. Richard himself escaped yet again, this time with just three companions, and rode hard in the direction of Austria. But the roads were watched and guarded, and our dearly beloved cousin Leopold, Duke of Austria, captured the King in a disreputable house near Vienna. He is now in our power. We know that this news will bring you great happiness.'

A long silence ensued after Coutances had finished. Alienor exhaled and drew a painful breath. The words had numbed her, but now anger seeped in to take its place.

'This is not to be borne,' she declared. 'That the German Emperor should write to Philippe of France and commit this terrible deed against a fellow sovereign and brother in arms is a disgrace. This is the work of men who disrespect God and are lower than maggots!' Her eyes flashed around the gathering. 'If the Emperor is holding Richard captive, then Philippe will turn on Normandy. We must prepare for war.' Her body shook as anger and fear became rage and terror. 'I shall write to the Pope immediately. We must discover where Richard is being held. And then we shall set about the matter of setting him free.'

'I shall find people to do that, and send them straight away,' said Walter of Coutances. 'At least the King is still alive, madam, praise God.'

She nodded grimly. 'And when he is found, we shall need

to know his wishes in the matter of government. There is no reason why he cannot direct us from where he is.'

Already she could not bear the waiting. She wanted to be there in Germany. She wanted to bend apart the bars of his prison and kill those who had imprisoned him. But that was all in her mind and she had to press it down; she had to have control. Richard was not dead, thank God. Hold on to that thought above all others.

35

Palace of Westminster, February 1193

Alienor woke from a ragged sleep in which she had been imagining Richard as a lion, fur matted, tangled up in chains and roaring with impotence, and found Amiria leaning over her.

'Madam, William the Marshal is requesting to see you. I told him you were resting and he said if that was the case he would return, but he has news he thinks you should hear. Shall I admit him or send him away?'

Alienor rubbed sleep from her eyes and sat up. Her throat was parched and raw both from dictating to her scribes and the weeping she had done in private with no one to see her grief and despair. William had not been present when the announcement of Richard's capture had been made, and she had written to him at his manor of Caversham on the Thames to tell him.

'Bring wine,' she said, 'and help me dress. Bid him wait.'

When William was ushered into her presence, she was gowned and composed but the sight of him, strong, tall and utterly dependable, brought tears to her eyes. She blinked them away and stopped him as he began to kneel to her.

'Come, sit.' She pointed to a chair by the fire. 'Give Amiria your cloak and boots. I can see it's been raining and you might as well be comfortable while you tell me what this is about.'

He did as she bade him. The maid spread the cloak across a coffer to dry and brought him a spare one lined with fur, and some soft shoes. William attended to the fire, adding some pieces of wood and giving it a swift bellow to make the heat flare up.

'You should have sent a messenger ahead and told me you were coming. I did not expect you at this time of night.'

'I wanted to reach you before any other messengers brought you this news, madam. You will not want to hear it and I am sorry to be the bearer of such tidings.'

'Tell me.' She sat up as straight as a lance.

William pushed his hair back from his forehead. 'I love and honour you and I would not tell you this lightly, but John has fortified Windsor and Marlborough with supplies and defenders, and gone himself to King Philippe to accept his offer of Alais for a bride and do him fealty for all of King Richard's lands across the Narrow Sea. There is no stopping him this time; he has already flown the country.' His expression was deeply troubled, perhaps even apprehensive. His own brother commanded Marlborough and it meant he had had to cut off his loyalty to family in order to support Alienor. 'He has not had the best advice. I have proof that he and Philippe are planning to invade England – I would not believe it on word alone.'

'What sort of proof?' Alienor asked woodenly.

'One of his messengers was caught recruiting Welsh mercenaries. I know this because my own man was out recruiting from the same source and ran across John's man who had letters promising good wages and rich pickings. Another of my agents tells me that the call is out in Brabant too. Madam, John is preparing to seize England for himself and the justiciars cannot allow him to do this.'

Alienor felt sick. She loved Richard with a passion, would

move heaven and earth to save him, but John was her son too. 'This cannot be true?' Her heart sank for she knew William would not come to her with anything less.

He looked her in her eyes and did not answer, but his expression was confirmation enough.

Faced by this solid wall of fact, her heart still pushed against it. She thought of John as a small boy busy with his abacus, calculating, looking suspiciously at the other children, but then giving her the sweetest smile. She thought of his charm, his intelligence, his constantly busy mind and knew that this was exactly how Henry would have behaved to steal a march on his own brothers and keep her down. That John should have this trait made her deeply sad. It was betrayal, yet she still sought excuses for him.

'He may have been led astray, but perhaps he is trying to make peace with Philippe and mediate.'

'That may be the case, madam,' William said diplomatically, 'but the matter must still be addressed and we have to decide what to do. If John is planning to seize power with Philippe's help, we must be prepared. If he is not, then we lose nothing.'

Alienor nodded wearily. 'I am worried to exhaustion and heartsick that my beautiful, valiant son has been cast into prison and slandered by his enemies, and that his brother would use the event for his own ends.'

William's gaze was filled with troubled compassion. 'Madam, indeed, I am sorry – and I am sorry I had to bring you this news.'

'And I thank you, but I will have your support in this, not your pity. Whatever happens, John is not to be harmed because he is still my son and it might set a dangerous precedent. I will deal with him in my own way. I want that understood.'

'Yes, madam.' William composed his expression to one of neutrality. 'I will do my utmost to fulfil your wish.'

She rubbed her brow. 'Nothing is as I wish, William, but I have to go on because I have no choice. The priority is to discover where Richard is, establish communication with him and find out how much his ransom will cost. I want you to arrange a watch on our shores so we are ready if Philippe does invade.'

'It shall be done.'

William rose to leave and she stood up to see him out.

'You are my rock, William.' She gripped his arm. 'I know you will stand firm whatever happens.'

'You can be certain of that, madam.'

He spoke with conviction, and she loved him for it, even while she knew he must be harbouring private doubts, for she harboured them herself.

At a meeting held at Oxford it was agreed that the Abbots of Boxley and Robertsbridge would set out to discover just where in Germany Richard was being held. Alienor was desperate to know Richard's location because without that knowledge he was still lost, and it would be all too easy for him to vanish for ever. She was well aware that an extortionate ransom would be demanded for his return. The best hope was that the Pope would put pressure on Leopold of Austria and Emperor Heinrich to release Richard without payment, but that was unlikely to happen. Her task, while the abbots were about their mission, was to find out how much she could raise and what resources they required for the defence of the realm.

She looked round the circle of sombre justiciars. 'We must be circumspect in this. Our enemies must not know what resources we have, and I trust to your discretion.'

The remark received immediate nods of agreement because it was an easy decision to make.

'What of the Count of Mortain's crossing the Narrow Sea to negotiate with the French?' asked William Briwere, taking the bull by the horns. 'What are we to do about that?

Even against such damning evidence Alienor raised her voice and prepared to protect and defend John. 'Philippe of France is a spider weaving his web. I feel that I have to ransom both my sons. If there is an invasion, it will be at Philippe's behest because he has John under his influence. Let all vassals take an oath of fealty to Richard and stand by it. I will have everyone so swear throughout the land.' She looked round the gathering. 'Whatever happens, I will not have John harmed. He must be brought to safety and I will deal with him – nobody else.'

'But madam,' said Briwere, daring where angels feared to tread, 'he is a danger to the country and the livelihood and safety of us all. If you could see your way to having him confined so he can be dealt with by the law, then we shall all sleep more easily in our beds at night.'

Alienor glared round the group but they all avoided her gaze. 'He is your prince,' she said with regal anger, 'and all princes have their wild oats to sow. It does not mean he is without worth and calibre for the future. I shall deal with him – I want that understood by all.'

William Marshal had said little thus far, but now he stirred. 'The Count of Mortain can still be contained without imprisonment and surely his mother is the best person to bring him to reason. Our main concern is to keep the French from landing any substantial forces and a shore watch and local militia have already been set up for that purpose under the Queen's instructions. Beacons are being prepared on the hill tops and the coastal defences are being strengthened.'

She sent him a grateful look. 'As my lord Marshal says, measures are being taken while we await news and in the meantime we shall seek diplomatic solutions and ways to remove John from French influence. Once we have made contact with Richard and know more, we shall not have to mark time.'

A few weeks later, the same group reconvened at Westminster. The days had begun to draw out and although the late February day was still dank and raw, the pallid sunshine hinted at spring. The first lambs were gambolling beside their mothers, and folk had started to poke their noses out of their doors, sniff the air and think about planting seed.

Alienor rose wearily from her prayers in her private chapel and swayed on her feet, made light-headed by exhaustion, lack of sustenance and worry. There had been no news from Germany and she was at her wits' end. Surely the Abbots of Boxley and Robertsbridge must have found Richard by now or discovered what had happened to him? Was she going to keep sending people only to have them disappear too? In April she would begin her seventieth year on this earth, and at the moment she felt every one of those years and their burden grew as her flesh withered and shrank. Where had her life gone, and to what purpose? She dared not think on the futility of it all.

She had taken an inventory of the funds available in the kingdom and had looked at how much she could draw from her own finances, and had a feeling it would not be enough, because Heinrich of Germany was the kind of man to cut to the bone and then keep on cutting. She had already decided that John would contribute a substantial sum from his own lands. He had just returned to England from France but she had not yet been able to pin him down and talk to him about precisely what negotiations he had been conducting with Philippe of France. However, he had requested this meeting at Westminster with her and the justiciars and now she would learn more.

Her chamber had been prepared for the meeting. The fire was redly aglow and flagons of good Gascon wine stood on a trestle together with a jug of clear spring water for those more dedicated to Lent. There were dishes of dried fruits and nuts as well as bread and smoked fish should anyone be hungry, which knowing William Marshal would be the case. A table had been set up with long benches for the men to sit on and for herself a curved chair.

One by one the justiciars began arriving and were offered food and wine and directed to their places. Of John there was no sign. Glances were exchanged but nothing said. The conversation meandered over routine matters – talk of the weather and the likelihood of a good spring sowing. William Marshal, as Alienor had predicted, applied himself to the bread and smoked fish with alacrity.

John timed his eventual arrival to ensure that everyone knew they had been kept waiting at his leisure. A clerk accompanied him and set down a small leather satchel on the table at his lord's place.

'My lords.' John gave a formal but perfunctory bow to the justiciars and then knelt to Alienor. 'My lady mother.'

Alienor sensed the antipathy in the way the justiciars responded to him with cold, correct courtesy and knew this was going to be difficult. 'Be welcome,' she said. 'I am glad to see you and hope you are here today because you have a sincere commitment to resolving our differences and coming to an amicable solution.'

John accepted a cup of wine from a servant and took his place with a regal air. 'Indeed, I hope so too.' His gaze flicked in assessment over the men seated at the trestle. 'I have been trying to help everyone. I do not know why you misconstrue my actions. I only have the best for England at heart.'

Alienor sensed the justiciars' dislike of this reproachful tactic. She heard a soft growl, but could not tell who had made the sound. Walter of Coutances was tight-lipped. William's face was studiously blank.

'We all need to recognise our positions, and with Richard gone, I am the one holding the forces against the tide,' John continued. 'Without me, what would happen to these lands? Who would come to the throne? You should cease opposing me and unite against the common threat. I know my mother supports me in this.'

Alienor sat up straighter; it was the first she had heard of this, but she would not deny John before everyone. However, she warned him with a look.

'Indeed,' Walter of Coutances said smoothly, 'we have the

country's interests at heart too and we need to know that you in your turn support us. We have made many sacrifices and compromises to come to this point and you will find no broken link in our armour when it comes to protecting England against the foe.' He considered John with cold blue eyes. 'We shall do this until the King returns because that is the task with which he entrusted every one of us.'

John drank, lowered his cup, and gazed around the board with an expression of impatient scorn. 'He's not going to return; you are all deluding yourselves. He is dead.'

Alienor stifled a gasp and put her hand to her mouth.

John grimaced. 'Mama, I am sorry, I was hoping not to have to tell you this, and that matters could have been settled another way, but I have letters.' He reached to the satchel the scribe had placed on the trestle and produced a folded parchment bearing the seals of Philippe of France and Heinrich of Germany. 'Read for yourself. The Abbots of Boxley and Robertsbridge will bring you the same news when they return. Richard no longer lives, and here is your proof.'

Walter of Coutances took the letters into his hands as if they were venomous and stared at the seal tags. Alienor's throat closed until she could barely breathe.

'Sire,' said Coutances, 'I see no proof here, only words on a page that might or might not have meaning. There is nothing to convince me that the King is dead and that any of us should swear fealty to you as his successor.' He flicked one of the seals with his fingertips. 'These could easily be forgeries.'

Making a tremendous effort, Alienor drew herself together. 'As my lord Archbishop says, these documents may well be false. We must evaluate them and come to a decision. Should it prove the case that they are true, then by due process we shall put the proper ceremonies in place.' But it couldn't be true, it couldn't!

Coutances leaned back, lips pursed, gaze watchful. 'There is no reason for haste in this matter. The country is in no difficulty despite what you say, sire, and we cannot act on the hearsay of these letters alone. When more news arrives, when we have solid confirmation, then we shall be in a better position to judge. Let the Abbots of Boxley and Robertsbridge return to us first and let us know more than this letter tells.'

'Then you refuse me?' John banged down his goblet on the trestle and surged to his feet. 'Even with proof before your eyes?'

'We need to know that this is genuine, sire,' William Marshal spoke up. 'As my lord Archbishop says, there is no haste. Even should it prove the tragic case that the King is dead, it is prudent to wait a few more weeks to be certain. Those who act in haste, repent at leisure.'

John glared round the assembled justiciars. 'You will see that I am right,' he said roughly. 'Richard is never coming back. If you will not accept it, there is nothing more to say and I will continue my preparations apace.' Grabbing the satchel, he stalked out.

In the immediate silence after his leaving, Alienor leaned her elbows on the trestle and put her head in her hands.

'It is a blatant forgery, as the Count of Mortain must well know,' Walter of Coutances said with contempt. 'I think we are all in agreement that we shall do nothing until we know more, save to guard the realm from the depredation of wolves.'

'And if he is right?' Alienor said bleakly, lowering her hands. 'What then?'

'Then, madam, we have clear consciences and know we have steered a careful and judicious course.'

Another fortnight passed without news of Richard or the two abbots who had gone in search of him. Alienor kept herself intensely busy sorting out finances, organising, administrating and writing numerous letters. She thought of Richard constantly, but she never stopped, because moments of stillness brought unbearable thoughts and visions.

John had stormed off and locked himself up in Windsor

which, together with Wallingford, was now being besieged by the justiciars. She knew John had to be contained, but she was worried, because if he did become King, men would view him as someone they could challenge and defeat, and thus the entire dynasty would be undermined.

She was sorting through a pile of parchments when William Marshal arrived to see her. With a broad smile on his face he deposited a small barrel on the trestle in front of her.

'A contribution from the King of France, madam, delivered to our own shores by an escort of Flemings in a fine seaworthy ship.'

Alienor raised her brows.

'Three shiploads of Flemish mercenaries beached near Shoreham, but the local folk were waiting to deal with them. This was on board one of the ships.' He prised off the lid to show her a mass of silver pennies. 'Fifty marks all told. Two of the ships have been commandeered for either use or sale and the sheriff gave the smallest one to the captors with a shilling each for their vigilance and stout protection.'

'Should we be alarmed?' she asked. 'Was this a forward investigation of our defences?'

He shook his head. 'The shore watch is diligent and the only reports are of isolated raids and small groups trying to make their way to Wallingford and Windsor. Another group of ten was taken on a fishing boat the day before yesterday, so it appears there is not going to be a great invasion.'

'That at least is good news. I am pleased our vigilance is paying off.' She put her hand in the barrel and trickled the top layer of coins through her fingers. 'There is no news from Windsor?'

'No, madam.'

Unspoken between them lay the knowledge that the siege, although being pursued, was not biting hard because she had ordered the justiciars not to force John to a humiliating defeat. She wanted him to sue for a truce of his own accord and for an amicable agreement to be reached, although for that to happen he had to change his attitude towards Richard. 'I . . .' She stopped and looked up as an usher entered the room and hurried over to her, almost tripping in his haste, his face red with excitement.

'Madam, madam! The Abbots of Boxley and Robertsbridge are here, and the Bishop of Salisbury!'

Alienor's heart lurched. Hubert Walter, Bishop of Salisbury, had been with Richard in the Holy Land. Now she would have her answer for better or worse. 'Bring them to me straight away.' She turned to William. 'I want you to stay and hear what is said – and sustain me if it is the worst news.'

'Of course, madam.' He bowed.

The men were shown into the room and made their obeisances. All three were travel-weary and grey with dust but in good heart. 'Madam, the King is alive and in strong health and spirits all considering,' said the Abbot of Boxley. 'He is being held in the castle of Trifels and he sends you greetings from there and begs that you move all forward to expedite his release.'

'I have letters.' Hubert Walter placed a satchel before her. He was tall, urbane and handsome with a mind as sharp as a razor and a formidable head for figures that meant he could out-calculate most men when it came to fiscal reckoning. He had been journeying home via Rome and, having heard what was happening, had diverted to Germany to join the other clergymen.

'I knew he wasn't dead.' Alienor swallowed tears. Knowing that these men had seen Richard filled her with a desperate hunger to do that for herself, and knowing she could not was torture. 'What do we have to do to gain his freedom?'

Hubert Walter's handsome features contorted with displeasure. 'There is a ransom demand, madam, and also a demand for hostages.'

'As expected, and we have been preparing.' She sent a servant to bring food and wine for the men, and opened the letters, but her eyes were too blurred with age and tears to read them, and she passed them back to Hubert Walter. 'Read,' she said.

The Bishop cleared his throat. His voice was deep and resonant – the kind to hold a congregation in thrall.

Richard addressed her as 'Sweet mother', and Alienor clenched her fists at those words. He said that all was well, but he needed her to secure his release as swiftly as possible. The ransom terms had been agreed and once the sum of seventy thousand marks was paid he would be freed, so long as hostages from his own family were provided as surety for another thirty thousand.

Alienor stared at Hubert Walter dumbstruck. 'A hundred thousand marks?' That was well beyond her reckoning.

He met her appalled gaze, then flicked his own briefly to William, who was impassive. 'Madam, I am afraid so. We could not negotiate a lesser sum. Indeed, I am sorry to say there is more, for the King also agreed to give the Emperor fifty galleys and two hundred knights for a year.'

'That is ridiculous!' Alienor snapped. She had always known the Emperor would make Richard pay and not release him easily, but this was out of bounds. The sum demanded would nigh on beggar them and make them weaker – which was what Heinrich probably intended. 'What else does he say?'

Hubert Walter applied himself to the letter again. Richard recommended him as the next Archbishop of Canterbury and suggested that she give him a key role in helping to raise the ransom. He also expressed a desire for William Longchamp to be involved in delivering the hostages and the money to Germany. Alienor nodded as she listened. Longchamp was an insufferable nuisance, but his loyalty to Richard was not in doubt and at least he would be positively utilised. She had no objection to Hubert Walter being Archbishop of Canterbury and was happy to promote his election.

'On the matter of the Count of Mortain,' Hubert continued, 'the King says that his brother is not a man to win his lands by the sword if anyone should offer him the slightest force in resistance and he says not to worry, he will be easily over-come.'

'Nevertheless it is best to negotiate a truce. We need peace if we are to raise this ransom, not strife.' Alienor touched the barrel of silver pennies.

'Indeed, madam. The King leaves it in your hands, and asks that you write to the Pope in the strongest terms.'

'It shall be done immediately.'

The food and drink arrived, as did Walter of Coutances, out of breath. The letter was read out again, and soon they were embroiled in discussing how to obtain the massive ransom. Alienor was appalled by the size of it, by how much of the country's resources would be drained, and also by how unpopular it was going to be. It was one hill to climb after another and she felt like a beast of burden with the world on her back.

As they were discussing how to raise money from wool clips, taxes and donations, one of Hubert Walter's knights entered the room bearing a heavy leather sack that jingled as he put it down at the Bishop's feet. Two squires followed the knight with a stand and two poles.

'I have the King's hauberk,' Hubert announced.

Rolled up inside the leather was Richard's mail shirt, which Alienor had last seen him wearing as he rode out from Vezelay three years ago. His helm and coif were there too, his chausses, and even one of his swords. Hubert directed the squires to arrange the gear on the poles. The hauberk had areas of rust and tarnish from confinement and travel, and in places torn links hung down like iron tears.

'The King says it is to be put on public display in London and then it is to be sent around the kingdom in order to encourage everyone to contribute to the ransom,' said Hubert.

Alienor shivered, because it truly seemed that Richard's presence occupied the room.

'It will have to be cleaned,' said Walter de Coutances, frowning. 'No one will believe that this is the armour of a king.'

'But it needs to be seen to have been worn in the service of Christendom,' William Marshal said, turning to Alienor. 'If you will trust me, madam, I shall see it refurbished to fit status, yet retaining the marks of honourable battle.'

'Thank you.' Alienor's eyes prickled with tears. 'I would trust you the most of all my lords to perform this task. You know my son, and you have been a soldier for Christendom yourself.'

'It will be my honour, madam.'

When the meeting ended and everyone went their separate ways to their duties, William remained behind to help his own knight Jean D'Earley return the hauberk to its leather sack.

'It will take some work,' D'Earley observed, rubbing the back of his neck.

William was undaunted. 'Nothing that a vigorous rolling in a barrel of sand won't cure.'

Alienor picked up Richard's arming cap. The linen was slick with the dark grease of constant wear mingled with iron filaments from the coif. 'This should stay as it is. It speaks as much if not more than the rest. Here is a man who has fought and toiled for his saviour, who has sweated and bled and been brought low by vile traitors. They need to see this as much as his sword.' She managed to stop herself from pressing the coif to her face.

William nodded agreement. 'You are right, madam. Sometimes the smaller details point up the greater ones.' His eyes were troubled. 'I am sorry you have this grief on your shoulders. Seeing these things must distress you even while they are a comfort, but we will raise the ransom, and he will return.'

'Yes,' she said fiercely. 'I will move heaven and earth for that, William.'

Later, sitting in her chamber, Alienor wiped away the tears trickling down her face and drank her wine. It was her third cup in a short time and she knew she should slow down. She had spent the last hour with diplomat and court scribe Peter of Blois, drafting a letter to the Pope. Several times she had had to stop because the emotions coursing through her were too painful, but on each occasion she had rallied and moved on. Peter of Blois was renowned for his eloquence with a quill, and she knew he would turn the piece into a work of art.

Pope Celestine was eighty-seven years old and she had her doubts about how effective her letter was going to be even if it were the most persuasive on earth, but she needed to say these things. Today had been terrible. Trying to keep a balance between the justiciars and John was an impossible task. John was her son; she loved him dearly, and tried not to think she was making excuses for him. But the justiciars thought she was, even William, who was staunchly loyal to her. But what else was she to do? Have one son imprisoned in Germany and another here? Have no sons at all?

'Read it to me,' she commanded with a wave of her hand.

Peter of Blois had written the letter on a series of wax tablets and now he laid down his stylus and shuffled through them to the first one.

'*To her revered Father and Lord Celestine, highest pontiff by the grace of God, Alienor, a wretched and to be pitied – if only she were – queen of the English, Duchess of Normandy, Countess of Anjou, begging him to show himself the father of mercy to the suffering mother.*'

Alienor nodded and bit her lip. 'Go on.'

'*I am in such anguish within and without that my words are filled with grief. I am wasted away by sorrow until the very marrow of my bones is dissolved in tears. I have lost the staff of my old age and the light of my eyes and it would answer my prayers if God condemned my eyes to perpetual blindness so they might no longer see the ills of my people.*

'*Holy Mother of mercy, look on my misery, and if your son, an endless font of mercy, exacts the sins of the mother from the son, let Him only exact them from me, not the innocent. Let Him destroy me, let Him not spare me. Pitiful and pitied by no one, why have I come to the ignominy of this detestable old age, who was ruler of two kingdoms, mother of two kings? My family is carried off and removed from me.*

327

The Young King and the Count of Brittany sleep in dust, and their most unhappy mother is compelled to be irredeemably tormented by the memory of the dead.

'Two sons remain to my solace, who today survive to punish me. King Richard is held in chains. His brother, John, depletes his kingdom with the sword and lays it waste with fire. My sons fight amongst themselves, if it is a fight where one is restrained in chains, and the other, adding sorrow to sorrow, undertakes to usurp the kingdom of the exiled by cruel tyranny.'

Peter of Blois paused reading and looked up. Alienor swallowed and wiped her eyes again. There was compassion in his gaze and shrewdness also. 'Do you need a moment, madam?'

She shook her head. 'No, continue – unless of course you do.'

'Madam, I am able,' he said, 'but there is indeed great power in these words.'

'Let us pray enough to move mountains. I would do that and more for my child.'

Peter of Blois took a drink from his cup, cleared his throat and resumed, pushing one tablet aside, picking up another.

'Why do I, wretched, delay and not go to see the one whom my soul loves conquered by poverty and iron? How could a mother forget the son of her womb for so long? But if I go, deserting my son's kingdom, that is laid waste on all sides with grave hostility, it will be deprived of all counsel and comfort in my absence. If I remain, I shall not see the face I most desire, of my son. There will be no one to zealously procure the freedom of my son and, what I fear even more, with the impossible quantity of money, is that my son will be driven to death by his tortures.'

Tears spilled silently down Alienor's cheeks as Blois' voice continued, soft but clearly enunciated and eloquent. In the gentle spring dusk, rain whispered past the open shutters.

'Father, why do you delay so long, so negligently, indeed so cruelly to free my son, or do you not dare? Bind the souls of those who hold my son in prison and set him free. Give my son back to me, if you are a man of God and not a man of blood.

'Legates have now been promised to us three times but have not been sent. If my son were prospering, they would swiftly come, because they

would expect rich benefits from the public profit of the kingdom. The wolf broods over the prey and the mute dogs do not wish to bark. You compel me to despair who alone after God is my hope. The highest pontiff suppresses the sword of Peter which he has replaced in its sheath and his silence is taken for consent.'

Alienor nodded her approval as Blois reached the end of the last tablet. 'I trust you to see that this is written in fair copy and to add or remove such as you need to bestow the necessary power.'

'Madam, it is very powerful already,' he said with a gleam in his eyes, 'but I shall do what I can to add a final burnish.' With quiet efficiency he gathered his equipment together, bowed and left.

Wrung out, but satisfied, Alienor retired to bed, but she could not settle because her mind kept returning to Richard. She thought of him in his prison cell, and remembered the days when she was walled up at Sarum. A pattern was repeating itself and there had to be an end to it. She ought to be doing something now. Sleep was a waste of time while Richard was a captive. Closing her eyes she reached out to him across the miles, knowing he was there. Even when people had told her he was dead, she had never believed them because she could still feel his heartbeat within her. Once she had carried that beating heart inside her body and sustained it with her own life blood, and she would give that blood for him now, every last drop.

36

Palace of Westminster, Summer 1193

John knelt to his mother and set his lips to the ruby ring on her right hand. He had just formally given into her keeping

the keys of the castles of Windsor and Wallingford and acknowledged a truce between himself and the justiciars so that the
ransom could be collected without strife.

Alienor stooped to give him the kiss of peace, the gesture
cool and political. She still loved him because he was her son,
but after his most recent behaviour she was hurt and wary.
However, since they needed his cooperation while the ransom
was being raised, and he had to provide a share from his own
estates, she was prepared to conciliate.

'I am glad we are reconciled. Perhaps now you will accept
that Richard will be returning and is capable of governing
through messengers. The business of the realm can go forward
as usual.'

John inclined his head. 'Of course, Mama. But you understand my concern. It is true what you say, but without Richard,
the country is still vulnerable.'

He was turning matters around as usual, but in the interests
of fostering the fragile peace, she said nothing. 'Yes, and the
sooner he is home, the better. We need your help to raise the
ransom.'

'Whatever I can do, Mama.'

He spoke too suavely for her liking.

'You know that the Emperor demands hostages from us?'

'I certainly hope you are not suggesting I go!' He smiled
to make a joke of his remark, but his eyes were hard.

She shook her head in exasperation. 'I have no time for
your levity, although it would serve you right if I said I was.
However, you can send your son.'

The smile dropped from John's face. 'What do you mean,
my son?'

'Richard, what other one is there? He has your brother's
name and he is ten years old and that means old enough to
bear himself well and weather the journey. Your nephews
Otto, Wilhelm and Lothar are going, and so is your half-
brother William. The clerks are already preparing the list.'

'And if I refuse to let him go?'

'You do not have that choice. It will do much to mend the rift between you and Richard if you send your boy. If the ransom is paid swiftly, he will not be long from home.'

A muscle ticked in John's cheek. He made no answer but his anger and consternation were obvious.

'Yes,' she said, 'when something you deem precious is put at risk or removed from your reach, it hurts, doesn't it? Learn from this, John. You have greatness in you, do not ruin it.'

He narrowed his eyes and set his jaw. She left him to think on the matter, and hoped that he would indeed learn, because there was always hope.

Richard's hauberk glinted like a snakeskin in the rays shafting down from Westminster Abbey's stained glass windows, the riveted rings glowing with the light of God. William Marshal had made a magnificent job of refurbishing the armour. The mail shirt gleamed without a trace of rust and had been coated with a light sheen of oil. Underneath a gambeson of quilted linen, packed out with fleece, gave the impression of the bulk of the King's body. A small tear in the links remained in the heart area and a few more damaged rings splayed the right shoulder. The sweat-stained coif had been left in its original condition. The rust had been burnished from the helm, but the dints left in situ. A shield bearing Richard's device of three golden leopards on a blood-red background hung on a stand beside the hauberk. The shield was new because Richard's original had been lost on the journey, but William had had one made and added a few nicks and scrapes so that to the onlooker it seemed as though it had seen hard service on the battlefield. A well-worn leather sword belt girded the hauberk and the scabbarded sword pommel bore the symbol of a pelican shedding its blood for its young in representation of Christ shedding His blood for mankind. Another stand was draped with Richard's cloak, a white linen cross stitched over the breast.

'This is your uncle's armour,' Alienor told John's ten-year-old son Richard who stood at her side. He was a good-natured child, intelligent, and eager to please. He reminded her strongly of Harry when he had been that age, but in a more subdued way. Certainly he was nothing like John. 'It is a poor thing to stand in lieu of the King, but it has its own power and it will greatly help to restore him to us.'

The boy gazed at it with awe and admiration. 'The King is a great man, Grandmère.'

'Yes, he is.'

Two other youths stood with Richard, admiring the armour – Henry's bastard son William FitzRoy, thirteen years old, and her grandsons Otto, Wilhelm and Lothar. The boys were in London preparing to accompany her to Germany as hostages in exchange for Richard's release, and the older ones were viewing the task as an adventure. They were men going out into the world to do their duty.

The first instalments of the ransom payment were almost complete. Another consignment had just arrived and would be re-counted and weighed before being locked away under Alienor's seal. Clerks from the treasury were busy at the counting tables, watched closely by the German officials Heinrich had sent to observe the proceedings. Not a single penny or item of treasure escaped their eagle eyes and all had to be precisely weighed and measured. Alienor forced herself to be civil to these men because it was better to make allies than enemies, and they were only doing what Heinrich had instructed them to do.

Hamelin had been helping to collect and coordinate the sums involved and stood beside one of the German officials, watching as another barrel containing a hundred marks of silver went under the seal. Hamelin's once sandy-gold hair was thin and grey and the years had weathered deep lines into cheeks and brow, although his eyes still shone with life, and he remained healthy and vigorous. He was busy and satisfied in his role of supervising the treasure collection, and Alienor was grateful to delegate it to his charge.

The barrel sealed and the table clear for a moment, he

joined her. 'We have almost half the ransom.' He lightly tousled his grandson's hair and then gestured to the armour. 'This will make a difference to the contribution.'

'I hope so,' Alienor said. 'Halfway still means half to go and I hope to be on my way to Germany before Epiphany.'

'You will be,' Hamelin reassured her. 'The funds arrive at a steady trickle day by day.'

'Yes, but I have hopes for a river.'

Alienor looked round as a courier arrived and knelt to her, proffering a letter bearing Richard's seal. Her heart quickened. Excusing herself, she retired to her chamber and summoned a scribe to read what was written. There were several pages. Saluting her as his 'sweet mother' and begging her to make haste so that he might be set free in order to deal with matters at home. He did not mention the depredations of Philippe of France; he did not have to.

One of the parchment sheets was a song he had written to while away the hours of captivity, and he asked that she make it known beyond the chamber and sung throughout the land. Alienor ordered her scribe to make copies and summoned her musicians to sing it for her here and now.

The words were an emotive cry from the heart of a prisoner, lamenting that his friends and faithful followers had forgotten him, and exhorting them to come to his aid. Read aloud by a scribe the song struck Alienor to the heart, but now, hearing the plangent tune brought to life with lute and voice, she was devastated and sobs tore through her body. When her women moved to comfort her, she waved them away. 'No,' she said. 'Let my tears fall, and let others hear this song so that it may move them to pity and anger too. Let it be sung in every town and castle and cathedral from the borders of Scotland to the Pyrenees. Let all hear it and respond to the cry.'

In his chamber at Marlborough, John was taking a bath. Eyes half closed, he drowsed in the warm tub, the scent of rose water rising from the steam. The relaxation, the sheer luxury never failed to set his world to right and help him to think.

Belle stood near the fire, patting her hair dry between two warmed towels. She had made her escape from her ailing husband and come to him in a fashion supposedly clandestine, but in reality everyone knew and just pretended they did not see. John suspected she would like to be with him all the time, but his philosophy was why have an apple from just one tree when there was an entire orchard of fruit waiting to be plucked and tasted? Still, he was enjoying her company for now. She had shared the tub with him and they had had pleasure of each other.

The window was open and from the courtyard came the sound of someone singing a mournful lament.

'That accursed song,' John growled. 'Does no one know anything else?'

She looked over her shoulder at him, amused, still gently patting her hair. 'I think it is very beautiful. Do you not like it?'

He grunted and swished the hot water over his chest and shoulders.

'Or are you jealous?' she purred. 'Even in prison, Richard is still garnering all the attention and displaying his vast talents.'

'The justiciars might be dragging his armour around England raising money,' John scoffed, 'but there's still no man inside it. It's a hollow fantasy.'

She sang the tune to herself: *'I have many friends but their gifts are poor. They show me no honour if for want of a ransom I am held prisoner here for two more winters.'*

'It will be much longer than that. For Christ's sake shut the window.'

'My father says not.' She sauntered over to the window and in her own time did as he asked.

'Your father's an old fool. He says a lot of things but he's not always right, is he?'

'Neither are you.'

John eyed her darkly. 'You are one to speak.'

Belle picked a handful of cherries from a silver bowl and bit into one. 'But if Richard returns, what then will you do?'

He shrugged. 'Nothing that I am prepared to discuss with you. Make yourself useful and put in more hot water.'

She fetched the jug from the hearth and topped up his bath until he held up his hand. Steam rose around him as if he were in a cooking pot. She handed him a fresh cup of wine.

'I worry for you,' she said on a softer note and touched the damp hair curling at his nape. 'I know it is a foolish thing to do, because anyone who holds out their hand to a wolf deserves to be bitten, but I cannot help what I feel.'

He grabbed her hand and closed his teeth on her index finger, hard enough to make her yelp and try to draw back, but he gripped her fast. 'Very foolish indeed, because you know I will only bring you pain.' He released her. 'You should go. I will see you later in the hall.'

She withdrew, rubbing her hand, and with a toss of her head retired behind the bed hangings to dress.

John closed his eyes, wishing her gone. He did not want to think about Richard, he wanted to have a moment away from doing so, but like a rotten tooth it was a constant pain that he had to keep touching. He could be a far better king than his brother if given the opportunity. All Richard had to do was die in prison and everything would resolve itself.

Belle emerged again wearing a gown of forest-green linen and fastening her wimple. Although he was impatient for her to be gone, he still enjoyed watching the way she secured the fabric, pins twinkling in her fingers.

'You are a respectable matron now – on the outside at least.'

'I play my part. You should think about what to do to make people respect you. People look at your brother's armour and they marvel, but it is upheld by the reputation of the man. Would they do the same for you, my love? I wonder.'

'Bitch,' John said softly as the door closed behind her, but without too much malice, and then he leaned back to finish his bath.

He was being dried when an attendant interrupted his toilet to announce that a messenger had arrived. 'He says he will give the words he bears to no one but yourself, sire.'

John arched his brows. 'Indeed? Very well, send him in.'

By the time the messenger was admitted, John was dressed in a loose robe and soft sheepskin shoes. With a wave of his hand he dismissed his servants and eyed the man who knelt before him. He wore sober, ordinary garments, nothing to mark him out as being unique or valuable, and his features were pleasant and nondescript. He had been divested of sword and dagger before being admitted to the chamber. The letter he handed to John was sealed with the small, private ring seal of Philippe of France. When John broke the seal and opened the letter, it was blank.

'Nothing was written, sire, in case I was intercepted, but I am bidden to tell you from the lord King of France that you must look to yourself for the devil is loose.'

John stared at the blank sheet while he absorbed the words. It could only mean one thing and it was no use to question the messenger, who for the sake of security would have been told nothing. John's stomach clenched. What this meant was that a final agreement had been made between Richard and Heinrich, and that as soon as the ransom was delivered, Richard would be on his way to England.

'Go,' John told the messenger. 'Return to your lord and tell him that I shall bring the reply myself.'

The messenger bowed and departed. John shouted for his servants, and when they arrived he ordered them to start packing his baggage. If Richard was soon to be released, he needed to stop the process and secure his own position before it was too late.

Instead of going to the hall to deal with various matters of business and play dice, he changed into travelling garments, donned his cloak, and called for his horse to be saddled.

Belle caught him in the courtyard, his foot in the stirrup as he gathered the reins.

'Where are you going?' she demanded.

'To settle a few matters. Do not make a fuss. Go back to your husband.'

He gained the saddle, reined about and spurred his mount.

Left standing in his dust as he galloped away, Belle's heart sank. Was this how it was always going to be? That he would use her and leave her at his convenience, never hers? She lifted her chin and returned to the hall. People gave her sidelong looks and she knew full well what they were thinking. She told herself she did not care, but it wasn't true. She cared far more than she would ever admit, and she hated him.

37

Southampton, December 1193

Alienor stood on the wharfside at Southampton, preparing to sail for Germany. The first instalment of the ransom had left for its destination in the autumn with officials from Heinrich's court and now she was preparing to embark with the hostages and the balance of the payment and bring Richard home.

A frigid wind was blowing hard, but at least it wasn't a gale and it was in the right direction, which was a good omen. Their crossing would be swift. The treasure had been distributed between several ships so that should a storm blow up in the Narrow Sea, there was less chance of everything going to the bottom. It made the consignment harder to guard, but she had sufficient good men to the task.

The youths who were going as hostages were being very

manly, but they were excited too. Seeing them gathered together, talking animatedly, hearing a laugh ring out, she realised that what to her was a driving matter of life and death, and the desperate need to go to her child, was for them a fine adventure.

There had been no word from John. She did not know where he was or what he was doing, and neither did anyone else – save that he had departed Marlborough and crossed to Normandy. The sea was navigable today but at this time of year it was capricious and news was sporadic. She did know that Richard had written to John, instructing him to take command of key castles in Normandy and hold firm against Philippe of France, but the Normans had rebuffed him and refused to yield their fortresses to anyone but Richard. But after that there had been nothing and she was worried.

Her grandson Richard joined her, his complexion a wind-freshened pink and his blue eyes shining with the joy of the adventure. 'Has Uncle Richard's hauberk been packed with the baggage?' he asked.

'Of course it has,' she said with a smile. 'It is part of him after all.'

He chewed his lip. 'Will he punish my father?'

Alienor set her arm around his shoulder. 'That is between your father and your uncle. There have been misunderstandings and bad decisions on both sides, but it is not your place to worry about them and not your burden to bear.'

Richard gave a pensive nod. Alienor added with humour to lighten the moment, 'Perhaps we could ransom one of the Earl of Norfolk's hats. I think it would fetch a fine price.'

Grandmother and grandson shared a mutual smile as they watched Roger Bigod, Earl of Norfolk, arrive at the dockside with his entourage. His reputation for flamboyant headwear was borne out by the peacock feather plumes fluttering from the crown of a brimmed concoction of scarlet felt.

Bowing to them, the Earl doffed the glorious creation with a flourish.

'That is a very fine hat you are wearing today, my lord,' Alienor commented.

He gave a self-deprecating grin. 'Better on my head than being crushed in the baggage, madam.'

'Indeed, unless it blows off into the sea. I would hate you to have to jump in after it.'

'It is well secured – more so than a wimple I would say.'

Alienor laughed, acknowledging his riposte. 'It will be a swift crossing, and once we are there, I pray for good weather and a trouble-free negotiation.'

'Madam, I shall do what I can for my part.' He was sober now.

'I know, and I thank you.' Alienor was fond of Roger Bigod. Like William Marshal he was trustworthy and reliable. Although less outgoing than William – except in the matter of his hats – he remained constant and calm whatever crisis was thrown at him. He was also highly skilled in the law, one of the reasons he was on this journey.

Roger gallantly assisted her to board ship and once again she felt the sway of a deck under her feet. Walter of Coutances had been designated a hostage too, and he arrived swathed in furs and holding his crosier like a warrior's baton. The winter chill had set his cheeks ablaze and fluffed his white beard to fullness. Walking with him was Baldwin of Bethune, lord of Holderness, and several knights and attendants. Some would stay in Germany as surety for the ransom and others would return as escort for herself and the king.

As the tide reached its zenith and turned, the treasure ships embarked and headed for the open sea, furrowing through the dark grey swell. Alienor sat in the shelter that had been constructed on deck, cushions and furs piled around her. Clutching a cross, she prayed for a safe journey and her son's imminent freedom.

Alienor warmed her hands at the fire in her chamber at Speyer, and shivered. Outside the ground was as hard as horseshoe iron and tiny pellets of snow filled the air like scurf, but the weather was not responsible for her sense of cold.

She had spent the feast of Epiphany at the tomb of the three kings in Cologne and had made offerings of gold and frankincense as she lit candles and prayed for her beloved son. Now she had arrived in Speyer, and although she had been greeted with deference by court officials and housed in comfort, she and her entourage had yet to meet the Emperor and she had not been permitted to see Richard. In some ways she was as much a prisoner as he was. Today, she had been promised that all would change. She wore her finest robes, and knowing how much store the Germans set by display, she dripped with jewels, many of them formerly belonging to Henry's mother the Empress Matilda.

A delegation of courtiers arrived to conduct her and her entourage to the Emperor's presence. Alienor straightened her spine and walking with a regal, measured pace allowed herself to be escorted to the great hall.

The room blazed with candle light and an enormous fire crackled in the hearth. Fine textiles and hangings curtained the walls, reflecting the heat back into the room, but still it seemed a long, cold walk to Heinrich's throne set on the dais, where he waited, wreathed and gilded in state, watching her approach with a speculative look in his hooded eyes. He was a snake, she thought, nothing but a viper dwelling under a rock. But she knew what she must do, and on reaching the foot of the steps to his throne she knelt and made a deep obeisance.

After a long moment to emphasise his dominance and her prostration, he rose and came down the steps to lift her to her feet and give her the kiss of peace. 'Welcome, madam. I trust you are being well looked after during your stay?' He indicated that she should take a chair at his side – a smaller one, and a little below his in height.

'Indeed yes, sire,' she answered neutrally. 'We have been afforded every comfort and hospitality.'

She took the jewelled goblet of wine Heinrich presented to her and wondered how much it was worth. She had been able to think about nothing else these past months. What price each item would fetch when set in the balance against Richard's freedom. This would bring a hundred marks at least.

'In truth, sire, my life has been wearisome of late. I am an old woman, burdened by many sorrows. I hope you have some good news for me as you have written, and that I may see my son very soon, or my heart will break for certain.'

Heinrich eyed her with calculation. 'Indeed, madam, I hope so too, but alas there is more to this than meets the eye.'

'I do not understand. What do you mean there is more?' Alienor gripped the stem of the goblet and felt the cold edges of the gemstones under her fingers. 'We have fulfilled all your terms and done all that you asked. Do you now play us false and demand more?'

His expression was inscrutable as he rubbed his forefinger back and forth across his top lip. Sitting there in his jewelled dalmatic he reminded her of a Byzantine prince, and she knew how false they could be. 'Madam, shall we say that the situation has become more delicate since our last negotiation. I have recently received a letter from the King of France, and from your son the Count of Mortain.'

Alienor's stomach lurched. 'Indeed? May I know what is in this letter?'

'Of course.' He flicked his fingers and a scribe came forward, knelt at Heinrich's feet and presented him with a parchment sheet, the seals dangling. 'Read it and you shall see the dilemma that faces me.'

He handed the letter to Alienor who in turn gave it to Walter of Coutances.

It was addressed to Heinrich by Philippe and John and they made him three offers of which they hoped he would find at least one acceptable. One was a thousand pounds a month if

341

he would keep Richard in prison. If that did not suit him, then Philippe would give a cash sum of fifty thousand marks and John thirty thousand to keep Richard a prisoner until Michaelmas. The third suggestion was that they would give Heinrich one hundred and fifty thousand marks between them if Heinrich would agree to detain Richard for twelve months or deliver him into their hands.

The details were utterly damning, and as she listened to them Alienor grew numb.

'I am sorry,' Heinrich said with false apology, 'but now you see my difficulty. It is a very tempting offer is it not?'

By a supreme effort of will Alienor retained her composure. 'I can see that this is mischief of the most malicious order, and I am astonished you would even consider it. I have come to you in good faith as a grieving mother, bearing all my worldly goods to pay you for my son's release, and now you set more grief on me with this news.'

'In showing you this letter, I am being honest with you. I could have withheld it from your sight, but I believed it was something you had to know.'

'You need not have said that it gave you pause for thought when I am here to redeem my son with a ransom already agreed. You could have said you would not countenance such a treacherous betrayal. Where do you think my son will obtain such sums when he is locked out from England and all the strategic fortresses in Normandy?' she demanded. 'John has no money to give you no matter what he offers. His promises are chaff in the wind, and I say this as his mother. I am the one who controls his finances. Perhaps you want to take me for ransom too? Shall I hold out my own wrists so that you can put them in fetters?' She extended her arms, fighting for her life, fighting for her son. 'I tell you to accept the bargain you arranged with me, because you will never see the money they offer you. If you choose to sup with the King of France, then you might as well sup with the devil himself.'

Silence filled the room after her last word rang out. She stood before him, wrists still bared.

'Now,' she said, her voice trembling, but with the force of anger, not tears, 'bring me my son. Let me see him.'

Heinrich had recoiled at her impassioned outburst, but rallied now with a look of icy disdain. 'Madam, indeed you may see him, but first I would have you walk with me and speak a moment in private.'

Alienor set her jaw. 'As you wish, sire.'

Heinrich escorted her from the hall and into the frozen January air. His men followed at a discreet distance, near enough to be summoned but removed from hearing. Heinrich strolled along until they came to a well, and here he paused, his breath rising in thin white vapour. He looked over the edge of the housing into the glinting darkness below.

'I suppose you are wondering where Richard is,' he said pleasantly. 'For all you know he could be at the bottom of this well.'

'You have brought me here to play pointless games.' Alienor was contemptuous. 'You know full well that if he is dead, then no ransom will be paid.'

He raised a blond eyebrow. 'I could maim him if I so chose. I could crush his sword hand and leave you the rest. That would not renege on our deal, would it?'

Alienor maintained a neutral façade although she was terrified of what this vile, vindictive man might do.

'Or I could pull all of his teeth and leave him without the wherewithal to chew meat at the table, yet I would still be due the ransom.' He shot her a glance. 'Or you, madam,' he added softly. 'You might fall down this well and who would know the difference? Who knows, perhaps you might even meet Richard down there. I could still have the treasure and your hostages into the bargain could I not?' He glanced at the men gathered behind him. One of them half drew his sword to show her the gleam of the blade.

Alienor was determined not to be intimidated. Henry had

343

done this to her often and she had faced him out and survived – but she had been younger then. Just now she felt every single one of her seventy years. And she was frightened.

'You don't know what I can do, do you?' He gave her a long look, then turned and walked away from the well, continuing to a nearby doorway. 'You wanted to see your son? Let me oblige.' He gestured another guard to unlock a heavy wooden door that opened on to a staircase.

As Alienor followed Heinrich up the twisting stairs she was thoroughly prepared to see Richard clad in rags, fettered to the wall and rats running about; however, beyond another barred and guarded door was a well-appointed chamber with a good fire blazing in the hearth and hangings decorating the wall. Richard stood facing the door and had clearly heard their approach, for he was tense and ready, with fists clenched. To Alienor's utter relief he looked well, if thin and fine-drawn, and his surroundings, while not luxurious, were adequate. She gasped his name, but she could not run to him because Heinrich's soldiers barred her way.

Heinrich turned to Richard. 'You have a visitor you must be eager to see,' he said, 'but first, by your oath, if you would see the light of day, put your hand on the table.'

Richard did so and Heinrich drew his dagger and poised it above Richard's wrist.

'No!' Alienor cried. 'By all that is holy, I beg you!'

Heinrich shot her a threatening look. Richard was impassive, although his jaw was rigid.

Heinrich slowly withdrew the dagger, although it remained ready in his hand. 'If anything should happen before we come to an agreement over the ransom, then my threat shall be carried out. Do not think to cheat me or engage in subterfuge and schemes for I will know and you will pay the forfeit.' He signalled, and the soldiers stood aside. 'You may visit with your son, madam, and I will send someone to fetch you in a little while.' He departed, leaving two guards at the door.

Alienor stumbled across the room and threw her arms around Richard, crying his name, stroking his hair and touching his face, needing to make contact with his physical presence to make sure he was real and not a figment of her imagination.

'Mama, it is all right,' Richard soothed. 'He enjoys posturing, that is all. Whatever he threatens and however he blusters, the eyes of all Christendom are upon him, and he very much desires to have his ransom and be rid of me.'

'And yet nothing happens!' she said with bitter frustration. 'I have entreated the Pope and he does nothing! And now we are trapped here.'

Richard gave her a gentle shake. 'I have the measure of the man. He enjoys toying with people and this is amusement and power to him. He is drawing out the last moments of his relish. It's not worth a turd.'

Pulling back, she wiped her eyes on her sleeve. 'I thought I was never going to see you again,' she said in a watery voice. 'I thought at times you were dead.'

'It would take more than Heinrich has to kill me.' He drew her to a bench by the hearth. 'I do not deny I have been through darkness and my host has not always been considerate even while he houses me in comfort. All he has had to feed on is what I show to him, and I have been very careful. He does not know me even now.'

Alienor took her son's hand as he sat down beside her and gripped his warm, strong fingers in hers, clinging to his life and vitality. 'After what I suffered at your father's hands for so long the last thing I would wish is for any of my sons to be a prisoner.'

'I understand what you suffered at Salisbury and Winchester more clearly now, Mama, that is for certain,' Richard replied wryly.

'I wrote to the Pope but I might as well not have bothered. Celestine is as ancient as the tomb and fears to draw the sword of Peter on the Emperor.'

'I would not have expected it either. But truly you are a miracle worker, Mama, to have raised the ransom.'

She gave the first genuine smile of their meeting. 'I would have moved heaven and earth to reach you. You know that.' Her hands were still trembling. Richard seemed remarkably composed but she wondered at what lay beneath. 'It still might not be enough.'

'Because of John you mean?'

She gave him a keen look. 'You know about that?'

He looked disgusted. 'Oh yes, Heinrich showed me yesterday at dinner and had every intention of making my response his own meal, but I gave him slim pickings.'

Her stomach clenched with grief and anger. 'I cannot believe John would do this to you. And for what? Very little can come of this. Philippe of France would do anything to drive a wedge between the two of you and he has worked on John so successfully that he has duped him into this.' She looked down at her hands. 'If I think anything else, then it becomes unbearable, and I am so tired.'

Richard clasped her arm in a comforting gesture. 'We will cross that bridge when we come to it, Mama – what to do about John.' His lip curled with contempt. 'He cannot stand against me, and neither can Philippe. I will set all to rights as soon as I am released. Heinrich likes to play games, but he is not God. From where is John going to get the money he has promised? By spinning straw into gold?'

'But how long before Heinrich makes up his mind?'

'It must be soon. Leopold of Austria will be demanding his share of the payment and he will not wait and the eyes of Christendom are on Heinrich in judgement. Besides, he needs the money and cannot have it until I am released.'

'He will want more concessions though.'

'Undoubtedly,' Richard agreed. 'If he had his way, we would leave here as naked as the day we came into the world.'

'Or not at all.'

Richard shook his head. 'There are too many eyes on

him now. If he were going to kill me, he would have done so in the early days – that was when I was most at risk. I am wary of him, Mama, but I do not fear him – and God sees all.'

There was a brief silence, and Richard bowed his head.

'I did not see Jerusalem,' he confessed, his voice pitched low. 'We came within eight miles and with a clear view in the distance, but I covered my eyes rather than look upon that which I could not rescue. If I had had the men and if my allies had not all proved to be traitors and deserters, we would have succeeded.' His face contorted. 'Perhaps this imprisonment is my punishment for failing God.'

'No!' Alienor was emphatic. 'Never think that. You have not failed God. Your captors are the evil-doers who stand accused of that. When they come before the throne of God they will be punished. You will wear your crown again and be cleansed of this disgrace that is truly the disgrace of others.'

Richard rubbed his palms over his face. 'The first thing I shall do when I am free is to hold a crown wearing in England and go on progress to show that I am still alive. You shall ride beside me, Mama, and wear your crown also.'

Alienor flushed with pleasure even while realising there was a glaring omission in his plans. 'What of Berenguela?'

His face became impassive. 'You are the one who has dealt with the matter of my ransom. You are the one who is here now to pay it and see me released. The accolade should be yours for all you have accomplished and endured. Berenguela will have her moment.'

This was not the moment to ask about their relationship. Clearly their time in the Holy Land had not resulted in a child before they parted and that was disappointing.

'You must send to her as soon as matters are settled.'

Richard set his jaw. 'Yes, Mama, I intend to.'

The flat reply, the tight expression told her not to pursue the matter, nor was she given the chance because an escort

347

arrived to return her to her entourage, although thankfully this time Heinrich was not with them. She embraced Richard once more, inhaling the scent of him. 'I will see you again very soon,' she promised. 'Whatever it takes to gain your freedom, I will do it, and not count the cost.'

Three weeks later Alienor came to Mainz with Richard and her household for the final consultation and to hear the result of Heinrich's leisurely deliberations over the ransom payment. Another three weeks in which England and Normandy could have fallen into the abyss for all anyone knew and there was nothing they could do except trust to the men she had left at the helm.

Heinrich faced Alienor and Richard across a broad trestle table spread with a white cloth. He looked like a cat that had just wiped cream off its whiskers and his lips were curved in a condescending smile. Pale February light leaked into the chamber; the sun was shining but as yet there was little warmth in its rays. Alienor's hands tingled as they absorbed the heat from the hearth and she could see William Longchamp trying to ease his swollen, arthritic limbs. The ride from Speyer to Mainz had been hard on many.

Wine was poured and everyone prepared to do battle. Alienor adjusted her sleeves, folded her hands on the table, and looked at Heinrich. 'Well,' she said, 'are we here to make my son's release official, or are you going to keep us waiting another month?'

Heinrich continued to smile and looked around at his lords. 'I sincerely hope, madam, that by the end of today all will have been resolved. I am having horses and baggage prepared even now in anticipation.'

'That is excellent news, sire. Then may we conclude this swiftly. Let us to business.'

'Indeed, madam, but first there is one small matter.' He gestured to a cleric who gave him a length of parchment with the seals dangling. Alienor stiffened as she recognised it as the letter from John and Philippe of France. 'The fact that I have had this offer made to me reveals the store that certain people set upon detaining the King of England as my guest for a while longer. Therefore it behoves you to have me as an ally.'

Richard narrowed his eyes. 'Naturally,' he said with flat sarcasm. 'I could think of nothing more terrible than having you for an enemy.'

'Quite so,' Heinrich said smoothly.

'How much?' Alienor demanded.

Heinrich looked pained. 'To foster lasting relations between the King of England and myself, I desire to make your son my vassal for that country together with a tribute payment of five thousand marks a year. I believe that seems fair.'

Alienor remained very still, although inside she was furious and dismayed. Richard flushed crimson and the veins stood out on the side of his neck as though he were choking.

William Longchamp spoke up. 'My lord, those are harsh terms. And they are on top of the demands you have already made upon us and which we have agreed to in good faith.'

'Circumstances change,' Heinrich said. 'What is true today may not be true tomorrow or next week. I desire these new concessions as proof of your good faith and to ensure we will continue as allies. The King of France has offered me much for my support.'

'Which he will never pay as well you know,' retorted Walter of Coutances.

'The fact that he is willing to offer it, along with King Richard's brother, means you need to keep my goodwill – which you shall have for this one last thing.'

Alienor drew a deep breath and laid her hands flat on the table. The marks of age mottled her skin like spots on withered autumn leaves, but the gold rings of authority shone brightly on her fingers. 'Pray allow us a moment to consult and consider, sire.'

Heinrich made a gracious gesture. 'As you wish,' he said, and left the room with his courtiers.

Richard exhaled hard. 'He desires me to kneel to him as his vassal!' He glared at Alienor and the two bishops. 'I have had all I can stomach of his weasel words, dishonour and untruth, and I refuse to swallow any more.'

Alienor reached over to touch his arm. 'Everyone has, but we have come so far that we cannot stumble here.'

'He may be bluffing for the pure enjoyment of seeing us dangle,' Coutances said, 'but do we take the risk of finding out?'

Richard's mouth twisted as if he had just taken a mouthful of vinegar. 'I will not be bound to this man. It would defile me.'

Alienor's touch became a grip. 'You do not need to be, my son, but in order to ride away from him you must do whatever is necessary. You know this in your heart. You said as much to me on our first meeting at Speyer.'

Richard swallowed convulsively.

'No one else need know about it. The only ones to hear are your kin or else staunch allies and they will agree to be bound to silence. Even if Heinrich demands this, once you are away from here, those imperatives will fade. How much is your pride worth? I have gone through hell to have you restored to me; do not set all my striving at naught.' She fixed him with pleading eyes. 'What good is having the heart of a lion if you cannot roar?'

Richard grimaced, but eventually he sighed. 'Very well, Mama, but only because you ask it of me. I do it as a boon for you.'

Alienor made a small sound of relief that was almost a sob. At least this way Richard could play by the conceit that it was to please her – a concession to her, as a woman, mother and queen making her request in the traditional role of peace-maker. If she took responsibility, it did not impinge on his honour so much.

The next day, Richard knelt before Heinrich, who sat in full regalia on his imperial throne. He put his hands between the Emperor's and swore to be his vassal. The words emerging from Richard's lips had a defiant ring, as if they were swords, and the kiss of peace between the men was more like a form of branding to seal the promise.

Following the oath taking a great feast was held to celebrate the event. Alienor noted the number of dishes and the elaborate table cloths and settings and knew that this event must have been in preparation for some time. Heinrich had always known Richard would capitulate. Some of the goblets and platters she recognised as her own – items she had yielded as part of the ransom payment – but she composed her expression and endured.

The following morning, Alienor and Richard departed Heinrich's court, leaving behind some of the hostages against the remainder of the ransom payment, although not any of the children. Heinrich magnanimously granted that they might return home. He bestowed gifts of good horses for their journey, sacks of food, fine cloaks and items of clothing to see them on their way as though they had been valued guests all along and never under any kind of personal threat.

It was a joyful company that set out, but there was an underlying anxiety to the journey and a real fear that at any moment they were going to be pursued and made prisoners again. However, as they took the road to Cologne, the light in the east was clear and the scent of spring filled the air. Alienor did indeed feel as though she had been into hell to reach down and pull Richard out of the devil's jaws. She was exhausted, having lived on her wits and used up reserves that would have to be paid for. Just a little while longer, she told herself, just enough to see Richard established as King once more, just enough to build a reconciliation between her sons, and then she could retire and close the door on the world except for a few select guests.

38

Winchester Castle, April 1194

The crown of gold flowers and sapphires was so heavy that it created a band of pain across Alienor's brow and temples, but she had no intention of removing it until the moment she retired to bed. She had worn this crown at her own coronation beside Henry forty years ago when she was still young and full of dreams and she had worn it again at Richard's crowning. But this was a new beginning.

If Richard's first coronation had been glorious, then this second celebration was Alienor's finest hour as she presided over a great feast in the hall of St Swithin. She sat in a place of high honour as the accepted Queen of England. Berenguela was in Anjou and Alienor had precedence. She was the triumphant Queen Mother whose efforts had restored her son to his rightful place: the Lionheart's mother with the heart of a lion herself. Everyone looked upon her with fondness, respect and trust in her wisdom.

Richard was already preparing to sail for Normandy. John had been summoned to court to answer for his behaviour but unsurprisingly he had not appeared. When the confrontation did eventually come, Alienor knew she would have to play peacemaker and bring the brothers together in order to face the real enemy.

She looked fondly at Richard who was laughing at a remark William Marshal had just made. Hubert Walter, the new Archbishop of Canterbury, had joined them, and Ranulf, Earl of Chester. Richard looked well, if still too thin, and he was as sharp as a honed sword, eager for battle. He had already tested that blade at the siege of Nottingham, fighting on the walls and helping to defeat the garrison that had been holding out for John. Alienor suspected he was making up for all the time wasted in prison enduring Heinrich's snide insults. He was restoring his balance and manhood as well as the country. She could appreciate that, but her heart quailed at the risks he took.

She was joined by Isabel de Warenne, moving slowly because of her stiff hips. Her face wore fresh lines of age and care, but she had a smile for Alienor. 'I prayed for you and for Richard every day. This is indeed an auspicious moment.'

'It is,' Alienor agreed. 'I owe a debt of gratitude to Hamelin for his toil in helping to gather the ransom. It could not have been done without him.'

'Yes. I am so proud of him. It has been difficult for him since Henry died. He mourns him deeply. Even if they argued, they were always brothers and they were close.'

'I know that Hamelin loved him. There were times when I loved him too, even as much as I hated him for what he did to me,' Alienor said sadly. 'Time passes and scars thicken over the wounds. I shall visit him at Fontevraud soon and see that he has a fitting effigy and prayers said for his soul.'

'Time for you to have a little peace too.'

Alienor gave a wry laugh. 'Do you remember when Henry wanted me to retire to a convent? You said it was a good thing and we quarrelled?'

Isabel eyed her warily. 'Yes, I do.'

'I was not ready then, but I am now in ways I was not before – and Henry is at my mercy, not the other way around.'

After a moment Isabel said, 'I do not know if you were aware because you were so busy working for Richard's release, but Belle's husband died last summer.'

'No, I had not heard; I am sorry.' Alienor was cautious, trying to gauge Isabel's reaction.

Isabel glanced round to check who was within earshot and lowered her voice. 'You knew she was still John's companion at times?'

'No, I did not. Had I been aware I would have tried to prevent it.'

'She tried to keep it from me too, but I knew. Hamelin suspected but never took it further – I think he could not bear to know. I wanted to tell you that Gilbert L'Aigle of Pevensey has offered for her in marriage. He knows that she is the mother of John's son, but he says she will be an honourable wife to him; what happened before should be laid to rest. They are to be wed as soon as we leave Winchester.'

Alienor wondered if the past could ever truly be buried, but she was tactful. Perhaps they would make a good match. Gilbert L'Aigle was much younger than Belle's first husband, and a man of purpose. 'I am pleased,' she said warmly. 'I shall make certain to congratulate her and give her a marriage gift.'

Isabel thanked her. 'She finds L'aigle pleasing and I hope she has grown up at last and learned what matters.'

Alienor murmured an appropriate platitude.

Isabel touched her arm. 'I hope you can find a way to reconcile your sons.'

'So do I.' Alienor noted that Isabel still had a deep need for family perfection; that had not changed with the years. 'It is time John grew up too. He is not blameless and some things even a mother finds hard to forgive, but I will endeavour to do so. I do not expect him and Richard to embrace each other in love, but they must unite against Philippe of France and not allow him to drive a wedge between them ever again.'

She had said enough, and changed the subject to ask about Hamelin's castle building project at Conisbrough. Isabel immediately began talking with enthusiasm about the fine chamber Hamelin had built for her and the conversation settled into calmer waters.

On a spring evening in early May, Alienor and her escort approached Lisieux. The almondy scent of hawthorn blossom hung in the air, and breeze-scattered petals drifted across the road like snow. Although she was in her seventieth year, Alienor still felt the haunting sweetness running through her veins and was a little tearful even though she welcomed the spring with an open heart. Every single one was precious because they no longer spread out before her in an endless vista.

She was travelling to Lisieux without Richard who was dealing with matters elsewhere but had promised to join her on the morrow. Earlier in the week, mother and son had received a message from Jean d'Alençon, castellan of Lisieux, informing them that John was staying there and desired to speak to her. Alienor and Richard had agreed that she would go and talk to him and prepare the ground first before Richard arrived.

'God knows, I want to string up the little runt by his heels and cook him over a slow fire for what he has done, but that is exactly what Philippe wants me to do,' Richard had said. 'I shall set the fear of God in him instead and then forgive him – not for my sake, Mama, but for yours, and for the stability of our lands. Go, do what you can to smooth the situation, but he is to know that my forgiveness is not unconditional.'

News of her coming had gone ahead and the town and castle gates were open so that she arrived with her escort at a brisk trot, banners flying. Grooms dashed out to tend the horses and an attendant helped her to dismount.

Jean d'Alençon emerged to welcome her and kneel in salute. He was beginning to go bald, and having been out in the sun without a hat, his pate glistened like pink marble. 'Madam, I am pleased to welcome you and serve you in any way I can,' he said. 'And I look forward to welcoming the King also.'

As she bade him rise, Alienor could see how ill at ease he was – and no surprise given the guest he was harbouring. 'The King will be here tomorrow,' she replied. 'For now you have me.' She set him at his ease with a smile and a light touch on his arm. 'All will be well, I assure you. Perhaps you would conduct me to my chamber.'

'Madam.'

He led her to a room near the top of the keep. A gentle fire burned in the hearth and small dishes of incense perfumed the room with fragrant white smoke. An attendant placed a jug of scented hot water and a towel on a chest at the side of the room.

'Leave me,' Alienor commanded d'Alençon, 'but send my son to me when I request.'

He bowed and departed, clearly relieved to be away.

Alienor settled into her chamber. Belbel gently washed her feet and rubbed them with unguent before slipping on pale silk stockings and soft kidskin shoes. While her attendants made up the bed with her own sheets and covers, Alienor went to sit in the window embrasure to gather her thoughts, and finally, when she was calm and prepared, she sent for John.

He came in quietly and hesitated in the doorway, one hand resting on the wrought ironwork of the decorated hinges. And then he braced his shoulders and advanced to kneel at her feet and bow his head.

She had thought herself ready for this meeting, but looking down at him, she still felt a hammer blow strike to her heart. This was her last son, the one always in waiting who had never had a niche that suited him, yet who, despite all his faults, possessed so much potential.

'Get up,' she said. 'Abasing yourself to me might do for a start, but how can I talk to you when I cannot see your face? Look at me, my son. Look me in the eyes and show yourself.'

John slowly raised his head and met her gaze. His eyes, quenched green with a glint of blue in their depths, held a boyish innocence. She had been drawn in by that expression too many times before and she was on her guard. But his face was thinner, a little sunken under the cheekbones, and she sensed his tension.

'I have forgiven you many things,' she said, 'but I do not know if I can forgive you this. Are you so desperate for power that you would trample on your brother's backbone and make pacts with our enemies? You have torn a great hole through all we have worked for by what you have done.'

His eyes glistened with tears, and she hardened herself.

'Many times I have asked why without an answer, or not one that I wish to be true, but what else am I to think?'

John put his hands together in supplication. 'I believed Richard truly was dead, Mama. And when I heard he had been imprisoned, I thought he might never be released.'

'Thought or hoped? You are not going to tell me you did what you did for the good of all? I am not that naive, John.'

'Yes,' he admitted, 'I wanted to be King. I knew I could rule well, and Richard was gone and might never return. When I went to Philippe to make a peace treaty, he offered to help. He told me about all the things Richard had done to him in Outremer, and how Richard often said how worthless I was, and that he would promote Arthur above me.' Anger suddenly flashed in John's eyes, and he continued self-right-eously, 'Was I supposed to work with someone who broke the faith with me?'

'Indeed, that is what I am asking myself at this moment,' Alienor retorted coldly. 'Your words cut more ways than one.'

John dropped his gaze.

Alienor sighed, raised him from his knees, and gestured him to sit at her side. 'Ah John, I may find it hard to forgive what you have done, but hard does not mean I cannot, and it does not lessen the love I bear for you. It is over; it is finished; a new page must be written. But how are we going to shape it?' She gestured to a nearby trestle. 'Go and pour wine.'

He went to do her bidding. Watching him with his back turned, he reminded her so much of Henry in his mannerisms – the curl of his hair, even if it wasn't vibrant red; the shape of his ears and angle of jaw – and she experienced an odd mingling of tenderness and apprehension.

'Richard will arrive tomorrow,' she said, as he turned round, 'and you must both come to an understanding. I can mediate, but ultimately it is Richard's decision as to whether he has you seized and cast into prison or forgives you your trespasses. You were summoned to Northampton to answer to him and you did not come – nor would I have expected to see you there. This truly is your last opportunity. You need to convince Richard that you will serve him faithfully from this day forth. I have spoken on your behalf, but I can do no more.'

John gave a wordless nod and handed her a cup.

'I know it will not be pleasant for you tomorrow, but you must face the consequences of your actions. My advice is to shoulder your burden and do all you can to make amends. Stand firm with Richard to set matters right. Count this as a lesson learned and your last chance to be the man I know you are and not the boy you have been.'

John reddened and took a gulp from his cup. She sensed the temper in him, barely held in check – that was like his father too.

'I want both of my sons to cooperate. As soon as this matter is concluded, I am going to retire to Fontevraud for a while. I need to rest.'

John eyed her sharply.

'Oh don't stare at me as if you think I'm going to drop dead,' she said testily. 'I have no intention of fading away or taking the veil. I shall expect to receive visitors including you and Richard, and I shall keep abreast of the matters of the world, but I need time to dwell in peace.'

John raised a sceptical eyebrow.

'The Bible teaches us that there is a time and season for everything. What was not right for me before is right now. And speaking of being right, I am reminded of your cousin Belle.'

John was immediately on his guard. 'What of her?'

Alienor fixed him with a stern look. 'I know you have continued to see her on occasion and as more than the mother of your son. Do not deny it. Everyone has turned a blind eye – her husband was in no position to do anything else. But now she

358

is wed to Gilbert L'Aigle of Pevensey. It is a good match for her and I want your promise that you will leave her alone. People will say I am mad to set store by your word, but as a personal token to me, I hold you to keep this one intact.'

John opened his hands wide. 'If that is what you wish, of course. I swear I will not go near her. It was over anyway.'

'Mayhap, but I know you. You always want what belongs to others.'

'I promise.' He placed his hand on his heart. He felt different now anyway, because his view of Belle was now as his leavings – the gnawed bones after a meal.

'Well then,' Alienor said, 'Richard will be here tomorrow, and you will take what comes. At least since you have recently been in the company of the King of France you know his plans and will have the best notion of how to counter and outwit him.'

Richard arrived late in the morning the following day with his full troop and Alienor was waiting to greet him with Jean d'Alençon. As she curtseyed to him they exchanged meaningful glances, knowing their part, although what was actually going to be said remained open to speculation.

In good spirits, a hawkish gleam in his eyes, Richard swept through to the great hall where the tables had been prepared and a meal was waiting to be served. For a short while Richard set aside his military concerns and applied himself with good appetite to food and conversation with his mother.

During a gap between courses, d'Alençon approached Richard with hands clasped before him in entreaty.

'Sire, you may already be aware of the fact, but I must tell you from my own lips that your brother the Count of Mortain is here in the keep. I have offered him succour under my roof in the hope that you and he might be reconciled.'

Richard made an open, almost casual gesture. 'Let him come forward and have no fear of me. My sword is at rest and I am too busy dining to go and fetch it to cut off his hands.'

D'Alençon bowed and departed.

Alienor placed her hand on Richard's sleeve and he smiled at her and pressed back. 'Do not worry, Mama. I do not intend mutilating him unless it be with words.'

John was a long time arriving and when he eventually entered the hall, silence fell behind his progress towards the dais like a shadow chasing the sun. He wore plain dark robes and a black leather belt girded round his waist so that the impression was sombre and penitent. A man facing his sins and admitting to them. Reaching the dais steps, he prostrated himself, arms outstretched and head bowed. 'Forgive me,' he said. 'I have done you wrong and I am at your mercy. I swear that I did not realise it would come to this.'

'You mean you hoped it would never come to this,' Richard retorted, eyes bright with ruthless amusement. 'You are indeed at my mercy. As I recall, our great grandfather imprisoned his own brother for the rest of his life for conspiring against him, and that is the least I could do to you for treason is it not?'

There was a brief silence accompanied by a shudder from John. His voice emerged from the darkness of his prostration. 'I know I have not done right by you. If you choose to imprison me, then I will gladly go.'

'I doubt the word is "gladly". I certainly did not go gladly when I was imprisoned, and I am sure our mother did not either when she was shut away in Sarum for all those years.' He allowed the silence to draw out before continuing. 'For that very reason, because I know how terrible it is to be a prisoner of someone else's schemes and in another's power, I will not do that to you, John. I would treat you better than you have treated me because you are my brother, and since I am indeed the King it behoves me to be merciful in victory.'

John said nothing, just kept his head bowed and his face against the wooden dais steps, breathing in the dusty air.

Richard leaned over the trestle and changed his tone to something softer, although far from merciful. 'Still, I think you were led like a little calf to the slaughter by the King of France. He is the real perpetrator and it is he and those who gave you bad advice and took advantage of your naivety that should be punished. You are nothing more than a foolish child duped by the machinations of others more cunning.'

John raised his head for the first time and looked at Richard, his face red with chagrin and humiliated anger. 'Then pray allow me to take my revenge on them for so misleading me,' he said through gritted teeth. 'I would never have harmed you of my own accord, I swear it on my soul.'

Richard arched his brows. 'I am inclined to believe you. Even if I do wonder if the state of your soul is not a little scorched around the edges by how close to the infernal pit you dance. Come, give me the kiss of peace. We shall say no more about it and we can sit and plan our campaign while we eat.'

John looked stunned at how easy it had actually been but stood up and stepped onto the dais. Richard rose from his chair, took John's upper arms in a bruising grip and kissed him hard on either cheek before escorting him to his place at his right-hand side. John paused to stoop and kiss Alienor who sat on Richard's left, smiling but wary. The worst seemed to have been weathered but there was still time for things to go wrong.

'I do not understand why you have forgiven me,' John said as a servant presented the high table with a large freshly cooked salmon, gleaming on a silver salver amid fronds of parsley.

'Because I know you were not equal to the task and it was my fault for over-estimating your ability to steer a straight path. As a king, it also behoves me to be lenient to the weak.' Richard gave John a benevolent smile.

John silently ground his teeth. 'Tell me one thing: why did you name Arthur as your heir?' There was a sudden glitter of true tears in his eyes. 'You talk of betrayal, but you betrayed me too.'

'I had no choice at the time if I wanted to succeed in Sicily,' Richard replied with impatience. 'The only way to make Tancred an ally was to promise Arthur to one of his daughters. It will never happen, and now you have a chance to prove your worth. We shall confront Philippe and you will have plenty of opportunity to redeem yourself.' He lifted a portion of glistening pink salmon and presented it on a large flat knife to John as a token of favour. 'Come, let us celebrate.' He directed an attendant to pour fresh wine into his goblet and stood up to raise a toast. 'To our future,' he cried. 'May it be glorious!'

Every man in the hall roared the toast back at him.

Richard drank and passed the goblet to John who set his lips to the exact same place. 'To Richard!' he cried. 'Vivat Rex!'

Again the cheer rolled around the room in a wave of sound, crashing back to the dais: 'Vivat Rex! Vivat Rex!' Men pounded the table with their fists and the hilts of their eating knives, even if some of them were eyeing John narrowly. For now they were prepared to follow Richard's lead and move on.

Richard turned to Alienor and raised another toast. 'My incomparable mother, without whom I would not be standing here among you now. To whom I owe my birth, my liberty, my very bones and blood. Vivat Regina!'

Amid deafening roars and table thumping, Alienor took the cup and drank, tears brimming in her eyes. 'To my sons,' she said. 'To brotherhood!' Amid another surge of cheers she made a graceful exit from the hall so that the men could do what men did at such times without having to stand on the ceremony of her presence.

As she returned to her chamber, she swiped away her tears and felt weak with relief. Her sons were reconciled even if they were never going to be bosom friends. At least they would cooperate for now, and the rift, if not healed, had been securely bandaged. Richard had raised a cup to the future and she had to trust that he and John could take it forward.

39

Abbey of Fontevraud, Summer 1194

On a perfect morning in mid-June, the warm breeze on her face and the first dust of summer sifting the roadside grass, Alienor glimpsed Fontevraud Abbey through the trees and drew rein, her heart lifting and expanding. The pale stone buildings waited to embrace her as they had always done, and now she came gladly, of her own free will.

'I am ready for this,' she told William Marshal, who had undertaken the duty of escorting her. 'I have lived seventy years in this world, and now it is time to take stock and nurture my spirit.'

'God grant you that tranquillity, madam,' William replied courteously, the reins slack in his fingers. His powerful bay shook its head against the flies and swished its heavy black tail.

She tilted him a smile. 'I shall still want to hear of the world's doings and how the lives of those I care about are progressing.'

William laughed gently. 'I did not think you were going to withdraw altogether.'

'Indeed not. I expect you to visit and keep me informed.' She teased him with a severe look. 'These days you may be the Earl of Striguil and a great magnate, but you will always be my hearth knight.'

He gave her that certain smile that always melted her heart. 'Madam, you could not keep me away.'

She meant what she said about him being her knight. His courteous, attentive manner and their shared sense of humour lifted the burden of her years and made her feel young and attractive.

As they arrived at the abbey gates, a robin perched on a low wall puffed out his chest and warbled a full-throated song of joy. 'There,' Alienor said, with delight. 'That salute is more fitting than any fanfare I have ever received.'

A welcoming party headed by the Abbess emerged to greet Alienor and her cortege, and conduct her to the guest house. Alienor prepared to alight from the mare, and because her mind was so buoyant she expected her body to be the same, but her joints were stiff and slow to respond. As William assisted her from the saddle she almost fell, and only his swiftness and strength held her upright.

She brushed off the moment with a rueful laugh. 'I should remember that these days my body does not do as I bid without a deal of urging, but I would not have ridden in a litter today for anything.'

'Madam, you are too eager and we are not quick enough to keep up with you,' William said gallantly, but his gaze was concerned because he saw her frailty even if she did not. Although she was in a fine humour and good spirits, she needed to recuperate. She was like a fine candle without enough wax to sustain the wick.

That night Alienor dined with William in the guest house and they talked of their shared past. He donned the persona of the young knight to please her, setting aside the magnate and soldier burdened with heavy responsibilities, and she flirted with him and was the vivacious, alluring woman from days long ago in Poitiers when she had bought him horses and armour, and raised him to prominence in her household.

She asked him to sing for her as he had so often done back then, and he obliged, standing tall and puffing out his chest like the robin on the wall. His voice was richer and stronger than in his youth but had retained the pure tone she remembered, and she loved him for it, particularly the way he improvised the tune, making up extra parts, changing the words here and there, all on the spur of the moment.

When he departed the next morning, he presented her with

a pair of embroidered gloves and a set of red leather reins. There was a small braided whip as well, and some dainty ladies' spurs, all of which he had carried in his baggage without telling her until now. 'For when you choose to ride out, madam. You once gave me fine harness and equipment, and I wish to return the same to you. Send me the gloves if you have need and I will come to you.'

She watched him ride away with a tinge of sadness in her heart but it was wistful rather than grieving, and although her eyes were wet, she was smiling too.

As Alienor settled into the daily routine of life at Fontevraud, she gradually recovered her stamina and her balance. The light returned to her eyes, and she looked forward with relish to rising each morning rather than struggling through a fog.

The lay women who dwelt at the abbey became her court and her companions, and she enjoyed hearing their stories and sharing their lives. She often received messages and visitors from the world outside and was only as isolated as she chose to be. She could go hunting with her gyrfalcon if she wanted, take daily rides in fine weather, and enjoy the gardens to her heart's delight. And there were healing and contemplative moments of prayer every day in the abbey church. Now and again she would glance at Henry's unadorned tomb and consider employing a stone mason, but the days passed and the task remained in abeyance. She would know when it was time, but for now she was not ready to make his presence more prominent.

On a golden autumn afternoon when she had been at Fontevraud for almost two years, Richard arrived at the gates with his entourage. He had sent harbingers ahead to inform her of his coming and she was waiting in the guesthouse courtyard to greet him. He dismounted somewhat stiffly from his dun palfrey and his face contorted as he set his left foot on the ground.

'You are injured?' She was immediately concerned.

'Ha, it was one of those foolish things. An almost spent crossbow quarrel nicked my leg under the shield.' He spoke with casual indifference.

Alienor tasted fear. 'Have you had your chirurgeon look at it?'

'Of course.' He gave a dismissive shrug. 'It's healing well. Most of the power was spent when it struck me.'

'You should not put yourself in danger, let others do that.'

He kissed her cheek. 'I am all right, do not fret. It is nothing.'

He looked so alive and vital that it made his words easy to believe, even knowing that they were all in the hands of God's mysterious will. 'I am glad to hear it. Come, I have food and wine laid ready.'

As they ate and drank in her chamber, he gave her the news of his campaigns against Philippe of France and the good progress he was making.

'And John?' she asked. 'Are you both cooperating?' She had heard very little from her youngest son since coming to Fontevraud. A couple of brief letters, a gift of a fur cloak at Easter and oil for her lamps, but nothing that spoke of John himself.

'He is proving a model adjutant.' Richard's expression was sardonic. 'Thus far he has done everything I ask of him and I have no complaints. If he has any to make of me, he has not said. I am sure he has his little proclivities tucked away in a dark corner somewhere, but nothing that causes me alarm – for the moment.'

He swallowed the mouthful of bread he had been chewing. 'I am building a castle on the island at les Andelys,' he continued. 'It will curb Philippe's ambitions. When I am finished it will be impregnable and guard the approach to Normandy so that nothing will get past it from France.' His expression grew fierce with enthusiasm. 'You have seen those fortresses in Outremer, Mama. The great ones that can withstand sieges for years on end. Gaillard will be such a one. I

366

am hoping just the threat of it will make Philippe turn tail and run. He is like a carrion picker – always slinking around the edges waiting his moment but he won't confront me face to face. Gaillard will serve warning that I am watching him.'

'And how much will it cost?'

'As much as it needs. The sooner and stronger my frontiers are shored up the better. Let Philippe skulk in Paris and venture out at his peril.'

He proceeded to tell her about his plans for Gaillard, as eager as the excited parent of a newborn child. Alienor listened keenly because she admired his skill and the defence of their lands against the French was vital. She was so proud of him, but even so other matters could not be neglected and in their own way were just as important as the great stone turrets of a proposed new castle.

'Berenguela has written to wish me well and make sure I have everything I need.' Alienor gave Richard a meaningful look. 'She tells me she holds you in her prayers and hopes you will soon visit her.'

'As I hold her in mine,' Richard replied, avoiding her gaze.

'You should go to her,' Alienor pressed. 'If you intend building great castles to oppose the French then you should have heirs of your own body to inherit them. I am not meddling, I am being pragmatic, and so should you be.'

'Yes, Mama, I will put it in hand.'

She could tell from the set of his jaw that he was merely paying lip service to humour her. Perhaps it was time she began writing letters and considering what might be done about an annulment, although there was no need to broach the matter with Richard at this point.

'I have also been wondering about Joanna. Have you any thoughts about her marriage? She has been a widow long enough.'

The guarded look left Richard's eyes. Clearly he was more comfortable discussing his sister's marital future than his own situation. 'One or two, which is part of the reason I am here.

I thought I might use my recuperation time to talk with you and see if you had an opinion – which I'm sure you do.'

Alienor smiled. 'What makes you think that?'

He waved airily. 'You are always one step ahead of everyone else . . . and since I have been pondering the notion of Joanna's marriage, I thought you might have heard that Raymond of Toulouse has put aside his wife and hopes to make new alliances.'

'As it happens I have already written to Joanna on the subject.'

Richard eyed her sharply. 'Indeed?'

She gave him a superior look. 'It is only natural that I exchange letters with my daughter. Strange as it may seem to you, there are some areas where women have as much influence as men. Joanna will do what is right for the family and our dynasty. She knows a union with Toulouse is to our advantage.'

'Has she replied?'

'She wrote to say she would consider the matter. Certainly it is a better suggestion than the one you had of wedding her to Saladin's brother when you were in Outremer,' Alienor said pointedly.

'That was just verbal jousting,' he dismissed with a wave. 'It would never have come to fruition; it just showed a willingness to bargain on both sides.'

'Perhaps, but the very fact that it was mooted is bound to cause misgiving.' She leaned back in her chair. 'You know how long I have worked to restore Toulouse to our affinity, and I greatly desire this, but Joanna is a grown woman and she is entitled to her say.'

After their meal they visited the abbey church to pray and pay their respects. Richard gazed at his father's tomb, still adorned with the same blank slab from seven years ago.

'Sometimes I come and talk to him,' Alienor said. 'And what pleases me is that he cannot talk back. Now he is the one who has to listen while I speak.'

Richard made an amused sound, but then sobered. 'I am surprised you have no effigy for him.'

Alienor grimaced. 'I think of it often, but somehow I feel it will bring him out of his tomb and back into the light if I do, and I am not ready yet. When it is time I shall know and he shall have the best stone mason in Christendom to carve it.'

Richard nodded with pursed lips. 'I understand, Mama.'

'He was mighty in life, and his effigy demands magnificence in death, but not yet. Let him rest in peace, and let me live in it.'

Three weeks later Joanna arrived at Fontevraud having ridden up from Poitiers with a full retinue of knights and servants. Richard had already departed north to deal with matters of government, and Joanna was to follow him to Rouen where she had agreed to wed Raymond of Toulouse.

Alienor swelled with pride at the sight of her daughter in the full flower of her beauty. Joanna was tall, graceful and glowing with vitality. She became stronger and more upright herself just by looking at her daughter – at the continuation of her lineage in this wonderful flesh-and-blood young woman.

'I am so proud of you,' she said as they walked in Fontevraud's gardens together, 'and of what you are doing.'

Joanna watched the fabric of her gown kick out and flare with each step. 'It is my duty to my family is it not? This opportunity to unite with Toulouse will not come again.'

Alienor said nothing. She strongly desired this marriage and to bring Toulouse into her affinity, but she was torn, and surprised to be torn. Marriages were always made for political alliance and the greater good of the dynasty, and as Joanna said, it was her duty. But at the same time, remembering her own unions, Alienor was unsettled about pushing her daughter into one that might not be made in heaven.

Joanna gave her a sideways glance from intelligent grey eyes. 'I can achieve what neither Papa nor Richard have been able to do with all their military might. I can restore Toulouse through marriage. If God is good, I will bear sons and I will raise them to know their bloodline.'

There was an edge to Joanna. Unlike her sister, Matilda, she did not have that softer maternal aspect and Alienor was pleased by the air of hauteur. It showed her daughter's mettle and that she had the strength, courage and passion for the task – a lioness to Richard's lion, which she would need to take on Raymond of Toulouse.

'And Raymond?'

Their walk had brought them to the abbey, and now they entered and moved silently down the nave until they stood before Henry's tomb.

'He is a man as all men, but not such a one as my father. Raymond is made of more malleable clay.' She sent her mother a look that twinkled with humour and knowledge. 'I am not without experience. I will endeavour to be a good wife to him, and I will foster relations between Aquitaine and Toulouse for all I am worth because I know full well that Philippe of France will do his utmost to destroy that link.' Her lips curved in mockery. 'To think that Philippe courted me in Sicily . . . the opportunities I have been offered these last few years astound me. I could have been Queen of France or wife to a sultan, and now the bride of a man who has long been our enemy.' She laughed as Alienor eyed her askance. 'I mean to bring peace if I can. You need not worry for me.'

'But I do,' Alienor said. 'I worry for all my children. That is the lot of a mother.'

Joanna gave her a spontaneous hug that took Alienor a little by surprise. 'I am glad you came to Fontevraud, Mama. I have loved it ever since I was a little girl. It feels so clean and light. I am glad Papa is here now even though he had planned to lie at Grandmont.'

Alienor made a face. 'Indeed, and he has had the last say as always because it seems that we shall now lie side by side in eternity, and I did not think that would ever happen.'

40

Abbey of Fontevraud, April 1199

The maid untwisted the last strands at the end of Richenza's plait, set the blue silk ribbons aside, and prepared to apply a fragrant lotion of rose water and ground nutmeg to her mistress's thick, wildfire hair. Copper and gold rippled in the light, with darker shadows of ruby and garnet, amber and topaz. The antler comb had wide teeth to work through the strands, and Richenza had had a special brush made from bristle to smooth it down and control the energy.

'Your hair has so much life!' Alienor laughed, stroking its abundance. It looked as if it would be coarse, but it was soft and silky – a marvel to touch. She put a hand to her own locks which shone like thin silver thread. 'Even when I was a young woman I could not match your glory!'

Richenza gave her a gentle nudge. 'Oh that is not true, Grandmère, you were a beauty in your own day, do not deny it! I have heard the tales and many a troubadour song made in your honour. How many songs do you think I will have in comparison to yours?'

'You are young yet, you have time,' Alienor replied with warm affection. Richenza was visiting Alienor for a few weeks and both women were enjoying the sojourn immensely.

'Who will sing a paean to my wild vixen hair? Yours was as smooth as gold. Mama often spoke of it and how she used to try out all the preparations and unguents in your coffer and hope they would make her as beautiful as you.'

'I remember her doing that.' A lump came to Alienor's throat. 'Although I never knew she wished such a thing; I thought it was just her curiosity: she always had to pare things to the bone to understand them. And she was beautiful.'

'Yes, she was.' A silence of memory followed, filled with unspoken words of love and regret.

Thomas, Richenza's small son, came to join in. He was not quite six years old, a handsome little chap made in the image of his father. His own hair was well-behaved, smooth and blond like Geoffrey's.

'Have you heard from Joanna?' Richenza asked.

Alienor shook her head. 'Not for a while, but I have no doubt I will and then in a screed. When Joanna writes letters, they take half a day for my scribe to read them to me.'

'How old is her son now?' Richenza tweaked Thomas's nose playfully.

'Two years this summer. He was born nine months after her marriage to Raymond, so she fulfilled her duty to provide an heir straight away. She seems content enough with him from what she writes, although as usual their vassals are creating difficulties and men will be men.'

'And Berenguela? Do you hear from her?'

Alienor's lips tightened. 'Occasionally. She has settled at Le Mans, but there is no sign of her and Richard coming together to make an heir. She does not encourage him, and he seems to have little interest in her.' She knew of the speculation about Richard. There were rumours of roistering and whores. He had twice confessed to sins of debauchery and had sworn in public to abjure such pastimes. He did not keep mistresses but he had a son – supposedly, although he had never mentioned the child to her and she had not broached the matter, not after what John had told her. If Richard wanted to bring the boy to Fontevraud then that was fair enough. She was praying that after the summer campaigning season Richard would settle down and attend to the business of begetting an heir. But she had thought that last year and the one before that.

The maids started plaiting Richenza's hair, Thomas helping them, although his attempt made the tress look like frayed rope.

Alienor fetched her jewel casket. 'I have a gift for you. I was sorting through these the other day and I found this.' She gave Richenza a gold band set with blue cabochon sapphires and milky pearls worked into the points of a star. 'I used to wear it on my little finger sometimes, but it no longer fits. The Empress of Constantinople gave it to me as a gift when I was there with Louis.'

Richenza tried it on and it fitted perfectly. Seeing it on her granddaughter's smooth, unblemished little finger, Alienor imagined her own hand when it had been like that.

'Have you seen the latest fashion in headdresses?' Richenza asked. 'I think it might suit you, Grandmère.'

Alienor gave a wry laugh. 'What makes you think I am interested in new fashions, my dear? They are for younger women who still desire to dazzle the world.'

'You still receive regular visitors and you will go out visiting yourself when the weather is fine,' Richenza said. 'And you will always be a queen.'

Alienor gestured, conceding the point with a smile. 'Very well then, what is this fashion? Show me.'

'You need a piece of linen like a swaddling band. Thomas, pass me my sewing basket.' The child obliged while Richenza pushed her dressed plaits over her shoulders out of her way. Opening the basket she found a strip of linen to suit and dextrously created an accessory that went under Alienor's chin and was pinned on top of her head and then the veil secured over it with more gold pins. 'There.' She showed Alienor the effect in a small silver hand mirror.

'So it binds up a sagging jawline,' Alienor remarked. 'Like a corpse.'

'But it frames the face and it makes you look regal,' Richenza said with undiminished enthusiasm. 'Truly, I would wear it.' She swiftly improvised one for herself, and Alienor had to admit that it did add dignity and gravitas. It also emphasised Richenza's eyes which were a deep ocean-blue swept by long dark auburn lashes.

'And this is what women in the world at large are wearing now?'

'Not all of them, Grandmère. There are still few enough that you would not be following everyone else.'

'And at the same time it is suitable for an old lady in a convent,' Alienor said, but with a teasing twinkle in her eyes. She loved having Richenza here. Her youth and vivacity brought light and laughter to Alienor's daily life.

Later the women visited the abbey to pray, although not for too long because Alienor knew Richenza was exactly like Henry and unable to stay still above a few moments. Contemplation and tranquil deep thought were not her strengths. She needed practical things to engage her mind.

Alienor showed her some slabs of tuffeau stone standing under cover of a lean-to shed. 'At last I have ordered the stone for your grandsire's tomb . . . and my own.'

A worried expression crossed Richenza's face. 'You're not going to die yet, Grandmère. I won't let you!'

Alienor chuckled. 'Bless you child, I hope not, but that is in God's hands, and He will take us all when He chooses. But I haven't yet lost the will to live and I hope He will give me time to instruct the masons.'

A look of relief crossed Richenza's face. 'What do you want?' She stroked the slab of Caen limestone and then rubbed the powdery dust between her fingers.

Alienor pursed her lips. 'It would please me for others to know who I was. Perhaps I shall have the sculptor portray me reading a book, and leave folk in the future to wonder which pious work I am reading aloud while Henry listens – or they may think perhaps I am keeping my knowledge to myself.' She flashed Richenza a mischievous smile. 'And a crown to show I was a queen. In truth it is worldly display but then it is for the living, not the dead. Hah, and a chin strap of course.'

Richenza laughed and shook her head. 'What of my grandfather?'

'I do not know yet. He was a great king and he shall have

374

that dignity, for himself and for his dynasty.' The twinkle left her gaze. 'It will not be easy to give instructions about your grandsire. Once I would have said it was because my heart was empty, but that is not the truth. I would do it tomorrow if that were the case. I hesitate because my heart is too full.'

In thoughtful mood the women left the chapel and returned to Alienor's quarters. They were drinking wine and eating some small savoury tarts when a messenger arrived, sweaty and travel-worn. Alienor saw him in the courtyard through the open door and grimaced. 'I do not want to be bothered now,' she told Belbel. 'Whatever it is can wait until after we have eaten.'

Belbel went out to do her bidding and send the messenger to wait but before she could address him, the man pushed past her and prostrated himself at Alienor's feet.

'Madam, you must come at once,' he panted. 'The King has been sore wounded and he asks that you come to him.'

Alienor's breath locked in her throat. 'What has happened? Where is he? Tell me!'

'Madam he is at Chalus in the Limousin, besieging the castle,' the man gasped, his chest heaving. 'He was walking the perimeter checking the placements of the siege engines and was struck in the shoulder by a crossbow bolt from the walls.' He pressed his hand to his collar bone to show her the area. 'The head lodged in the bone and the chirurgeon had to dig for it. Now wound fever has set in and the inflammation has spread. The King was in the grip of fever as I left him, but clear enough to ask for you. Madam, I am so sorry to bring you this news.' His eyes squeezed shut and two tears plopped onto his cheeks.

'Give him a drink,' Alienor said peremptorily. This could not be happening, and yet somehow she had been waiting for this moment for a long time. 'You will lead the way back by the swiftest route,' she ordered him as he drank from the cup Belbel had handed to him. 'Go and make ready and have a groom saddle you a fresh horse.'

Tense but focused, she made ready to leave. If she could get to Richard in time, she could make a difference she was sure. She had been denied that access to Harry and Geoffrey, but it would not be too late this time; she would not allow it, not with Richard. She needed very little, just a cloak and a spare chemise and gown swiftly rolled into a leather sack strapped to her horse. Other things could be brought by slower sumpter beasts and she delegated one of her knights to sort it out. She sent a servant running to find her physician, Magister Andrew.

'I am coming with you,' Richenza said, bundling her own requirements into a baggage pannier. 'Thomas can stay here with his nurse. You need a kinswoman and companion.'

Alienor nodded brusquely. 'Yes, but make haste. Belbel, you as well. You're a good rider and practical. No one else. I cannot afford to be slowed down.'

Murmuring an excuse, Richenza hurried to find the messenger who was standing in the yard bolting down bread and meat as fast as he could and swigging from a pitcher of wine. A groom was saddling a bad-tempered bay that kept lashing out with a vicious hind hoof but was full of spirit.

'How bad is it?' she asked him. 'Tell me true for my grandmother's sake so that I may help her.'

He gave her a look from eyes dark-ringed with exhaustion, and shook his head. 'My lady, it is a hundred miles to Chalus. We might get there in time.'

His words hit Richenza like a blow, but she absorbed it and kept her composure because she had to have strength for her grandmother.

Alienor mounted her grey mare, gathered the reins and turned onto the road leading to the abbey gatehouse. She wanted to push the horses but had to hold her impatience and settle for a steady trot because they had many miles to cover and their mounts were not in condition these days for long journeys and would go lame. She was not in a strong physical state herself, but her need to get to Richard overrode all other concerns.

The party from Fontevraud rode until dark and halted when their mounts began to stumble on the path. Under a fine, clear sky her knights made a fire and raised tents. The horses were picketed with nosebags of oats, and hobbled to graze on the sweet April grass.

Alienor could not eat the bread and cheese in her bundle; the mouthful she did take almost choked her and she abandoned the rest. But she did drink wine, into which Magister Andrew mixed herbs and honey to give her strength.

While the others ate, she paced up and down, sending thoughts and prayers to Richard, imagining them as strands of golden healing fire in the night. He would recover. She refused to countenance any other outcome.

She summoned her scribe and dictated letters to her vassals by lantern light, telling her lords to hold firm for Richard and ignore any foolish rumours they might hear about him being injured. He still lived and they must continue in their loyalty. She wrote also to Hubert Walter and William Marshal, informing them what had happened and warning them to be prepared.

Eventually, in the early hours of the morning she lay down, but slumber was as far away as the stars shining palely over the camp.

'You should try to sleep, Grandmère,' murmured Richenza, who was sharing her tent.

Alienor shook her head. 'How can I close my eyes when my son needs me? How can I not be there for him? No, I must keep watch.'

'Grandmère—'

'Say nothing more.' Alienor held up her hand. 'Let me endure in my own way as best I can and take your own rest.'

'If you will not sleep, I shall keep vigil with you in prayer,' Richenza said with quiet determination. Gripping Alienor's hands in hers, she began a prayer to the Virgin. After a hesitation Alienor joined her, and their voices rose towards the dimly lit roof of the tent, one old and cracked with age and exhaustion, the other young and light as springtime. Alienor fixed her gaze on a stitched square where a rip had been patched so that it was whole again. Why could a tent be mended and not a man?

Some time later, Richenza fell asleep in mid-prayer. Alienor folded a blanket over her and then continued her vigil silently, mouthing the words, refusing to close her eyes for an instant.

Before dawn she was out and about, chivvying her company to saddle up, to eat and make ready. Messengers set off with the letters she had dictated the night before. Richenza emerged from the tent binding up her hair, her face puffy and eyes dark-circled.

'You should not have let me sleep, Grandmère! I wanted to keep vigil with you!'

'Do not take on,' Alienor said shortly. 'There are more important things to worry over. Go and finish dressing and see that our tent is struck. That will be the most help now.'

Chagrined, Richenza bit her lip. She curtseyed to Alienor, then threw her arms around her and kissed her before turning to her duties.

As the light brightened in the east and burned a line between night and day Alienor left a handful of men to finish breaking camp and set out again, begging Richard to stay strong, to hold firm – she was coming.

Alienor arrived at Chalus towards noon of the third day and was passed straight through the pickets and guards to the centre of the encampment. Impatiently she waited for one of her knights to help her from her horse because her limbs were set and stiff from the ride, and then, formalities brushed aside, she hurried as best she could towards the large, pale tent with the red and gold triple-lion banner waving from the top. People were blurred shapes, bowing, standing aside to let her pass.

Stepping through the entrance with its folded-back flaps,

the taint of rotten meat struck her, powerful as a city shambles despite the fumigation of incense and herbs. Her throat closed for she knew what it presaged.

Moving further into the tent she saw Richard lying on a bed, covered to the waist by a linen sheet, his pale flesh naked above it. An attendant was bathing his chest with a moist cloth and wiping his arms. Richard's face was scarlet, and his hair clung to his scalp in matted tendrils, so dark and flattened with sweat that the wonderful auburn lustre resembled a thatch of dirty straw. High on his shoulder was a horrible wound, all suppurated and reeking with bloody pus. The flesh had been cut in the shape of a cross in order to extract the crossbow bolt, and the edges were blackened and disintegrating. A physician was placing maggots into the wound in the hope that the creatures would devour the foul materials leaking from the inflamed and rotting flesh. A long groan escaped Richard's throat but it was obvious he was almost unconscious. The physician raised one of Richard's eyelids and the blue iris rolled upwards, opaque and unseeing. 'Sire,' he said, 'sire, your lady mother has come as you asked. See, here she is.'

The man looked at Alienor and his gaze said everything without words. Alienor ignored him, denying that knowledge. It couldn't happen, she would not allow it. Not to Richard.

'Richard?' She took his hand and its heat almost scalded her. Against her fingers she felt the rapid beat of his blood, hotter than the sun. 'Richard my heart, I am here, I have come. All is going to be well now, I promise you.'

He groaned again. The physician covered the wound with honey-soaked bandages. Another attendant was rubbing Richard's feet and legs with an astringent herbal unguent. Slowly, Richard's eyes returned to focus as though from a great distance, and he looked at Alienor with a semblance of recognition. His lips moved, but she could not tell what he said, although she thought it might have been 'Mama'.

'Yes, I am here,' she soothed, stroking his hand. 'I have come, and all is well.'

He gave the faintest nod, and she felt a tremor run through his fingers and into hers.

'Rally for me, Richard,' she whispered, trying to force her own living will into him and give him the vitality to fight. 'I know you can do it. Do it for yourself, do it for your heirs – for my heirs unborn of your seed.'

Another infinitesimal acknowledgement and a faint squeeze of her fingers.

If she looked at the area of the wound she knew it was hopeless, so instead she gazed on the unharmed side of his body and willed all of him to be wholesome and firm. She projected to everyone within the tent that this was what was going to happen and locked her gaze on his, trying to hold him in the world and turn the tide.

For a while she thought she was succeeding, but he was beyond the point of return and the grace that had bound him in the moment was not enough. By slow but inexorable degrees he slipped away from her. His gaze disconnected and his eyes rolled back in his head again. His breathing began to slow and stutter, the rise and fall of his chest growing more erratic.

Her own breathing constricted. 'Give him a drink,' she said. 'In God's name give him a drink.' She snatched a goblet out of someone's hands and held it to his lips, but the liquid spilled from his mouth and slid across his cheek like watery blood. Murmuring prayers, his chaplain pressed a cross into his other hand and folded it upon his breast.

Numb with disbelief, Alienor watched as her beloved child died before her eyes. As the breath flowed out of Richard, so the belief flowed from Alienor, and as his breathing faltered she felt as if she too were falling into death, open-mouthed and bewildered.

A final breath shuddered out of him and he was still. The physician placed a mirror against Richard's lips, before shaking his head. Alienor ignored him and everyone around her. Still she held Richard's hand, and looked into his face. And then the reality hit her.

'No!' she wailed aloud and put her head down on her son's silent chest. 'No, no, no!'

Luke of Turpenay gently touched her shoulders. 'Come away, madam,' he said gently. 'He is with God now.'

'No!' She raised her head, tears streaming down her face. 'I cannot! He needs to stay here with me!'

The Abbot persisted. 'Madam, there are things that must be done for the King. I pray you, come away. Let the priests and physicians care for him now, and you shall return when they are done. Indeed, let someone care for you.'

She heard his words as though from a great distance and wiped her eyes on the back of her hand. 'He can't be dead. How do I believe something like this?' She rose unsteadily to her feet. Assisted by two of Richard's knights, she left the tent, but as she entered the open air and the public arena, long training made her stand erect and regal even though she had received a mortal blow. All was blackness, pouring down and engulfing her. Her light had gone from the world. Everything she owned, every hope for the future she had ever harboured.

The baggage had arrived and her tent had been raised. Richenza was waiting for her but Alienor held out her hands to fend her off. 'Do not speak,' she said. 'I have no words for this. Is my bed prepared?'

'Yes, Grandmère.' Richenza was pale but resolute.

'I want to lie down, and I don't want to be disturbed by anyone.'

'At least let me unbind your hair and take your gown. You will rest more easily that way.'

Alienor surrendered to her granddaughter's capable ministrations and was grateful for her pragmatic obedience. She could not have borne sympathy or tears. How well she now understood how people could turn to the wall and die of grief, but that indulgence could not be hers because Richard's death had immediately increased her burdens and responsibilities.

She was facing a world without Richard and the only way to cope was to be numb. Three days ago she had been content

381

at Fontevraud, playing jewel games with Richenza. Why had she not felt the crossbow bolt at the moment when it struck him? Why had she not known?

Once Richenza had helped her to undress, Alienor lay down on her camp bed, crossed her hands over her breast like an effigy and closed her eyes. *Oh my God, oh my love. Oh my child, my child.*

Richenza sat by her grandmother and prayed, tears rolling down her face. She could not believe her uncle Richard was dead because he had always been larger than life. How terrible it was for Alienor – far beyond grief. How did you come back from something like that? How would she feel if she were to lose her Thomas? The thought brought her grief so close to the surface that she choked.

Fearing that her sobs would disturb Alienor, she left the tent to compose herself. A chill evening breeze tugged at her skirts and made her shiver. Glancing across to Richard's tent she saw that the crowds from earlier had departed, but several people remained inside. An orange glow of candle and torchlight shone through the open flaps. Priests including Luke of Turpenay stood within, praying and chanting, and the air was misty with incense. Other men were gathered around a raised trestle, busy at some task. Lifting something that dripped; putting it in a box.

The man who had placed the object in the box now moved away from the trestle and stepped outside the tent and she saw that it was Richard's mercenary captain Mercadier. He stooped and swilled his bloody hands thoroughly in a bucket of water, and as he stood up, Richenza saw the dark blood-stains on his tunic too. Their eyes met across the torchlit space as Mercadier dried his hands on a rag tied to the tent rope.

'My lady, this is no place for you,' he said.

Richenza turned on her heel and fled back inside the women's tent where she sat down on her stool, trembling and nauseous. She did not want to think about what she had just seen, but knew it was taking place. That dripping thing she had seen in Mercadier's hand was Richard's heart. They were dismembering the King's body with their knives, unmaking the shell in one last service. His entrails were to remain here in the Limousin, his heart was to go to Rouen Cathedral to join his older brother, and his body was to rest at Fontevraud with his father.

Teeth chattering despite the warm spring evening, Richenza got into bed with Alienor and put her arm protectively across her grandmother. Alienor did not move.

In the morning, prayers were said over Richard's body as he was carefully placed on a bier in a cart lined with cloaks and covered with a silk cloth provided by Mercadier. He had been dressed in robes of scarlet and ermine. His hair had been washed and combed and restored to gleaming red-gold waves, and a jewelled crown had been set upon his head. His hands, adorned with rings, were folded in an attitude of prayer over his breast and all signs of violence to the body were concealed under the folds of his gold-pinned cloak. His entrails had been buried in a short ceremony at the church in Chalus and his embalmed heart, sealed in a lead casket, rested above his sword on the bier.

While the men made ready, Alienor walked about the camp checking all was in order. With Richard gone, she had to take on her son's role as well as her own and exert her authority. She had already ordered Mercadier to serve her as he had served Richard – at least until matters were more settled.

'As you wish, madam,' he had replied, his eyes dark-shadowed because like Alienor he was in hell. Indeed, there were hollow eyes throughout the camp. The walking dead bearing the dead to burial.

When the moment came to set out on the hundred-mile return to Fontevraud, Mercadier brought her horse forward, but Alienor refused to mount. 'I shall walk,' she said. 'Even if my feet crack and bleed, I shall walk every step of that road.'

The mercenary gave her a long look, but whereas others would have tried to dissuade her, he merely nodded and gestured someone to take the palfrey away.

Alienor went to the side of the cart and there removed her headdress and unpinned her hair, letting it fall around her face and stream down her back in dishevelled white strands. Gripping the curved metal bar on the side of the cart where cauldrons and sundry items were usually hooked, she gave the order for the procession to begin.

Richenza joined her, declining to ride her own mount in support of her grandmother. She too removed her wimple, but left her hair in its plaits.

It had been a dry April and the ground was decent underfoot, although the road was at times lumpy and potholed. Alienor barely noticed, except when the pace changed or the cart jolted, and then she was concerned for Richard, that it shouldn't disturb or undignify his kingly slumber. For herself it mattered nothing and she walked for mile after mile. One foot in front of the other, gripping the handle of the cart, hearing the creak of the wheels, the clink of the harness and snort of the horse between the shafts. The birds were singing, the sky was as blue as the Virgin's cloak, and the leaves unfurling on the trees were a tender spring green. And in all this beauty and life, her son was dead.

She stumbled on a stone and fell to her knees. Richenza hurried to help her up, and Alienor pushed her away.

'Grandmère, you should rest.'

Alienor shook her head stubbornly. 'No, I will walk every step of the way.'

Richenza handed her a leather wine bottle. 'At least take a drink.'

Alienor did so and the liquid burned down her gullet and made her cough. It was hard to swallow knowing that her son would never drink a cup of wine again.

Fortified, she stumbled on for another two miles, but finally her legs gave way and she slumped on the ground at the side of the cart, head hanging, lacking even the strength to weep.

Mercadier picked her up with the tenderness of a rough shepherd for a foundling lamb. 'In Jesu's name, madam, your son would not want you to do this.' His voice was gritty with emotion. 'Your son would have you ride.'

'No,' she whispered.

Mercadier frowned in thought and then bore her to the horse drawing Richard's bier and lifted her across its back. 'So,' he said, and with a brusque nod returned to his palfrey.

They set out again. Alienor clung to the sun-warmed leather, feeling the rocking motion of the sturdy horse beneath her and the quiver of the cart behind.

Folk who stood aside to watch them pass witnessed a cavalcade of mourners, men wearing full armour, banners lowered, and the ends trailing the dust. On a cart, draped in rich textiles, a waxen-faced king lay clothed in splendour. Astride the horse drawing his bier hunched an old woman, a hag almost, her wild white hair screening her face. Some of the knights in the party cast silver coins into the throng and the cry went up: 'Make way for the King! Make way for the King!'

41

Abbey of Fontevraud, April 1199

Kneeling at prayer by her open window, Alienor felt the warmth of the spring sun on her body, and was indifferent to it. It was a beautiful day with pale showers of blossom petals drifting across the gardens, and the green scent of growing things in the air – and she did not care.

Three days ago she had buried Richard in royal pomp and splendour and now his body lay in a lead coffin, closed off from the light, and she was existing in a numb void because it was the only way she could survive.

Richenza had stayed to give her comfort and company, as had Luke of Turpenay, for which she was grateful. Hugh, Bishop of Lincoln, had been a stalwart. Arriving at Fontevraud she had found him waiting for her, for he had heard the news of Richard's death and had been close enough to divert to the abbey, where he had helped to officiate at the funeral.

She had sent out letters every day, urging her vassals to stay staunch and swear their allegiance to John. She had worked until she was comatose with exhaustion because it was the only way she could survive, and the moment she woke she immediately immersed herself in toil again.

She prayed constantly because prayer was the closest connection she had to Richard now. Kneeling beside his tomb, she exhorted God to bless his soul and keep it safe in His hands.

She was praying now in her chamber, repeating the words over and over, making of them a comfort mechanism and rocking herself forward and back to the rhythm of her own beating heart. It took her a while to become aware of a gentle but persistent touch on her arm.

'Grandmère, are you all right?'

Glancing up, a little dazed, she strove to focus. 'Yes,' she said wearily, 'what is it?' She expected it was about food. Richenza kept trying to push sustenance on her, even though she had no desire for any of it.

'There's a messenger. Uncle John is here and asking to see you.'

Alienor's belly churned. She had been expecting him, but did not know how she was going to feel when she saw him. Her sole surviving son. 'Give me a moment to compose myself. Let me finish my prayers first.'

'I can tell him you are indisposed,' Richenza offered.

Alienor shook her head. 'I am well enough for this.' She pressed Richenza's hand. 'Bless you, child, go on.'

Richenza left the room and closed the door, and saw John walking along the path towards her, almost swaggering. Belatedly realising she should be kneeling to him, she made her obeisance.

A patronising smile on his lips, he gestured her to stand up. 'Where is my lady mother, niece?'

'She is at prayer, sire,' Richenza answered, 'but she knows you are here and will see you presently.' She planted herself firmly in front of the door.

An irritated look flashed across John's face. 'Then I shall wait. There is no need to stand there like an angel with a drawn sword. My mother is perfectly able to defend herself, and I mean her no harm.' He chucked Richenza under the chin in an avuncular way, pinching just a little too hard, and, setting her aside, entered the room.

Feeling the draught at her back, sensing John's presence, Alienor deliberately continued to pray. Only when she was finished did she rise and turn around.

Despite being prepared, the sight of him still jolted her and she found herself searching his face for traces of Richard. Perhaps there was an echo in his eyes and something about the way he stood, but most of all she saw Henry. 'I knew you were coming, but I had not expected you so soon.'

He remained where he was and she wondered if he was expecting her to kneel to him. She would do it in public formality, but not in her own private space. Going to him, she set her arms around him. 'I am glad you have come,' she said. 'You have been in my thoughts and prayers.'

He returned the embrace awkwardly, and his body was stiff. 'I could not believe the news about Richard,' he said. 'I never thought . . . it was so sudden. It's like always having a mountain in your life and suddenly it is no longer there when you look up.' Drawing away, he straightened his tunic and avoided her gaze.

'Do not think because you are the youngest, you are the least,' Alienor said, wondering if that was the source of his

387

discomfort. 'You have my support and I will do all I can to protect and sustain you in your kingship now it is your turn.'

'And I thank you, Mama. I rode hard to get here, but I cannot stay for long. I have much to do and little time to mourn. In the gap between the death of one ruler and another taking the reins there is always grave danger, and I do indeed need your cooperation in all things.'

She was taken aback by his direct approach, but then that had been how his father had reacted in the face of death, brushing it aside, pretending it did not exist.

'I have secured the treasury at Chinon, but there are rival claims to my power. Already Philippe of France has moved towards my borders, and so has my dear nephew Arthur with his mother. Constance would have Anjou and Maine for her brat.'

'Arthur is your brother's son, and my grandson,' Alienor reminded him.

'But he's still a brat.' He eyed her with suspicion. 'I take it I do have your support?'

'Of course you do! I would not prefer Arthur over you, ever. You are my son, flesh of my flesh. In my eyes, my heart and mind, Arthur has no right in this except Brittany, but it still does not stop him from being my grandson.'

'Whether he is kin or not, he will try to take what he can.'

Alienor felt as though she was a cushion with all the stuffing dragged out. It was difficult to care about anything, but she tried to rally. 'Just tell me what you want and I will do it.'

'I want you to keep watch over Anjou and Normandy. I want you to contain any unrest while I have to be elsewhere. Use Mercadier; he knows what to do. Employ the best messengers and send news to me swiftly of everything you do because then I can decide how to act. It is imperative you keep your own vassals in order. I need you to go to Aquitaine and take their homage and then go to Philippe of France and swear to him for Aquitaine. But leave the big decisions to me.'

Once Alienor would have bridled at being thus addressed.

She would have fought tooth and nail for the right to be involved in those decisions, but that was before her spirit had been brought low by Richard's terrible, premature death. Rekindling the fire from John was never going to happen. 'As you wish,' she said wearily.

He gave a curt nod that encompassed acknowledgement and departed to his own lodging.

Not long after John had ridden away leaving Mercadier on guard in Anjou, and Alienor preparing for her visit to Poitiers, Berenguela arrived at Fontevraud with her entourage to pay her respects at Richard's tomb. Alienor had hoped she would make a fine and fertile queen for Richard, but the marriage appeared to have been a thing of role and external show, barren within. Now Berenguela came as a widow with claims of dowry. She had proved her tenacity on their journey over the Alps and Alienor suspected she would bring that fortitude to pursuing what was owed.

Alienor welcomed her courteously, but seeing Berenguela brought tears to her eyes and made her wounds bleed all over again. 'You must be tired after your journey,' she said, swallowing down her grief as they embraced. 'Richenza will show you to a chamber where you can rest and refresh yourself.'

'Thank you, madam.' Berenguela's own eyes were wet. 'For all the difficulties we faced together crossing mountains, this has been the hardest journey of my life.' Her gown was sombre, almost nun-like, and the first fine age lines etched her face in the clear spring light. She clasped her hands prayerfully. 'I was sorry not to be here for the funeral, but I knew you could not wait.'

Alienor said nothing. She had grieved herself raw, and the pain was bottomless. It would have made no difference whether Berenguela was there or not. Tears trickled down her cheeks and she let them run.

'I always feared he would die untimely in warfare,' Berenguela said, biting her lip, 'but there was no stopping him.'

'He was born to do what he did. It was his nature, like a hawk is born to fly or a lion to hunt. Take away that nature and he would not have been whole.'

'He was always courteous and chivalrous towards me,' Berenguela added, wiping her face delicately with her cuff. 'Even in the battle camp, he made sure I was looked after. He spared that thought.'

Alienor nodded. Their eyes met, communicating without words the things that could not be openly said for to do so was to tread on the thinnest glass.

'May I see his tomb?'

'Yes, of course.' Alienor could not bear the thought of accompanying her there. It was difficult enough to shoulder her own emotions, let alone be burdened with whatever Berenguela might display as she knelt at Richard's grave. 'The Abbess will show you. You will wish to spend some time alone with him, but forgive me, I am not well enough to accompany you.'

'I understand,' Berenguela said. 'And thank you.' She held Alienor's gaze for a moment longer then curtseyed and withdrew, her step graceful and self-contained, but with an air of sad resignation.

Later, when Berenguela had refreshed herself and paid her respects at the abbey, the women dined together in Alienor's quarters. As they ate a light meal of chicken spiced with honey and pepper, Berenguela gently raised the subject of her dowry – as Alienor had known she would.

'You must write to John on the matter,' Alienor said. 'It is in his hands now.'

'I thought you might write too and add your words to mine,' Berenguela requested. 'I know he has many concerns and this must seem a small one to him, but I need the means to sustain myself.'

'Indeed, I shall do so.' Alienor inclined her head. She did not want to think about it because although as one woman to another she had sympathy for Berenguela's circumstances and payment was due according to the marriage contract, it was another drain on an already depleted treasury. It was like paying coin for goods from which there had been no satisfaction even while it was not entirely the vendor's fault.

After they had finished their meal, Berenguela took out her sewing and the women sat together on the window seat. Alienor watched her work with painstaking care, embroidering small gold lions onto the cuff section of a man's blue silk tunic. One sleeve was complete, the other half finished.

'I was making this for Richard,' Berenguela said sadly after a while. 'I cannot bear that it should be incomplete even though he will never wear it.'

Alienor's throat closed as all the grief welled up in her again. 'Leave it,' she said in a tight voice. 'He is dead. What will you do when it is finished but put it away in a coffer? It should be like his life and remain undone.'

'No.' Berenguela shook her head with firm vigour. 'This is for me, and I shall finish it because it is my duty and my last gift to him as his wife. I have to finish it, because how else shall I steer my life?'

Alienor pressed her lips together lest out of her bitter grief she said something terrible about the duties Berenguela had not performed while Richard was alive. Her daughter-in-law might just give her a reply she did not want to hear.

'I am sorry,' Berenguela said. 'I should not have brought it forth in your presence. It was thoughtless of me.' She folded the tunic with careful, tender hands and returned it to its basket.

'Perhaps,' said Alienor, recovering a little, 'but we each do what we must to continue.'

'I should retire if I am to be on the road early tomorrow, and I have my prayers to say.' Berenguela stood up.

Alienor rose too and did not try to prevent her from leaving because there was no more to say that would not intensify the grief and bitterness. 'I am glad you came.'

'So am I – and it was more than duty.' Berenguela performed a deep curtsey. 'My lady mother, I honour you.'

'And I you, daughter.'

Alienor gave Berenguela a formal kiss on either cheek, and then a warmer embrace that spoke of the ties they had shared, but she was relieved to see her depart. Tomorrow she would wish her Godspeed on her way and send her out of her life.

Almost as soon as Berenguela had gone, Alienor departed Fontevraud herself with Richenza and rode south, leaving Mercadier to deal forcefully with the Angevin vassals whose loyalty was suspect and to push Constance and Arthur out of the province and secure the territories for John. She received reports and sent messages by return as she rode from castle to castle, taking stock of her domain and homage from her vassals. Condolences and respects were paid to her, and anxious questions asked to which she issued reassurances. She was their duchess, they were to trust her. She was here and ready to listen to their concerns. Forced to take up the reins, she clung to her work because there was no one else; she had always done her duty and she was a duchess and a queen.

The spring sun warmed her bones as she rode through old haunts and the familiar places of her youth. Deep sadness and nostalgia settled on her like a heavy cloak, but there was something in the sensory detail that uplifted her too, like a gold thread hemming the garment's border. Glimpses of child-hood enlivened her soul, and even though her body was old and stiff with years, she remembered how it felt to be limber and sprightly. To climb trees, and run. To dance with swift steps, heel and toe, circle and spin.

She visited the bustling port of La Rochelle and drew the salty tang of the ocean into her lungs while she watched the trading vessels dock and embark. And then on to Talmont, one of the hunting preserves of the Dukes of Aquitaine. Ghosts awaited here of long-ago picnics, childhood romps, and flir-tations. Barefoot at the sea's edge, her toes lapped by the white lace of spent waves, and the sun sparkling on the water like coins. A man's laughter as she chased him with a ribbon of darkly shining weed. She could still hear the old songs faintly on the wind. Time had not stolen her memories but enhanced them, making them perhaps better than they were, but she would settle for that and not complain.

Everywhere she went she took the homage of her vassals and made the point that she was and had always been the Duchess of Aquitaine. Before. Now. Until her heart stopped beating. Her sole task was to survive.

In June she came to the town of Niort, two days' ride from Poitiers, and rested there for a few days. On the second morning, not long after she had risen from prayer, Alienor received news that her daughter Joanna had arrived at the gates in distress and was asking for her.

Alienor dismissed all the servants but Belbel and having embraced Joanna drew her to a cushioned window bench. Through the gap in Joanna's cloak the swell of pregnancy was unmistakeable, and her daughter looked tired and harassed.

'Come, come.' Alienor signalled Belbel to bring a footstool. 'What are you doing here when you should be resting in Toulouse?'

'There is strife among my husband's vassals.' Joanna wearily passed her hand across her forehead. 'Dear God, when isn't there strife? I came to bring troops to the besieged castle at Casses, but Raymond's own knights betrayed me. They turned rebel against us and burned the camp. I had to flee just as I am.' Her chin trembled. 'I came to ask help from Richard, but now I hear rumours that my brother is dead. Is that true, Mama? I do not want to believe it . . . but what are you doing here otherwise?'

Alienor took Joanna's hand. 'Oh, my love, I am afraid it is true.' She struggled to hold back the tide of grief so that she could speak. 'Of a crossbow bolt that festered in his flesh, taken at a petty siege that he need not have been conducting. I reached him before he died, and I brought him back to rest at Fontevraud a few weeks ago.'

'No,' Joanna said in a choked voice. 'Not Richard.' She put her hand to her mouth and heaved.

'I say that to myself over and over. I cannot accept it, yet I must.' Her voice cracked and she gripped her hands together. Striving, holding on. 'Your brother John is King now. We have to look to him.'

Joanna staggered to the laver basin and was sick, retching and sobbing. Alienor went to support her, an arm across her back. Joanna was taller than she was now, and it seemed a strange thing to be holding someone so much more robust. 'Come now, come now. For the child's sake do not upset yourself. You must lie down and rest.'

Joanna rallied, stifling her tears and wiping her eyes and face on the towel above the laver. 'I cannot.' Her voice was scratchy with tears. 'I do not know which way to turn. My husband is at war somewhere in the field and nowhere is safe. I had placed my hopes on Richard but . . .' She made a helpless gesture.

'You have succour here with me,' Alienor said firmly. 'John will help you. For now you are safe and do not have to worry about your immediate welfare. Perhaps if you went to Fontevraud and rested while I finish what I must do here.'

Joanna returned to her chair, and was consoled enough to take refreshment and prop her feet on the footstool. Alienor did not want to talk about Richard. It was too painful and she was anxious about Joanna's situation.

Joanna shook her head. 'I never thought on the day I became Countess of Toulouse that I would find myself fleeing with nought but my immediate baggage, and this new babe less than five months in my womb. God pray that my son is safe. I left him in Toulouse with his nurse.'

'You are overwrought. He is succoured, and so are you, and that is all that matters for now. John will aid you, and you have my protection for as long as you need.'

Joanna swallowed. 'You are a rock, Mama. When all else is torn away by storms, you will still be standing.'

Alienor felt the burden of Joanna's trust settle upon her like another load on a pack horse. 'You are my daughter,' she said. 'I will always stand in the storm for you.'

As Joanna made her way to Fontevraud, Alienor rode to Tours and there knelt to pay Philippe of France homage for Aquitaine. She had never met Philippe before and would not have done so now unless forced by circumstance. She esteemed him as a rival and an astute political player, but it did not make her loathe him any the less. She would never forgive what he had done to Richard. It was burned into her, soul-deep. She could not trust him an inch; he was without honour.

Outside the cathedral in Tours the summer heat beat down like a smith's hammer upon the anvil, but it was shadowed and cool within the sheltering stone walls. Philippe had a look of Louis about the mouth and jaw. He was slim like his father but did not have his height, and both eyes and hair were light brown, the latter receding to show a shiny pink scalp beneath. No one would have marked him out as a king in a crowd of people; only his fine clothes and rings revealed his rank. But when she looked into his face, she met the expression of someone who only played to win – inscrutable and soulless even while professing pleasantry as he greeted her.

Alienor slowly knelt before him to pay homage for Aquitaine and stifled a gasp at the pain from her stiff joints. She was sick with bitterness that he should be alive while her beautiful Richard was dead. There was no justice in the world. But at least in making this oath and remaining Duchess of Aquitaine she could keep John safe and close the door on Arthur's claim to Aquitaine. While she lived and held the sovereignty, there was no question.

Having stooped to give her the kiss of peace, Philippe was solicitous and helped her to her feet with courtesy and concern. But then he could afford to bide his time, and that knowledge was also part of her bitterness. She well recognised his ploy. Making it seem to others that she was ailing and frail served to lessen her authority and hinted that she might soon die. Alienor accepted his help but stood tall and walked at his side with regal dignity to give the lie to such hints.

Philippe's son Louis was present to mark the ceremony – a handsome youth of twelve years who greatly resembled his grandsire of the same name. Although wary of his father, she found herself liking the youth. He was ungainly because of his age but well-mannered and polite, and Philippe was clearly immensely proud of him.

At the formal banquet after the oath taking, Alienor sat at Philippe's side, and it was almost as difficult as the time she had had to keep company with Heinrich of Germany, who was now thankfully dead. She made a pretence of enjoying the food, even though it almost choked her to swallow. Tomorrow it would be over. Tomorrow she could return to Fontevraud to see how Joanna was faring before going to Rouen to await John's return from his coronation in England.

Philippe presented her with a tender morsel of venison. 'It is a pity there has never been a marriage alliance between our houses that has endured. My father always wished us to be united and have peace from strife – as I do too.'

Alienor held the meat daintily between her forefinger and thumb. How she was going to eat it she did not know. She had never welcomed such an alliance herself. Having once been married to Philippe's father, she had wanted to sever all ties of blood. Henry had never seen it that way. He had viewed it as an opportunity to seize in both hands. She thought of how Philippe had briefly chased Joanna in Sicily and concealed a shudder of distaste. 'Perhaps God did not mean it to be,' she said.

'Mayhap,' Philippe acknowledged, 'but I was thinking that a marriage alliance now would help to heal what has gone before.'

Alienor somehow dealt with the sliver of venison. 'Between whom, my lord?'

Philippe cut another slice of meat from the haunch. 'Between my son and one of your Castilian granddaughters. It is a generation removed and you might have fewer objections to such a match?' He glanced at his heir and smiled. Louis remained politely silent, although his gaze was watchful.

'Such a decision is not up to me, but to my son,' Alienor said impassively.

'But even now your word carries wisdom and weight.'

'Even now?' Alienor raised her brow at him in bleak amusement. 'My flame has not burned out yet, my lord.'

'Indeed I meant no insult,' Philippe responded smoothly. 'The point I was making was that you might or might not choose to speak, and your decision on the matter would make a difference to what happened.'

'Perhaps,' she replied, having served warning that kneeling to him did not mean she was beaten down. 'I shall say nothing for now save to acknowledge you have mooted the idea. I will decide later whether to think upon it.'

Philippe inclined his head. 'As you wish.' There was humour in his gaze and speculation, as if something he had taken for granted had sprung a hidden surprise.

As soon as she could, Alienor made a graceful exit from the meal. 'I beg your leave to retire,' she said. 'I have some long journeys ahead of me and an early start on the morrow.'

Philippe was content to bid her goodnight, but looked taken aback when she asked that his son should light her to her chamber instead of one of the squires. 'If I am to think on certain matters, then I might find such a service instructive,' she said as she rose to leave, attended by Richenza.

Philippe eyed her warily, but gestured with an open hand. 'Of course. I trust that neither of you will lead the other astray. Louis, attend the Queen and see her safely to her chamber.'

Louis left his place at the table, bowed to Alienor, and summoned a servant to go before them with a lantern.

'I have never been to Aquitaine,' he told her as they walked side by side. 'I would like to see it. My tutors often speak of places beyond my father's domains, and then I wonder about them – not just Aquitaine.'

'Well, perhaps you will get your wish.' Alienor wondered if he was plotting somewhere in his adolescent mind to expand the French dominions, just as Henry as a youngster had once plotted his own rule which now, ten years after his death, was gradually imploding.

'I hope so.' He gave her a half-shy, half-assessing look. 'My father told me you were a good horsewoman.'

'How would he know that?' Alienor demanded with surprised amusement.

'He says you went to the Holy Land with my grandfather who said you were as sturdy in the saddle as any man.'

Alienor laughed. 'Yes, that was true once upon a time.' She rather liked the youth who seemed genuinely interested and curious even if he had been sired by a snake. Perhaps Philippe had not meant it as a compliment that she had mannish tendencies, but the boy had phrased it as one. She suspected he was sharply political like his father, but he had a mind of his own.

At her chamber door she thanked him for his escort and he bowed to her and departed. 'A personable youth,' Alienor remarked to Richenza, and thought it a pity that she would not live to see the kind of man he would become if God spared him to grow up.

'What did you think of the marriage suggestion, Grandmère?'

Alienor pursed her lips. 'That it bears thinking about, but not just now.'

At Fontevraud Joanna had rested during Alienor's absence, and since she felt much improved, was determined to accompany her mother to Rouen.

Alienor told Joanna about the French offer of marriage with Castile.

Joanna raised her eyebrows. 'Will you advise John to pursue it?'

'It will depend what France offers in return. It is John's

398

decision to make, not mine. I have other matters to deal with when I am in Rouen.'

'Yes, Mama,' Joanna said sombrely, 'I know.'

Alienor thought about the casket sitting before the altar in the abbey church. Richard's heart had been embalmed with preservatives, herbs and precious spices and encased in a rock crystal reliquary before being sealed in lead. Just a few months ago it had beaten within her son's body, giving him life, driving him forward. In Rouen she would see to its interment beside his brother's tomb and she was dreading the duty, but it must be done. And then she would return to Fontevraud and begin work on the effigies. It was time.

42

Rouen, Summer 1199

Alienor studied her remaining son thoughtfully. John had been crowned King of England two months ago and now, in his feast hall at Rouen, wore a golden diadem set with sapphires and rubies, reminding everyone of the fact that he was King, including himself. He was in a magnanimous mood because Alienor had just ceded her rights in Aquitaine to him, reserving her sovereignty.

The assembled barons sat at a lavish banquet at which no expense had been spared. Silver gilt goblets, spoons and dishes adorned the dais table with its white linen cloth. Dishes of roast meats and fish from sea and stream were arranged down the middle of the board, interspersed with boats of colourful piquant sauces and loaves of fine white bread. Numerous varieties and hues of wine had been provided, from a red as dark as pitch to the palest Poitevan gold, and one from Normandy that sparkled on the tongue.

Occasionally John sent morsels from the high table to be presented to the less exalted retainers lower down the hall, and a couple of times he ordered the squires to take baskets of plain bread and loops of smoked sausage to the crowds loitering outside in hope of alms.

John had been delighted to see Joanna and was feting her at the table, sharing his dish and cup, calling her his dearest sister and promising that as soon as he was able he would come to her aid in the matter of Toulouse. Joanna basked in John's attention, and as they indulged in banter and reminisced about their childhood, Alienor delighted to see them bonding as adults.

William Marshal sat close to Alienor. John had rewarded him with the title of Earl of Pembroke for his support immediately following Richard's death and he was riding a crest of golden favour. He flirted gently with Alienor, making her laugh, and resurrecting echoes of the past when she had felt young and desirable. He was solicitous of her welfare, but not in a way that suggested she was an old woman, and she loved him for that.

'I have to thank you for supporting my son,' she said. 'Without you and the Archbishop of Canterbury, his path would have been much less certain.'

William directed an attendant to refill her cup with more sparkling wine. 'He is our rightful lord and a man full grown. I knew it was your wish and the late King's, madam.'

'It is not over yet. Aquitaine is stable for now, but the rest is in a state of flux. There is conflict over the Vexin, and the King of France will continue supporting Arthur in order to try and weaken us. I have done what I can in speaking with Philippe and doing homage for Aquitaine, but John must address the situation himself.'

'I will do my best to advise the King, madam, but he has his own notions of procedure.'

Their conversation ended as William was called upon to sing, and he had perforce to rise and oblige the request. His voice had deepened with the years, but the tone was clear and true as he sang a composition written by Alienor's own grandsire, a poet of renown. The exquisite melody, the verses describing the joys of spring lifted Alienor's heart and made her tearful but in an uplifting way, particularly when he came to the last verse and sang with his eyes on hers:

> Open-hearted, her manner free,
> Bright colour and golden hair,
> God who grants her all sovereignty
> Preserve her for the best is there.

That night she slept in a large bed piled with swansdown mattresses and dressed with the finest linen sheets, Joanna one side of her and Richenza the other. Her slumber was deep and dark, without dreams. She was slow to wake in the morning and stiff because she had barely moved all night. Richenza was already up and about, but Joanna was still abed and slow to her own stirring. She gave Alienor a sleepy smile and yawned widely like a cat.

'I think there must have been something in the wine last night,' Alienor said, opening and closing her right hand to restore feeling because she had been lying on the limb all night.

'I woke up to use the pot and you never stirred. The child was restless and kept me awake.' Joanna flapped aside the covers, and as she left the bed Alienor noticed a few fresh red blood spots on the back of her chemise, and a small mark on the sheet.

Joanna turned at Alienor's murmur of concern and the daylight from an open shutter shone through her fine linen chemise and illuminated her swollen belly.

'I think we should send for the midwife and the physician,' Alienor said gently so as not to alarm her. 'There is a little blood on your chemise.'

Joanna twisted and grasped the back of the garment to look at the marks.

'Are you in pain?'

'No, Mama.' She lifted the garment to reveal a few further smears on her upper thighs and staining her pubic hair. 'It happened before, two days ago, but it was like this and only a little.'

The physician and the midwife arrived and gently examined Joanna. The former studied a sample of her urine and declared her to be healthy but that a tisane of camomile in wine would be advisable for her to drink. By now the bleeding had stopped and Joanna, although a little puzzled and anxious, was not in discomfort. Both the physician and the midwife were confident that the baby was alive and vigorous.

While Joanna took a warm, prescribed bath in salt water, Alienor drew the midwife, Dame Hortense, to one side and demanded more detail.

'It is too soon to tell, madam,' said the woman with careful neutrality. 'It depends upon the Countess of Toulouse's progress from now until the birth. She should rest in bed for a few days and not do anything to exert herself.'

'What do you mean "too soon to tell" – to tell what?'

The midwife folded her hands. 'Madam, the child is lying sideways, but there is time for him to turn. It usually happens, but . . .' She hesitated. 'But many times when a child lies sideways, there is bleeding before the birth.'

Alienor's stomach flipped with fear. 'And if the child does not turn?'

Dame Hortense's brown eyes were steady and compassionate. 'If all is well then the child will turn of his own accord and will be born living and breathing, but the spots of blood indicate that the Countess may bleed a lot at the birth and should be nourished and cared for so that she is strong.'

'And if all is not well?'

The woman's shoulders tightened, but she continued to hold Alienor's gaze. 'Then the bleeding will worsen and when true labour begins only a miracle will save the Countess and her child.'

402

Chills shivered up and down Alienor's spine. 'Leave me,' she commanded. 'That is enough. Go.'

The midwife curtseyed and left, followed by the physician. Composing herself, Alienor went to Joanna who had just stepped from the bath. Her hair was piled on her head in two heavy bronze-brown plaits, and small, wet strands curled at the nape of her neck. Her breasts were round and full, her belly too, of life . . . and potential death.

'Well,' said Joanna with a strained smile, 'I can now be utterly lazy and not be castigated for it. You must all come and fete me at my bedside.'

Alienor forced a smile in return. 'Just because you have to stay in bed does not mean you cannot sew and dictate letters, my girl. I intend to keep you very busy.'

Joanna made a face at her and laughed. 'I suppose not. In truth such work will keep me from becoming bored. I had better write to my husband, wherever he is, and let him know.'

'Indeed, it should be your first task. Come, I will dress your hair.' Alienor picked up an ivory comb from Joanna's toilet items.

'I always loved it when you combed my hair when I was a little girl,' Joanna said as she sat down to let Alienor work. 'You were better than any of the maids.'

'Yes, you would have sat for ever if I had let you.'

Alienor's throat tightened as she worked on Joanna's thick tresses, shining with life. They were nowhere near the magnificence of Richenza's blazing wildfire, but still truly beautiful, and Alienor was filled with terror and the desire to protect her daughter, while knowing that everything was in God's hands.

The blood spotting continued intermittently over the next few days, and by the time a week had passed it was clear that the symptoms were not easing and indeed the flow had become greater despite the bedrest and warm baths that had been prescribed. Dame Hortense was reassuring and comforting when she visited Joanna, but when not facing her patient her expression was increasingly anxious. The baby remained sideways and showed no signs of turning, and it was becoming too late for that to happen.

In the second week, with no improvement, Alienor came with Dame Hortense to Joanna's bedside. Sitting down on the coverlet, Alienor took her daughter's hand in hers. 'We have something to tell you, something I wish did not have to be said, but you must be forewarned and prepared.'

Joanna looked between them, alarm blossoming in her eyes.

Dame Hortense curtseyed. 'Madam, the child is lying sideways in your womb. His head his here' – she indicated Joanna's left-hand side – 'and his feet here. The way he is lying is causing you to bleed.'

As the words sank in, Joanna's alarm increased. 'Can the baby not be turned round?'

'It would be very difficult at this stage, madam, and unlikely to succeed.'

'But if the child is not turned, then how will it be born?' Joanna looked at her mother.

Alienor squeezed her hand. 'You must pray to God Almighty and to the Holy Virgin and St Margaret, patron of women in travail.'

Joanna swallowed. 'You are telling me I am doomed,' she whispered. 'If the baby cannot be born, then he will die, and I will die with him. I cannot give him life, that is what you are saying.'

'Nothing is certain, my love,' Alienor said, 'but you must prepare for the possibility and that is why we have told you – so you may set your affairs in order.'

Joanna put her hand to her womb and touched the area where the midwife had shown her the baby's head. 'But there is nothing you can do.'

'I will stay with you, I promise.' Alienor did not think her heart could break into any smaller pieces than it had done when she lost Richard, but she had been wrong. Just now it was being pulverised. 'You will never be alone.' She pulled

Joanna into her arms and held her tightly as if she could protect and shield her by such an act.

That night as she lay beside Joanna in bed, neither of them sleeping, Joanna, who had been holding a cross in her hands throughout the day and was still gripping it now, said softly to Alienor, 'If this is to be my end, then I wish to die as a nun of Fontevraud. I wish to take the veil.'

Alienor sat up and gazed at Joanna in the glow from the lamp above the bed. Joanna had insisted they keep a light burning because light meant life. Fear glistened in her daughter's eyes, and determination jutted her chin.

'I want to be closer to God, Mama. I want His light to shine on me when I die, and if I am a bride of Christ it will help my cause. Certainly I can no longer be a wife to my husband.' A single tear rolled down her cheek.

'You will need your husband's permission to take the veil,' Alienor said, being practical through her shock. 'Is he likely to give it?'

Joanna shook her head. 'I do not know, but I have to hope. It will be best for the child too, because it will convey status upon him whether he lives or dies.' Her chin trembled. 'I understand there is a small chance they may save him even if they can do nothing for me. Summon the scribes, Mama, and I will write to him now.'

Alienor looked at her askance. 'It is the middle of the night.'

Joanna's mouth twisted. 'Soon enough it will not matter. Who knows how many more days I have?' She set her lips. 'I will write to the Abbess at Fontevraud too because her dispensation is necessary, and the Archbishop of Canterbury. You may go back to sleep if you wish, Mama; this need not concern you.'

'Of course it concerns me,' Alienor snapped, angry now. 'I do not know how many tomorrows I have either. If you cannot sleep, then better this than lying awake and counting the hours.'

She summoned more light and gave orders. A bleary scribe

arrived, stumbling, his hair sticking out around the edges of his coif which was tied askew. Alienor gave him some of her own wine to drink and opened the window so that the fresh air would awaken him further. Outside the night was black and still, a blanket of cloud smothering the stars.

The scribe sat down at a small lectern and, opening one of the wax tablets he had brought with him, reached up for the brass stylus that was tucked behind his ear.

Joanna dictated two letters, one to her husband and one to the Abbess of Fontevraud, begging to be allowed to take the veil. A third was sent to Hubert Walter, Archbishop of Canterbury, with the same request. The scribe would make fair copies which would be impressed with her personal seal and sent out at dawn.

Still she was not ready to lie down. 'I need to make my will,' she said, 'so that my wishes are clear.'

A small sound of grieving protest escaped Alienor's throat before she pressed her lips together. She gave Joanna a fierce hug and sat staunchly beside her as point by point her daughter disposed of her worldly goods. A thousand marks went to Fontevraud. Her personal jewels she left to her son for his eventual wife save for a red belt sewn with small golden lions that was for Richenza.

Finally, as dawn broke over the Rouen skyline, she was finished. Eyes blue-circled, Joanna attended mass and confession, and at last, wrung out and exhausted, curled up on the bed, fighting sleep. 'Watch over me,' she whispered. 'I am so afraid.'

'Always, my love, always. You are my dearest daughter and I have so sworn.'

Exhausted herself, Alienor held Joanna's hand until her daughter finally succumbed and slept. Alienor got into bed with her and folded her in her arms. She felt the baby kick against her, and had to suppress the howl of grief that rose out of her very core.

* * *

Joanna retreated within herself, and despite everyone's atten-
tiveness and the spiritual comfort of her chaplains her eyes
stared with fear because she knew she had but a short time
to live and could not contemplate the notion of no longer
being in the world. Not to taste food and wine, not to see the
sky or the changing seasons. No winter for her, no Christmas
feast. She would never see her little boy grow up, and the
child in her womb was almost certainly doomed.

A fortnight later a messenger arrived with a letter from her
husband, furious that she should speak of taking the veil and
refusing his permission. He wanted her in the world, not
removed from it and him. She should never have run off to
her kin in the first place and it was no good making bargains
with God now.

'He can still be overridden,' Alienor said. 'The Archbishop
of Canterbury has granted a dispensation.'

'I knew he would refuse,' Joanna said, swallowing. 'He does
not understand. He thinks I am pretending. Dear God, I wish
I was. Mama, when I . . . when I am gone, will you go to
him and explain?'

Alienor had no wish to do so, but she took Joanna's hand.
'All will be settled as you wish. Of course I shall.'

Joanna swallowed. 'He does love me in his own way,' she
whispered. 'I do not want you to be angry with him.'

'Do not worry; I will do what is necessary.' She would not
be angry with him, she would damn him, but she was not
going to say that to Joanna. Let all be smooth for her on this
terrible path.

'I just want it to be over,' Joanna whispered. 'Waiting is the
worst suffering. I wish I could have seen my husband and son
one last time.'

'I will let them know you were thinking of them.' Keeping
a steady voice at this time was one of the most difficult
things Alienor had ever had to do. 'That goes without
saying.'

*   *   *

Two days later, pale as a ghost, the blood flow a constant slow trickle, Joanna's glorious ruddy-brown hair was shorn to her scalp in the manner of a nun. Garbed in a plain dark robe she was borne into Rouen Cathedral on a litter to take the veil in the presence of Hubert Walter, Archbishop of Canterbury. September sun shone through the windows upon the tomb slab of her eldest brother, and the new marker over the lead casket holding Richard's embalmed heart. Her wedding ring was replaced with the gold band of a bride of Christ as she made her vows and was taken into the order of Fontevraud for the succour of her immortal soul.

It was over. Alienor had hoped against hope, like playing with loaded dice and thinking that they still might fall in her favour, that the physicians and midwives had been wrong, that by a miracle Joanna might survive the bleeding and the baby be born alive. But holding her dead daughter in her arms, she had to face the truth.

'Why, God, why?' she demanded, tears streaming down her face. Here she was, wrinkled, brittle, old, her bony arms clutching this beautiful young woman who should be alive. She put her head down on Joanna's cold brow. The sheets concealed what they had done to her after she had died, cutting open her womb to remove the baby. It had been a little boy, perfectly formed. The midwife had claimed to see him breathe and he had been swiftly baptised Richard for his uncle. The woman had washed him and wrapped him in swaddling and placed him at his mother's side. The room reeked of blood, thick and heavy even though the windows were wide open on the golden September morning. This was not the way it was supposed to be. Superimposed on this ghastly moment, Alienor imagined a different outcome with Joanna sitting up in bed, proudly showing off the pink newborn baby in her arms, and tears rolled down her cheeks and were lost in the wrinkled creases of her own enduring years.

After the midwives had cleared away the blood-saturated

towels and linens, Alienor fetched a small ivory pot from a trestle, and taking Joanna's hand started rubbing the rose water unguent it contained into her flaccid palm and fingers. As she worked, she sang to her softly. A mother song, a reassurance song, one she had learned from her own mother, and she wondered who would be there to hold her hand and sing for her when she died. She had borne ten living children and eight of them had predeceased her.

Richenza joined her, lightly folding her arms around Alienor's shoulders for a moment of shared sorrow and comfort before sitting down across from her. Taking Joanna's other hand and a dab of unguent, she began to work the same as Alienor, and she too sang for Joanna. Beyond her pain, in a corner so small it almost didn't exist, Alienor acknowledged a tiny spark of comfort.

43

Palace of Poitiers, Winter 1199

Standing in the middle of the fine great hall at Poitiers, Alienor gazed around the completed building, begun three decades ago when Henry was alive and John just two years old. Now the arcaded walls were hung with rich embroideries and furnished with luxury. Great candelabra spiked with beeswax candles gave light and cast shadow across carved chests and benches covered with embroidered cushions. Her great chair dominated the dais at the end, a length of red and blue tapis rising up the steps to meet the two great bronze leopards perched in regal disdain either side. The beasts had once been Henry's but Richard had taken them for himself – and now they were hers.

Swathes of cloth powdered with gold stars canopied the dais seating and servants were busy draping the dining trestles with white cloths, and arranging silver gilt boats on them containing eating knives and spoons.

Alienor turned to John who had entered the hall and was looking around as he stripped off his gauntlets.

'Most of the cups and plates went to Germany to pay Richard's ransom,' she said. 'But I am slowly replacing them.' Her lip curled. 'Much good they did Heinrich.' He had died of malaria in Messina three years after Richard's release, and all his ambitions were dust in his grave. It all came down to dust in the end.

'Indeed, Mama.' A pained expression crossed John's face; he disliked being reminded of that time. 'It is a majestic space, even now I am grown.' He tucked the gauntlets in his belt. 'I thought it might look smaller.'

'I was ambitious in those days,' she said with a deprecatory smile. 'I had such great plans. I wanted to show your father that Aquitaine was great in its own right, and so was its Duchess. It will be here long after I am gone and the sound of my footsteps across the floor are lost in time.'

John gave her a sidelong look. 'Do not grow maudlin on me, mother.'

'I would never do that – there would be no point. But I have my regrets and disappointments, as do we all.' She faced him. 'I hear you have negotiated a truce with Philippe.'

He brushed at a speck on his cloak. 'Yes. He has acknowledged my rights and withdrawn.'

'But you have to pay him a fine? Twenty thousand silver marks is a great deal of money.'

Irritation flashed in his eyes. 'You have busy spies, Mama.'

'Merely a matter of government. My informants are no busier than yours.'

John turned from her and wandered around the hall, looking at this and that, fingering the wall hangings, touching a statue of St Peter that stood in a niche. When he returned to her he chose not to comment on the twenty thousand marks, but she had known he would not.

'I rode past Fontevraud on my way and paid my respects to the dear departed. It's becoming quite a mausoleum, isn't it?'

Alienor bridled at his flippant tone, but bit her tongue on the comment that his respects had rarely been paid in life. He was exactly like his father in that detail. 'When I return from Poitiers I shall have the tomb effigies carved. I have had a mason recommended – from Chartres – who will do them justice.' It hurt her to think on the subject of the burials at Fontevraud and yet they were constantly in her mind. She had borne Joanna's body to the abbey on her way south and with a numb heart had seen her interred at Henry's feet. It still seemed impossible to her that they were all dead and that she lived still.

John pinched his chin between forefinger and thumb. 'I wanted to ask you about that.'

'About the tombs?' She looked at him in wary surprise.

'No, about returning to Fontevraud. I have a favour to ask of you before you go.'

'What sort of favour?' Now she really was wary.

John took two paces away from her and swung round. 'The truce I have agreed with Philippe and the settling of matters between us involves more than just a payment of silver. We have agreed a marriage alliance to seal the matter, as you must know, between Philippe's son and my niece Urraca.'

'Yes, I was aware.' Indeed Alienor had known the gist for longer than he had. 'What is your favour?'

John drew a pattern with his toe on the flagstones. 'I thought you could go to Castile and bring the girl to her marriage.'

'You wish me to go to Castile?'

He nodded. 'We are in Poitiers and it is not that much further, Mama. I thought you would like to see Alie and your grandchildren before you return to Fontevraud. The opportunity will not come again.'

All that was true, but Alienor was still slightly dismayed. 'But now, in winter? I do not know if I have the strength.'

411

'It has to be now. My truce with Philippe allows five months for the wedding to take place. You can spend a few weeks in Castile and come to know the girl. Take a full escort with you and take Richenza to meet her aunt and cousins.'

Alienor felt a faint stirring of excitement, countered by weariness. She was so tired.

John folded his hands around his belt and said impatiently, 'You went over the Alps in the middle of winter to bring Berenguela to my brother, and then all the way to Messina after that. You went to Germany to bring Richard's ransom. Am I less to you? Will you not do this for me? For the future of the dynasty? Your granddaughter will be Queen of France.'

'I was a few years younger then,' she said. And less worn down by the world – and she would have sold her soul for Richard. But she did not say that to John.

'But you are still strong, Mama, and in good health.'

'Am I?' She gave a snort of bleak amusement. 'I am glad you believe so.'

She sighed deeply. He was indeed her last remaining son, and if it would bring peace and calm troubled waters then she could not refuse. Besides, he was right. It was her final opportunity to see her daughter.

'Very well, I shall go. What does it matter if I spend the last of my life's flame doing this for you? You would see how much I have already done for your sake if you were to count up the times instead of thinking you had been stinted. You need not have brought Richard into the matter. You too are my flesh and blood; my son.'

Although her eyes were clouding, she could see the strands of silver in his beard. Her lastborn child was almost thirty-three years old. Her life had moved too swiftly, like a single year of seasons, and now it was late autumn moving into winter and the last goblet of wine had been poured from the flagon.

'I must leave you to your own devices for a while.' She patted his cheek. 'I am flattered that you think me indefatigable, but I need a few moments before dinner to rest. After

412

that you can regale me with all your news.' She was amused to see alarm flicker in his eyes. 'I know full well you will filter the information and I will only hear what you wish to tell me, but since I know this already, I shall not be disappointed.'

'You know full well I did not want Joanna to become a nun.' Raymond of Toulouse glared at the will Alienor had just given to him. He struck the parchment with the back of his hand. 'You went against my specific wishes that she should not take the veil.' His dark brown eyes were bloodshot and a little wild.

Alienor was visiting her widowed son-in-law in Gascony on her way to Castile, and had brought him Joanna's will and her effects. 'It was what she wanted, and I was disposed to help her attain her dying wish for her soul's comfort.'

'Hah, and her headstrong ways led her to lose her life,' Raymond snapped.

'She did not plant the child in her womb by herself,' Alienor pointed out with icy restraint. 'There is nothing anyone could have done; it was in God's hands.'

'But it might have had a different outcome if she had stayed here in Toulouse instead of fleeing to her brother who was already dead. What prompted her to such folly? This is judgement on her.'

'The child was lying sideways in her womb; there was no hope when he settled that way.'

'If she had stayed here it might never have happened,' he repeated obstinately.

'She had no choice; her safety with you was compromised and she was trying to help you both by seeking aid from Richard. She wasn't to know he was dead.' Alienor gave him a hard look. 'You are being unfair.'

Raymond's jaw worked and tears shone in his eyes. 'She should have come back to me. And now she has paid the price – and so have I, and our son, because now he will grow up motherless. Do you know how bitter I feel that the nuns have her when I do not? Do you know what that does to me?' He struck his chest. 'I feel betrayed and deserted that she turned her back on me. Can you comprehend that?'

'Your feelings have nothing to do with the truth. She neither betrayed nor deserted you. She loved you and she wanted to survive, even though it was not to be. Her thoughts were all of you and your living son in her last days, and they were more kindly than you have shown to her.'

He turned away from Alienor and knuckled his eyes, his shoulders shaking.

Alienor drew a deep breath. 'I will not quarrel with you and it is not what she wanted. Too many harsh words have already been spoken, and I am too heartsick with grief to be burdened with more. She was my daughter and your wife. Let us at least pray together and part in understanding.'

After a moment Raymond turned round, and nodded wordlessly, too choked to speak. She could see he was far from forgiving, but he was a man of sharp tempers that were swift to blow over, and he would come to terms with his anger and grief. He would see it better as he gained perspective and distance and would come to understand in time, she hoped.

On a fine, blue-skied morning in late February, Alienor sat winding silk thread onto a bobbin in her daughter's chamber in the palace at Burgos in Castile. She had been there for ten days now and was enjoying her stay. The spring was more advanced here, and the weather was being kind to her old bones.

Her daughter, christened Alienor and called Alie as a child, had taken the name Leonora when she married young Alfonso of Castile twenty years ago, and now inhabited that identity. She was a woman of Castile and spoke the language fluently; indeed, it was her French that bore a foreign inflection. She had Henry's wide cheekbones and grey eyes, but otherwise she resembled Alienor, being tall and graceful with a fine long nose and firm jaw. She reminded Alienor greatly of herself as a young woman in her ways and mannerisms and being with her was a healing experience, for Leonora was fulfilled. She was strong and healthy and had a close bond with her husband, Alfonso. They were the same age and had matured together. Alfonso clearly honoured his wife and heeded her opinions, although he was still his own man and expected high standards of their offspring.

The Castilian court was formal and proper but at the same time had a fluid quality like clear water, and much of it was Leonora's doing. She had a particular skill for managing situations without being harsh or dominant. A light touch here, a word there, a gesture and a smile, and all was woven to her design. Seeing her about her work, Alienor was admiring and immensely proud. Indeed she had started to wonder if her blessings might be in her daughters and their progeny rather than in her sons. There was greatness in the female side of her line, and if she could nurture it and enhance its lustre, then she would.

Currently she was considering her two granddaughters, Urraca and Blanca, who were sewing at her side. Everyone knew why she was here in Castile, and she was expected to make an announcement soon about Urraca being chosen as the future bride of the heir to France. However, Alienor was in no immediate hurry. Since both girls were of marriageable age she would make her selection based on the one with the most suitable qualities and take her time to observe their personalities and characteristics before she decided.

Urraca was the oldest at fourteen, a little taller than her sister and physically more developed. Her rich brown hair was braided and pinned neatly under a virgin's embroidered cap. She had clear hazel-gold eyes and full pink lips that formed a natural pout whatever her mood. Although still a child in many ways, she was swiftly becoming a woman and was very aware of court life and how to play it. Alienor was slightly reminded of her niece Belle, and although it was no more than a distant echo, it made her wary.

Urraca's sister Blanca had lighter hair, ranging in hue from honey-brown to deep gold depending on the light, and her eyes were sea-blue like Alienor's. She was long-limbed and graceful in her movements. Blanca took time to consider before answering questions so her responses came more slowly but were less by rote than Urraca's. It was clear, though, that both daughters had been well brought up and Alienor had nothing but praise for Leonora and Alfonso.

'I was your age when I became Queen of France,' Alienor told the girls. 'I had to leave my home in Poitiers and go to Paris with my Louis. I was a young girl just as you are, and just as your mother was when she came to Castile to marry your father.'

'Were you afraid, Grandmère?' Urraca asked, leaning forward a little.

'Yes,' Alienor said. 'I felt like a straw on the flood because everything had happened so swiftly and the changes were so great, but I was excited too, and I was in love with my husband and thought we could rule the world. There are many things I wish I had known then, but they have only come with the wisdom of old age.'

A pink flush stained Urraca's cheeks. Alienor could see that she was animated by the idea of young love. She turned to her mother, eyes bright. 'Were you afraid when you went to marry Papa?' she asked.

Dimples appeared in Leonora's cheeks as she smiled. 'A little, but it was more apprehension than fear. I knew the worst to expect and the best; your grandmother had prepared me well.' She sent Alienor a warm, slightly rueful glance. 'And I too loved my husband dearly.'

Blanca said thoughtfully, 'What did you wish you had known, Grandmère?'

Alienor was delighted by Blanca's perception. 'That spring-time does not last for ever and that the fine seasons should have their harvest gathered and stored against harsher times. That you should choose your battles wisely. You cannot fight everything and win. Sometimes the price of losing is beyond what you can afford to pay, but that applies to winning as well.' She narrowed her focus on the girls. 'Be very careful and think before you act. Make friends with those who you know will stay true to you and reward them fittingly.'

Blanca nodded with parted lips, and Alienor could see her soaking up the wisdom like a plant absorbing nutrients and putting fresh growth into its leaves.

Their father, Alfonso, arrived to engage in a brief moment of conversation and fetch the women to dinner. He had a couple of squires with him in attendance, and Alienor noticed Urraca glance at the taller of the two. Her flush deepened and the young man returned her look and then dropped his gaze. Alienor put aside her sewing and, rising stiffly to her feet, gestured the handsome young squire to assist her to the great hall. As they walked, she gently questioned him, discovering that his name was Jaime and that his family had estates twenty miles outside Burgos. He was well-connected and stunningly handsome with brilliant dark eyes and a soft beard outlining a firm jawline. The sort to turn any young woman's head, but no match for a Castilian princess.

At the table, Urraca sat one side of her and Blanca the other so that she could give both girls her scrutiny. Blanca was attentive, seeing that Alienor had everything she required and engaging in conversation, but at the same time was aware of her surroundings and directed her focus to peripheral matters too – qualities desirable in a queen. Urraca was more concerned with social display, and her conversation, although appropriate, lacked depth. While Blanca made a point of being solicitous to the other ladies at their table, Urraca had less awareness. She was the King's daughter and that was sufficient. What more did she need to do? Jaime was serving at table, and when he stooped to arrange a dish or pour wine, she sent him coy glances, although they were quick and Alienor would not have noticed had she not been attuned.

Following the meal, the girls went to play a board game together in a window seat, leaving Alienor and Leonora to talk.

'You have two very beautiful and worthy daughters,' Alienor said. 'I am a very proud grandmother. You have done so well in raising them.'

Leonora looked satisfied. 'I hope so. Urraca is becoming a lovely young woman. I do wish you could have met our eldest, before she went to her marriage. Our Berengaria would have loved to meet her famous grandmother.'

'I am glad you said "famous" and not "infamous".'

Leonora smiled and gestured the comment aside. 'Mama, you inspire us all,' she said; but then her expression grew sombre. 'It is sad to have daughters leave the nest, greatly so – and also when you lose them. I have grieved for my siblings.'

'Yes,' Alienor replied, and for a moment mother and daughter shared mutual sorrow for the losses they had endured. Eventually Alienor drew a long breath. 'The cracks in your heart never mend, but even so, your daughters have healed mine as far as anyone can, and Richenza has been a godsend. I am greatly blessed in my grandchildren.'

'Indeed, Mama. My own heart will crack when Urraca goes to France, but it is such a great opportunity for her and I am glad that Louis is of a similar age. That eases me a little.'

Alienor drew back slightly. 'I know you have always assumed Urraca would be the one to go, but I have to tell you, my dear, that I lean towards Blanca.'

Leonora's fond expression froze and then changed into something set and imperious. 'Of course Urraca must be the one to go. That is what is expected and why you told us you were coming. She is the oldest and it is only right that her turn comes first. We have prepared her trousseau with that in mind.' Her gaze sharpened. 'Has she done something to displease you, Mama?' She glanced at the girls at their game.

'Not in the least,' Alienor replied swiftly. 'They are both beautiful girls and I am as proud of them as you are, but I must be governed by which one will best suit the circumstances. Urraca is a regal and lovely young woman, but I think she may find it difficult to adapt to life at the French court.'

Leonora said nothing, but her jaw tightened and she thrust out her chin.

'Urraca may already have plans for herself anyway,' Alienor continued. 'If I were you, I would be careful about her relationships with certain young gentlemen of the court. Where looks have been cast, it may become more than looks in time.'

Leonora's eyes flashed with anger. 'My daughters are well brought up and chaste.' Her voice was pitched low and did not carry but nevertheless was furious and to the point. 'They know their place and what is expected of them and they will go to their marriage beds as virgins.'

Alienor inclined her head but did not back down. 'You are a diligent mother, but still they may form attachments of the heart in a way that young girls are wont to do. Indeed, I wonder if Urraca has the best sort of focus for the task in hand.' In the days since her arrival, Alienor had reached the conclusion that Urraca had a limited understanding of hearts and minds and the strategies to deal with them.

Leonora shook her head. 'Mama, I am astonished you would consider not choosing Urraca. Everyone is expecting her to go as the bride of the prince of France – including the French themselves. What will they think when you present them with her younger sister?'

'Nothing is cast in stone with the French.' Alienor summoned her patience. 'Only that the bride should be one of your daughters, and both girls are of marriageable age. Blanca sees more. She listens properly to what is being said and when she answers my questions her replies are fully considered and more than platitudes in order to please me. She speaks with honesty, but she is not foolish or senseless about it. She watches people and knows how to respond to them, whereas Urraca has less grasp of such skills even though she behaves in a noble and fitting manner. Blanca will cope with whatever is put before her.'

Leonora firmed her lips. 'But Urraca is the older, and she has the comportment of a queen as you say. Why take Blanca when Urraca is more ready to fledge the nest?' She opened her hand towards her mother and there was hurt in her eyes. 'Blanca still has time to grow in my tutelage, but not if you take her now. I was hoping that with Urraca wed, I could devote more time to Blanca's education.' Her expression hardened. 'Have you considered what it will mean for me and Urraca? Matching her will be more difficult now. People will wonder why she has been passed over as Queen of France. They will wonder what was wrong with her that she was not chosen. What will they think of us? In effect you are devaluing my eldest daughter.'

Alienor reached out to Leonora, trying to be patient. 'I am not doing this to make things more awkward. I know the French as you do not and I have met the prospective bride-groom. Blanca is the more suitable match, that is all, and I must do the best for the long term. Other more fitting matches will come for Urraca, I promise you.'

Leonora dug in her heels. 'If you choose Urraca then you will be giving something to all of us, but if you continue with this decision to choose Blanca, you will be taking something very precious away.'

Leonora's hurt was palpable, but although she understood it, Alienor was not prepared to change her mind; she knew her decision was the right one. 'I am sorry,' she said. 'I have been charged with this duty and I must do what is best for the political weal of future generations, and I feel that Blanca has the necessary grasp.'

Leonora briefly closed her eyes. When she opened them again and looked at Alienor, her expression was resigned and cool. 'I do not see it your way, Mama, but since you have been charged with the task, and from my brother, I am bound by your wishes.'

Alienor touched Leonora's sleeve. 'I do not want us to quarrel over this. If Urraca was the one best suited, I would have chosen her.'

'Yes, I know,' Leonora said woodenly, 'and I wish that my elder daughter was that choice.'

Alienor kissed Leonora and felt her resistance, but eventually Leonora softened and accepted the embrace, not wholeheartedly but at least in token. Alienor hoped the rest would come when she had had time to consider, for she was politically astute.

'We shall need to make swift preparations for Blanca.' A challenging look entered Leonora's eyes. 'Even if I yield to you in this, Blanca shall not have the jewels and gowns that were made for her sister.'

'Indeed not. You may call upon my purse to ensure Blanca has everything she needs.'

Alienor glanced across at the girls who were still oblivious of their fate as they sat over their game of chess. They had been born to be pieces on a board, but whether pawns or queens depended on the skill with which they played the game, and how clever their opponents were. Urraca might indeed be a player as she matured, but Blanca already possessed that quality.

Two days later, Alienor sat with Blanca, watching her embroider a golden fleur-de-lys border onto a blue silk pouch she was making for Louis, her future husband.

'You have a swift needle, my dear,' Alienor said, 'and some skill.'

Blanca flushed at the compliment. 'It seems strange to be embroidering the arms of France instead of those of Castile.' She rested her needle. 'I wonder what life at the French court will be like.'

'Different to what you know at the moment,' Alienor said, 'but there will be some similarities, and you will soon grow accustomed to your role. We can talk about it on the journey.'

The announcement to the girls had been made the same evening as the discussion between Alienor and Leonora, and the reason given for the choice was that Blanca was the younger and would more easily adjust, and her name was more suited to French adaptation. She would become Blanche. Urraca had reacted with dignity, and although a few tears had been shed, Alienor suspected that her elder granddaughter was secretly relieved – and very pleased to receive a pet monkey with a jewelled collar in compensation.

Blanca had been surprised and shocked, but had rallied swiftly whatever her thoughts on the matter and Alienor had been pleased at her response which had served to confirm that she had made the right choice. Blanca was looking down now at the ring on her middle finger that Alienor had given her at the time of the announcement – an irregular sapphire edged with gold set between two creamy pearls.

Alienor said softly, 'I have been watching you these past few weeks and I have seen that you know how to comport yourself in any situation and that your mind is sharp. You will be a great queen and a good one, the true line of your mother and grandmother; I recognise that in you. You are our hope for the future.'

Blanca nodded, her expression serious, but a gleam in her eyes. It was as though all the praise, information and advice Alienor was imparting to her was opening up wonderful new horizons, and while she was fearful, she was eager and excited too.

44

Burgos, Spain, Spring 1200

In mid-March, Alienor and Blanca set out from Burgos on their three-week journey to Bordeaux. Farewells had been said in private with tears and embraces, but in public the departure was formal but joyous with a great parade and fanfare to salute the company on its way. The packhorses were laden with gifts of silk and spices and the fragrant white soap for which Castile was justly famed. There were caskets and boxes, and a priceless rock crystal flagon carved by Moorish craftsmen.

Blanca rode a coal-back palfrey led by a groom dressed in scarlet cloth. Alienor's mount was a white Andalusian mare, a gift from Alfonso and Leonora. She had been offered a decorated litter but had politely refused. She might be fast approaching eighty years old but she had ridden here on horseback in the depths of winter and intended returning the same way in the first warmth of spring. She noted how well Blanca rode, confident and lithe in the saddle. Her smile for the crowds was natural, but not familiar; already she was projecting a queenly aura.

Once the city was behind, they increased their pace. Alienor remembered other journeys she had made, travelling the long distances with intrepid fortitude. The great venture to the Holy Land with Louis when she had ridden from Paris to Jerusalem, enduring mortal danger, hardship and utter heartbreak. A very different, wiser young woman had returned to France from that experience.

There had been that first crossing of the Narrow Sea in December with Henry at her side as they sailed for England. She remembered the powerful explosion of spray against the ship's prow, the capricious wind, and Henry's wide, exultant smile. Their son in her arms, his brother in her womb and crowns waiting to be claimed. Everything had been possible on that day.

More recently there had been the hard journey over the Alps and down to Sicily with Berenguela. So many hopes turned to dust. And this, her last expedition, once more fetching and escorting a bride and bidding farewell to her last daughter. Riding away from Leonora, she knew she would never see her again in this life, and that had been hard. Once she had delivered her granddaughter to the French, her tasks would be complete. She would retire to Fontevraud, oversee the creation of the effigies and live out her final days in prayer and contemplation. Sadness came upon her like a cool spring wind, but it felt right and she embraced it.

Alienor continued to instruct Blanca as they travelled, but it was difficult distilling the wisdom of eight decades into three weeks. She could only pray that the girl, like a seed given water and nourishment, would flourish and blossom of her own accord.

A fortnight after setting off they crossed into Aquitaine and came to the ancient fortified town of Dax which was famed for its healing springs of warm mud, beneficial for rheumatic bones and skin disorders. Richard had built a castle here and there was a fine welcome for the party and comfortable beds for the night.

Blanca was unsure about immersing herself in one of the pools of warm grey mud but, determined to overcome her trepidation, bit her lip and, wearing her shift, her hair bound up in a linen turban, followed her grandmother and Richenza into the wallow.

'Come, come,' Alienor encouraged, 'this opportunity will not come again and you should experience such things while you are young. The more knowledge you have, the better you will govern.'

'Yes, Grandmère.' Blanca wafted her hand through the silty grey liquid.

Alienor studied her, noting the girl's mingled curiosity and reluctance. During their journey Blanca had been cheerful and responsive on the surface, but there were moments when an almost forlorn expression would cross her face and a couple of times there had been tears, concealed but not swiftly enough.

'You must be missing your family,' Alienor said with sympathy, 'especially your mother and your sister. It is no easy thing to make great changes in your life with so little warning.'

Blanca nodded. 'Yes, Grandmère. I know my duty and will try to learn from everything you say.'

It was the right response but Alienor could see it was lip service and that Blanca was speaking to please her. Alienor well understood her anxieties for she had suffered the same when she went to Paris with Louis, and at least she had had her sister to accompany her when she became Queen.

'You have courage beyond your knowing, child,' she said. 'And you have proud blood in your veins. Even if you do not think it now, you are expanding.' She smiled at her. 'It is like being small and your mother gives you clothes that are a little too big so that you have room to grow into them. That is what you are doing; you are filling that gap, and soon they will fit you perfectly, you will see.'

Blanca gave her a considering look and once more Alienor watched her absorb the information like a plant taking in nutrients.

'Of course,' Alienor said to lighten the moment, 'for all his great learning, your grandsire Henry never took the mud of Dax, so in that you are ahead of him. Your twice great grand-mother Dangereuse did though. I will tell you about her . . .'

Alienor and Blanca arrived in Bordeaux after just over three weeks of steady travel. Around them spring was in full bloom, the grass fresh and green at the roadside and the air warm and soft but without the heat of May and June.

Alienor brought Blanca to the Ombrières palace on the banks of the Garonne river, and because her young grand-daughter was seeing it for the first time, Alienor too experienced the moment with the eyes of a thirteen-year-old girl, and everything became new and magical again.

She stood with Blanca on the battlements on their first evening and together they watched the sun set over the river in a sheet of beaten gold, and gild the stone turrets with the last of the light.

'This is where I saw my husband for the first time,' Alienor said, pointing out across the water. 'The French camp was over there, and they crossed to our side in a barge draped with silks of every hue. I could not tell which one was Louis among all the people, but I met him in the cathedral soon after and thought him the most handsome youth I had ever set eyes upon.' She touched her stomach. 'I felt a clenching here, and fear in my heart, but something greater too. The river was bringing me my destiny and I had all my life before me to live it.'

And now it is almost spent. The thought was so loud in her head that it was as though she had spoken it. The wheel had turned full circle and here she was with a granddaughter of thirteen standing at her side, soon to marry the heir to France and become its future queen. God willing it would turn out well this time and set all to rights that had been awry before. Gazing at Blanca's slim shoulders and sleek golden hair, Alienor thought she could indeed be herself from all those years ago. She had to think how best to give this child what she needed and what she herself had never had – advice from older female relatives in the face of so much change and responsibility.

As if sensing her pensive mood, Blanca looked round. 'Grandmère?'

Alienor shook her head. 'I was losing myself in the past and the future at the same time and that is never wise.' Smiling ruefully, she set her gnarled hand to Blanca's breeze-blown hair in a tender gesture. 'I did not know what was before me when I stood here all those years ago – all my tasks and all my children. Should you have need of me, I will be here for as long as I am able. Even if I am not, others of your kin will answer your call. Never think you are alone.'

'No, Grandmère.'

'You must not let people mistreat you. You must stand up for yourself and what you know you are worth. Do not let them treat you for less. Remember that, and you will be a great queen; this I tell you, and this I know.'

Blanca met her gaze directly and Alienor realised how much the girl had matured even in these last few days – ever since the bathing pool at Dax. Blanca was growing swiftly into those clothes that had been too big for her. It was not so much that she had been removed from her old life, but that new horizons were opening up with the potential to spread the world at her feet if she played the game with sufficient skill.

Three days later the French entourage arrived in Bordeaux to take Blanca north to Paris and her new life. At the time of parting, Blanca clung to Alienor for the final moment, the last one of her childhood, and then drew herself upright, raised her chin and went with the French envoys in the true way of a queen in waiting, gracious but not haughty, projecting her worth in every step she took.

Alienor watched her leave and sent hopes and prayers winging in her direction, like flinging a young gyrfalcon into the sky and wishing her a glorious maiden flight, free of her leashes.

When Blanca had gone, Alienor returned to the palace to prepare for her return to Fontevraud. She still had work to do, for there were several slabs of pale tuffeau limestone awaiting her attention before she could truly rest and say that all her tasks were complete.

Mercadier had been attending to his own business while she visited Castile, but had promised to escort her to Fontevraud. She had spoken to him earlier that morning, and he had assured her all would be ready by noon.

Before setting out, Alienor visited the cathedral of St Peter to pray and light candles for the repose of the souls of her children, and for Blanca's safe journey to Paris.

'I was married here to Louis of France,' she mused to Richenza once they had attended to their spiritual business. 'It fills my mind's eye even now.' The colours were brilliant in her vision, like an illuminated manuscript – herself standing outside the cathedral in her golden gown and Louis at her side in a tunic of blue and gold, his fair hair nimbused with light. The crowds of cheering people. She had felt soaring elation and raw, painful sorrow, because it was her wedding day and she was mourning the loss of her father and trying not to sink as the politics and ploys of powerful men threatened to close over her head.

'Were you happy?' Richenza asked.

'No, although God knows I wanted to be. I was excited, certainly. I loved my gown and the splendour of the occasion. I thought my new husband was very fine and beautiful – he was a handsome youth, whatever he became later.' She could remember her anger and resentment too, because she had been Duchess of Aquitaine in her own right and everything had been taken from her; what she gained in return was not a good bargain. At least Blanca would not have to contend with such a poisoned chalice.

Mercadier was waiting for her outside the cathedral as promised with the horses saddled up and the sumpter beasts loaded. He was wearing his mail and his coif was neatly pushed down to rest on his collar bone. An imposing sword hung at his left hip.

Alienor noted that he seemed preoccupied and his lips were set in a grim line. When she asked what was wrong he shook his head. 'Nothing, madam, or nothing that concerns your journey and my duty to see you safely there.' He settled his features into a polite mask, but his eyes remained hard and watchful.

She began to walk towards her mount, stiffly because her left hip was painful today, and she refused to use a stick for it reminded her of her mother-in-law the Empress Matilda forty years ago. Mercadier diplomatically tailored his step to hers and clasped his hands behind his back.

In a sudden blur of motion a man clad in the quilted tunic of a serjeant at arms ran out from the shadows at the side of the cathedral, spun Mercadier round and with one swift slash of a hunting knife, slit his throat. 'For Brandin, you whoreson!' he snarled.

Hot blood splashed across Alienor's face and she recoiled with a scream. Mercadier staggered, clutching his throat, and went down, jerking, struggling, already in his death throes. Pandemonium ensued as Mercadier's men grabbed the assassin and wrestled him to the ground. Alienor's knights rallied around her but before they closed off her view with their bodies, she met Mercadier's dying gaze in the moment before his eyes rolled up in his head and his last breath bubbled out of his open throat.

Richenza was half gasping, half screaming, blood spatters covering her gown, face and hands. Alienor seized her in her arms, partly to support herself and partly to prevent Richenza from tipping over the edge. Belbel placed herself in front of them, arms outspread in a protective gesture.

The murderer was on his knees, hands behind his back, the dagger torn from his hands. 'This is a message from my lord Brandin,' he repeated, unrepentant, eyes alive with the fire that had fled Mercadier's. 'So are all men served who break their word!' He spat on the ground an instant before he was clubbed unconscious by Mercadier's mercenaries.

Priests came running from the cathedral but it was too late to administer the last rites. Mercadier's soul had departed without salvation and flies were already buzzing in the sticky blood around the corpse. Someone fetched a hurdle to bear him into the cathedral. Alienor, Richenza and Belbel were taken there too, to another room where they could wash off the blood and clean their gowns.

'Why?' Alienor asked. She was trembling with reaction now. 'Why? I do not understand.' It was one blow after another. The suddenness had been shocking. Mercadier had obviously been the target, but it could so easily have been her. The mercenary captain was one of her closest links to Richard, had been there when he died. She had relied on his pragmatic solidity and now he was gone in an instant and she was left stumbling.

'It is too much,' she told Richenza, 'and I do not know how to stop it. So many people have left me and I never know who and when the next one will be. God rest his soul, God rest his poor soul.' He was a mercenary, a soldier of fortune, in need of more prayers than most, but she refused to entertain the thought of him in hell. More than ever she wanted to return to the spiritual security of Fontevraud, but she could not leave until Mercadier had been buried with the requisite prayers for his soul. She owed him that and much more.

Drawing on reserves that were close to depletion, she went outside to give instructions concerning what was to be done.

In the morning Alienor attended Mercadier's funeral and gave alms for his soul. The murderer when questioned was eager to volunteer the information that Mercadier had been involved in a dispute with another mercenary leader named Brandin whose honour Mercadier had slighted. As Brandin's kinsman he had been sent to deal with the matter by killing Mercadier and redeeming the family honour.

Live by the sword and die by the sword, Alienor thought bleakly. Greatly saddened, she departed Bordeaux, leaving behind her the grave of the most famous mercenary captain of his age. The body of the serjeant who had murdered him in a single blow swung in the breeze as she rode past the gibbet without looking back.

45

Abbey of Fontevraud, Summer 1200

Jean D'Ortiz the sculptor was in his late forties, a slim man, sun-browned and wiry yet muscular from wielding mallet and chisel. A slight wheeziness in his breathing attested to the nature of his occupation. With him was Matthew his son-in-law, blond and broad-shouldered with piercing light blue eyes, creases fanning from the corners.

D'Ortiz removed the sacking covers and crouched to study the blocks of tuffeau limestone. He ran his hands over them, assessing grain and quality, like a horse coper examining the legs of a horse for soundness. His sensitive fingers were tactile and swift as he read the stone by touch. He had brought Alienor some samples of his painted carving including a decoration for a corbel of a small, delicate face with realistic flesh colours and golden hair peeping out from dense green foliage, and also a queen with an enigmatic smile tipping her mouth corners.

'How soon before you can begin work?' Alienor asked.

The mason rose to his feet and dusted his palms, but more as if feeling the grain than brushing it off. He was a little awkward for usually he would have talked to her intermediary rather than Alienor herself, but she had wanted to speak to him personally regarding her commissions. He was the best and she would have nothing but the best, although his skill meant he was in demand and already had plentiful work.

'I can come in the winter months, madam,' he said, 'but in the meantime I shall make preliminary sketches and submit them to you. I shall need to know the colours you desire and how the people should look. It will take more than one season.'

'It will take as long as it takes, messire, although I would hope not for ever. I would like to see them complete while I am still in the world.'

The mason cleared his throat with a wheezy cough and struck his chest. 'Indeed, madam.' He flicked a swift glance at his son-in-law.

'They must look at rest but alive. They must laud and exalt the dynasty. I need to know that you and your household are capable of rendering what I want, and that you have a passion to do so. I wish those who look upon your work to see kings at rest, not gone from the world. Can you do that?'

He took his time to reply, and she respected him for it. It would have been easy for him to rush in and agree. Rubbing the back of his neck, he nodded slowly. 'Yes, madam. Indeed, it shall be my honour.'

Having asked for details of what she required, Master D'Ortiz made sketches on parchment, took measurements, and departed. As he was riding away with his son-in-law, two messengers arrived to inform Alienor that her son the King

431

would be here by evening, bringing his new bride with him – Isabel, daughter of Aymer, lord of Angoulême.

Alienor was dumbfounded by the news. As far as she knew John's most recent marriage plan had involved a Portuguese bride and envoys had been sent there to discuss the possibility. Aymer of Angoulême was one of her more troublesome vassals, and John must have a reason for the marriage, but she was utterly taken aback. Drawing herself together, she issued brisk orders for food and lodging to be prepared, although with so little warning they would have to make do with what there was or else provide their own, and pitch tents outside the abbey walls. She was even a trifle irritated because although she desired to see John and his new bride, she had reached a stage where surprises like this were an intrusion rather than a diversion.

'Madam.' Isabel of Angoulême made a demure curtsey to Alienor who found herself facing a fair-haired, blue-eyed slip of a girl with dainty features and clear, glowing skin. A gown of blue silk in the latest fashion for tight-fitting sleeves revealed that her figure had begun to develop, but that she had much growing to do before she could be called mature, and certainly there was no question of child bearing.

'I am pleased to meet you, child.' Alienor raised her to her feet and kissed Isabel's cool petal cheek. She noted the wedding ring on her finger and the jewels twinkling like small stars in the net of meshed gold covering her braids. Alienor was not sure that she was pleased to meet her but the courtesies had to be observed. This girl would not be ready to fulfil the role of Queen for a long time to come. What did John think he was doing? 'All this must be new and strange for you.'

'Yes, madam, but I am learning every day.' Isabel cast a tense glance at John who was standing beside her, an enigmatic smile on his face.

The girl's words, although spoken by rote, were nevertheless a valiant effort. *Are you a pawn or a player?* Alienor wondered. And who would train her? She would have received some instruction at the hands of her mother's household, but not the kind to prepare her for being a queen consort.

'Come,' she said. 'Help me to sit down. I am not as limber as I was.'

Isabel took her arm and walked with her to a window seat that looked out on a lawn of turf and daisies.

Alienor discovered over the course of the next half hour on the sun dial that Isabel of Angoulême was modest and reticent, but as hard as she worked she could not strike a spark of personality from the girl. She was either guarding herself well or she was truly a blank page. Eventually Alienor sent her off with Richenza to speak to some of the other ladies from the abbey and summoned John to her side.

'Now,' she said to him, 'why this one?'

John folded his arms and gazed out of the window. 'You know full well I was never going to remain with Hawise of Gloucester.'

'Indeed not, but you told everyone you were looking to Portugal.'

'That was the story I put about, yes. Isabel was betrothed to Hugh de Lusignan but if Lusignan and Angoulême unite who before have been enemies they will have a block of territory that will create a far greater threat to me, and make them more likely to turn against my rule.' He gave her a keen look. 'This marriage keeps them divided and fighting each other. I gain the girl's dowry and a strong ally in an area where I need it.' His mouth twisted. 'Some people accuse me of besotted indulgence, but I have sound reasons I promise you. When we reach England, she shall be crowned Queen before all.'

Alienor pursed her lips. *All hail the Queen of England*, she thought cynically. *One a crone at the end of her years and the other still a little girl.*

'What of Philippe of France? What trouble can he make from this?'

'I do not care,' John said tautly. 'It is not his business. I shall deal with him as I must.'

He left her and went to circulate among his courtiers, and William Marshal took his place.

'You are looking well, madam.'

'For my years?' she said with a grim smile. 'For a crotchety old woman?'

'For both of those.' His own smile was full of humour. 'I would not lie to you, for you are my liege lady.' He took her hand and kissed the back of it. 'It is good to see you.'

'Yes,' she said, and sadness welled within her. 'I always wonder if it is for the last time, but on each occasion I find there is always the grace of one more.'

'And many such to come I hope.'

'We shall see,' she temporised. 'What do you think of this sudden marriage?' She narrowed her eyes and added sharply, 'Did you counsel him to marry her?'

William shook his head. 'No, madam, he had already made up his mind to the matter when he told us. It suits my lord's political needs and that is all we need to know.'

'Political needs.' She exhaled forcefully. 'Abetted by a sprinkling of lust and the pleasure of putting down an opponent. I am not sure about this at all. My son has gambled and the dice have yet to land. Ah God, who would think I would still be alive after almost four score years and all but one of my sons would be dead. I am tired, William, and the world has lost its savour. I am too rusty to dance.'

'I do not believe that, madam, not for a moment.'

'It is the truth, but delude yourself if you will.' She studied him. He was in his late prime now with grey in his hair and beard, and lines on his face, but the fire still burned within him, steady and bright. 'How are Isabelle and the children?'

'Very well, madam. We have another daughter, born in February and named for her mother.'

'Your nursery is a busy place.' Her smile glinted with sorrowful nostalgia as she remembered her own nursery, how full it had been and how it had become an empty nest far too soon.

He told her that John had given him permission to visit

Ireland. 'I have been promising Isabelle for so long that I don't think she believes me,' he said wryly.

'It is never wise to make promises to a woman and then delay them beyond her expectations,' Alienor scolded him gently. 'Your wife is forbearing and fair. Do not take her for granted or you will lose her trust.'

'I do not, madam. If not for love of my wife, I swear to you I would not be contemplating crossing the Irish Sea in late autumn.'

Alienor laughed, even while her sadness at the passing of things increased. 'Have a care, William. I have been far in my life, even to Jerusalem, as have you, but I have never been to Ireland nor shall I. Count it as a blessing and an opportunity to explore pastures new.'

'In your honour, madam,' he said with a bow.

'In my memory,' she replied, and they looked at each other in perfect understanding. 'Look after John for me. We both know his ways – his strengths and his weaknesses. It is no easy or light thing I ask of you, but there are so few people I trust enough to lean upon. Give to him the service you have given to me. That is all I ask.'

William inclined his head. 'It shall be done, madam. My service is yours.'

His words comforted her. His assurance was another loose end woven into the tapestry of her life and secured for the time when she was no longer in the world.

46

Abbey of Fontevraud, June 1202

Alienor sat in the shade of a canvas awning and watched Jean D'Ortiz working with delicate precision on the sword lying beside Richard's effigy on the bier of draped stone. Now and again D'Ortiz would pause and look to the actual item for reference. It was one of Richard's favourite blades with an unusual octagonal pommel and had been at his bedside at Chalus when he was dying and then borne beside his body on the bier. The red leather scabbard and the belt gleamed with a polish of pride and care, but no one had drawn the sword since Richard's death, and Master D'Ortiz had had the reverence to keep it that way.

Mostly Alienor watched the sculptor work and did not interrupt him, but occasionally she would make a point of note, or he would ask her a question. Her presence and the working silences had become comfortable for both of them. The younger man, the son-in-law, was a little less at ease, but accepting, and their apprentice lad was cheeky and cheerful but good at heart, even if he had to be thrashed every now and again to keep him in order.

They had arrived late to their commission because Master D'Ortiz had been unwell with a chest ailment. They were still promised to the cathedral at Chartres and were dividing their time between the two projects, although recently Master D'Ortiz had been spending more time at Fontevraud, where the air was better for his lungs. Even so, every breath he took was accompanied by a dusty whine.

Alienor too had been unwell with a fever and cough in the spring and had taken to her bed for several weeks – something unknown to her apart from times of recovery from hard childbirth. She had wondered if this was to be her end; however, as the spring progressed she had rallied, even though she felt as fragile and insubstantial as thistledown.

Henry's effigy was complete except for the painting which Master D'Ortiz intended working on once all the carvings were finished. He had chiselled Henry's features to Alienor's exacting description, and the clothes were Henry's coronation robes rendered in drapes of stone. His had been the first effigy to be carved because he was the head of the dynasty and his

436

position gave all the others of his line their status. Whatever Henry had done to her, he had still been a great king. She had narrowed her focus to that. The prestige and the dignity were all. She would create a proper family in stone to supersede the flawed one of the flesh.

Alienor glanced up from watching Master D'Ortiz work on the sword hilt as Richenza, who was visiting her, arrived leading a young man by the hand. He was tall and handsome with warm brown hair and blue eyes like her own. His beard, decently grown for his years, glinted with copper lights in the summer sun. He was wearing a sword belt minus the weapon which, as with all visitors, had been surrendered at the gatehouse.

'Grandmère,' said Richenza, smiling, 'see who is here to visit.'

Alienor frowned and narrowed her eyes the better to focus, but still it was a long moment before realisation dawned. John and Belle's bastard boy, almost fully grown. 'Richard?' The word was strange and bittersweet on her tongue. Any excuse to say it.

'Madam my grandmother.' Smiling, he knelt to her.

'Dear God, when did you become a man?' she asked in amazement and even a little dismay at such rapid passing of time. She kissed him on both cheeks and bade him stand up. 'You are so tall!' Taller indeed than his father and grandfather. His hair grew the same way as Hamelin's and he had a similar jut to his jaw. 'How old are you now?'

'I am twenty, madam.' A red flush spread upward from his throat into his face.

Taking pity, she stopped embarrassing him. 'What brings you to Fontevraud?'

'Grandmère, I have news for you. It is not good, but my grandmother asked me to deliver it personally rather than send a messenger. She has a letter for you.' He handed over a parchment secured with Isabel's seal.

Alienor's heart sank. Was there ever going to be good news? 'At least it has brought you to me. Clearly you know what is

437

written and your voice is better than my eyes, so you might as well tell me what it is.'

He swallowed. 'I am sorry to tell you that my grandsire Hamelin died at the end of May. He had been unwell with a cough since the winter. We thought he was getting better with the spring but he died suddenly at Lewes from pains in the chest. He has been laid to rest in the priory and I have come from his funeral to let you know.'

Pain surged in Alienor's own heart. She and Hamelin had often had their differences, but she had been fond of him. Isabel must be utterly devastated because Hamelin was her world. 'I am sorry to hear such news, may God rest his soul. He was an honest man who always gave of his best and he was my dearest brother by marriage. How is your grandmother?'

He grimaced. 'She is not well and in deep mourning. She is at Lewes, spending time in prayer for his soul and preparing his tomb.'

Such irony. That she and Isabel should now be in the same position. Old women sitting at the gravesides of their dead husbands.

'My mother is comforting her.'

'I am glad to hear it.'

He hesitated, then added, 'They have made amends with each other and my mother was fully reconciled with my grand-sire before he died. My half-brothers and -sisters are at Lewes also.'

Alienor had not kept abreast of Belle's second marriage to Gilbert L'Aigle. 'Your mother has children?'

'Gilbert and Richer are five and three, and Alais is nine months old. My mother is well and sends you her duty and regards.'

Alienor gave a thin smile. Belle would indeed do that, but how sincerely was a matter for debate. 'I thank her, and am glad,' she said, and after Richard had looked at the progress on the effigies, she brought him to her chamber to offer him refreshment.

'Where will you go now? Back to England?'

He nodded. 'Yes, Grandmère, but first I shall visit my father. He will already have the news by swifter messenger, but I wish to see him for his own sake.'

Alienor patted his arm. Not many people would say that about John and it warmed her to hear Richard speak in such a way. By whatever quirk, he had done well by this bastard son of his.

'You know there is still trouble between your father and Philippe of France? Your cousin Arthur is not as dutiful as you are, and is creating difficulties. Only yesterday news came that he has been knighted and is preparing to make another attempt on your father's domains.'

'Yes, I had heard.' He gave a dismissive shrug. 'Everyone knows he is a pawn of the French.'

'Yes, but even pawns can be dangerous.' Alienor sighed wearily. 'I have been thinking this morning that I should go to Poitiers and bolster the resolve of my vassals – it might be safer at the moment than here.'

His eyes widened. 'You think Arthur would attack Fontevraud?'

Alienor gave an acerbic smile. 'I doubt he would call it attacking, but I am concerned that he may choose to pay a more forceful visit on his grandmother and the tombs of his ancestors than you have.'

'I could escort you to Poitiers if you wish.' He bowed, and when he raised his head, his eyes were bright and alive. 'Indeed, it would be my honour.'

Alienor felt amused and tender. He had not completely mastered the art of concealing his thoughts and emotions behind a courtly façade. Here was a young man off the leash and eager to taste some of the world before he returned to mundane things. He would be a knight errant, protecting his grandmother and being useful at the same time. Amid all the heartache and shame his conception had engendered, good had come from it. She smiled, her spirits lightening despite the seriousness of their discussion. 'Then it will be my honour to have you ride at my side and be my escort and equerry,' she said.

Two days later on a sticky morning, Alienor set out for Poitiers. She wore a gown of cool, pale linen and a straw hat over her wimple, and rather than ride this time she opted to journey in a decorated cart with Richenza and her ladies, escorted by knights. Richard rode alongside the cart in pride of place astride the glossy golden palfrey Alienor had especially given him for the journey.

Alienor watched the countryside roll by through the open arch at the back of the cart. She had her own grey palfrey in the train and could ride it if she wanted, but for now she was content to be passive. The cart jolted when the road was uneven and potholed, but she was well bolstered by cushions and fleeces. Indeed she was so comfortable that she dozed for a while, then woke and dozed again. At one point she woke to find Richenza watching her with a fond smile.

'I used to think it comical the way old people fell asleep the moment they sat down,' Alienor said with self-deprecation. 'I had no patience, but now I am one of them and it is not so amusing.'

'You are entitled to rest, Grandmère.'

Alienor gave a small snort. 'But there is no rest for the wicked they say and I must have been very wicked at times in my long life.'

'I do not believe that!' Richenza declared with staunch indignation. 'Others have wronged you, not the other way around.'

'Oh, I have done my share.' Alienor waved her hand. 'There were times when I hated your grandfather so much that I prayed for his death. I expect he prayed often for mine too though.' She looked at Richenza, who was clearly deciding how to respond. 'My grandmother, now there was a lady who lived her life as she chose. Her name was Amaberge, but my grandfather called her Dangereuse.'

Richenza laughed. 'Why did he do that?'

'Because she was, I suppose. She was no great beauty but she had a glamour about her that forced everyone to look at her – and she was fierce. She cared little for what people thought.' Alienor chuckled at the memory. 'Petronella and I were terrified of her when we were children, but we were fascinated too. She used to wear gowns with great hanging sleeves – they are out of fashion now, but they were the style back then. She taught us how to use them to convey feelings without words – the lightest sweep and a turn of the wrist to flirt with a man.' Alienor demonstrated with her age-mottled hand, yet the movement she made was alluring and graceful. 'And then to perhaps drape that sleeve across his face as an invitation to greater intimacy.' Her smile hardened and her action became a sudden swipe. 'Or to express contempt and anger. We learned all that from her. How to command an audience. My grandmother was always the centre of attention and could not bear for others to have it. She was unpredictable and wild. I remember her screaming at my grandsire and throwing laden dishes from her table at him, one after another, until there was food splattered all over the walls. He let her, because he knew after that they would go to bed and it would be like the mating of lions.'

Richenza listened open-mouthed.

'They left their given spouses to live with each other,' Alienor said, enjoying her tale. 'They were the fire and nothing else mattered when they were burning together.' She smoothed her gown over her knees. 'My mother was very different, but that is often the case. The children either become like their parents or else they flee in the opposite direction. My mother was a gentle soul who had no desire to flaunt herself before others. I am both of them and neither. Your uncle John is exactly like his father.'

She closed her eyes again and almost instantly fell asleep.

It was dusk by the time they arrived at the small walled town of Mirebeau, and despite having slept for much of the journey,

Alienor was still tired. She decided to stay a day to recover and then move on to Poitiers. Age constricted the world to what could be done with a weak flame and a candle stub. Once she could have ridden astride like a man for more than thirty miles and still been ready to dance and politic. Now all she wanted was some decent wine, a little food, and her bed.

Climbing to the top chamber at Mirebeau was an ordeal, but she forced herself to the task even though each step was agony to her hips and knees. Her reward was a well-appointed and airy room with a comfortable bed that the servants were already making up with her own mattresses, sheets and coverlet.

She took a light meal with Richenza and then retired, but left the bed curtains open and the shutters too, so that she could observe the deep blue bowl of the night. There was a tinge of murky purple to the clouds, and occasional flashes of dry lightning. Thunder rumbled in the distance. Storms had never bothered her. She enjoyed their wild spectacle providing she was safe behind walls.

At the other end of the room Richard and Richenza were talking softly as they played chess. The sound of their laughter and easy camaraderie was comforting and made her feel secure.

She was only vaguely aware of Richenza coming to bed later. The storm had brought rain, but the direction meant that it was not blowing into the chamber, and its steady sound was soothing. Feeling the soft brush of Richenza's lips on her cheek, she murmured a sleepy response and turned over.

Once more the darkness took her down. She wanted to dream of Richard as a baby, a boy and then a grown man in all of his beauty; she wanted to dream of being young, vivacious and unfettered; but there was only darkness with faint ripples on the surface. Not unpleasant, she could float in comfort, but it was heavy and thick.

She woke in the morning to the pain of stiff joints, a dry mouth, and the bleariness of too heavy a slumber; it was an effort to sit up in bed and call for a drink. Belbel was swiftly at her side to provide the necessities, see to her dress and comb and braid her thin white hair.

'Where is Richenza?' Alienor looked round as she left the bed and walked stiffly into the main chamber.

'She went out a few moments ago, madam. Messire Richard summoned her, but I know not why.'

Alienor sipped her watered wine and went to the window. The air smelled fresh and green after the storm and the sky was forget-me-not blue. A day that once would have sent her running down the stairs in search of adventure.

A servant entered the room bearing fresh new bread and a crock of honey, and Alienor's senses began to stir and move away from the darkness. She was attending to her meal when Richenza and Richard returned.

'Ha, you scented the new bread!' Alienor said with a laugh, but grew serious as she saw their faces.

'Grandmère, there is an army approaching led by Arthur of Brittany,' Richard said. 'They are crying the warning in the town. Several hundred strong coming along the road from Tours.' He swallowed. 'The walls are not strong enough to hold them.'

His words jolted Alienor's senses into full awareness. 'He is clearly not paying a social visit to his old grandmother. Send the seneschal to me and secure the gates.' She had known she was vulnerable. In Poitiers she was safe, but en route she was a tempting target. She turned to Richard. 'Take the fastest, freshest horse in the stables and ride to the King. Tell him as he values Aquitaine, he must come to me as fast as he can.'

Richard shook his head and puffed up with indignation. 'I cannot leave you, Grandmère, it would be desertion and cowardice!'

'No it would not,' Alienor snapped, her candle burning high now. 'Do as I say and abandon your foolish notions of chivalry. If you do not reach your father and he does not come, what do you think will happen? There are others here

443

who can better defend me. Make haste – already you have no time.'

Richard's ears reddened at her rebuke, but he rose to the occasion and with a swift nod strode to the coffer and snatched his cloak off the top. He fumbled to gird on his sword and dagger and Richenza hurried to help him.

'Take bread,' Alienor ordered, and tied her breakfast loaf into the cloth on which it had been served. Belbel grabbed a leather bottle from a hook in the wall and filled it from the flagon of watered wine.

Alienor removed her favourite, distinctive topaz ring from her middle finger and presented it to him. 'Give this to your father. He will know what it means.'

Richard slipped the ring onto a cord around his neck, knelt to receive her kiss of blessing, and was gone at a run.

At least now her grandsons would not be fighting each other, Alienor thought, and Richard was the best person to send anyway.

'It will not be the first time someone has tried to capture me,' Alienor told Richenza who was biting her lip. 'I became wife to Louis of France because my father died and they dared not leave me unwed. Your grandfather's own brother tried to abduct me when my marriage to Louis was annulled and then William the Marshal saved me from ambush by the Lusignans more than thirty years ago.' She laughed with angry amusement. 'Time and again I have known how powerful I am just by the efforts made to seize and imprison me, although I must admit I never thought I would be facing siege from my own grandson.'

'What will happen if Arthur captures us?'

Alienor picked up her cup again and sent Belbel for more bread. 'That I do not know. Indeed I would say I do not care, but it affronts me that a youth of his years should have the disrespect to besiege his aged grandmother, no matter who is influencing him. He wants me to yield him Aquitaine, but hell will freeze over first.'

'I do not want to frighten you, Grandmère, but what if you die in his care and he claims you have ceded Aquitaine to him?'

Alienor pursed her lips, deepening the spider lines surrounding them. 'No one will believe him except Philippe of France. However, I have no intention of falling into his hands. Help will come.'

'But—'

'Enough!' She drew herself up, becoming a queen, filled with regnal power and ready to fight to the death. 'I will hear no more, do you understand me?'

Tears shone in Richenza's eyes, but she set her jaw. 'Yes, Grandmère, I do.'

Richard didn't take the fastest horse in the stable even though he was tempted by a rangy black courser with long, thin legs. He needed speed, but it had to be tempered by strength and endurance. He required a horse that could go forever at a swift and steady pace. His grandmother's grey had the stamina but it was too small for him, and his own mount had already travelled a recent long journey. He eventually took a strong bay palfrey with a fat rump, arched neck and Roman nose that belonged to the constable and was fresh – indeed fresh enough to buck and kick as Richard gained the saddle, but he was a good horseman and drew in the reins and gripped with his thighs.

Leaving the castle at a trot he rode swiftly through the town. He had to force his way through fleeing people with their belongings and livestock, the word having spread that an army was imminently going to fetch up against their walls. Richard's heart was pounding and his mouth was dry, but he restrained the urge to push the horse because he would need its power later.

Knowing that the enemy would have scouts on the main routes he took to little-used side tracks and worked his way round, using the sun as his compass. He was conscious of the passage of time but there was no point in rushing headlong into the path of the enemy and risk being injured or caught so he bided his time and ate a quarter chunk of the bread his grandmother had given him, washed down with some wine.

Two hours later he judged it safe to begin working his way back to the main track leading to Le Mans. A distant dust cloud and fresh horse dung in the road revealed that Arthur's army had recently passed that way. The birds were singing and Richard's heightened senses detected no danger. Clicking his tongue to the bay, he urged it to a strong pacing trot and set out to eat the miles to Le Mans, hoping he would be in time.

47

Castle of Mirebeau, Poitiers, June 1202

Arthur's army arrived at Mirebeau shortly before the morning sun reached its zenith. The light glittered on mail shirts and harness, on surcoats and silk banners. Arthur, recently knighted, rode near the head of the array on a lively Spanish stallion, decked out in red and gold harness, against the white satin hide.

The constable, Pons de Mirebeau, brought the news to Alienor as she dined in the great hall with Richenza and Belbel as though all was normal.

'They have a stone thrower with them, madam, and siege ladders,' he reported. 'The gates are barred against them, but they will not hold for long.'

'Then let them hold as long as they may, Messire Pons. Concentrate everything here in the keep.' She raised her chin. 'I do not fear them.' She was filled with iron-cold conviction. No matter what happened, that part at her core was inviolate.

'Riding a white horse you say?' Her lip curled with scornful amusement.

'Yes, madam, and wearing mail.'

'Well, we shall see how much of a soldier he is. A stripling comes to lay siege to his own grandmother in her dotage. What a brave and chivalrous young knight he is indeed.' She took a sip of wine and did not know if its sourness was the state of the wine itself or a taste that was already in her mouth. 'I pray that my other grandson is more of a man.'

She continued to eat, but had only taken a few bites when a request arrived from the enemy camp that she receive their messenger to discuss terms.

Alienor looked at the piece of parchment on which the request had been written. She was a player on the chess board for probably the final time in her life. Knowing that every minute she delayed made more time for Richard on his road, she left an hour before replying and then had her scribe write that she was unwell and indisposed, but she would discuss the matter in the morning. She made sure that the message was worded in such a way as to offer encouragement, because a blank refusal might precipitate their besiegers into an outright attack now.

Once the message had been sent, she gathered everyone together in the hall and, mustering her reserves, stood before them on the dais, frail but upright and resolute as she addressed them like a battle commander.

'We are under siege from my grandson Arthur, the Count of Brittany,' she said. 'I blame him insofar as he has been misguided by the King of France, who has a serpent's tongue and a particular talent for misleading the young. The Count of Brittany probably thinks that an old woman and her small escort is easy meat, but never was he more mistaken.' She paused, drew a deep breath and put increased strength into her voice. 'This particular old woman has crossed the Alps and the Pyrenees in the thick of winter, and has ridden all the way to Jerusalem and back under attack from arrows,

447

scimitars and the political games of the Emperor of Constantinople. She is a queen and has borne children who have been and are kings and queens. He has had no time to make anything of his life – has barely left sucking from his wet-nurse's pap.

'Yes, he is my grandson, and I acknowledge that bond of kinship, even if he does not. I shall humour his request and parley with him, but in truth I shall never yield even if it means my death, and I hope and pray that all here today who know and love me as their liege lady will stand firm. Help is coming, I promise you, and when it does, our attackers will rue the day they ever drew rein before these walls and dared this calumny. When this is over, I promise that each man shall receive a mark of silver from my own hand!'

Loud acclaim rang through the hall and the atmosphere immediately grew more martial and bristled with energy. Leaving the men to their strategies, Alienor retired to her chamber. They knew what had to be done; she had laid their cause out to them. These walls would not stand long; Arthur's force would take the keep within a couple of days if not sooner. They had to stand firm for as long as they could.

With brisk authority she ordered servants to bring water up to her chamber and food supplies that would keep for a few days – eggs, cheese, root vegetables, flour and honey. They could make soup and bread. She also commanded materials to be brought upstairs to make barricades. Even if the keep was broached, there were still final defences.

Richenza rolled up her sleeves to help and dove in with enthusiasm. 'I should have a sword,' she said as she stacked jars of soap near the door, ready to spill their contents down the twisting turret stairs.

Alienor eyed her with wintry amusement. 'I have one of Richard's in my coffer, you can use that.'

'I mean it,' Richenza said stoutly.

'I know you did, and so did I.'

Richenza blotted her forehead on the back of her hand

and tucked a loose curl back under her wimple. 'He will gain nothing from this save condemnation.'

'It is war,' Alienor replied with a shrug. 'I doubt he cares. I have seen it all before – many times. Too many.'

In the morning, Arthur's messenger arrived and was admitted to the great hall. Alienor permitted him no further because she knew he would be looking around, assessing everything and reporting back. Her own men had told her that Arthur had assembled his trebuchets and was already shooting experimental rocks and boulders into the town.

Arthur's man was in his early middle years with a grizzled gold beard and fierce clear blue eyes. He had handed in his sword at the door and wore an ordinary tunic, not mail, to show he came in peace.

'Madam, the Count of Brittany fears for your safety,' he said with a Breton lilt in his voice. 'He asks you to trust to his mercy and yield yourself into his keeping where he will protect you and keep you from harm.'

Alienor offered him wine and when he declined she opened her hand. 'As you please, but I am going to have some and I must sit down. Richenza, if you please . . .'

Richenza helped her to the window seat, casting a reproachful look at Arthur's man, as if to say how could he be part of a host that dared to make war on this fragile old woman? She assisted Alienor to ease down onto the cushioned bench, and then met her sharp and lucid gaze. 'We may have no time,' Alienor whispered, 'but we also have all the time in the world to play with this one.'

As Alienor had suspected, Arthur's envoy was glancing around with keen eyes, assessing the defences and counting up the number of men in the hall. 'Now then, sir.' Alienor raised her voice. 'Come and tell me again what you just said and speak up, because my hearing is not what it was.'

He had no choice but to approach the window seat and repeat his tale. Alienor absorbed it slowly, often asking him

449

to go over his words again. She sat back and waited while the wine arrived and was poured. 'But I already feel safe where I am,' she said in a perplexed and querulous voice. 'I have these walls around me and good men for protection. Surely my grandson would not dream of attacking me.'

Although the messenger had refused wine initially, he was presented with some and was forced out of courtesy to take an obligatory swallow. 'Indeed, madam,' he answered with determination, 'and your grandson desires to protect you, but it cannot be done while you are within this keep. You must emerge at some point, so why not now? There need not be any siege. You and the Count of Brittany could enjoy each other's company and banquet together instead of you lacking all succour and comfort.'

'So all of this is in order to invite me to a banquet? Dear me, young man.' Alienor gave him a sweet smile edged with thorns. 'Well then, tell your lord he is most welcome to partake of our generous rations if he wishes to dine as my grandson and not my opponent. Take that message back to him for I would hear his reply. That is all I have to say for now. And now I need to retire and think the matter over for a while because this is all too exhausting for me.'

Arthur's messenger had no recourse but to rise and take his leave. All the time he was making his farewell his eyes were busy absorbing every last detail. Alienor remained in the hall and had a footstool brought so that she could put her feet up.

'He won't agree,' she said to Richenza, 'but he needs to salve his conscience and say that he has tried negotiating. The longer we can draw it out, the better chance we have.'

Arthur's messenger returned within the hour. Alienor made him wait the time it took a fast pacing horse to go four miles. The man declined the wine fully this time and while courteous was tight-lipped. 'My lord says that he is only your opponent if you make him so, madam, and he has no desire to be at odds with you. If you will yield the keep, all shall be well.'

Alienor spent a long time playing with a ring on her right forefinger, and after a long pause – another quarter of a mile – replied, 'Then if your lord is not my opponent he is welcome to enter my gates. All that I ask is that he arrives without weapons of any kind – as you yourself have come to me – and that he will agree to kneel at my feet and by proxy swear fealty to my son the King.' Suddenly she straightened up and her gaze was fierce, almost hawkish. 'Tell him that, sire, and if he agrees, then all indeed shall be well.'

The messenger met her gaze, and she saw realisation dawn in his eyes, and perhaps a glint of respect. 'Madam, I shall do so, but I do not think he will like it.'

'That is his decision. I am not responsible for his likes and dislikes. He has his answer, and on his own head be it. Tell him if he does not choose to do as I suggest, it would be better for him to leave, because I expect a visit from my son imminently. If you are sure you will not take some wine?'

'Thank you, madam, no. I must report to my lord.' The messenger performed a stiff bow and departed.

There was a brief silence after he had gone. Alienor rose unsteadily to her feet. She was trembling, but with effort and anger, not distress. 'They will come at us now,' she told Richenza. 'Bar the windows, close the shutters, and let us retire and make ready.'

Richard rode into Le Mans a day and a half after setting out. The bay gelding was lame and staggering by the time they arrived at the castle and Richard almost fell out of the saddle as a groom came to take the reins. 'Look after him,' Richard said. 'See he has the best.'

Sweat-mired, filthy with dust and exhausted, Richard stumbled into his father's chamber on the heels of the startled usher who was announcing him.

John, who had been in conversation with some of his mercenary captains, looked at his son in astonishment.

'Arthur is besieging Queen Alienor at Mirebeau,' Richard

gasped. 'I got out just in time before he arrived with his troops. It won't hold above a couple of days, and I've spent half that time getting to you. You must come!'

Following on from utter astonishment, his father's expression grew thunderous. 'What?' He shot to his feet, strode to Richard and shook him hard. 'What are you saying?'

Richard swayed. John grabbed the cup that William de Braose was about to drink from and thrust it at him. 'Here.'

Richard took several deep, desperate gulps and then, spluttering, repeated his information. 'They won't hold,' he reiterated.

'God's sweet death! Why in the name of Christ's nails did she have to leave Fontevraud?' His father began barking orders in every direction. Horses were to be saddled, rations assembled and soldiers ready to ride within the hour. Messengers were sent in haste with verbal commands for there was no time for written ones. 'The misbegotten runt,' John spat between commands. 'I will put an end to this once and for all. By God he has gone too far.'

'I want to come with you,' Richard said.

John looked him up and down, then nodded brusquely. 'You're in no fit state, but I won't stop you. Find yourself a fresh horse and get something to eat. You'll have to keep up. There'll be no room for stragglers.'

Arthur and his troops broke down the gates and entered the town just before noon of the following day. The women had been listening to the whump of the trebuchets hurling boulders and flaming missiles into the town. They had been seeing and smelling smoke all morning, but now they heard shouts, cheering, and the clash of battle. With the town taken, only the wall ringing the keep and the keep itself lay between Alienor and capture. How close was help? Too far away if she searched her heart, but she tried to remain focused and deal with what was immediately before her and not what might be.

In short order siege ladders shot up in several places around the outer walls and Arthur's knights and serjeants launched a concentrated assault that Mirebeau's tiny garrison and Alienor's small entourage had no chance of resisting. Despite a valiant effort, the defenders were forced to fall back to the keep while the archers on the battlements tried to pin down the attackers and keep their own men covered. The last man reached the postern door and then it was barred and barricaded.

'Help me up.' Alienor gestured to Richenza and struggled to rise from her chair.

'Grandmère, you cannot go back down, it is not safe!' Richenza protested.

'Tush, it is safe enough for now,' Alienor responded. 'They will regroup before they attack again and they know we will make them pay dearly so there is bound to be another round of parley. There are wounded men below and they shall know that I care about their welfare.'

With Richenza's support she gained her feet and made her way stiffly to the door and then slowly, with great care, down the twisting stairs to the chamber two storeys below where the soldiers were assembled. An older knight had suffered a broken arm, another a deep gash from a sword. There were cuts and bruises aplenty, but as yet no deaths. Alienor spoke to the wounded, giving them brisk encouragement and comforting words, but in a matter-of-fact way. It was a soldier's lot and being wounded in the course of duty was an accepted hazard. She helped to hand out food and wine and doled out reassurances that relief would arrive. The latter she declared in a firm voice that held absolute conviction, because while she believed, so would they.

Pons de Mirebeau urged her to return to her chamber, but Alienor refused. 'I will go when it is necessary, sire. I shall at least eat and drink with the men, and tackling all those stairs is a tiresome business.'

'Even so, madam, perhaps you should think about—' He broke off and turned as a guard arrived to announce that the messenger had returned and desired another parley.

'Admit him,' Alienor commanded. 'Let us indulge in a little more banter, shall we?'

When the messenger was shown into the hall, she stood regally in its centre, surrounded by her knights, just a single opening giving access to her presence.

'So,' she said when he came and knelt to her, 'what message does your lord have for me this time, messire? Has he changed his mind about my offer of a banquet?' She kept him on his knees.

He raised hard blue eyes to hers, and when he spoke he made certain that everyone could hear. 'My lord the Count of Brittany desires that you surrender the castle to him immediately. It is clear that you will be taken sooner or later. If your garrison resists, then they will be hanged to a man, but if you surrender now, then my lord guarantees clemency to all.'

Alienor met him gaze for gaze. 'So now we come to the crux of the matter. My grandson declares that he is not my opponent but he damages my property and would slaughter my people as if they were no more than animals. Tell him that I thank him for his generosity and that my son will repay him tenfold when he arrives. My advice to you, my lord, is to save yourself while you still have time.'

A muscle ticked in his cheek but he persisted. 'Madam, I beg you to reconsider. You cannot win this.'

'Indeed not,' she agreed, 'because there are no winners in this sorry state of affairs. We are all losers; we are all diminished.' She allowed the moment to draw out. Her instinct was to spit in his face and say she would rather die than yield, but that might bring on an assault straight away and she had gone as far as she dared. She allowed herself to slump a little. 'I need time to consider because it is no small thing you ask of me. At least let me have until tomorrow dawn to decide.'

The messenger hesitated. 'Madam, why drag it out that long? Let me speak bluntly and say that help is not coming. Better to yield now for the good of all.'

'But not for the good of my pride and dignity. Tomorrow

at dawn I will open the doors, and that is my last word.' At last she bade him stand.

The messenger bowed. 'So be it, madam, I shall convey your words to my lord and return with his answer.'

He walked swiftly from the room as though expecting to receive a blade in the back. When he had gone, Alienor looked at the men surrounding her, and took in their varied expressions – shock, surprise, and speculation. One or two even looked grimly amused. 'Of course we're not going to yield at dawn,' Alienor said, 'but if he accepts our terms then we have bought ourselves more time.' She swept her gaze around them. So few, even if they were the best, and she knew what she was asking of them. 'I thank you all for your good service and loyalty, but if any of you wish to depart, I grant you leave. But go now, because these doors will not open again until the fight is over one way or the other.'

There was a momentary hesitation, but only for the time it took for the men to process the words into thought, and then in a rustle of garments and jangle of armour they knelt to her almost as one, and she had her answer.

'Thank you.' Two tears rolled down her face, but she did not wipe them away. 'Thank you. May God reward you, even if it happens that I am unable, and may God be with us all now.'

Alienor retired again to her chamber, her joints throbbing from all the stair climbing; she'd had to pause on the narrow stair wedges to gain her breath and keep her balance. By the time she crossed the threshold she was dizzy and near to collapse.

Above her head she could hear the guards in the roof chamber that led out on to the battlements, and below, in the stairwell, the sound of barricades being dragged into place – mangers filled with stones, upended tables. The soap was poured down the stairs, making them more slick and slippery than flagstones on a frosty day. This, then, was to be Arthur's banquet.

The chamber door was locked and barred. Richenza kilted

up her skirts like a peasant girl and helped to drag a coffer across it, and then filled that coffer with stones brought in earlier before the bailey fell. They had barrels of water and food. And there were three knights and an archer in the room with her who would fight to the death to protect her.

Blackness washed over her and she stumbled. Fortunately she was close to the bed and she landed half against it before slipping to the floor. Richenza was swiftly at her side but Alienor thrust her off. 'I am all right,' she said crossly. 'Do not dare to burn feathers under my nose or I shall never speak to you again!'

'Grandmère, you must rest.' Richenza's eyes were full of concern. 'Come, lie down and be comfortable for a moment.'

She grudgingly allowed Richenza to help her fully onto the bed and endured the plumping of pillars and bolsters at her back.

'What you have done, I could not do, Grandmère.'

'Tush, of course you could if you had to. It is not so difficult and you are young while my strength is not what it was.' Alienor closed her eyes. 'I never thought that the end of my days would find me besieged in a tower by my own grandson – although I have been locked in towers of various kinds often enough. I lived in a great one in Paris when I was first married.'

Her mind drifted as she dozed. She was looking out over Paris on a warm morning in early autumn and her lustrous tresses were the colour of dark honey. Louis was lying on the bed, gazing at her with adoration. Those were the days when he had thought her beautiful and they had been innocent and in love – before the world invaded and changed everything.

And then another husband, a red-haired, vital young lion. Her long legs were wrapped around his waist as he rocked into her, and the sun was cascading through the windows over their gleaming naked bodies. They were creating life and she felt vital and filled with vibrant joy. It was long, long ago, but she could see the sunlight sparkling on their sweat and taste him as if the moment was now in this room.

The scene changed abruptly. She was kneeling beside Richard in his tent, looking at his terrible wound, and his lips were moving even though he was dead and he was telling her that it didn't matter. That all flesh was corruption anyway.

She jerked awake with a gasp as the dull blow of a trebuchet missile shivered against their walls, followed by a muffled cheer.

Richenza flew to her side, her eyes wide with fear. 'They agreed a truce until the morning. Why are they attacking us?'

Alienor pushed herself up against the pillows. Everyone waited, breath held, but the silence continued, heightening the tension, until at last it dissipated as nothing else happened.

'Their messenger returned while you were asleep and agreed to the truce,' Richenza said. 'I do not understand, Grandmère.'

'They are doing it to make a point and cow us into submission on the morrow. They are telling us they can strike as they choose and we cannot stop them. Pay no heed.' She thought, seeing Richenza's white face, that it was easier said than done. The waiting was the hardest part. They were like flies trapped in a spider's web, waiting for a bird to come and eat the spider. She wished William Marshal was here; he always knew how to pass the time and had a fount of stories and anecdotes to lift the spirits and make everyone laugh. 'Come, play chess with me,' she said. 'It may not take our mind off what is happening, but it is something on which to focus.'

The long night passed. Alienor played chess and merels with Richenza and talked in a desultory fashion. There were no more trebuchet shots, but if they listened at the shutters they could hear the men in the camp and there seemed to be a lot of laughter and even carousing. Eventually she persuaded Richenza to come and lie down at her side on the bed, and stroked her granddaughter's thick red hair with a tender, gnarled hand until Richenza fell asleep. But there was no sleep for her: she lay in vigil, waiting for the dawn, and behind her eyes the memories ran like a thread to the heart of a labyrinth.

* * *

457

Richard was almost dead in the saddle. His muscles kept going into spasm and his thighs were chafed raw. His father had set a ferocious pace and was moving almost as fast with his army of mercenaries as Richard had done alone to bring the news. Halfway there they had been joined by the baron William des Roches who had promised to help them capture Arthur on the condition that he had a say in dealing with him once he was in custody, and his father had readily agreed because it swelled their numbers and assured them of victory.

They had ridden all night, pausing briefly to water their horses, feed themselves and stretch their legs. No camp had been made and the troops had just sat on the ground to eat their rations. Back on the road, Richard had tied himself into the saddle to stay astride. They were jolting along too fast for him to fall asleep, but he was not sure if he could physically remain on his horse for much longer.

In the grey light heralding dawn they were less than two miles from Mirebeau. The soldiers halted to check their arms and weapons, securing helms, adjusting shield straps and scabbards. Richard's mouth was parched and he reached to the leather water bottle on his saddle. His gut was churning with the nausea of exhaustion mingled with apprehension and excitement.

'You have done well.' His father, clad in his mail shirt, had joined him, speaking man to man. 'I am proud of you.'

'Thank you, sire, but it was my duty.' Heat burned Richard's face at the compliment and he tried to sit up a little straighter.

'Many know their duty, but they do not perform it,' his father said with a twist of his lips.

A returning scout arrived and dismounted almost before he had drawn rein to make his report. 'Sire, the town is taken and half burned down. The gates are broken and no one has yet shored up the gap. They're wide open to us – they have no notion we are here.' He flashed chipped teeth in a broad grin. 'They're breaking their fast round their fires – roast pigeon from the nearest loft if I am not mistaken.'

John returned the scout's grin wolfishly, tossed him a coin and turned his horse. 'It would be rude indeed not to join them at their feast. I am ravenous and I am sure I can persuade my beloved nephew to provide us with hospitality.'

Towards dawn Alienor left the bed to visit the privy. Task accomplished, she went to the window where one of the knights had been watching throughout the night. The light was greying towards dawn but the sun was still below the horizon. Spirals of smoke were rising from the revived campfires of the besiegers, and their cheerful voices carried up to the window together with a scent of roasting meat.

'Everything was quiet last night after that single stone from their stone thrower, madam,' the knight, Guillaume of Poitiers, said, 'but they will come once they have enough light.'

'Let them. We are strong enough to beat them back at least once or twice. They will seek out our weak spots to pummel and soften us first.'

Guillaume gave a taut smile. 'You know much about siege craft, madam.'

'I benefited from listening when my husband and sons were either talking of warfare or waging it, which was most of the time.' It was ironic, she thought, that the greatest of them had died at a petty siege of a castle not much greater than Mirebeau.

A thin band of light began to glow in the east, like a box opening to show a gleam of treasure. Alienor wondered if this was the last dawn she would ever see. Many of the knights would be thinking the same thing as they knelt before the priest to be shriven. God pray she was not sending them to their deaths.

From the camp there came a sudden shout, and then another, followed by yells of warning and alarm. As men ran to grab weapons, mounted soldiers in full mail galloped in among them, smashing down the tents, scattering the fires, and wreaking destruction and mayhem.

'Dex ai le Roi! Dex ai le roi!'

The unmistakeable war cry of the King rang out, and although Alienor's eyes were blurred with age, she could make out John's banner of blazing red and gold as his standard bearer waved it aloft.

Richenza joined her, hair dishevelled and eyes cloudy with slumber but wide with anxiety. 'What is it? Are we under attack?'

'They've come!' Alienor exulted. 'Richard got through, praise God!' She made a sound halfway between a laugh and a gasp. 'I said they would come did I not? We are rescued! I played for time and now the tables have turned!'

John's troops had burst through the open town gateway and galloped through the deserted, half-charred settlement to the keep, through the broken defences and into the midst of Arthur's men. Richard caught sight of his cousin in shirt and braies, a stunned expression on his face, the roast pigeon in his hand dripping grease into the dust. Two knights seized him, clubbed the food to the ground and pinned his arms up high behind his back. He yelled and kicked and fought until one of them struck his temple with a clenched fist, and he slumped between them, half senseless.

The besiegers were utterly caught out by the speed and surprise of the assault. The soldiers in the keep surged out to lend their assistance, and Arthur's small army was crushed like a nut under a hammer.

Strengthened by the heat and swiftness of the moment Richard forgot his pain and exhaustion. He dismounted and ran to the keep, immediately coming up against a piled barricade of stone-filled mangers, tables and huge pieces of tree trunk at the foot of the stairs. He started dragging the barricades aside, and others joined him. From somewhere above on the twisting stairs came the sound of thumps, bangs, and then sloshing water.

Moments later, Guillaume of Poitiers appeared round the newel post, clinging for dear life to the wall, followed by two compatriots, all taking similar care. By this time John had arrived and stood, hands on hips, looking askance at the goings-on.

'It's the soap, sire,' said Guillaume of Poitiers.

'Soap?' John raised his brows.

'The Queen ordered it to be tipped down the stairs. We've managed to sluice off the worst with the water we were storing, but it still needs more. Thank Christ you have come. We could not have held out more than a few hours.'

'Grandmère was determined,' Richard said with admiration.

'Oh, your grandmother knows how to fight to the death,' John said, casting his gaze heavenwards.

Gingerly he began to climb the steps, and Richard followed in his wake.

Alienor stood upright facing the open door as John negotiated the final steps and entered the chamber. He still wore his mail and was breathing heavily from his climb.

'Thank God!' She rushed to him. 'Thank God you came in time!'

He took her hands and kissed her cheek.

'We thought it would be much closer than this; we thought we would have to endure a day of assaults.'

Grimacing, he left her to take a towel from beside the laver and wipe the soles of his boots before tossing the cloth to Richard, who did the same. 'Well then, it seems for once I exceeded your expectations, Mama.'

'You often exceed my expectations,' Alienor replied with asperity, 'but I can truly say I have never been so pleased to see you as I am now.' She turned to Richard. 'And you are a hero! You must have ridden faster than the wind, and now to return with your father – that is indeed a feat. You look exhausted.'

He smiled at her, his features alight despite the dark shadows beneath his eyes. 'I care not, because we were in time. I can sleep in a while.'

'Well, at least have some wine. I had the best barrels brought up here. If the keep was broached I had no intention of letting the rabble swill the good stuff.' Her voice was bright, but it was brittle too. Like her grandson she was enduring by the power of her will and pure determination.

Richenza presented her uncle and cousin with goblets, and gently tugged Richard to the window seat and made him sit down.

John said, 'Thanks to your summons we have captured Arthur and his accomplices Hugh de Lusignan and Savaric de Mauleon, among others.' His eyes gleamed and there was a smug curl to his lips. 'I could not have set a better trap if I had thought it up myself rather than it being happenstance. God has done me a great favour. Now Philippe will have to retreat because his pawn has been knocked from the board.' He took a drink from his cup and gave her a sharp look, as if suddenly remembering something. 'Even so, Mama, what were you doing here?'

'I was travelling to Poitiers.' She tensed, for she recognised that look on his face, and these days the tables had turned; she could no longer command him. 'I thought it safer than Fontevraud when I heard Arthur was ravaging with an army.'

'Two hundred knights is not an army,' he said. 'And since this has happened to you, it clearly was not a safer option than remaining at Fontevraud. You are too frail for this, Mama. I thought you had retired to a life of contemplation, but then I find you riding around like a nomad and desperately pleading for succour. What would have happened if Arthur had captured you?'

'But he did not and instead you have captured him which is a happy outcome,' she retorted. 'Do not seek to scold me. Yes I am old, yes my body is failing, but my spirit is as fierce as it was on the day I married your father, and if I thought it best to go to Poitiers, it was my choice.'

John inclined his head. 'I was concerned for you, that is all,' he said silkily. 'But now that Arthur and Hugh de Lusignan are in my hands, I think it would be best if you returned to Fontevraud rather than continuing to Poitiers. No one will attack you now. As soon as Richard has recovered from his heroic rides, he will escort you back there.'

She thought about being contrary just to irritate him, but in truth, and in spite of her fighting words, after today's ordeal all she wanted was the quiet of her chamber at the abbey, and gentle tending. However, she was not done yet.

'Yes, you are right, and besides, I need to speak with Master D'Ortiz about the effigies.'

'Good.' John put down his cup and made to leave.

'But first I want to see Arthur,' Alienor said. 'I want to see my grandson.'

John's expression narrowed, but he shrugged. 'As you will, Mama, although God knows why.'

'Because all the time we were under threat of siege, my exchanges have been with his messenger. Now I want to put a face to the words I received from him.'

John had business to attend to and Alienor had to wait until the stairs had been thoroughly washed down so as to leave not a trace of the slick and slippery soap. An hour later John returned and brought her to the commander's small chamber off the guard room where Arthur had been confined alone. He sported a black eye and his face wore a red flush of new bruises. From the way he was holding himself she suspected he had been kicked in the ribs too. Her grandson, who had threatened her and would have used her without mercy as his pawn. Now he was in John's hands and a pawn himself. She saw a gangly adolescent, tall and thin with oily blemishes on his cheeks. His hair was a dirty blond and his eyes pale grey and watchful.

'I hope you have learned your lesson from this,' she said. 'Now you see the consequences of your folly and what happens when you go against your kin. You need to change your ways. You must submit to your uncle the King and adhere to him, not Philippe of France.'

Arthur scowled at her and she felt the hostility emanating from him in waves. He was sullen, a caged animal, and she had no patience with him.

'Why should I?' His voice grated in the space between boy and man. 'My father was the older brother. The right is mine more than his.'

'You have no choice. What use are such claims without the wherewithal to fulfil them? Swearing your allegiance and making your peace would benefit you far more than this childish defiance.'

He said nothing and turned his head away.

'Charming, isn't he?' John remarked.

'He is no ruler,' she said scornfully, 'nothing but a boy with a desire for entitlement.' As John had once been himself. She pushed that thought aside. 'What are you going to do with him?'

John shrugged. 'I do not know, Mama. For now all that matters is that he is no longer free to make his mischief.' A savage glint entered his eyes. 'As far as his allies are concerned, I do not care if they rot in the deepest dungeons known to man.'

'Have a care,' Alienor warned. 'Enemies in your power are tools to be used. Consider well whatever you do.'

'Yes, Mama.'

She heard the impatience in his voice and felt tired. This was a triumph for him and she could sense it buoying him up in a dark and gloating kind of way. Henry had been like that at times, never Richard, whose dealings with his enemies had always been clean and astringent. Both sons were beyond her reach now in different ways.

The effort expended over the last few days had taken its toll and she had drunk her reserves to the dregs of her cup. All she wanted was to return to Fontevraud, retire from the world, and rest.

48

Abbey of Fontevraud, April 1203

Alienor looked at the cleric who had just been shown into her chamber. He was tall and thin with piercing dark eyes, long cheeks and a straight mouth, held in a tight line. He had presented her with a letter and now stood with hands folded before him as Richenza read it out to Alienor.

'*We send to you Brother John de Valerant who has seen what is going forward with us and who will be able to tell you of our situation. Put faith in him respecting these things whereof he will inform you. Nevertheless the grace of God is with us even more than he can tell you.*'

'What is your information?' Alienor asked. 'I take it that it cannot be committed to parchment.'

John de Valerant bowed. 'Indeed, madam, the King considered the information would be best told to you rather than written. He bids me say that the succession is determined and cannot now be set aside. An agreement has been reached that cannot be undone. He bid me show you this as proof.' He withdrew a ring from his pouch and handed it to her.

Alienor's eyesight was not good but she could see that it was a personal seal ring, similar to the one Richard had once possessed, and set with a red intaglio. Her son Geoffrey had had one too. 'To whom does this belong?' she demanded.

'To Arthur, Count of Brittany,' de Valerant replied tonelessly. 'I am to tell you that all is settled, and that the King is now confirmed in all of his lands. You have no further need to worry on this matter.'

Alienor looked down at the ring and wondered what John had done now. Something had clearly happened, presumably to Arthur, and by design not accident, for if the latter de Valerant would have said so. She did not have the strength to go delving, and knew even if she did she would either not get to the truth or she would find out and wish forever she had not. From the careful tone of the cleric, whom she knew to be one of John's spies, she suspected the worst. He would not tell her and there was no point in pushing him. The news was worthless except to build up a layer of acceptable fabrication. Since she had no energy to sort it out, she must look the other way.

She returned the ring to him and rubbed her hands together as if washing them. 'Thank you,' she said. 'I do not wish to keep this. You may go.'

He bowed and departed, clearly as eager to be free of her presence as she was for him to leave.

Richenza was biting her lip. 'Grandmère, what did he mean?'

Alienor turned to her granddaughter. 'I think you know perfectly well what he meant.'

Richenza looked stricken. 'But what if—'

'I do not wish to talk of the matter, and if you are the sensible young woman I think you are, you will not dwell on it,' Alienor said firmly. 'It is out of my hands. There is nothing I can do, especially for something that is already a fait accompli – nothing, that is, except pray for all concerned. If you cannot put it from your mind, then lock it away and do not speak of it. The world is a harsh place where terrible things happen every day. Be thankful for what grace we have.' She gestured. 'Come, help me up, I would walk in the garden.'

Alienor struggled up from her seat, Richenza aiding her one side, and her walking stick the other. She had always sworn she would never use one of these things, had stuck to that determination all the way until the winter after Mirebeau when at last she had capitulated when struggling to walk between her dwelling and the abbey. The alternative was to be carried and she would not tolerate that. Each day she tried to walk a little way if the weather was kind, but it was becoming progressively more difficult. Her eyesight was failing too and she had to rely on Richenza and Belbel more and more. Each journey was one from seat to seat, respite to respite, but at least if she was concentrating on setting one foot in front of the other and keeping her balance it pushed their visitor and his news from her mind.

William Marshal stood in the choir of the great abbey, his breath misting in the chill December air. The clear pale light from the windows enhanced the rust-red hue of his cloak and the contrasting blue and cream of the squirrel fur lining. His gloves and soft hat were folded over his belt. He had been gazing for some time upon the completed effigies of King Henry, Richard and the kneeling Joanna, praying at her father's feet.

'They are magnificent likenesses, madam,' he said to Alienor. 'They do indeed look as though they are at rest but only sleeping for a single night, not eternally.'

Alienor nodded. 'That was my intention. They may be dead, but I have their replicas in stone, and people shall look upon them and marvel as they pay their respects.'

He had arrived to visit while she was here in the church, sitting by the tombs in the chair that was always left for her there and where she spent an increasing amount of her time.

She had given up receiving news of the outside world a short while after Brother de Valerant had come from John. The last she had heard before shutting herself off was that John's affairs were going from bad to worse as town after town fell to the French. Such information made her even more determined to remove herself from the world and all the pointless striving that came to naught. She had also heard around the time of her decision that Isabel de Warenne had died and been buried beside Hamelin at Lewes Priory. That had hit her hard because Isabel had been her sister in many ways even if they had grown apart in later years. She had brought out the shawl her friend had once given her, finely woven from the wool on her estates, and she had wrapped it around herself, seeking comfort in its plaid folds, but finding it hard to come by – threadbare. That was when she had finally withdrawn. Enough. She was wearing that shawl now, fastened with a silver brooch that had also been Isabel's gift.

'King Henry does not have a beard.' William gave her a questioning glance.

Alienor smiled a little. 'When I first knew him he often did not have one, and I want him to be remembered in his youth and strength.' Unspoken between them lay the awareness that Richard was bearded and thus to an onlooker might have the greater gravitas of the two men. 'The robes are the ones he wore at his coronation when we had all our future before us and everything was possible.' She set her hands to the chair arms. 'Help me to my feet.'

He was immediately attentive but treated her as he always had, with deference to her rank and not her age.

'It is so good to see you again, William, although in truth my inner vision is better than my outer one these days – and I would rather live that inner life.'

'It is good to see you too, madam. You are always beautiful and gracious,' he said.

She gave a small snort of amusement. 'Not always, but I welcome your courtesy. Come, I wish to show you another effigy.'

She led him slowly from the church and brought him to the shed where the masons had been working in the summer months. 'Master D'Ortiz died of the lung sickness before he could finish this one, and perhaps it is fitting that it has not yet been completed. The masons will return in the spring and someone else will complete the work. Lift the canvas . . . I am all right.' She placed both hands on her walking stick.

He left her side and crouched to pull away the sheeting that covered the unfinished effigy of a woman reading a book. The block was roughed out, but there was still much work to be done.

'The others of his household have the plans,' she said. 'They have the colours and the gown I desire to wear. It's the one I had in Poitiers that summer I took you into service.'

'The pale silk with the red jewels and green embroidery.'

'You have a good memory.'

'That day will be with me always. How could I not remember?'

She saw him swallow. 'Do not dare go maudlin on me, William,' she warned. 'I did not choose that gown for tears and mourning.'

He made an effort, and when he faced her his eyes were dry. 'No,' he said. 'It will celebrate your beauty and power, and yet be entirely fitting to the surroundings. It will be perfect. If I am sad it is because of what I have to tell you.'

She gripped the rock crystal knob on top of the walking stick. 'Be careful what you say to me, William. I meant what I said, that I would rather live the inner life. If your news is bitter then I do not wish to hear it.' Her look sharpened. 'I mean it.'

'Perhaps we should go within, madam, it is very cold.'

She eyed him suspiciously but then capitulated for he was right. She had not realised how chilled she had become sitting beside the tombs. She was like a stone herself.

'So what is this news of yours, or have you decided to keep it to yourself now?' she demanded as they entered her chamber. The servants had built up her fire and spiced wine was warming on the hearth. For a moment the contrast with outdoors knocked her back. William helped her to her seat by the fire, fetched a stool for her feet, and poured her a goblet of the spiced wine. The scent of cinnamon and honey rose on the steam and she took an appreciative sip.

He sat down opposite her. 'I came to see how you were faring because the Christmas season is close. You must know there are difficulties in Normandy and that the King of France continues to make inroads on our territories.'

She nodded stiffly. 'I hear things even when I do not wish

to, but if you are going to tell me of some calamity, my ears are closed. The ocean is rough beyond my walls these days and I have lost my taste for sailing. I strove for many years to keep Philippe of France out of our territories. I fought for Richard – I would have died for him. I even fought for John until that spark went out of me. When I do think of such matters now – which I would rather not – I wonder if all the time I have been riding the wrong horse.'

'Madam?'

'If Philippe of France does prevail, then his son will succeed him, and his son's wife is mine – child of my child, and chosen by me to fulfil her role. Blanca will be Queen of France as I once was long ago.' She looked at William. 'Sometimes a river runs on the surface and sometimes it runs underground, but always it is present. Even if you do not see it, you can feel it.'

'That is true,' he said gravely.

'What were you going to tell me? My mind wanders along its own pathways these days. You had not finished.'

'Only that the King is returning to England to spend Christmas and while there will make preparations to ship more resources to Normandy. I am returning with him and bringing Isabelle and the children. I had not visited you in a while.'

She gave him a tired smile. 'And you wanted to say farewell while I still lived? Ah William, you may give whatever courtier's answer you wish, but we both know the truth – and it no longer matters, although once it would have done.'

He gave her the look of a supplicant. 'I confess I am not ready to let you go. You mustn't depart yet. I would see you laugh again.'

Alienor gave a weak imitation of the sound. 'I no longer have it in me,' she said, but because she wanted to comfort him, and give him a parting gift to remember, added, 'You are dearer to me, William, than you will ever know. You have never failed me – ever. You are my man; you have always been my man, from the day you fought off my attackers in Poitiers and sacrificed yourself to let me go free. I want you to carry that with you. You are more to me than a queen's equerry.'

'Madam, you are my liege lady, and I will serve you in whatever way you ask.' He rose to his feet, but only to kneel at hers and bow his head.

'Then pray for me, William, and keep me gently in your thoughts.'

'Until we meet again.' His words had the sense of either this world or the beyond.

Despite her desperate need for rest, Alienor insisted on seeing him on his way. As he mounted his bay stallion, her blurred vision was suddenly crystal clear and she saw a young knight, in all the beauty of early manhood, riding the horse she had given to him when he first entered her service, and she thought that when they met again perhaps he would indeed look like that, and she would be a young woman, unburdened and joyous.

49

Abbey of Fontevraud, April 1204

Alienor felt a soft breeze on her face from her open chamber window, scented with blossom and new grass. There was distant birdsong, and the nearer throb of a dove, which she knew must be perched on the thick stone windowsill.

She found the light too bright for her eyes these days and so she kept her lids closed and dwelt in the peace of darkness, turning ever inwards. Earlier she had confessed to her chaplain and received unction. It had become a daily routine recently, although she was bedridden and the only opportunity she had to commit sins was in her thoughts, and they were slow and turbid. She had been ready for a while now, but each morning the dawn came and she was still in this chamber, fettered inside her body. She was fully attended, all her needs seen to as she waited for each breath to come and go, each muddy heartbeat to thump and stir her sluggish blood.

'Grandmère?'

She turned her head slightly at the sound of Richenza's voice, soft but with notes of mingled fear and concern. An arm slipped behind her shoulders and she caught the scent of musk and spices. Raising her lids, she made out a hazy outline.

'Can you take a sip of water?'

Alienor tried for her granddaughter, but it was difficult to swallow and most of the liquid dribbled down her chin. Richenza gently wiped her lips and then sat down at the bedside and took her hand. Alienor felt the smooth young skin against her own, the strong fingers, and for a moment it was as if they became her own.

'You must eat and drink,' Richenza said tearfully.

Alienor forced her eyes to stay open, even though the light upon them seemed as sharp as vinegar. 'I am beyond that,' she whispered in a dry voice. 'But sing for me if you will. I would like that.'

'What would you have me sing, Grandmère?'

'Something joyous. Something from Aquitaine, of April and love – and I do not want you to cry when you are doing it. There is no reason to cry.' The effort of speaking made her so exhausted that her eyelids seemed like lead weights and she had to close them again.

'It is spring now,' Richenza said. 'You should stay to see it for yourself, Grandmère. I swear the grass has grown half a foot in three days.'

'Better to leave the world in a time of beauty and renewal,' Alienor said weakly. 'When . . . when I am gone, I want you to look after Snowit for me.'

Richenza squeezed her hand. 'Of course I will,' she said in a strangled voice.

'And go to Blanca in Paris – Blanche as she is now – and give her my crown, the one with the sapphires and pearls. John's wife will have crowns and coronets enough in her time, but Blanca should have this one for herself. Promise me.'

'Yes, I promise – I know the one.'

They were interrupted by the sound of dashing young feet and shouts of play as Richenza's young son Thomas charged into the room with a small friend and played chase around the furniture, ducking and dodging. 'Can't catch me!'

Richenza rounded on them angrily. 'What have I told you both?' she snapped. 'Thomas, your great grandmother needs peace and quiet. Go elsewhere and make your noise!'

'Let them be,' Alienor whispered. 'It pleases me to hear them while I still can. They are the future, and when else in their lives will they be able to do this?'

'Well then I am glad you are not disturbed, Grandmère, but they should know better.' Turning to the boys, she gave them a stern look. 'Grandmère does not mind you playing, but go outside.'

The sound of their boisterous play faded but did not vanish entirely as they resumed their game under the window. Disturbed, the dove on the sill took to her wings with a sound of clapped air. Alienor began to drift away on a sea of slumber, scented with green spring air, to the joyful shouts of children at play.

Richenza stroked Alienor's hand. 'I need you here,' she whispered. 'What will I do without you? I need your guidance. Please don't leave me.'

Alienor gave a dry swallow. 'You have to let me go, my dear. You will find your own way. It is what we all must do. Just sit with me awhile . . . and sing. That is all I ask.'

Richenza hesitated, a hitch in her breathing as she controlled herself, but after a while she cuffed her wet eyes and raised her voice, clear and steady, with a wistful tone like gentle rain.

When the soft breeze blows and speaks of love
As April turns its face to May,
And on a flowery branch above
Sings the nightingale his praise.

When each bird gives his sweetest call
In the freshness of the morn
Sings, joyful of his bliss of all
Delighting in his mate, at dawn.

As all things on earth rejoice
And sing to see green leaves appear,
Then I recall my lover's voice
And yearn for him all through the year.

By past custom and by nature's rule,
The time is nigh when I must turn
Where soft winds my memories unspool,
And my heart must dream and yearn.

Alienor was vaguely aware of people entering the room. Her chaplain, she thought, and the Abbess; she recognised their voices. Outside the children continued to squeal and play, but it was a distant and fading sound. Others had entered the room; she could sense them even though she could not open her eyes, and she felt their presence as a shiver through her body for they were not of the fleshly world, although they had been once.

Her hearing strengthened and Richenza's voice soared.

Open-hearted, her manner free,
Bright colour and golden hair,
God who grants her all sovereignty
Preserve her for the best is there.

The song was overlaid by the hoarse cry of a gyrfalcon, and although her eyes were closed she could see Snowit dancing on her perch, secured by the leather leashes tied around her slender legs. She spread her pinions in a white fan and flapped and bated.

'Set her free,' Alienor entreated, but could not tell if she had spoken aloud or not. If she had, then no one had heard her, for the gyrfalcon continued to beat her wings and fight the leashes.

Someone pressed a cross into Alienor's hand and there were whispers of concern like the rustle of dry, dead leaves.

She struggled to leave her bed and release the falcon herself because she could not bear it. Where was her stick? Why couldn't she move?

She became aware of a girl at the bedside, a young woman clad in a gown of ivory-coloured silk damask patterned with gold, her warm tawny hair decorated with jewels. Alienor thought that she had once owned a dress like that. The girl smiled at her, and her eyes were as blue as the sea in the bay at Talmont. Alienor felt her joy, the vibrant life pouring through her lithe body. The girl turned away in a shimmer of hair and jewels, and took the falcon onto her wrist. Her hands were long and fine, young and smooth. She bore the gyrfalcon to the window, unnoticed by the crowd gathered around the bed. Drawing up her skirt to show a froth of pale silk under-gown, she stepped up onto the window seat, light in her kidskin slippers, and leaned forward to the open casement. She looked briefly over her shoulder at the bed, at the people leaning over the wizened shell lying upon it, and then with a smile on her lips and a wide sweep of her arm that floated her sleeve she sent the gyrfalcon soaring free into the blue.

Watching her fly, Alienor felt utter joy in her heart, and the sensation expanded outwards until she was one with the girl and the bird. High above the abbey, spiralling inside the light. Prisms of colour like the rainbow refractions in the rock crystal vase she had once given her first husband as a wedding gift splintered and came together, and expanded again. She saw others in the lambency, welcoming, reaching out to

475

embrace her, and as she opened herself to their love she became one with them within infinite coils of light in a never-ending labyrinth where all was as one.

Epilogue

Abbey of Fontevraud, April 1205

A year later, Richenza stood before her grandmother's graceful, enigmatic tomb in the abbey choir. The effigy had been completed in the winter following Alienor's death, a different sculptor having added the fine details to her figure. Although it had been a necessity owing to Master D'Ortiz's demise, the subtle difference of style caused Alienor to stand out from the others and seem more active in the hint of movement over the knee draped in its blue cloak and the way the hands were raised to support her book.

The sun streamed through the church windows and picked out the rich colours of the garments. Alienor's jewelled crown shone with points of reflected light. She wore a pale dress with a lozenge pattern picked out in green and red. The effect drew the eye to her first, even if Henry had been intended as the leading figure. It seemed that her effigy glowed with life. While Richenza's grandfather and uncle lay in deep slumber, Alienor was awake. Joanna's representation, kneeling at her father's feet in prayer, was lifelike too. The women were active, the men passive, and that made Richenza smile as she absorbed wisdom in that moment. Her grandmother had often been told she did not know her place, but truly she did.

'God grant you peace in heaven, Grandmère,' Richenza whispered. 'May you have been reunited with those you loved in your life.' She kissed the cool stone cheek of the effigy, did the same to Henry, Richard and Joanna, and went outside to join her waiting entourage. The chess board was gathering for momentous moves. Alienor might be gone but others had taken her place and in their turn were engaged in playing the great game.

All around her the April spring was flourishing. The cherry blossom had blown from the trees, leaving the new green fruit to set. Richenza had no tears today. She had shed and dried them many months ago, and although she mourned, she was coming to terms with her loss. 'There will never be another such as you,' she said softly, with a look over her shoulder, 'but you will be remembered for as long as memory endures.'

She mounted her horse and, leaning down to her falconer, received Snowit onto her gloved wrist. The gyrfalcon uttered a single piercing cry, bated her speckled wings, and then settled.

With Fontevraud's pale abbey buildings behind her, Richenza took the road north towards Paris and Blanca.

Author's Note

Writing three novels about Eleanor of Aquitaine – Alienor as she was known in her own lifetime – has been a wonderful and enlightening journey for me. I have learned so much along the way and at the same time discarded a great deal of what I thought I knew.

The Autumn Throne covers the thirty years of Alienor's life between her imprisonment at what is now Old Sarum (the original Salisbury) by her second husband Henry II and her death at the Abbey of Fontevraud in April 1204.

It is often said that she was incarcerated at Sarum from 1174 to Henry II's death in 1189, but while she did indeed spend many years there, she was at times held under house arrest at castles including Winchester, Berkhamsted and Dover. She also visited Normandy to attend family gatherings and rubber-stamp (so to speak) Henry's policies.

At one point in the early period of Alienor's imprisonment Henry actively considered annulling their marriage and consigning Alienor to a nunnery. It is interesting that around that time the Abbey of Amesbury became an English colony of Fontevraud. Did Henry have Alienor in mind as a putative abbess while still confining her to his island kingdom? Perhaps.

From being set free following Henry's death in 1189 to her own death in 1204, Alienor scarcely had a moment to draw breath as she was hurled into the thick of diplomacy and government. As well as governing England, she crossed the Alps in midwinter to bring Berenguela of Navarre (also known as Berengaria) as a bride to Richard the Lionheart in Sicily.

After a respite of only three days she had to set out for home via the papal court in Rome to sort out problems caused not least by her youngest son John.

Following Richard's imprisonment by Emperor Heinrich of Germany she made immense efforts to raise his ransom and then rode to bring him home. The letter in chapter 35 with Peter of Blois where Alienor writes to Pope Celestine castigating him for his passive response in the face of her desperation comes from her actual correspondence. All I have done is condense it slightly. Richard really did have his armour returned to England to be put on show as a fund raiser, and he also composed while in prison, the beautiful, sad song I mentioned. It still exists today. If you search the internet for 'Ja Nus Hons Pris' you should be able to find several versions.

Alienor's retirement to Fontevraud in 1194 was interrupted when Richard was struck by a crossbow bolt in the Limousin and died after the wound festered. While researching I discovered that a few years earlier he had taken a hit from a crossbow to one of his legs. Clearly he was an insurance risk in that department! Arriving at his deathbed Alienor had no time to grieve but immediately had to throw her efforts into supporting her remaining son John as he inherited the vast but splintering Angevin empire. As well as Richard's death she had to cope with the loss of her daughter Joanna in childbirth. We don't know the difficulty that caused Joanna's death, but whatever it was she had time to make her will and gain permissions from the Church to take her vows. I have gone with placenta praevia – a complication of late pregnancy whereby a low-lying placenta, depending on its position, can prove fatal for mother and child.

Having buried Richard, the 'light of her life', at Fontevraud and Joanna too, Alienor had to cross the Pyrenees in winter, now aged around seventy-six, in order to bring one of her granddaughters from Castile back to France as a bride for the Dauphin Louis. The expectation was that Urraca, the oldest, would be chosen, but Alienor preferred the younger one,

Blanca. The latter, renamed Blanche, was to become a formidable Queen of France and rule as regent during her son's minority and later during his absence on crusade. She was certainly cast in the mould of her famous grandmother.

On returning from Castile Alienor retired once more, but during the strife between her remaining son John and her grandson Arthur, posthumous heir of her son Geoffrey, she found herself being besieged by the youth at her castle of Mirebeau. She was rescued in the nick of time by John, who was around ninety miles away but covered the distance at such speed that he surprised the besiegers as they were breaking their fast on roast pigeon, and turned the tables on his nephew – who was to die at his hands in suspicious circumstances the following year.

Alienor returned to Fontevraud to live out her days. Some sources say she took the veil before she died; others make no mention of it. I have chosen not to portray her becoming a nun at the end of her life as I don't feel personally she would have done so.

It is thought that Alienor was responsible in part for designing her own effigy and those of Henry II, Richard and her daughter Joanna (the latter has been lost). Alienor is depicted reading a book and is thus more active than her menfolk who are lying passively in state clutching their rods of office. It may be that she is reading aloud to them for their edification from what is highly likely to have been a book of a religious nature. Reading aloud was the usual mode of medieval reading, rather than silently as we do now, and means that for once they have to listen to her!

I noticed when researching the effigies that Henry II lacks a beard. There are a couple of portrayals of him in life and on both those occasions he is bearded. Richard the Lionheart is certainly bearded on his effigy. Did Alienor want to portray Henry as the handsome young man she had married, who might not have been hirsute at the outset? Or perhaps she wanted Richard to have a greater authority than his father.

In the medieval period, a beard was equated with gravitas. I do not suppose we shall ever know.

The debate about whether or not Richard the Lionheart was homosexual is still strongly argued and everyone has an opinion. I have left mine open in *The Autumn Throne*. From this far a distance we don't know, and in truth it doesn't really matter. Philippe of France and Richard are reported as having shared the same bed but that wasn't unusual in the medieval period and was a sign of trust and prestige between high-status individuals. It's our modern mindset that has imbued it with homosexual connotations. However, I did use the bed-sharing detail to put forward a different theory. Richard is reported to have been a debaucher of women and to have behaved with lustful depravity – sufficiently for him to have performed public penance for his deeds. A ménage à trois would fit neatly into this. Richard is reported as having a son, Philippe of Cognac, but he disappeared from the scene soon after John came to the throne. John is recorded as paying him a single mark in documentation, so obviously was not about to cultivate him and never acknowledged him as his nephew – although given John's track record with nephews, perhaps one should be suspicious.

On the subject of names, I called Geoffrey's spaniel Moysi. It means 'Mosaic' in Anglo-Norman and I envisaged his coat as being mottled.

Alienor's gyrfalcon is called Snowit. I had to use this name somewhere in the novel. One day while browsing a legal document of circa 1200 I came across a lady called Snowit, which today we would translate as 'Snow-White'. I had always thought the name an invention of the Brothers Grimm, but no, she had once been a living woman, dwelling in Middlesex, the wife of William le Parmentier. At times like this I love the research!

Alienor's granddaughter Richenza changed her name to Matilda when she returned to the Angevin court. Frequently women did change their names when they married; she is not the only example. Henry I's queen changed her name from

Edith to Matilda, and of course another of Alienor's granddaughters became Blanche instead of Blanca when she married Louis, heir to the French throne. I made the decision to remain with Richenza to avoid a confusion of Matildas.

Since there were so many ladies called Isabel in the novel, I used the name Hawise for John's first wife, Isabel of Gloucester. Over the years she has been called both Hawise and Isabel by sundry historians, but Isabel would appear to be her correct name. However, I've gone with older custom, as I did when retaining Richenza, in order to lessen the confusion.

Still on the subject of names, 'L'Histoire de Guillaume le Mareschal', a poem about the life of the great William Marshal, tells us that Alienor's name had the meaning of 'Pure Gold' (it's also a pun on her mother's name, Aenor, because it has the meaning of 'another Aenor'). The 'Histoire' reveals the depth of the friendship between Alienor and the Marshal which lasted in strength and honour throughout their lives. Even when others were blackening her name following her death, the 'Histoire' holds true in its praise.

It was interesting researching Richard FitzRoy (later in life also recorded as Richard of Dover, Richard of Chillham and Richard de Warenne) and weaving him into the story. We do not know which of Hamelin's three daughters bore him. I have gone with Isabel (Belle), the eldest daughter. Richard named his own daughter Isabel, and although it was his mother-in-law's name too, and he may have been pleasing her, it may also indicate family ties from his own side of the blanket. There is no evidence that he was with his grandmother at Mirebeau, but this is where a writer of historical fiction plays on the space between the lines.

Alienor's two maids in the novel, Amiria and Belbel, are taken from life. Amiria, we know, was from a Welsh Marcher background and was the sister of a baron called Hugh Pantulf of Wem. Circa 1194 she entered the convent of Amesbury. Belbel is more elusive. There is an entry in the pipe roll for her which lists clothes for both her and Alienor in the same entry and says 'for the King's use'. Some historians have jumped on this detail as evidence of Belbel being another of Henry II's mistresses, but to me it's skating on ice so thin that it holds no weight. It's a massive leap to go from listing clothing to presenting the woman in the role of mistress. To me it's far more likely that the reference is to one of Alienor's ladies and that 'for the King's use' is concerned with the garments in some way rather than listing a concubine!

I now commend Alienor to her reading at Fontevraud and hope that the light I have shed on her life has illuminated a few unknown facets among the familiar.

Select Bibliography

For those wanting to read further I have included a short list of the books I found the most useful and grounded while writing Alienor's story. In particular Michael Evans' superb *Inventing Eleanor* was indispensable when it came to untwisting the mythology both ancient and very modern that entangles Alienor. (My thanks also to Akashic Records consultant Alison King.) For any readers interested in viewing my full research library, it can be found here:

http://elizabethchadwickreference.blogspot.co.uk/

Aurell, Martin, *The Plantagenet Empire 1154–1224*, translated from the French by David Crouch (Pearson Longman, 2007), ISBN 978 0 5827 8439 0

Evans, Michael R., *Inventing Eleanor: The Medieval and Post-Medieval Image of Eleanor of Aquitaine* (Bloomsbury, 2014) ISBN 978 1 4411 6900 6

Farrer, William and Charles Travis Clay (eds), *Early Yorkshire Charters, Volume 8: The Honour of Warenne* (Cambridge University Press, 2013 edition), ISBN 978 1 1080 5831 5

Gillingham, John, *Richard I* (Yale University Press, 2002) ISBN 978 0 3000 9404 6

Holden, A. J. (ed.), *History of William Marshal*, with English translation by S. Gregory and historical notes by D. Crouch, vols 1 and 2 (Anglo-Norman Text Society)

Kaye, Henrietta, *Serving the Man that Ruled: Aspects of the Domestic Arrangements of the Household of King John 1199–1216*, a thesis submitted in September 2013 to the University of East Anglia

Trindale, Ann, *Berengaria: In Search of Richard the Lionheart's Queen* (Four Court's Press, 1999), ISBN 978 1 8518 2434 2

Turner, Ralph V., *Eleanor of Aquitaine* (Yale University Press, 2009), ISBN 978 0 3001 1911 4

Warren, W. L., *Henry II* (Eyre & Methuen, 1973), ISBN 973 0 4133 8390 3

Wheeler, Bonnie, and John C. Parsons (eds), *Eleanor of Aquitaine Lord and Lady* (Palgrave Macmillan, 2003), ISBN 978 0 2306 0236 6

Acknowledgements

I have a few people to thank wholeheartedly for their help either direct or in the background while I have been writing my Eleanor of Aquitaine trilogy.

My agent of many years, Carole Blake, for her clear-sighted advice, her drive and determination. We are enjoying a long and fruitful partnership and although we will never see eye to eye on wine versus tea, we have found common ground in gin! My thanks to all the other enthusiastic members of the Blake Friedmann agency too.

While I was in the middle of writing the trilogy, my then editor Rebecca Saunders moved away and I want to extend my appreciation to her for all her work. My thanks now go to my new editor Maddie West and I raise a toast to our continuing collaboration. Also to Marina de Pass for dealing with the day to day editorial business and Dan Balado-Lopez for the external copy edit. Any errors that remain are my own! My thanks also to the lovely Stephanie Melrose who deals with the publicity side of matters and Cath Burke for being there if I need her. Also my appreciation to the rest of the team at Sphere.

In these days of swift communication and the internet, I want to thank my lovely readers for all the support, fun, madness and fascinating historical discussion that goes on daily on my Facebook pages and groups. You're a great community and I treasure you.

I must thank my husband, Roger, for all his love and quiet background support which keeps the house functioning around my day job. Also the dogs, Jack, Pip and Bill, for their not so quiet background support, and my dear friend Alison King for true friendship – and adventures in time travel.